400 HORSEPOWER
OF THE APOCALYPSE

I0689557

ERICA LINDQUIST &
ARON CHRISTENSEN

LOOSE LEAF
STORIES

Cover by Bookfly Designs
Edited by Amber Presley & Lacey Waymire

Find more of our books at LLStories.com

*For everyone out there
riding the rough roads.*

PROLOGUE

Last night, I had the dream again. The two sides were still locked in endless battle – fighting over what, or for how long, I couldn't even guess. Forever. Since before forever... This war was older than the concept of time, and had been fought through more iterations than there were numbers to express.

How the hell did I know that? Dream logic, I guess.

I hope.

But I couldn't tell if this eternal battle was a one-on-one duel or the epic clash of two vast armies. It was sure as hell the biggest fight I had ever seen, outshining the worst hair-pulling, face-scratching bar-room brawl. I couldn't tell much more than that, though...

The timeless war raged back and forth through a void so empty that it defied even twisted dream-logic. There was nothing for scale as the two sides fought, and I could only vaguely sense the great blows being dealt with power and weapons incomprehensible to my tiny mortal perceptions. I would have called the clashing factions *forces of nature*, except that these strange warriors went far beyond nature. Nature was a force of *them*...

Or maybe I just had a few too many beers before bed.

There was only one thing I knew for sure in all of the weirdness and confusion of my dream – *nothing* was more important than victory in this eternal war. It was a fight between darkness and light, of order against utter chaos, and I had no idea who would win.

CHAPTER 1

Dreams end, though, even the weird recurring ones. And now it was time to get my butt out of bed.

My cell phone blared an endless loop of the most obnoxious ringtone I could find. It *had* to be one I hated – nothing else would wake me up at five o'clock in the morning day after day after day.

I fumbled the phone out from under my pillow and groaned a few choice curses at it. The damned thing had already been going for nearly ten minutes and I hoped that I hadn't woken anybody else. That late start probably should have come out of my shower or breakfast time – but I wasn't willing to cut either one, so I grabbed a bottle of coffee from the fridge and chugged it while I waited for my shower to heat up.

And waited... I was twenty-three years old, but my parents had bought that water heater long, long before I was born. So I waited some more.

Once the shower was warm – *hot* was right out of the question – I gulped down the last mouthful of coffee, but it was bitter and gritty because I had forgotten to shake it first. I made a face at the empty bottle and left it on the bathroom counter.

Welcome to the life of Jasmine O'Neil. *Jaz* to my friends, or people who think they're my friends. Or anyone who is too lazy to just say my whole damned name.

I showered and dried off quickly, then tied a bandana over the fluffy black curls of my damp hair. With a last-minute bagel clamped between my teeth, I climbed into my dad's car and backed out of the garage. I drove across town while wolfing down my bagel in four huge bites.

So why was I up before the sun? Well, people usually needed to stop by my work before they headed out to *their* job. I was a mechanic at Golden Touch Auto, one of those boring chain car garages where they change your oil, rotate your tires and upsell you on semi-useful and over-priced maintenance plans.

And by *they*, I mean me. I was always the first GTA employee into the garage because nobody else wanted to be up that early. Neither did I, but I was the newest hire in years, the youngest and the only girl in a workplace that was otherwise an utter sausage fest. So I got stuck with *all* of the shit work.

But I dutifully unlocked the GTA front door with my security code, turned on the lights and booted up the ancient computer system so that people could drop off their trucks and cars before heading out to their own jobs at a more reasonable hour.

The day only went downhill from there. The guys came in around nine o'clock. By ten, Craig had made no less than three different comments about women having no brain for machines, including a snappy one-liner about how I should be spending more time in the back seat of cars rather than under their hoods.

When I turned to tell Craig to shove it, I caught my coveralls on the corner of a bumper and tore the knee right open. Craig laughed at me.

"Damn, Jaz," he said. "I was going to suggest you get a job down the street waiting tables, but now I'm not even sure you can do that."

"No, I can't," I snapped at him. "Because I'm a mechanic, not a waitress."

I spun back to face the car that I was working on, hopefully before Craig said anything else. My cheeks were flaming and even with my dark brown skin, I was pretty certain that everyone could tell. Bob made some joke that I only half heard over the rush of blood in my ears, but I flipped him off anyway. When I returned to wrestling the bolts out of the old Ford's transmission, though, my hands were shaking and the wrench slipped. I smashed my finger and cursed some more.

The other mechanics were all laughing again. What the hell were they doing gathered around me, anyway? Didn't they have their *own* jobs to do? Not that I trusted Craig to change a windshield wiper.

An hour and a half later, though, it was finally and thankfully lunchtime. I didn't get to leave the garage, of course, but everyone else went up the street to the bar. Lucky Jaz got to stay behind at GTA... New girl and all that.

I'm not complaining – okay, I am – but I wouldn't have gone out to lunch with Craig and the other guys, even if they invited me. Not just because they were all assholes, but because it was cheaper to eat a bagged lunch and I needed to save every last dollar if I was *ever* going to escape this place.

This place was Crayhill, Kansas. Or as I tended to think of it, *Craphole*. Look, there are really nice places in Kansas. Beautiful, peaceful places – and for some people, maybe Crayhill was even one of them.

Ugh, sorry. That made me throw up in my mouth a little.

Crayhill was a tiny town, with a population of perhaps two thousand. It used to be larger, but that was back when there was a major motorcycle factory here. Both my parents had worked at that plant, met and fell in love there. I grew up playing with their socket wrenches and calipers. But then the economy crashed, the factory closed down and pretty much everyone in Crayhill lost their job.

Anyone who could afford to moved out of Crayhill, but that still left a shitty, broke little town full of people who had spent their entire professional lives designing, building and repairing motorcycles. I got the job at Golden Touch Auto because I'm a damned good mechanic... and because I was willing to come in at the ass-crack of dawn to work ten-hour days for minimum wage. I couldn't afford to take my crappy job for granted, though. In Crayhill, I was all too easily replaceable. But I hadn't gotten a raise in... ever, and most of what I earned went straight to helping my parents with the bills.

I had my *own* plans, however. Once I was sure that Craig and the other guys were all safely gone for lunch, I went out to the cracked concrete pad behind the garage and pulled a tarp up off the motorcycle parked back there. It wasn't a secret or anything, but I didn't always have the time to work on the bike and Craig got cranky if I stored it inside.

I ran my hand along the chrome handlebars of the Triumph Bonneville 790. The previous owner abandoned the motorcycle when he couldn't afford the repairs and it took seven months of working on the side to get it running. And I managed it all with minimal parts, scavenging and machining every single little doodinkus all on my own because I'm twice the grease-monkey that any of the other GTA mechanics are.

My Bonnie was still a rough ride, though... The bike badly needed new shock springs and a set of Ikons cost four hundred dollars that I didn't have.

I crouched down to inspect the wheel fork. It had been just this side of mangled when I started work on the Bonneville, but it was looking pretty damned good now. The motorcycle was a cruiser, not a racing bike, with a dark blue and purple body, and chrome highlights that I always kept brightly polished.

Someday I would finally jump onto my Bonnie and ride the hell out of here. Hopefully before it was too late... There was a gravity to Crayhill and the last handful of eligible men in town were all eyeballing me expectantly. By the time I hit drinking age, I had already slept with the three or four guys worth taking to bed. Only two of them were worth doing the deed sober, and none of them merited a second go. But if I didn't escape Crayhill, I would eventually give up and marry one of them, then likely drink myself into a slow, early death so that I wouldn't realize how miserable I was.

Nope. Not today, and not without a fight.

I gave my Bonneville another loving pat and straightened. There was still a Corolla up on the lift, but I figured changing its transmission fluid could wait until I was done with lunch – and maybe a little daydreaming.

There hadn't been enough time to pack a sandwich or anything that morning, so I grabbed a candy bar from the half-full lobby vending machine and sat down in front of the reception computer to browse eBay for some new shock springs. It's not really a part you can buy used, but maybe some bike shop had an old set sitting on a stock shelf and wanted to offload them for a few bucks.

No dice. I put my chin in my hand and sighed. Oh, well. Just another frustrating day in Crayhill.

Or was it...? I leaned over the counter and squinted out the lobby window. Something felt strange today – something in the air, like there was a storm coming. Whatever it was, the sensation crawled up my spine and seemed to grab on, pulling me with invisible hands in the direction of the approaching storm. A tornado, maybe?

But the sky was still clear and a pale blue color scrubbed nearly white by the bright sun. I took another bite of candy bar, wondering if I should check the weather app on my phone. But I never got the chance.

Last night's dream of cosmic battle came suddenly rushing back over me with such force that I choked on chocolate and caramel. Light bloomed across my vision, colorless but blinding in its intensity. There were elemental forces battling for the soul of the entire universe and something incandescently hot raced through my body like a lightning strike.

Holy shit, was I having a stroke? Can you get a stroke from frustration?

But a second later, the light, the battle and everything else simply... vanished. The rush of blood in my ears was replaced by the loud roar of a motorcycle engine – something a lot bigger than my little Bonneville. I dropped the remains of my candy bar and jumped to my feet to get a look out into the parking lot.

Any trace of morning coolness had long since dispersed and the asphalt shimmered in the midday heat as though the very air were trying to escape Crayhill. A big black motorcycle turned into the GTA parking lot and stopped just outside the front door. The bike's rider pulled off his helmet and uncovered short, wavy brown hair. He peeled off a leather jacket, too, then stuffed it into one of the saddlebags slung over the back of his motorcycle. His arms were thick with muscles and tattoos.

Damn, the guy was an eyeful – six foot something, with deep brown eyes and dusky skin. Neither his complexion or hair were as dark as mine, but he definitely had the look of a man who spent a lot of time outside, and probably somewhere way more exotic than Kansas.

The bike was a fine specimen, too – a 2014 Packmaster CVB, if I was any judge. And I was. Black leather and chrome finish, with beautiful blood-red detailing. Both motorcycle and rider were well-crafted machines of barely-restrained power in sleek packaging.

Alright, maybe I was letting my imagination run away... But hey, it was the only part of me that got to.

The biker pulled a cell phone from the pocket of his jeans and dialed as he walked across the parking lot. I centered myself behind the counter, brushed any stray bits of chocolate off my shirt, and did my best to look professional as he pushed the door open. The automated doorbell let out a loud, sharp buzz meant to be heard all the way back through the garage and I winced, but my strange new customer didn't even appear to notice the ruckus.

"Yeah. See you soon," he said into the phone. "Call me if you run into any trouble."

His voice was deep, with a trace of Mexico in his accent not quite overwhelmed by the strong Chicago vowels. He smiled as he spoke, but stepped quickly up to the counter like he was in a hurry. I straightened to my fullest five-and-a-half foot height, then checked the bandana that kept my hair out of both engines and my eyes while the tall biker stuffed his cell phone back into his pocket. It was too warm in the garage and I had unzipped the top of my coveralls to tie the arms around my waist. Not exactly club wear, so I put on what I hoped was my best and brightest smile to make up for it.

Alright, Jaz, I told myself firmly. *Say something smart, maybe a little flirty. First impressions are forever.*

"Hi, Jasmine," I said, then felt my face go hot. "I mean, hello. I'm Jasmine. Jaz. Welcome to Golden Touch Auto. Do you need a jump?"

Good job, Jaz.

The biker's expression became confused, but he nodded.

"Leo," he introduced himself. "Leo Valdis. Can you look at my bike? The steering is pulling and my engine keeps surging."

Points to Leo for not assuming I was a receptionist. A lot of guys who came into the garage did – despite the coveralls and grease stains up to my elbows. Leo *might* not be a sexist douche-bag, or maybe he was just slightly observant.

"Sure, let's go take a look," I said.

I came out from behind the front counter and gestured to the door, letting Leo lead the way back out to his motorcycle. Not so I could watch his ass – well, not *just* so I could watch his ass – but I had never seen the guy in Crayhill before, and I was otherwise alone in the garage until Craig and the others came back. I wasn't about to turn my back on a strange man, no matter how sexy.

We stepped out into the hot Kansas afternoon and I gagged, but then forgot all about the heat and my suspicions when we approached Leo's bike. Wow, it really was a gorgeous machine... My initial assessment was right – 2014 Packmaster CVB.

The Packmaster was based on the classic Harley-Davidson Softail design, but with an extended gas tank and a longer back end made for hauling larger saddlebags. The Packmasters were popular with bikers who spent a lot of time driving cross-country, who wanted fewer stops for gas and some increased carrying capacity.

But *CVB* meant that this motorcycle was a special release. The manufacturer only made a few of them each year, and they were both more expensive and more powerful than the standard models.

Leo's Packmaster made my half-finished Bonneville looked like a beater by comparison. Well, to be honest, it *was* a beater, but I would have been jealous even if the Bonnie were brand new. The big Packmaster had a flawless red and black paint job, with sturdy-looking custom leather saddlebags across the back. Hard cases produced less drag on the road, but lots of bikers preferred the look of the leather, and they were collapsible when empty. These bags were far from empty, though – they were stuffed with something and bulged liked bunched muscles.

"Hmm, steering problems are usually tire problems," I said, crouching down to inspect the tread. "But... I don't see any uneven wear. Your fork doesn't seem bent, either."

"Did I screw up the alignment?" Leo asked.

I squinted. "Hmm... Maybe. Or the engine might be racked incorrectly. That's usually more of a problem with the touring models than the Packmasters, especially a CVB. But let's take it inside for a look."

I straightened and grabbed the handlebars to wheel Leo's bike into the garage. But as soon as I touched the motorcycle, the blinding light came back. There was a hollow boom like a thunderclap and the world spun all around me. I staggered away, wheeling my arms wildly as I struggled to regain my balance.

"Hey, are you okay?" Leo asked.

When I could see again, the biker was reaching out to steady me. I waved him off and blinked a few times, but the light was gone and so was the dizziness.

"It's alright," I said. "I'm fine... I think."

What the hell was that? Did I just get electrocuted or something? Maybe I should check over the Packmaster's electrical system, too.

"Want me to bring it inside?" Leo asked.

"Um... yeah," I answered. "Thanks. But be careful. I think it zapped me."

Leo frowned at his motorcycle before cautiously touching the back of his hand against the handlebars. Nothing happened, though, so he kicked up the stand, then followed me through one of the big roll-up doors into the garage. I pointed to a lift table, a much smaller and portable version than the lift with the Corolla still waiting for its new transmission fluid. Leo maneuvered his motorcycle into place while I pulled on a pair of worn leather gloves. I didn't want to touch the Packmaster without protection again.

Once my hands were safely covered, I strapped the motorcycle onto the lift table and raised it a few feet. I cracked my knuckles and nodded to Leo.

"You can wait up front, if you like," I offered. "I think there's still some coffee. It doesn't taste great, but the lobby air conditioning is better, at least."

Most customers opted for the uncomfortable chairs to either stare at their cell phones or page through old car magazines, but Leo shrugged.

"If I'm allowed back here, I'd rather stay," he said.

I didn't really like an audience, but I had been working with the other GTA mechanics while they taunted me for two years now. So I nodded and got to work.

I started out by sighting down the Packmaster's swingarm. That's the part of a motorcycle behind the exhaust muffler that holds the rear wheel in place. There were tick marks etched into the metal and the wheel alignment looked good. But those calibration marks were placed by the manufacturer and if their machinery was off, then so were the marks. Better to check the alignment myself just to be sure. I grabbed a tape measure from the tool bench.

"Have you bumped up over any curbs recently?" I asked. "Hit anything?"

Leo shifted his weight a little back and forth between his feet. Not shuffling, really – it looked far too deliberate for that – but like he was ready to move. Maybe to run.

"No curbs or meridians or anything," Leo said. "I take care of my bike, but... I ride hard."

"Yeah, I bet you do," I murmured to myself.

Luckily, Leo didn't seem to hear me. I unspooled the tape measure and checked the distance between the left swingarm pivot and the rear axle. I slipped my hand between the exhaust pipes to get the measurement on the other side. That usually required removing some of the body casing, but my hands were small enough to just maneuver around it.

Screw you, Craig.

But I shook my head. The measurements were identical on either side, which meant the alignment was dead on. No clues there why Leo's steering was off. Maybe I could at least solve the zapping problem.

I lowered the lift table and checked the Packmaster's headlight, but didn't see any sign of frayed or sheared wires. So what had shocked me? I dug through a toolbox until I found a big multimeter, one with a current clamp on the end. I hooked it around some of the exposed chrome of the Packmaster's handlebars, but the meter needle didn't budge. If there was any electrical current running through the metal, then it was too little for the multimeter to detect. Which probably meant it was too little to zap me.

I scowled at the meter and put it away, but I didn't take off my gloves.

"So far, everything looks fine," I reported. "If your steering is pulling to the side, it might be... maybe a bearing problem? That will take a bit longer to check, though. What about the engine issues? What's going on there?"

"It runs fine most of the time," Leo told me. "But every once in a while, the engine surges and the RPMs shoot through the roof. I jump up about ten or twenty miles per hour until I can throttle back down."

"Hmm..." I said.

The engine seemed fine from the outside – no signs of leaks or cracks or anything like that. I raised the lift table again to inspect the drive belt. I pinched the edge of the belt and gave it a gentle twist. It turned forty-five degrees without trouble, but not much further than that. The belt was at the correct tension and looked recently replaced.

"Put anything weird into the tank?" I asked. "Engine cleaner or the wrong gas?"

Leo shook his head. "Nope."

I frowned at his motorcycle. Alright, maybe fluid levels? But when I checked, the oil wasn't low. Even if it were, it wouldn't have made the engine surge. I lowered the lift again and finally pulled off my gloves, tucking them into the waist of my coveralls.

"Look, I know my bikes," I said. "But I'm not the motorcycle whisperer. I'll need to crack open the bodywork and primary case to figure out what's going on here. And that will take a little time."

"How long?" Leo asked.

"You should probably get a motel room. Crayhill isn't exactly a big tourist destination, but Highway 44 runs a few miles south of here, so there are a couple of motels for stopovers."

Leo nodded. "I was out on the highway when my bike started having trouble today."

"And you stopped in Crayhill...?" I asked, cocking my head curiously. "There are garages in pretty much every truck-stop town along the highway. Why did you come here?"

Leo shrugged and I shook my head.

"Get a room and come back in the morning," I suggested. "I should have some answers for you then."

At least, I hoped that I would. So far, all of the usual suspects were unusually absent. I just had to pray that once I opened up the Packmaster's engine, the problem would present itself. Leo crossed his thick, tattooed arms.

"Is my bike rideable?" he asked.

"Well... yeah," I answered reluctantly. "You rode it into town. But you don't want a major engine seize or steering pull at highway speeds."

"I can't stay here. I need to catch up with my friends," Leo said. "There's somewhere we have to be."

I sighed. "I can't recommend you riding very far on this beast until you find out what's wrong and fix it. I guess you could leave the Packmaster here and maybe buy another motorcycle from someone in town. There used to be a factory, so there are plenty of them around."

It seemed a little ridiculous to buy a whole new bike just to keep some appointment, but even I was surprised at the heat in Leo's answer.

"No," he growled. "I'm not leaving my steed behind."

Alright, I loved my motorcycle as much as the next girl, but *steed* was a bit excessive. Leo winced at his own intensity and he looked down at the oil-stained concrete floor for a moment. He let out a long, hissing breath.

"Another bike isn't really an option for me," Leo answered at last. He rubbed the back of his neck and gave me a rueful smile. "Sorry."

"I get it," I said. "I wouldn't give up my Bonnie, either. It's my only ticket out of Crayhill."

Leo glanced briefly at me, but then returned his attention to his motorcycle on the lift table. He shifted his weight again, as though his body had to play out the options running through his head. Leo pulled the phone out of his pocket and looked at it, then finally back down at me.

"I can't stay here... but my bike needs work," he said slowly. "So come with me. Do whatever repairs need to be done on the road. Keep me up and running, Jaz, and I promise I'll make it worth your time."

Maybe there was something wrong with my heart, too, because the RPMs shot through the roof. Look, I know that human hearts don't have RPMs, but the hottest biker guy I had ever seen just asked me to run away with him. Getting out of this shit town was all I ever wanted, but I fought to get my pulse down below heart attack levels.

"I... I have a job here," I stammered. "And I'm supporting both my parents with it. Trust me, I would love to go, but I can't just... leave."

"I can make it worth your time," Leo said again. "I'll pay you. Cash."

I blew out a long breath and shook my head. "I can't. Really. Not unless you happen to have thirty thousand dollars in your back pocket."

That was what my mom and dad still owed on their house, more or less. The social security checks just weren't enough to cover bills and food, not while they were paying the mortgage, too. Leo didn't laugh or roll his eyes, though.

"Not in my back pocket," he said. "But... thirty thousand? Is that your price to get me where I need to go?"

"Um... yeah?" I said. More like gasped.

Leo looked at his Packmaster again, deliberating, but only for a moment. Then he met my gaze with dark, intense eyes.

"Deal," Leo said.

Holy shit, I thought. *Oh shit, oh shit, oh shit.*

Thirty thousand dollars just for a mechanic? Leo must have *really* wanted to make this meeting. I wished that I could ask for a night to sleep on it, but Leo was already offering me thirty grand to avoid staying in Crayhill overnight. That was more than I made in an entire year working at Golden Touch Auto.

Was this actually happening? How could it be real? I had no idea, but I couldn't pass up this chance to get out of Crayhill.

"Deal," I echoed breathlessly. "Wait, what about some kind of deposit?"

I didn't want to ruin things by haggling, but if I was really about to skip town, I couldn't just leave my parents in the lurch. One of Leo's eyebrows rose a little, but he nodded.

"How about... ten thousand up front?" he asked.

"Yeah," I said. "Yeah, okay."

It was way better than *okay* – this was a dream come true. Leo went to his motorcycle and opened up one of the bulging leather saddlebags. His broad shoulders blocked my view of the contents, but when he turned back, Leo was holding a stack of hundred-dollar bills. They were still wrapped in a bank-branded paper band.

"Ten thousand dollars," Leo said.

"Holy shit," I breathed.

Leo held out the money. Benjamin Franklin stared up at me from the crisp new bills with a faintly accusatory look on his round face, as if to say *You know he stole me, right?*

I didn't know if it was a crime to accept stolen money, but what choice did I have? Stay in Crayhill and watch my mystery biker ride away with the only chance I might ever have to see the world tucked away into his saddlebags?

Screw you, Ben, I told the money.

Carefully, I took the cash in shaking hands. Leo snapped his fingers and grinned at me.

"Great," he said. "Do you need to put some stuff together?"

I nodded. "Umm, yeah. Give me... about an hour?"

"Quicker if you can. I want to get back on the road."

CHAPTER 2

I collected my tools, locked up the garage and drove back home as fast as I could without getting a speeding ticket. We had exactly four cops in Crayhill and I knew them all by name, but my hometown was so tiny that they could easily keep an eye on the whole thing. I didn't want to slow down for a single stop sign, but I couldn't risk being pulled over with Leo's stolen cash crammed into my pocket.

Apparently, I was still going fast enough to kick up gravel along my driveway and I came to a stop surrounded by a cloud of dust. I opened the garage, but Mom's car was gone. When I parked and went inside, the little modular house was quiet. Dad was already out fishing with some of the other guys from the old motorcycle factory.

There was a note on the refrigerator from Mom saying that she was over at Judy's house. Probably watching soap operas and gossiping... But I couldn't exactly blame either of my parents. There wasn't much else for them to do around Crayhill.

But that was about to change. I fumbled the thick stack of money from my pocket and counted out five hundred dollars. With sweating hands, I stuffed the bills into my wallet, then left the other nine and a half thousand on the kitchen table. I pulled my mom's note down off the fridge, flipped it over and scrawled a quick message on the other side.

Ran into some luck. I just got a paying job on the road, so I'm going to be out of town for a while. Maybe for good! More money coming soon.

I'm taking the Bonnie, so Dad's car is parked over at GTA. Sorry I couldn't leave it at the house. I'll call when I can.

It wasn't Shakespeare, but I didn't have time for poetry and my parents didn't need to know where I got all the money. They would only worry.

I added one last thing, though.

Love you both.
  – Jaz

I ran to my room and changed out of my GTA jumpsuit, into jeans and a clean t-shirt. Then I stuffed some more clothes in a backpack, followed by my toothbrush, a box of tampons, and a jar of shea butter for my hair. Finally, I grabbed my leather jacket, motorcycle helmet and toolbox. Of *course* I had my own kit, and if I was going to be Leo's personal mechanic, I would need it.

I replaced all my tools in the case. I would never have to steal them back from Craig again. The metal box was too big for my backpack, so I tucked it under my arm and hurried toward the door that led out into the garage. But I stopped with my hand wrapped around the dented knob.

Was I really doing this? I had lived in this house since I was born. The close, warm air was thick with smells of dust and my dad's roses blooming on the back porch. Could I actually just ride away from my whole life? Alright, it wasn't much of a life, but it was safe and predictable. Normal.

I didn't know anything about Leo. Well, except that he had a suspiciously large wad of even more suspicious cash. Not exactly promising when it came to my safety. My strange new customer could be an axe murderer, for all I knew. Something inside me shouted wordlessly not to do this, not to go with Leo. That it was suicidally dangerous.

But I knew one thing about Leo Valdis – he was my ticket out of Crayhill. I had no idea where I might end up if I rode with him, and I didn't care – as long as it wasn't here. I would be alright... If I could just leave Crayhill before its gravity sucked me into a decaying orbit of acceptance, I could do *anything*.

It was time to go.

I opened the door and ran into the garage, then dropped my backpack and toolkit in the passenger seat of my dad's station wagon. Barely resisting the urge to slide across the hood *Dukes-of-Hazzard*-style, I jumped into the driver's side and started the engine. I backed out and then drove away without looking back.

I made it across Crayhill to Golden Touch Auto again with twenty minutes to spare. My heart pounded as I pulled into the GTA parking lot, but Leo was still there, lounging against the side of his big black motorcycle and checking something on his cell phone. He looked up as I parked and then climbed out of the car.

"I was worried you wouldn't come back," Leo said.

"Yeah, so was I," I admitted.

Leo laughed. I locked up the car doors from the driver's side control and dropped the keys into the drink holder. I grabbed my backpack and tools, then kicked the door shut and jogged around behind the garage. There, I yanked the tarp off my Bonneville, stashed my toolkit in the tailpack – that's a case mounted on the motorcycle pillion behind the rider, rather than draped on either side like Leo's saddlebags – and then pulled my backpack on over my leather riding jacket.

I was actually doing it, finally leaving Crayhill. Just like I had always dreamed of since... ever. Since I was a kid, since before I could even remember. I was running away at last.

When everything felt secure, I walked my motorcycle out around Golden Touch Auto, but Leo was no longer alone in the parking lot. There was a beat-up truck parked next to the front door and I could already smell the familiar mix of beer and WD-40.

Craig and the other GTA mechanics had gathered around the closed door and were staring suspiciously at Leo. The big biker stood next to his Packmaster with tattooed arms crossed over his chest. I pushed my salvaged little Bonnie to a stop beside his motorcycle and tried not to feel self-conscious about it. I dropped the kickstand.

"Give me a minute," I said.

Leo nodded. "Yeah, sure. But make it quick? We need to get moving."

"This will just take a second," I promised.

I hurried over to Craig and his thick brows drew down. He gestured toward Leo and then the front door of GTA.

"Who the hell is that guy?" Craig asked, scowling. "And why is the garage closed?"

"I quit," I said.

Craig blinked and his face turned bright red. He looked like a tomato being squeezed and about to burst.

"Jaz, what the–?" Craig began.

I didn't wait for him to finish. "Screw you and screw this job. Try treating the next girl better, asshole."

I turned and walked away, showing Craig my middle finger over my shoulder. Leo grinned at me as I strode back across the parking lot to him.

"*Now* I'm ready to go," I said.

Leo unslung his jacket from the seat of his Packmaster and pulled it on. There were a pair of patches on the black leather, one on each shoulder. The right was an embroidered image of an old-fashioned helmet – not a motorcycle helmet, but the kind you see on *Game of Thrones* – with a flaming plume on top. The name *Knights of Hell* was stitched in silver thread underneath. I had never heard of them, but it sounded like a biker gang or club. Were those the friends Leo was so eager to catch up to?

But the patch on his left arm wasn't another helmet. It was a coiled rattlesnake emblazoned there in black and bronze, scales arranged in a hatched diamond pattern. Shit, I knew that patch, though I had never seen one in person. Most snakes were harmless, but some were truly poisonous and those dangerous few – like the diamondback rattler – gave the rest a bad name.

And that was precisely why criminal biker gangs wore the rattlesnake patch. Ninety-nine out of a hundred biker groups were completely legal and harmless, but one percent of them... Well, they were the dangerous ones.

I almost dropped my helmet. But what else had I expected? I could practically hear Benjamin Franklin telling me *I told you so* from my back pocket.

The smart move would have been to run. One whisper to Craig – and probably some serious groveling later – and we could have all of the cops in Crayhill here inside three minutes. Okay, so that wasn't very impressive... But a wrench across the back of the head would keep Leo down until they put him safely in handcuffs. I could see myself – vividly – holding the wrench and standing over Leo.

But instead, I asked, "Where are we going?"

"Down to Highway 44," Leo told me. He picked up his black helmet. "We'll meet my friends on the way. Then we're going west to San Diego."

"Great," I said. "I've always wanted to see San Diego."

Not specifically, but San Diego wasn't Crayhill and I always wanted to see not-Crayhill. And San Diego was all the way in California. I was going to see my first palm tree – on an endless white sand beach! I promised myself that I would order an over-priced mimosa as soon as we got there.

Leo swung a leg over his Packmaster and I climbed onto my Bonneville. We both put on our helmets and strapped them into place.

"Jaz!" Craig shouted.

Leo started his bike and if Craig had anything else to say, it was swallowed by the sudden roar of engines. The Packmaster revved and Leo pulled it through a tight turn, then raced out into the road. He turned south, toward Highway 44. I kicked the Bonnie to life and followed.

CHAPTER 3

I rode down Highway 44 beside Leo and finally lost sight of Crayhill over my shoulder. Which was actually kind of a feat in Kansas. Despite its name, there wasn't a single hill in Crayhill, so it took pure distance to swallow up my hometown.

I couldn't stop checking every few seconds. Some part of me was still screaming that this was a terrible idea, and I had to convince myself over and over again that I wasn't dreaming the whole thing, that I had finally left. But when I could no longer see Crayhill, I cheered into the dry summer wind. Leo glanced over at me, but I couldn't read his expression under the helmet.

We rode past wide, flat fields in alternating green and gold. I smelled hot asphalt and warm earth, the sharp stink of exhaust and the sweet scent of sun-baked cornfields. Engines and the wind roared in my ears, even under the protective padding of my helmet. They were the sounds of the open road, and it was the most beautiful music in the world.

Shut up. I was allowed to be a little poetic – I was actually leaving home and it felt *amazing*.

Well, mostly. My Bonneville's shitty shocks hadn't suddenly gotten better and I didn't own a pair of good motorcycle gloves.

It was only the middle of the afternoon – less than two hours after leaving Crayhill – and my hands already ached. I felt the hard vibration of the road in my lungs and guts. It just added to the exhilaration for now, but I was pretty sure that I would be over the sensation long before dinner time.

I gave Leo a sidelong glance. He wasn't watching the landscape streak by, but gripped the handles of his Packmaster with tension that I could see even through his leathers and helmet. Leo caught my eye and held up his hand, first finger raised.

I frowned. That was the signal to ride single-file. The highway wasn't empty – there were trucks hauling crops and tankers full of gasoline, all mixed in with smaller cars driving through my shitty little corner of Kansas without stopping – but there was plenty of room for two motorcycles to drive abreast.

Was this some kind of macho bullshit? Maybe Leo felt some alpha-wolf need to lead the way... I didn't know, but the man was paying me a lot of money, so I dutifully throttled back and fell in behind his Packmaster.

We crossed the southwest border of Kansas and into Oklahoma. I rode behind Leo until the sun began to set, turning the blue sky dark and purple. Our headlights cast bright blades of illumination out in front of us. Leo gestured again, this time pointing in the direction of the next highway off-ramp.

I didn't catch the name printed on the green sign beside the road, but I didn't care. The town we drove into couldn't have been any larger than Crayhill. It wasn't much more than an overgrown truck stop, but it was a new place, a not-Crayhill place. I called that a win.

Leo rolled into a shopping center parking lot and stopped under one of the streetlamps. I parked next to him, kicked out the Bonneville's stand and rubbed my aching hands. Time to start earning Leo's suspicious money.

"How did your bike do?" I asked.

Leo pulled off his helmet. He shook out the sweaty brown waves of his hair and frowned down at the Packmaster.

"Steering was a bear," Leo grunted. "It fought me the whole way."

Was *that* what had been going on? I didn't see the motorcycle swerve all afternoon, so I guess that Leo had been able to keep it under control. Must be those big arms...

"That's why I asked you to ride behind me before," Leo said. "My bike kept pulling toward yours, and I didn't want to hit you if I lost control."

"Oh," I answered. "Um... thanks."

So *not* some kind of stupid alpha-male shit. Well, that was something of a relief, at least. But what the hell was wrong with Leo's motorcycle? I pulled out my toolkit to check his tire pressure and alignment. Still fine.

I sat back on my heels. Too bad I couldn't have brought a lift table and some better lights. I settled for spreading my jacket on the ground and turning on my cell phone flashlight.

"Let's look at your head bearings," I said. "Give me a hand."

I directed Leo to hold his motorcycle level and steady while I found my jack. It was just a little one – small enough to fit into my toolbox – but we lifted up the front of the Packmaster. Reluctantly, I grabbed the handlebars. No electric zap this time, which was an improvement... Not that I had ever figured out why it happened in the first place.

Leo held his motorcycle while I rotated the front wheel to feel the movement of the bearing inside. Something felt wrong. The bike's steering grated and groaned in protest, and the effort of yanking the handlebars a few degrees made sweat prickle along my hairline.

But a tight bearing wasn't the only thing wrong. The sweat running down the back of my neck was ice cold and I had the sudden overwhelming urge to shove the motorcycle off the jack, over onto Leo. What the hell? I'm not really a violent girl and don't let Maisie Perkins tell you otherwise. She started that fight – I just ended it.

Sure, Leo was mysterious and his glitchy motorcycle was frustrating, but neither of them was trying to steal my favorite doll. So even if I *could* lay them both out on their asses there in the parking lot, it seemed like overkill. It had been a weird afternoon, so I just shook the sensation off and gave the Packmaster's handlebars another twist.

They barely moved. The bearings were way too tight, that was all. That didn't explain the swerving and pulling that Leo had described, exactly, but maybe forcing the over-tight steering had damaged the bearing further. Wrestling with it might have carved a notch into the metal... Well, I wouldn't know until I got in there to ease up the bearings and take a look. I let go of the Packmaster and rubbed my hands.

"I have a drift and hammer set in my kit," I told Leo. "I can loosen up that head bearing for you. It's not a complicated fix, but I'm tired and you're paying me too much money to do shit work on your ride."

"What do you need?" Leo asked. "A garage?"

"No, just dinner and maybe some sleep," I said. "You weren't planning to ride through the night, were you?"

Leo hesitated and drummed his fingers on the back of his motorcycle, then finally sighed.

"No, I guess not," he answered with obvious reluctance. "My friends have to stop for the night, too. We'll catch up to them tomorrow."

"Great. Then I'll take care of your bearings first thing in the morning."

Leo nodded and we lowered his bike back to the ground.

Without getting on the road again, our meal options were fast food or a country-style diner, so we chose the diner. It was just at the end of the parking lot and we left our motorcycles under the streetlight – after Leo double-checked the buckles on his saddle-bags, I noticed – then walked over to the diner.

It was getting late on a Tuesday night, so there were only a few truckers in the diner, loading up on grease and caffeine for the road. Most of the tables were empty and a server looked up from her coffee long enough to tell us we could take any seat.

Leo selected a nearby booth and slid into the far side, where he could keep an eye on the front door. I sat down across from him with a wince and waited for some menus.

"Are you okay?" Leo asked, frowning.

"Your motorcycle isn't the only one with problems," I said. "My shocks aren't great. The Bonnie's a rough ride and I've never taken it on the road for this long. My hands are kind of numb, and so is my ass."

"I don't think any of my gloves will fit you, but you're welcome to a pair if you want to try," Leo offered.

I shook my head. "Thanks, but your hands are like twice the size of mine."

Leo nodded and then stripped out of his jacket, laying it over the green vinyl booth seat. He smiled a little self-consciously as he peeled off his fingerless riding gloves, too, and tucked them into one of the pockets. Leo folded his tattooed forearms across the tabletop. Red and orange ink flames curled around his left wrist, up to the wheels of a bike of a similar make and model to his own. An armored figure rode astride the motorcycle on his bicep, with a few gleaming details picked out in white ink. The helmet had a flaming plume on top that disappeared up under the sleeve of Leo's black t-shirt.

"You've been working on bikes for a while, right?" he asked.

"Yeah, pretty much since I could lift a wrench," I answered. "Just for fun when I was little, a way to spend time with my mom and dad. But it wasn't like I could go to college, so guess what I ended up doing for a living?"

"And you seem good at it," Leo said.

I arched an eyebrow. "Uh, you've barely seen me work. And I have no idea what's causing your engine surges yet."

"I've been to see a lot of mechanics over the years," Leo said. "Most of them would have made something up by now."

"Ever had to bring one on the road with you before?" I asked.

A bit nervously, I have to admit. Leo *was* a criminal, after all, and I had nightmare visions of some other mechanic duct-taped to a chair somewhere back in Chicago. Leo smiled, though.

"Nope. This is a first for me, too," he said. "My uncle always told me that a buck spent on maintenance was worth a hundred in repairs."

I nodded. "Smart guy. Your uncle's right."

"He usually is."

Our server finally strolled over with a couple of menus, then brought us some drinks – coffee for me, cola for Leo – and took our orders. The diner did breakfast all day, so I asked for a skillet full of eggs, bacon and potatoes. My lunch was only half a candy bar and now I was *starving*.

"So why are your shocks so bad?" Leo asked when the server left again. "Seems like a good place for a little bit of that preventative maintenance."

"Money," I answered with a shrug. "Up until this afternoon, I couldn't afford new shocks. I only have the Bonneville at all because the owner skipped out on the bill and Craig let me work a bunch of unpaid weekends to buy it."

Leo nodded his understanding. He obviously had plenty of money now, but it was just as clear that wasn't always the case.

Leo's money was stolen, and I doubted he was about to start investing it in prudent stock portfolios. His bank account probably spent as much time in the red as mine... If Leo even had a bank account. I didn't want to ask him about that, though.

"Well, I have to move fast, and I need you to make sure my Packmaster can do that," Leo said. "That means we need *you* to be able to ride fast, too. How do we get your Triumph some new shocks?"

"In this place?" I asked, gesturing to the diner window and the narrow street outside. "We don't. When we ride through a bigger town, I can pick up new springs. I should be able to swap them in without much trouble. How soon I can do that depends on where we're meeting your friends. The uh... the Knights of Hell, right?"

I glanced down at Leo's tattoos. He caught my look and then nodded.

"Yeah. The Knights are heading toward San Diego, too, but they shouldn't be more than a town or two ahead of us. I'll give Audrey another call tonight and find out."

Now it was my turn to nod. I was just Leo's mechanic for this trip. Where we went and how fast was up to him. Unless Leo actually tried to get me to do anything illegal. I couldn't imagine any crime that he might involve me in, but what the hell did I know? This morning, my biggest dream was finding some out-of-date motorcycle shocks online.

"My friends will ride as slow as they can to let me catch up," Leo said. "But they can't stop to wait for us."

Yeah, I had kind of figured out that part. Chances were somewhere around a hundred percent that every rider in the Knights of Hell wore that rattlesnake patch, too. The mark wasn't unlike a diamondback's rattle, I supposed – it was a warning. Leo was dangerous and no matter how much cash he paid me, I couldn't forget that.

Literally... it was like something was shouting in the back of my mind to get the hell away from Leo Valdis. I willed that voice to shut up and took another drink of coffee. I was so amped and jittery that I doubted I needed any more caffeine, but it gave me something to do.

I ran my hand over the scarred wooden tabletop of the diner booth. This could have been any table in Crayhill, but it *wasn't*. Despite the longest, strangest day of my life – and my sore butt – I was very, very glad that I had accepted Leo's offer.

Our server appeared at the table like the patron goddess of food and I almost grabbed the skillet right out of her hands. She blinked at my enthusiasm as I began devouring heaping forkfuls of scrambled eggs. She dropped off a little pitcher of creamer for my coffee, too, and I stirred some into the mug.

Leo watched me demolish my dinner with a faintly shocked expression. I guess he had never seen a half-starved mechanic before.

"So... what's in San Diego?" I asked between mouthfuls. "Or are you just going there because it's not Chicago?"

Leo grinned. "Like it's not Crayhill?"

"Hey, I've got nothing against Chicago." I held up my hands. Well, one of them – the other was occupied grabbing a strip of bacon. "I want to go there someday, too."

"Chicago's a good city," Leo said. "I grew up there, but I spent every summer down in San Diego. To get away from things at home."

A shadow flickered behind Leo's dark eyes and I guessed I wasn't the only one at the table who wanted to run away from home. I was curious... but didn't risk pressing Leo. It didn't seem smart to poke a rattlesnake and besides, Leo didn't owe me any answers – he was the one paying *me*. I just needed to get him to San Diego intact, and then collect the rest of my thirty thousand dollars.

"Yeah, I get it," I told him.

"And San Diego's as much my home by now as Chicago," Leo said. He smiled at me again, but it didn't look as easy this time. "That's where my uncle lives. What about you, Jaz? Where are you going?"

"San Diego, apparently," I answered.

"What about after that?" Leo asked. "How far do you want to go?"

"As far as I can get."

After dinner, Leo picked up the check and paid in cash. I considered arguing with him, but Leo was the one with buckets of money. Until we got to San Diego, I had only the five hundred dollars in my wallet to see me through. And maybe to buy some shocks for my bike.

Besides, as Leo counted out the money, my cell phone rang and the screen lit up with my dad's picture. I took a couple of steps back from the register, but Leo was still watching me from the corner of his eye as I answered.

It was both of my parents, in fact, each speaking louder and louder to make *their* questions heard over the other. I covered my eyes with one hand, but I smiled. They were just worried.

"I told you I'd call when I could," I pointed out. "But I'm fine. Really. It's a short job on the road. I'll be back home as soon as I can, and I'll phone to let you know where I am. Okay?"

It took a few more rounds of reassurance that I was safe and that the money I left for them was legit, but after Leo had been waiting a few minutes, I was able to hang up and grin sheepishly at him.

"Parents," I said.

"Did you tell them where we are?" Leo asked.

"Uh... no," I answered. "Was I supposed to or something?"

Leo shrugged in noncommittal answer and I followed him out into the parking lot. We drove – carefully – down the street to the only motel in town and Leo bought a pair of rooms, also in cash. Finally, I groaned inwardly.

"I... really should pay for my own motel room," I said.

After all, I hadn't actually fixed Leo's motorcycle yet and a motel room – even a crappy one – was way more expensive than highway diner food. But lodging was going to eat through my remaining money fast. Maybe Leo could deduct the cost from my pay once the job was done...

"Call it traveling expenses," Leo said. "Don't worry about it. Trust me, Jaz, you're the one doing *me* a favor."

I didn't feel great about it, but I shrugged and wondered if Leo was feeling a bit guilty for stealing me away from my home and family – even though I had jumped at the chance. I didn't want to take advantage of his generosity, but neither did I want to screw up this one opportunity to actually earn some good money.

We walked our motorcycles down the single row of motel rooms. We stopped in front of two of the doors and Leo handed me one of the keys. I thanked him – hey, just because this whole adventure was weird as hell didn't mean I couldn't be polite – grabbed my toolbox and shouldered my backpack.

I let myself into the room that matched my key number and threw my things down onto the narrow bed. My hands were still pretty numb, but maybe a nice hot shower would help increase the blood flow. With any luck, the motel water heater was a slightly more robust model than the one at my parents' house.

The faded sky-blue window curtains were already closed, but they were only about as thick as Bible pages, so I grabbed the felt-lined blackout drapes on top to pull them shut. But Leo was still outside, straddling his big, problematic motorcycle with a thoughtful expression on his face. He ran a hand through his hair, let out a long breath and then pulled the cell phone from his pocket. Leo swiped the screen a few times, then held it up to his ear. The motel room walls were nearly as thin as the curtains and I could hear every word.

"Hey, Audrey," Leo said. "Are you still clear? Good. Yeah, I got some help. I don't know what's wrong with the Packmaster, exactly, but I hired a mechanic. She's riding with me. Where is everybody now?"

I couldn't hear the response, but Leo shook his head.

"No. No, don't come back," he said into the phone. "I'll catch up to you soon. And if I don't, you take the Knights and keep going west."

Leo glanced toward my window and I jumped. Could he see me through the drapes, too? I grabbed the blackout curtains and yanked them shut, heart pounding. What would Leo do if he caught me eavesdropping? He had been nice enough so far, but I hadn't for one second forgotten about that rattlesnake patch. Maybe Leo just wore it because it looked badass and didn't know the snake's significance.

Yeah, right. And the saddlebags full of bank-banded money were a birthday present from his uncle in San Diego.

But after a few minutes passed, Leo hadn't busted down my door and I couldn't hear his voice outside anymore. There was a thump – not very loud, but enough to make a framed map of the town bump on my wall – so I guessed that Leo had finished his phone call and gone to his room for some rest.

The same as I was supposed to be doing. I still felt like something was watching me, though, so I went into the bathroom and closed the door before stripping out of my clothes for a shower. Once the water was nice and hot, I climbed in and got to work scrubbing off the day's sweat and grease with the motel's bar soap. I washed my hair, too, but used my own shampoo for that.

The cheap miniature bottle provided by the motel just wasn't up to the challenge of dense curls like mine.

I lingered in the warm water for a little longer than I should have. Okay, a *lot* longer. But hey, I brushed my teeth while I was in there, so at least I was still accomplishing something. The shower began to cool down, though, so I turned off the water and wrapped myself in a towel. It was scratchy but clean, so I called that a win and climbed into bed.

It was finally the end of the longest, weirdest, and best day of my entire life. Tomorrow morning, I would loosen up the head bearings on Leo's bike. If that did the trick and fixed his motorcycle, then it would be time to get paid. I had a whole new life outside Crayhill to consider and plan. No way was I just going to sleep tonight.

But within seconds, I was fast asleep... and dreaming.

The eternal forces of existence were fighting their endless, repetitive war all over again. They clashed, circled and clashed again in the infinite void. No, not the void. Not anymore. There was a battlefield now. Wait, was it a cornfield? There were acres of wheat on the other side of the highway, rippling and golden in a blazing wind.

I was in the middle of Highway 44. Blue sky stretched overhead and flashed white with every blast of light. Something fought back and forth across the highway – four huge man-shapes riding astride even bigger stallions that seemed to have been forged out of nightmares and living chrome. Manes and tails of smoke snapped in the wind and sent glowing red embers up into the air.

The four horsemen rode out against three tall winged figures of blinding radiance. From on high, the trio of archangels flung lances of light and crackling lightning, and the demons tore their burning shots down from the sky with coils of shadow. The whole planet shuddered and quaked beneath my feet.

I threw my hands up over my face, trying to block out the sight of angels and demons fighting, of my world tearing apart at the seams. But my hands were glowing, too, and I held a blade of pure white light.

There weren't three angels – there were four.

CHAPTER 4

I slept in. Of course, six-thirty in the morning *was* sleeping in for me, so I was still awake by the time the sun had finished rising. Leo had already paid me a lot of money up front and I wanted to have something to show for it. The luxury of sleeping late and hope of diagnosing the Packmaster more than outweighed the night of intense, chaotic dreams and I was in a great mood.

I got dressed in some new jeans and a tank top, pulled on my jacket and headed outside with my toolkit. The early morning light was good, so I set down my tools in the motel parking lot next to Leo's big black motorcycle. I rubbed my hands together for warmth, then took out what I would need and sat on my toolbox. A lift table or a stool would have been a lot better, but I didn't have either one and had no desire to wear out my spine or knees before breakfast. With my Bonnie's shitty shocks and no gloves, it was already going to be a rough ride today. I had *just* gotten the feeling back in my fingers.

Checking the head bearings on a motorcycle wasn't hard and I had all of the right tools, but it did require unfastening and peeling away some bodywork to access the steering mechanism.

Time to get started on that, so I picked up my wrench set... but none of them fit the Packmaster's bolts. I switched to the metric set and then my torx keys, but they didn't fit either. I frowned at the bike.

Plenty of motorcycles had specialized parts that called for specialized tools, but just removing a few pieces of the body and cowling should have been easy. Leo's Packmaster was a CVB, which stood for *custom vehicle build*, and meant that the manufacturer made a bunch of changes for this edition... But custom bolts? I didn't remember ever reading about that before.

Had Leo installed them for some reason? He was clearly an experienced biker, but he didn't seem like that much of a grease monkey. That was what he had hired *me* for, after all. And why would anyone put in weird-ass bolts that didn't fit any tool?

Were they just covers or plugs or something? I can't tell you how many people called the garage in a panic because they were trying to change a tire and didn't realize that the actual bolts were *under* the hubcap. The little domed bits on the plastic cover are only for looks.

So maybe I wasn't screwed, just sleepy and dumb. I could live with that.

I selected a small flat-head screwdriver and worked it under a corner of the Packmaster's casing – carefully. Leo had a beautiful custom paint job and I didn't want to ruin it. Gently, I pried back the metal, but then jerked my hand away with a hiss of pain. A red line sliced all the way along my palm, blood welling up and oozing across my skin.

"Shit!" I said.

Well, *that* was going to make riding fun today. I flipped off the Packmaster and winced.

"Hey, everything okay?" Leo asked.

I jumped again, but in guilt this time instead of pain. I really hoped that Leo hadn't seen me give his motorcycle the bird.

"Your Packmaster bit me," I said.

"Is it bad?" Leo asked.

"No, I'll be fine," I answered quickly. "Maybe I should have had some coffee before getting to work. Did you have custom bolts put on this thing?"

Leo yawned and scratched his cheek. His face was freshly shaved and still a little bit pink along the jawline. But he shook his head.

"Nope," Leo said. "Just the paint. I haven't changed anything else."

I frowned. "Hmm…"

What the *hell* was going on with this motorcycle? I had no idea, but I didn't want Leo to think he was wasting his money on me. If he asked for his deposit back, things were going to get really awkward.

Leo circled his bike, patted the gas tank and then sat down on the curb to watch me work. No pressure.

I picked up my socket wrench again and got ready to explain the problem to Leo. But when I slipped the wrench over one of the bolts this time, it fit perfectly. I rolled my eyes and barely resisted the urge to flip the Packmaster off again. So it *was* just me being dumb.

I was still pissed off, but with the bolts finally playing fair, I quickly stripped back the bodywork to reveal the guts of the bike's steering. I grabbed the handlebars to find that notch, but they pivoted smoothly.

"What? This was stuck like glue yesterday," I groaned. "*Please* tell me you snuck out last night to lube up the bearing."

Leo shook his head. "No. I was in my room all night."

I was about to rename this thing a Packmaster PJO – *Piss Jaz Off* model. I growled at the motorcycle, which made Leo laugh. I was torn between wanting to punch him in the face for that and enjoying Leo's smile. It was a good one.

"Is the bike rideable?" Leo asked.

I sighed and then began bolting everything into place again. "Same as yesterday. So yes, but expect the same problems. I still don't know what's wrong with this beast."

"Then let's have some breakfast and get back on the road. Alright if we hit the same diner as last night?"

"Yeah, just let me grab my things," I said.

I went back into my motel room and washed my hand, then took a look at the gash across my palm. It was jagged and it hurt, but it wasn't too deep. I cussed a little more and cleaned it out with soap, then wrapped it in a towel until the bleeding stopped.

I collected my shampoo from the shower and stashed everything in my backpack again. Outside, I put my tools away while Leo returned our room keys. He came out of the front office just as I was stowing my toolbox into the Bonneville's tailpack.

"How's the hand?" Leo asked. "I've got a first aid kit in one of my bags."

I shook my head. "There's a grocery store right across from the diner. I'll grab some bandages and antibiotic there."

"You sure, Jaz?"

"Yeah, I'm good," I assured him.

I was supposed to be fixing Leo's problems on this trip, not the other way around. We drove carefully down the little town's single main road and stopped in front of the diner, in view of the windows. Leo headed inside to get a table while I went across the parking lot to the store. I picked out a couple of bandages, a tube of antibiotic ointment, and a big bag of beef jerky in case I needed a snack later.

I hesitated as I approached the check-out counter. My bank account had about five bucks in it and as cheap as this shopping trip was, the total would come to more than that. Which meant using the cash in my wallet – the stolen money that Leo had paid me.

Well, I couldn't ride all day with an open wound in my hand, so I held my breath and dropped my stuff on the conveyor belt. The teenage clerk in a store-branded red vest scanned each of the boxes and I handed him a hundred-dollar bill, which he regarded suspiciously. He tested it with one of those counterfeit pens, but that wasn't the part that worried me – I didn't think Leo and his gang had printed that money.

But the clerk nodded and slid the cash under the tray in his drawer, then counted out my change. I was pretty proud of how even my voice was when I thanked him before scooping up my purchases.

I left the grocery store and hurried back across the parking lot to the diner. There were only a couple of cars outside, and no other motorcycles. I decided that I didn't really feel like navigating breakfast with a bandaged hand, so I stuffed the medical supplies and snacks into my backpack for the moment.

Leo was already seated and his menu lay closed off to one side. Instead, he was staring down at his cell phone screen. The crease between his dark brows didn't look happy and my heart jumped up a few gears.

"Is everything okay?" I asked.

Wasn't that the first thing Leo had asked me this morning? But his hand wasn't bleeding and the biker set his phone face-down on the table.

"Yeah," Leo said. "Just expecting a text."

"Got a girlfriend or boyfriend waiting in San Diego?" I asked.

If I didn't already know that Leo was running around with stolen cash in his saddlebags, a girl or guy might have explained Leo's hurry to get out to California. I *did* know about the money, though... So I was just being nosy.

"When I got up this morning, I asked my friends where they were. But they haven't responded," Leo said. "So I was trying to find them on my mapping app."

That didn't exactly answer my question, but I didn't press Leo. He drummed his fingers on the tabletop until a waiter came by and took our orders. I got a stack of pancakes and eggs over easy, while Leo just ordered some coffee and a bagel. He alternated between staring out the window and down at his phone as he devoured his breakfast in record time. I'm not even sure Leo chewed that bagel.

I followed as much of my employer's lead as I could and ate like I was late for work. As soon as I was done, Leo asked for the check, put on his jacket and paid at the front counter. I didn't bother arguing about paying my share, but went straight to the parking lot and our bikes. By the time Leo joined me outside, I had already applied the antibiotic ointment to my palm and wrapped both hands in my new bandages. Leo closed the distance from the diner to his motorcycle in a few long strides, but paused as he put on his helmet.

"What happened to your other hand?" he asked.

"Nothing," I answered. I wagged my fingers and showed off my now-padded hand. "And I want to keep it that way. Still no gloves, but they shouldn't get as numb today."

"Good call," Leo said as he pulled on his helmet.

"You want me to take another look at that steering?" I asked.

Leo shook his head. "Maybe later. Right now, we need to get moving."

I put on my backpack, tightened the straps and then jumped onto my bike. Leo swung a leg over his Packmaster and stomped it into gear, making the engine roar like some kind of monster. He yanked the heavy motorcycle around in a tight half circle, leaving a faint black arc of rubber burned on the asphalt, and raced out into the road.

For a moment, I considered just letting him go. By the time Leo noticed that I hadn't followed him back to the highway, I could be long gone with the cash that he had already given me.

He probably wouldn't even bother chasing me – Leo was racing off to find his friends and didn't seem to care about much else.

I could forget all about Leo, about his stolen money and his rattlesnake patch, and let him vanish from my life as suddenly as he had appeared. I didn't even need to go back to Crayhill. I had five hundred dollars – minus the cost of some bandages and beef jerky. I could go somewhere else, *anywhere* else.

But I shook myself. Leo had paid me to figure out what was wrong with his weird-ass motorcycle and I wasn't done doing that. Besides, there were worse ways to spend the week than following a hot biker around and letting him buy my food.

Okay, I *really* needed to convince Leo to let me get the next bill. It was only fair, and I had no intention of relying upon some strange man.

I revved the Bonneville, turned it west, and raced to catch up with Leo.

CHAPTER 5

The bandages weren't as effective as real riding gloves, but a couple of hours later, I was too excited to care if my fingers fell right off into the road and got run over by a tractor.

Not that there were tractors here... I leaned over my handlebars and grinned up at the jagged city skyline. Leo and I were driving through Oklahoma City. It wasn't as big as Paris or Los Angeles, but Oklahoma City was a thousand times bigger than Crayhill. There were people here that had never met each other, who never would. I could walk into a bar in Oklahoma City and not know everyone sitting at the counter, and every one of the three shitty beers on tap.

There were whole *new* shitty beers here!

I wished we had time to stop and try one of them, but Leo was in a hell of a hurry and raced through Oklahoma City with barely a glance. I supposed that it was all pretty dinky compared to Chicago, but still... If I didn't have a job to do, I would have been gone in a flash, riding away through the shiny office buildings of the downtown commercial district. Bright, hot sunlight flashed off the glass and turned every skyscraper into a silver blade of radiance.

But I *did* have a job to do, and just trying to stay close enough to do it was proving a challenge. My Bonneville's engine put out sixty-two horsepower, which wasn't bad at all. A Packmaster had somewhere between eighty to ninety, maybe about a hundred if you threw EPA regulations out the window. It's not *that* much of a difference, but I struggled to keep up with Leo through Oklahoma City. Every few minutes, his motorcycle growled thunderously and surged ahead of me.

By the time we were driving out the other side of Oklahoma City, Leo had signaled for me to ride single-file again. I fell back with a frown and followed him at a distance. Okay, I *was* worried about Leo losing control of his motorcycle and side-swiping me, but what about him? If the throttle stuck and he couldn't brake, he was going to end up a biker-sized smear down the center of Highway 44.

Was Leo in *that* much of a hurry, or was his engine surging again? Making sure that his bike didn't crash itself or its rider was my job. And I needed gas, so I accelerated up beside Leo and raised one hand, gesturing for him to pull over. He nodded tightly and took the next off-ramp.

We stopped at a filling station on the western edge of Oklahoma City – that's a gas station if you're from the coast. It was the middle of the day in the middle of the week, and we were alone at the row of pumps. I parked in front of the first one, then ran inside the little convenience store and threw a ten-dollar bill on the counter. The man behind it collected my money and then flashed me a thumbs-up.

I hurried back outside as Leo was climbing off of his motorcycle. The Packmaster's extended tank probably wasn't as low as my Bonnie, but filling up was usually a good idea.

"What's going on with your bike?" I asked.

"Sorry," Leo said. He removed his helmet and ran one gloved hand through his hair. "My engine was surging."

"I'll take a look while we're tanking up."

"Thanks, Jaz."

Leo pushed the gas nozzle into his Packmaster's tank, then punched the button on the pump with one elbow. He pulled out his phone, ignoring the urban myth about cell phones setting fire to gasoline fumes, but he growled something in Spanish and jammed the device back into his pocket.

"Still nothing," Leo said. "What pump are you on? One?"

"Yeah," I answered.

"I'll go square us up."

"Wait, I've already–!" I began, but Leo had turned away and was stalking off in the direction of the store to pay.

Oh, well. I doubted that my Bonnie's little gas tank was going to cost much more than ten bucks to fill, anyway. So instead of chasing Leo down over a couple of dollars worth of top-off, I hunkered down and squinted at the Packmaster, trying to pick out some clue about whatever the hell was causing those weird surges of speed.

Leo must have paid, because the gas pump clicked and then the hose started to hiss softly as gasoline poured into the motorcycle's tank. But just a few seconds later, the pump let out a loud *ka-thunk* and then cut off. I looked up at the display. Only half a gallon... At the next pump, my Bonnie was still thirstily sucking down fuel.

Huh. What the hell? I reached up and gave the gas handle a tentative squeeze, but it thunked and stopped again.

Like the tank was already full.

I tapped my knee, thinking. Perhaps something was leaking into Leo's tank, something besides gas. That might account for the weird surges, if it was burning in the engine at a different rate than properly rated gasoline. Was there a crack in the tank?

I was hesitant to touch the Packmaster again, so I carefully pulled out the fuel nozzle and sniffed the tank valve. I didn't smell anything other than gas... but the whole station reeked of the stuff, so it might have been masking any useful scents.

Well, if there was a breach in the Packmaster's gas tank, then the fuel would be leaking somewhere. I inspected the tank, the seat behind it and the engine beneath, but there was no sign of dripping or oozing gasoline. Everything was shiny and perfect.

Fuel line, maybe? A hole in the line could cause surging and sputtering, but that would empty the tank, not leave it so full that Leo couldn't gas up. I considered popping the air cleaner cover to take a look inside, but while a blocked-up filter might explain the gas tank not draining, the Packmaster wouldn't even be running.

I was about done with Leo's damned mystery bike. I enjoyed a brief fantasy of hosing the motorcycle down with gasoline, then tossing a cigarette at it over my shoulder like in the movies. There was an automated chiming noise as Leo walked out of the station store, holding his cell phone up to his ear, and I suddenly wanted to burn that thing, too. And Leo for good measure.

Whoa, Jaz, I told myself. *Easy... No need to go all murder-happy over a glitchy motorcycle.*

"I haven't heard from my Knights since yesterday," Leo was saying into his phone. "Can you call me if you find anything?"

So he *had* managed to contact someone, but it didn't sound like one of his people. Leo nodded at whatever the other person said, even though I was the only one who could see it.

"Yeah," he said. "Thanks, tío. Bye."

Leo ended the phone call and then hurried back to his bike. Arson was a little extreme, maybe, but my hackles were still up. I knew that my new employer was a criminal and we hadn't talked about that at all. My ass was sore from riding, my cut hand hurt, and Leo's Packmaster was pretty much my mortal enemy. I tried and failed not to frown.

"Finally got in touch with somebody?" I asked.

I hoped I didn't sound as suspicious as I felt and doubted it. I've never been a very good liar. But Leo just nodded at me.

"I called my Uncle Carlos," he said.

"The one in San Diego?" I asked.

"Yeah. My mother's brother. He didn't raise me or anything, but I wish he had. Everything worth knowing in my life, Uncle Carlos taught me."

I wasn't sure what to say to that... I suppose even hardened criminals had loved ones and people who were important to them. Leo took something out of a jacket pocket and tossed it to me – a candy bar.

"Thought you might be hungry," he said.

I caught it and then smiled at Leo. The candy bar had the same branded brown wrapper as the one I had been eating at the garage yesterday. It wasn't my favorite or even high up on my candy list – yeah, I have a candy list – it was just the best on offer in GTA's crappy vending machine.

But Leo didn't know that.

"Thanks," I said.

"Still no word from my friends, though," Leo told me. "What happened with the gas? I barely had to take out my wallet."

"Your bike only took half a gallon," I said. "It won't fill and I can't figure out why."

I summarized my gas-related theories – and why they didn't make sense. Leo frowned down at his bike.

"What the fuck?" he asked. "Does it have anything to do with the engine surges?"

"No idea," I admitted, crossing my arms. "I swear I'm actually good at my job."

Leo ran his hand along the curve of his Packmaster like he was petting a horse. I skipped the horse phase that most little girls seem to go through and jumped straight to motorcycles. So had Leo, apparently.

"And I swear I'm actually a good rider," he said, then patted his bike. "But this big guy seems to have other ideas for both of us."

I laughed and tore open the candy bar Leo had given me. I wolfed it down in three bites while Leo closed his gas tank and pulled on his helmet again.

"If we hurry, we can make it out to Arrow," he said. "That's in Texas. Arrow's a big enough city that we should be able to buy some new shock springs for that Bonnie. My treat."

"You really don't have to do that," I said. "I can get my own shocks. You did pay me for this job, after all. You know, when I actually manage to do it."

Leo shrugged. "We'll split the cost, if you like. But it's in both of our best interest for you to have a smooth ride. You can't fix my bike if your hands are trashed."

"Alright, deal," I said. "And I need some gloves of my own. I'll buy those myself."

"Then let's get moving. My friends were heading for Arrow last night and with any luck, we'll be able to catch up to them by tonight."

Leo's friends. His *gang*. I swallowed the rest of my candy bar in a huge lump of chocolate, caramel and nougat.

"Yeah," I said. My mouth was suddenly dry. "Let's go."

I tossed the empty wrapper in the trash and hurried back to my motorcycle. I replaced the fuel nozzle and put on my helmet, then straddled the Bonneville. Leo gunned the Packmaster and pulled out of the filling station, driving smooth and straight.

For now.

CHAPTER 6

Oklahoma City vanished into the distance. I was sorry to see it go, and not just because it was my first real city. It would have been a great place to stop and buy some new shocks, but Leo had made it pretty clear that he had no intention of slowing down or turning back. He wanted to catch up with his friends, and he wanted to do it today.

And that's why I found myself clenching my teeth so hard that my jaw ached. Not because of the rattling ride, but up until now, it had been just me and Leo... which was a lot like being stranded on a desert island with a hot rich guy. But Leo's friends were a criminal biker gang.

Last night, I overheard Leo telling someone that he had a mechanic – me. Okay, they had some warning that Leo would be bringing an outsider. That was good... But that rattlesnake patch meant armed robbery, drugs and often prostitution. Some biker gangs ended up with murders attached to them, too, and serious vehicular manslaughter charges.

Was that something I really wanted to get involved with? Leo seemed nice enough – as far as I could tell – but what about the Knights of Hell? The name certainly didn't sound very inviting.

No matter how much I tightened my grip, my hands shook on the Bonnie's handlebars and it wasn't because of the shitty old suspension.

Leo had blown into Crayhill to change my whole life with a sexy smile and a heap of cash. Was I about to pay the price for that? Did I still have a choice? Maybe not, but I wasn't about to show up for what might be a tire-iron bludgeoning without at least asking a few questions.

We left Oklahoma behind and crossed into Texas as the sun began to set, painting the sky in brilliant red and purple. Traffic on Highway 44 was sparse this far outside of the cities, and only a handful of tail lights lit up the darkening evening in intermittent red embers like demonic eyes. The Packmaster had more or less behaved all afternoon and we rode side by side, so I raised my arm and pointed off with one finger, gesturing Leo to pull over again.

There wasn't a filling station out here, so we pulled off onto the shoulder. This stretch of Highway 44 was little more than a few miles of cracked asphalt, and my tires crunched over gravel as I stopped beside Leo. A pickup truck drove past and honked once at us, then vanished into the deepening evening and left me alone on the highway with Leo.

He removed his helmet and ran his fingers through his hair. That had quickly become a highlight of my day since taking this job, but right now my heart was jackhammering too hard to enjoy it. I left my own helmet on – not because I didn't feel like dealing with my wild collection of natural curls in the rising evening wind, but in case this conversation went south. I had to be ready to run.

"What's the problem?" Leo asked.

"Look, Leo..."

I had spent all afternoon silently rehearsing what I wanted to say, telling Leo that I knew what the rattlesnake patch meant, that I knew his money was all stolen and I needed some guarantee of safety once we caught up with the Knights of Hell.

But now I choked. My mouth was dry and I couldn't seem to suck enough air down into my lungs.

Leo's brow furrowed while he waited for an answer, but then his eyes went wide and the biker held up a hand as he snatched his cell phone out of his pocket. Damn that phone... But it wasn't a call. I craned my head to look at the screen. Leo wasn't reading a text message, either – it was some kind of map, and a red dot blinked in the center.

"What's that? One of your friends?" I asked.

"It's a location ping." Leo's voice was bright with excitement. "That's Audrey and she's close!"

"Wait, Leo...!" I said.

We still needed to talk, but Leo was already on the move. He jammed his helmet back on and kicked his motorcycle to life. Gravel sprayed through the air as he roared off in the direction indicated by his phone. I swore a few times and then raced after Leo.

It was a damned good thing that the cops didn't seem interested in this lonely stretch of highway – Leo had to be pushing a hundred miles an hour. I struggled to keep his taillight in view as he shot down the highway and then out along a narrow off-ramp. There was no name printed on the green metal sign – just a number – and the ramp dumped us out onto an empty single-lane country road. It was little more than a streak of darkness, without streetlights or even traffic markings on the asphalt.

Something smelled awful. I recognized the scents of burnt rubber and gas, but there was something else, something worse. The smell was sharp and rancid, making my stomach churn. It reeked like an infected wound. I gagged and slammed on my brakes as the stench hit me full-force.

What the hell *was* that?

Up ahead of me, Leo's motorcycle skidded to a sudden stop in the darkness, too. His headlight shone over something scattered across the road.

Bikes... and bodies.

Holy shit. There had to be twenty people laying there in the road, all unmoving. Blood sprayed the pavement around the dead bikers like dark wings where several of them appeared to have been thrown from their crashing motorcycles. Others were slumped over their bikes or crumpled right in the middle of the road.

Leo leapt off his motorcycle so fast that there was no way he could have set his kickstand, but the Packmaster remained upright as he ran down the road toward the carnage.

"Audrey?" Leo shouted in a voice loud enough to hear even over my Bonneville's engine. "Danny? Sam?"

But no one answered. Leo reached into his jacket and drew something that shone in the light of our headlamps. Was that a gun? Shit, yeah... Leo held a snub-nosed revolver pointed down at the ground with his finger on the trigger. He moved through the battlefield of bodies.

What the fuck was going on here? I wasn't sure, but I knew it was bad. Really, really bad.

"Leo!" I called out. "Don't!"

He either didn't hear me or just didn't give a shit. I yanked the bandage off my uninjured hand and clapped the rubberized cloth over my mouth. It wasn't exactly a respirator, but it helped a little with the eye-watering smell.

"Audrey!" Leo shouted.

I chased after him, but then stumbled to a stop next to the nearest body. It was a big, bearded white guy lying dead under a torn and twisted Harley. He wore full leathers, including a jacket with the same flaming helmet and rattlesnake patches on the shoulders as Leo's. Shit, so these *were* the Knights of Hell... But it wasn't the gang patches that brought me to a halt.

The motorcycle was smashed as though it had run full speed into a concrete wall – though there wasn't anything like that here on the open, empty country road – and the bearded biker's helmet had shattered. Beneath, his face was bloodlessly pale, but his veins bulged black under waxy white skin. His eyes were open and bright red with ruptured blood vessels.

I stared. Something dark flecked the corners of the dead man's mouth. More blood? But no, it gleamed with a blue-green shine... There were flies on the body, but they didn't move when I leaned in to get a closer look.

Even the insects were dead.

Suddenly, a bandage over my mouth didn't seem like nearly enough. I held my breath and backed away as quickly as I could, not stopping until I bumped into my motorcycle.

"Leo, get out of there!" I cried, but the bandage muffled my voice. "These guys didn't just crash. They've got Ebola or something!"

It didn't really look like Ebola. It didn't look like *anything* I had ever heard of before – but I knew cars and motorcycles, not diseases. Whatever it was, though, it sure as hell wasn't healthy and I didn't want to breathe any of it.

But Leo still wasn't listening to me. He ran from one body to the next, searching and calling out names with a rising edge in his voice.

"Jett? Shit... Shit!" Leo shouted. "Mason? What the fuck...? Audrey!"

He staggered across the shadowed road and fell to his knees next to one of the bodies, a woman with short red hair and a snake tattooed up the side of her neck. Leo threw his head back in a wordless howl of anguish and slammed his fists down into the pavement.

"We... we have to call someone," I stammered. I fumbled my phone out of my pocket and stared at the screen. "The police? What's the number for the CDC?"

Leo jumped to his feet and crossed the distance between us inside a single stuttering heartbeat. He still held the gun and I flinched violently. Leo slapped his free hand over mine, covering the cell phone.

"No, Jaz–!" he began.

But as soon as Leo's hand touched mine, I was suddenly plunged into my dream again. A demon charged at me down the dark country road, riding a black horse whose mane and tail were plumes of pale green smoke. Sparks flew with every strike of its hooves against the asphalt. The horseman sitting astride the galloping mount was tall and indistinct, but its eyes oozed sickly emerald light. Something inside me recognized the monster and roared.

Pestilence!

Leo and I both gasped, staggering away from one another. I stared at him and he stared right back, brown eyes wide. Dreams are only supposed to happen when you're asleep – that's what makes them *dreams*. When you start seeing shit while you're awake, those are hallucinations.

"What the hell was that?" I asked in a shaky voice. "Did you see... whatever that was?"

"The guy in a suit," Leo said. "With a racing bike and flies in his mouth."

"What? No, I saw some kind of demon on a horse... thing."

"I don't know," Leo told me. "I have no fucking idea what's going on!"

"Maybe whatever's in the air is making us see things," I said. "We need to–"

But Leo moved in close again and placed his hand over my cell phone screen once more, careful not to touch me this time.

His dark eyes burned with an emotion that I couldn't quite identify. And wasn't sure I wanted to.

"No police," he said. "Please, Jaz. Don't call the cops."

"We can't just do nothing!" I protested.

Leo's hand tightened around my cell phone. He didn't yank it out of my grasp, but the case creaked ominously in his grip. The phone was shaking, and I suddenly realized that I wasn't the one trembling.

"These were my friends," Leo said. "Let me... Just wait to call the cops, okay? Phone in an anonymous tip when we're gone."

"Gone? Leo, what if we're sick?" I asked.

But even as I said it, I doubted that we had contracted whatever fatal demon-flu had killed the Knights of Hell. Their bodies were scattered across the ground among the wreckage of motorcycles. Some of them clutched weapons in their hands – switchblades, concealable revolvers like Leo's, and a few bigger automatic guns. These people had died fighting, not trying to get to a hospital.

This disease or biological weapon or whatever it was had clearly hit the bikers fast. And violently. I stared down at my hand. There was no sign of blackened or bulging veins under my skin. Leo was still wearing his fingerless gloves, but while his face was pale, it didn't seem dangerously so.

If this thing was going to kill us, it would likely have started already. But other than being scared right out of my mind and nauseous from the smell, I felt fine.

"Just don't touch any of the bodies," I told Leo. "Or... or any of the blood."

He nodded once and ran back into the road. He counted the corpses scattered there in a choked voice. Did he hope that one of his friends had made it out of this open-air charnel house? But it didn't take Leo long to give up that hope. I could see it in the slump of his shoulders.

Instead, Leo began sifting quickly through the other bikers' saddlebags. He came up with handfuls of cash. Was he really worried about the money? But Leo was also carefully collecting weapons and wallets, too.

Cleaning up evidence, I suddenly realized. When the cops or fire department or whoever arrived, Leo didn't want his friends getting into trouble with the law, even posthumously.

He closed each of the switchblades and removed the bullets from the guns, then dumped it all into an empty backpack. After a final circuit of the scene, Leo came jogging back. His eyes were red and the bottom dropped out of my stomach. But that wasn't blood running down Leo's cheeks – he was crying.

"That's everything... I think," Leo said, and then took a deep, shuddering breath. "Alright, let's go. You can call the cops from Arrow and... and we'll deal with the rest later."

The rest...? Did Leo mean dealing with me, or was I being paranoid? Did *anything* count as paranoid in the middle of all this? My dream of running away from Crayhill to see the world with a pocket full of cash had just turned into a nightmare.

But I couldn't worry about that right now. All I could do was nod to Leo and climb back onto my motorcycle. We had to get out of this plague pit.

I would deal with the rest later, too.

CHAPTER 7

"Two rooms," Leo told the man behind the desk. "Ground floor, if you have them."

Arrow Lodge was a cheap motel a few miles off Highway 44 and the clerk had to be used to suspiciously late-night check-ins, but he kept one eye on Leo and maintained his sour expression. He clearly didn't approve of something, but I was way too tired to figure out if it was the hour, our leathers, or Leo's tattoos. Or maybe we just stank. The dead Knights of Hell were two hours behind us, but I still hadn't been able to shake the smell.

The clerk's disapproval eased a bit when Leo paid for both rooms in cash, and he slid a couple of flimsy key cards across the desk.

"Room number five," the clerk told us. "That's on the ground story. Eleven is right above it. Best I've got."

"That's fine," Leo said.

The man behind the desk gave us a final half-disapproving look before picking up his fishing magazine again and ignoring us. Leo grabbed the keys and we hurried back outside. He held out the little cardstock envelope with a number eleven written on it. I took it, but then stuck the key card into my pocket.

"Leo... we need to talk," I said.

He hesitated, but then nodded. We walked our motorcycles across the parking lot and left them next to each other in an empty spot facing a blue-painted door marked with a brass number five. True to the clerk's word, room eleven was upstairs, right overhead. I retrieved my backpack and followed Leo to his door. He took the card from its envelope and jammed it into the lock. A light flashed green and we went inside.

The room was small and basic, with a twin bed covered in plain white sheets. It would have fit just as easily into a hospital as a motel room. There were a few watercolor landscape prints framed on the wall, all faded into pastels by years of too much sunlight. Leo pulled the blackout curtains shut.

I dropped my bag next to the door and Leo set his own backpack down more gently on the bed. Was that because there were weapons inside? Or because they belonged to his dead friends?

Leo went back to the door and turned the deadbolt, then set the chain. Slowly, he unzipped his leather jacket and I caught a glint of steel just before Leo drew his gun again. It was a snub-nosed revolver, small enough to conceal but plenty big enough to blow a hole right through a terrified mechanic.

I gulped and stepped back until I hit the motel room wall. My heart pounded like it was about to fight its way out of my rib cage, but Leo only stripped off his jacket and set his gun on the bedside table. The tall biker slumped down onto the edge of his bed and put his face into his hands.

"You can call the cops now, Jaz," Leo said through his fingers. "They can call the doctors or... or whatever."

"Are you sure?" I asked. My voice cracked and I cleared my throat before going on. "Look, I know you're running from the police. Or at least avoiding them."

I pointed with a trembling finger down at the shoulder of Leo's jacket draped across the bed beside him. He dropped his hands into his lap, revealing eyes rimmed in red, and followed my gesture toward the rattlesnake patch.

"You recognize that?" Leo asked.

I nodded. "I've been playing with motorcycles since I was five years old. I know the gang patches."

"Alright, yeah," Leo said in a heavy voice. "I'm road captain for the Chicago chapter of the Knights of Hell. Every one of the people we found back there were my friends – and my responsibility."

Road captain? That wasn't the gang founder or anything, but it was a pretty high rank for a guy Leo's age. He wasn't much older than I was… He must have done something important. Or else he knew someone who had.

"Does all that stolen money have anything to do with what happened to them?" I asked.

Leo had slumped on the bed, but now his head snapped up and he snarled.

"What?" Leo asked. "No!"

I jumped at the sudden heat in Leo's voice, but pressed myself back against the motel room wall and kept watching him. Some kind of horrible nightmare had played out on that little road off Highway 44 and I needed to know why.

"Then… then what did you do?" I asked.

Leo hesitated. He reached out to touch one of the patches on his jacket. Not the snake, but the flame-crested helmet. His large hands were shaking again.

"We hit a bank truck," Leo answered at last. "That's where all the money came from."

"You stole from a bank," I said. I felt like someone had to state the obvious.

"Yes," Leo admitted. "But it's all FDIC insured. No one lost any money except the bank. Some executive's bonus might be a little light this quarter, but those guys already have more than they deserve."

No bank had ever done me or my family any favors, and I didn't feel particularly sorry for whatever white marble building Leo's gang had stolen a few hundred thousand dollars from... But what the hell had I gotten myself into? What did this have to do with all those dead bikers?

"What happened?" I asked. "Did you kill anyone?"

Leo shook his head. "No. That's not how I do things. A few broken bones and one of the guys Audrey hit is probably going to be seeing double for a while. You got a problem with that?"

"Uh, yeah. A bit," I said.

"Do you know the first job I ever did?" Leo asked suddenly.

He fixed me with dark, intense eyes and I somehow doubted he was about to tell me the story of flipping burgers at some Chicago fast-food joint.

"James was road captain before me," Leo said. "He got wiped out by some weekend driver who didn't think they needed to check their mirrors before changing lanes. Then they drove off and left James bleeding on the side of the freeway."

I winced.

"James survived the crash. Barely," Leo said. "But the medical bills were more than he could pay. So I called the other Knights and we hit a bank one morning, while they were still opening up. James can't ride anymore, but all his bills are paid now."

I leaned against the wall and wrapped my arms around myself to keep from trembling. Leo's expression was intense, but he wasn't shouting. What if that changed, though? The biker was twice my size and that gun was just a few feet away. Should I try to grab it? Try to shoot Leo before he could shoot me?

I did my best to ignore that line of thought, but the butterflies in my stomach were all puking.

"I don't know what went wrong this time," Leo said. Now his voice had dropped to something barely above a whisper. "We've done jobs like this a dozen times. We were just taking the haul to San Diego, like we always do."

"Why take the money to San Diego?" I asked. "That's a long drive."

"Because that's where my Uncle Carlos is," Leo said. "He's one of the founding members of the Knights of Hell. The original gang. He sponsored me for road captain after things went down with James."

So I had been right on both counts. Leo's loyalty to the old road captain must have impressed the other ranking Knights of Hell, but being related to a gang founder probably didn't hurt either. Somehow, I couldn't feel very proud of myself for gauging the situation correctly.

"We go to Carlos whenever we need to lay low for a while and get some cash cleaned," Leo told me. "My uncle knows a lot more people than I do, on both sides of the border."

That was who Leo had been talking to on the phone back at the filling station. There was a weight of history and all sorts of subtext when Leo talked about his uncle. Carlos was clearly an important man in Leo's world... But something had gone really, really wrong in that world.

And now the Knights of Hell were dead. Leo wiped his eyes. They were bloodshot and tears shone across his knuckles in the light of the bedside lamp.

"Leo..." I began.

What should I say? What *could* I say...? His friends were all dead. But if we didn't figure out what the hell was going on, we would end up the same way.

"Was the cash you stole... I don't know... mob money?" I asked. "Did someone come after them to get it back?"

Leo stared down at his tattooed hands and clenched them into fists.

"No," he said. "It was just the bank's money. Cash from the federal depository in Chicago. It didn't belong to any particular account. It was only going to sit in a vault until someone withdrew it. And my Knights weren't shot. They were... sick."

"The government, then?" I asked.

I stood and paced over to the window, peeking out through the drapes into the parking lot. Our motorcycles sat outside and it felt weirdly like Leo's Packmaster was glaring at me. I closed the curtains again.

"Jaz, the Knights didn't get into a shootout with the cops," Leo said. "Or state troopers. Not that Texas has those..."

"How do you even know that?" I asked.

Leo gave me a smile so weary that it barely qualified. "I've made this run a dozen times before, remember? But nothing like this has ever happened."

"Maybe it was some kind of biological weapon," I suggested. "The sort of weaponized super-virus you see in movies. But why use something like that against bikers who stole an insignificant amount of money?"

"Hey," Leo objected, but his heart just wasn't in it.

I crossed my arms. "On the scale that the government wastes money every day? Have you ever *seen* the federal budget? I'm pretty sure everything you've ever stolen is less than a drop in the bucket."

"Yeah... I suppose," Leo said. But he kept staring down at his clenched fists.

"Maybe it was something on the money," I suggested. "Some experimental deterrent?"

Leo's fists tightened until his leather riding gloves creaked and his knuckles popped like miniature gunshots. I flinched, but then shook my head.

"Wait, no," I said. "We've both been handling the money for a couple of days now. So have my parents... I haven't gotten any more panicked calls from my dad and I feel fine."

Well, that wasn't quite true... But I felt scared and lost, not sick. Leo finally looked up at me.

"What about that hallucination?" he asked. "That thing we both saw?"

The green-eyed demon on horseback was straight out of my worst apocalyptic dreams. Apparently, my nightmare was tired of being forgotten by the second cup of coffee.

"But you hallucinated something else," I pointed out. "You saw a man in a suit, right? On a motorcycle?"

Leo nodded slowly. "But it wasn't human. I think it was the same thing you saw. Just... in a different skin."

Well, *that* was a horrifying idea. I shuddered violently and tightened my arms around myself.

"How do you know that?" I asked.

"I don't know!" Leo answered in a deep snarl. "I don't know anything. All of my friends are dead and I don't even understand why!"

I didn't know, either. None of this made any sense, but whatever it was, it was dangerous. A bunch of badass bikers with guns were all dead and I really didn't want to end up the same way. Leo stood and began pacing the length of the motel room like a caged tiger.

"If someone or something did that to your gang, are they going to come looking for you next?" I asked. "Did they know where you were going?"

Leo stopped pacing to stare at me, the blood draining from his face.

"Shit," he said. "I need to call Carlos."

Leo grabbed his phone out of the pocket of his jeans and dialed, jabbing at the screen so hard that I worried he might shatter the glass. Leo paced away from me, but he turned up the volume loud enough that I could hear the line ring.

And ring. Leo gripped his cell phone until the case groaned. Finally, the ringing stopped and there was a click.

"Uncle Carlos?" Leo asked. "Are you there?"

"I'm here," said a voice on the other end. "What happened?"

Carlos' voice was far more accented than his nephew. It was deep and rough, like his vocal cords had been dragged behind a motorcycle for a few miles. Not exactly the voice of an angel, I thought, but Leo slumped in obvious relief against the wall of his rented room.

"I... I found my Knights, tío," he said, voice shaking. "They're all dead. Something killed them. They were all sick with something... unnatural."

"I know," Carlos answered.

Leo straightened up, his eyes wide and expression shocked. I suspected I looked pretty much the same. Carlos *knew*? What did he know, precisely?

Leo stepped in close to me and angled the phone so I could hear better. It didn't help much, but I appreciated the thought – especially since this whole thing was making me an accomplice in grand larceny and possibly biological warfare. It was the least Leo could do.

"What happened to them?" he asked. "How do you know?"

"I know who did this," Carlos answered. "And I know what's happening to you. I know about your dreams."

"What?" I blurted.

I wasn't sure if I was supposed to be quiet, but I couldn't help myself. Was Uncle Carlos talking about my weird-ass recurring apocalyptic nightmares? Was Leo having some kind of dreams, too? Leo caught my eye and I didn't think he could stare any harder, but I swear that I felt that look in my soul.

And it burned.

"You're not alone," Carlos said, and he didn't make it sound like a question. He had heard me, apparently.

"Yeah," Leo admitted.

"Who is it?" Carlos asked.

"That's Jaz," Leo said. "She's the mechanic who's helping me with the Packmaster."

"Has she been having the dreams, too? Of the war?" Carlos asked.

Leo looked at me and I nodded slowly.

"Yes," he answered.

"You felt it, didn't you?" Carlos said in his low, engine-growl voice. "The call. There were other garages and other mechanics. But you wanted *her*."

Leo's eyes widened and my heart pounded. We both stared at the phone.

"Yes," Leo breathed.

"Something is happening to you," Carlos said. "Both of you. But we can't do this on the phone. Come to San Diego as fast as you can."

"What?" Leo asked.

"Get your ass to San Diego. Burn up the road and be ready for action. I've got answers and solutions for you when you get here."

"I'll be there soon, tío. Be careful," Leo said.

"Drive fast and drive hard," Carlos told him. "I'll be waiting."

That seemed to be about as much of a goodbye as either of them were going to give and Leo hung up, pocketing his phone again.

"Umm, what the hell is going on?" I managed to stammer. "How does your uncle know about my weird nightmares? And... and you've been having them, too?"

Leo nodded. "Dreams about demons fighting angels? Yeah."

"For how long?" I asked.

"I'm not sure," Leo said. "But I never told Carlos about them. They were just dreams."

"Until today. Why the *hell* would we both be having the same dreams?" I asked.

"I don't know," Leo said. "But Carlos does."

"Do you trust him?"

Leo rounded on me with anger burning in his brown eyes.

"Carlos is family," Leo said. "He's the only reason I'm *alive*."

"Okay, okay. Easy on the gas there."

Leo sat heavily on the corner of the bed again. "I'm sorry, Jaz. You didn't deserve that. But yes, I trust Carlos more than anyone else on this planet. If he says he knows what's going on, then he does. And if we want to understand, we need to get to him."

I was scared, more frightened than I had been in my entire life and my heart was still seriously considering a coronary. My feet moved of their own volition, taking a step toward the motel room door. I had to get away from this whole terrifying thing. This wasn't just a weird dream anymore... People were dead and I didn't know why.

But Carlos said he had answers. If I ran now, I would never learn them.

"I can't get all the way to San Diego without your help," Leo said. "I need you, Jaz, and I need to know why this is happening. Don't you?"

I froze in front of the door. The urge to run away was overwhelming. Every muscle in my body was taut as a guitar string and my pulse raced... But when push came to shove – and I felt pretty damned shoved – I knew the answer to Leo's question.

"Yeah," I said. "I need to know."

Leo smiled a little. It looked tired and his eyes were still red, but he nodded at me.

"I'd like to get back on the road right now, but we need at least a few hours of rest," he said. "Then we'll leave first thing in the morning."

I shook my head. "If your bike will let us."

CHAPTER 8

Leo volunteered to call in the anonymous tip to the cops and I agreed. He knew what details to avoid that might implicate his dead friends. I lingered in the doorway just long enough to watch Leo dial 911 and listen to the harried-sounding dispatcher on the other end connect him with the local police.

I didn't want to make Leo recount the horrors that we had witnessed to a larger audience than was strictly necessary, so I went upstairs to room eleven and dropped my backpack onto the narrow bed, then flopped down into the covers next to it. Had I ever been so tired? Pretty sure the answer was *no*. Even my worst days at Golden Touch Auto hadn't involved apocalyptic visions, a highway plague pit full of bikers, and a temperamental motorcycle with mystery malfunctions.

Okay, my last day at GTA *technically* included the first weird-ness with Leo's Packmaster, but it had been a long, shitty and weird day. I think I was allowed a little hyperbole.

That stupid motorcycle... Maybe I should get up and go take another look at the bike. Leo said that he couldn't have gotten this far without me, but was that true? I still had no idea what was causing any of his mechanical problems – to say nothing of actually fixing them. All of the steering, surging, electrical zaps and now fuel tank overflow issues made absolutely no sense. They surfaced just long enough to make things difficult for us, but then vanished before I could pin them down and put a wrench to them.

I was tired, though, and trying to wrestle the Packmaster in the middle of the night seemed like a good way to get cut again. I resolved to deal with it in the morning.

I hadn't taken off my shoes or jacket, but I just threw an arm across my face and figured I would be asleep within seconds. But I found myself staring at the dim, colorless sparkles of light dancing behind my eyelids. Inwardly growling about the Packmaster was easier than thinking about what was going on with the motorcycle's owner.

How much did I actually trust Leo? Just because a hot guy walks in and offers you a lot of money to run away from home doesn't make him trustworthy. And then what about his Uncle Carlos? I knew nothing at all about him except that he was a founding member of a criminal biker gang. Carlos had offered answers, but I saw the dead Knights of Hell there in the darkness behind my closed eyes, their corpses bloated and mouths crusted in blood.

Was this worth the remaining twenty thousand dollars Leo had promised me? I left Crayhill to see the world and build a real future for myself, but that future wouldn't be a very long one if I came down with the plague or whatever had killed Leo's Knights.

I felt strange. Not sick, but like the hairs were standing up along the back of my neck. Wait, wasn't I more likely to contract a disease through an open wound or something?

I sat bolt upright in the motel bed and yanked the bandage off my hand. The cut left there by the Packmaster was a scabbed line across my palm, but it was no longer bleeding or even red.

Wow, that was fast... I frowned and flexed my fingers. The skin pulled tight, but there was no pain.

That was weird... but there was no sign of infection or creepy blackened veins, either. For now.

My Bonneville was parked right downstairs. I could still ride away from all of this bullshit. As long as I had my motorcycle, I had my freedom. Maybe I could strike out north for Colorado. Denver was a nice big city, chock full of opportunities for a fresh start. One without Leo and his mystery motorcycle or dead biker gang.

But could I really just... leave? I had told Leo that I wanted answers. And I did, but what if whatever had killed Leo's gang came for their road captain? We couldn't get any answers from Carlos if we were dead on the highway to San Diego. But how else could I find out what was going on?

Something is coming...

There was a soft knock from outside and I jumped, my heart pounding. I clambered up off the bed and ran to the door. Leo must have decided not to wait until morning to get moving. Unless there was something *else* he wanted in the middle of the night... I held my breath and looked out the peephole.

Nope. There was a little old white lady at my door. She had to be my grandma's age, wearing a buttoned-up cardigan and a purple felt pillbox hat like she was on her way to church. She seemed somehow familiar, but Crayhill was small enough that I knew every single person there by sight, if not by name. And this woman was none of them.

The little old lady seemed to stare right back at me through the peephole. She raised one tiny, bird-like hand and knocked again. Maybe she was lost... But before the thought had entirely formed in my head, I was unfastening the chain lock. I opened the door.

"Um, hi," I said. "Do you need something?"

"Of course," the woman in the pink knit cardigan told me. "We need you."

I blinked. "Not to be rude, but what are you talking about, lady? Who are you?"

"This vessel thinks of me as Gabriel."

"Gabriel who...?" I asked, frowning.

"Gabriel the archangel," the woman answered. "That name means something to your vessel, too, I believe. It seems to be a common paradigm in this part of the world."

She stepped toward the door and I moved to block her path, but the woman slid right past me. Holy shit, she was a fast little thing. The old lady glanced around my room without curiosity and then turned back to face me.

"It is time to depart, Uriel," she said.

"Hey, my name is Jasmine," I told her. "Not Uriel. And you're not making a lot of sense. I really think you should go."

My day was more than weird enough and I just wanted a few hours of sleep, preferably without any demonic dreams. I put a gentle but firm hand on the old lady's shoulder to steer her back out of my room.

But as soon as I touched her, I almost fell over as blinding light eclipsed my vision. The motel, the parking lot outside, the whole damned universe vanished and I was thrown back into my dream again. I was in a void, a place so vast and empty that I would never be able to properly describe it later. This wasn't the emptiness of a clear sky or a deep, dark underground cavern. There was *nothing*.

Yet I wasn't alone in the darkness. Gabriel was there beside me, a bodiless but powerful presence. I felt the other two archangels there with me... Michael and Raphael.

And facing us were the *other* four – the enemies.

But it wasn't time to do battle again. Not yet. Light and formless matter gathered between us in the heart of the great void, growing hotter and denser under the force of our combined will. And then, in an instant, the entire universe exploded outward through the darkness, glowing and coalescing into stars and nebulae and planets, blooming like flowers in a garden. All of creation spread out before us, waiting...

I staggered back away from Gabriel, gasping and grabbing my head.

"What... what the hell was that?" I asked.

"You were always the strongest of us," Gabriel said. "That is why you lead, Uriel. But your vessel is strong, too."

Yes, agreed a directionless, sexless voice. *I grow more powerful each day, but she has not yielded to my control.*

"It may be the horseman's proximity," Gabriel said.

"Wait, you can hear that?" I asked. "That... voice?"

Perhaps, said the voice, ignoring my question and answering Gabriel's instead. *Contact with the horseman did awaken me. But this vessel is reluctant to leave him.*

"Hey!" I shouted. "Stop that!"

I made a T with my hands, the universal signal to wait just a damned minute. Gabriel looked up at me with unconcern as I turned a quick circle, searching for whoever she was talking to. But there was no one else.

That voice was coming from *inside* me. Inside my own mind. Shit, was I hallucinating again?

"What the hell are you two talking about?" I cried. "What's going on? Why is there a voice in my head? What horseman? Is it here?"

"Death is upon us," Gabriel said. "Leader of the horsemen, our eternal enemies."

Those must have been the other four... things I felt when I touched her. The four horsemen.

If any of this was actually happening at all. Maybe... maybe I was just dreaming again. Had I fallen asleep on the motel bed?

God knew I was tired and all of this was plenty weird enough to not be real.

The four archangels and the four horsemen, said the voice in my head. *We shall gather our forces, and then it will begin.*

I jumped at the sound of the voice inside me and slammed into the wall. The fire exit map swung wildly and then fell to the floor with a thud.

"Shit, don't do that!" I said. "Then *what* can begin? What are you talking about?"

"The final battle," Gabriel answered far too calmly. "Come, Uriel. Our proximity strengthens us, but it will wake Death as well. We must unite all four of us before the war may finally be waged."

"What? No! I don't want to be in a war!" I protested.

Gabriel grabbed my hand in her tiny ones before I could move, but I didn't feel her lined and folded skin against mine. There was only the sensation of bright fire filling me and then stretching out into long wings of pure light. At least, I *hoped* it was only a sensation...

"We must go, Uriel," Gabriel said. Her arthritic hand gripped onto mine like a vice. "Pestilence has already come seeking its brothers. The horsemen hear the call, too, but you know they do not respect the law – even if they helped to craft it. If Death wakes now, it will not hesitate to strike you down and leave us to fight outnumbered."

"We have waited too long to risk losing the war now," Uriel agreed.

The voice in my head spoke through my mouth this time. That light, that force from my dreams was flowing through me, filling my very being and shoving me out of it. I floated somewhere in the bright haze, watching and unable to move. Now *my* body was leading, heading through the motel room door with the weird old lady in tow, and started down the stairs toward the parking lot.

"Come," Uriel said in a ringing voice. "We must go find the other two. I can sense them only faintly."

"They may have manifested far across this planet."

Uriel shook my head. "Then we need to move quickly. We will unite and prepare for battle. And then all of this shall finally end."

Uriel moved down the steps, propelling *my* feet with *my* legs. Bullshit. I did *not* escape Crayhill just to wind up trapped in my own body by some angel – or a voice in my head claiming it was an angel. I didn't have a tire iron or even my own arms to swing one, so I struggled and lashed out with everything else... whatever you have left when your body has been taken away. Every thought and sensation inside me was strange, soft and slow, but I resisted the powerful presence that had taken over. I thrashed and screamed and shoved with every last ounce of will.

Why do you fight me, vessel? Uriel asked. *The horsemen are the enemy and they must be fought. They must be destroyed.*

The archangel was answering me internally, not speaking out loud. That seemed like progress... I grabbed onto that tiny toe-hold and slammed the mental equivalent of my foot into the mental equivalent of Uriel's crotch.

"Get the hell out of my head!" I shouted.

The words came from my mouth and Gabriel released my hand, looking up at me. My body stood frozen on the concrete steps as the archangel thing inside me yanked back and forth for control.

"Uriel–" Gabriel said.

But then the downstairs door banged open and Leo stalked out. He must have been in the middle of getting ready for bed – Leo was wearing his jeans and boots, but he had pulled his leather jacket on over his bare, tattooed chest and his hair was wet. He held the revolver in his hand, but pointed the weapon down at the ground. Leo narrowed his eyes at Gabriel, then turned to me.

"Jaz...?" he asked. "What the fuck is going on here? Are you okay?"

"No, I'm not! Something weird–" I began, but the old lady stepped between us.

"Uriel, fly from this place!" she said. "You cannot fight Death while fighting your vessel, too."

Death? The leader of the horsemen? Uriel said that contact with Death had awakened them.

Did they mean Leo...?

A halo of light suddenly surrounded the little old church-looking lady that burned like a star. Apparently, I had enough control to throw my hand across my face and squint as light seared the motel parking lot. When the glow faded, the old lady wasn't an old lady anymore, or a woman at all.

Or even human.

Gabriel was at least ten feet tall now, a barely humanoid statue made of steel and feathers and glowing light. Four wings stretched out from the archangel's back like great blades of radiance. Leo's eyes flew open wide and he staggered, pressing one hand against his temple as though in pain. But the shirtless biker raised his gun and pulled the trigger. The shot sparked off Gabriel's metal skin and the angel didn't flinch.

"Uriel, go!" Gabriel shouted in a voice like church bells.

"Now is not the time for the final battle," Uriel said. Shit, the angel had control of my mouth again. "As soon as I am gone, flee this place."

Leo ran toward me, but Gabriel was faster and slashed one wing out in a blinding arc of light. It slammed into the nearest vehicle – my Bonneville.

"No!" I cried.

My motorcycle flew through the air toward Leo in pieces. He threw himself under the stairs as flaming chrome rained down over the parking lot and a smoking bike tire crashed through the window of his motel room. My Bonneville was only burning shrapnel now.

"Go!" Gabriel said again.

"Jaz, what the fuck is this?" Leo shouted.

He darted out from behind the motel steps, aimed and shot at Gabriel again. The archangel pounced and crashed into Leo like a lightning strike. They slid out across the asphalt in twin streaks of light and darkness, smashing together right through a parked car.

"Shit!" I cried. "Leo!"

I ran toward Leo like a suicidal idiot. I was back in control of my body. For now, at least. But what could I do? Leo had already shot Gabriel twice, but the angel seemed about as bothered by his bullets as mosquito bites. And I couldn't get away – my bike was a heap of smoldering slag.

I do not require your vehicle, Uriel said from inside me. *Yield control of your body, vessel.*

"Shut up," I told the voice in my head. "Leo!"

I couldn't see him through Gabriel's brilliant glow or the smoke billowing up from the car they had smashed into. Was Leo even still alive?

"What the hell is going on out here?"

The suspicious clerk from the Arrow Lodge front desk came stalking out of the office. He was working in the middle of the night in Texas, so he gripped a shotgun and waved it angrily at us. But this was no good guy with a gun stops a bad guy with a gun scenario. This was... mayhem.

"Get out of here!" I screamed. "Run!"

Gabriel rose from the blackened tangle of metal that used to be someone's station wagon, unfurling four long, burning wings.

The motel clerk's eyes went so wide that I could see the whites all around and he yanked up the shotgun. He pulled the trigger, spraying Gabriel in buckshot.

The archangel glanced back at their new attacker – at least, Gabriel's featureless glowing face *seemed* to turn toward the clerk – and swept one wing in his direction. A spreading arc of white light blazed out across the parking lot, sheering right through the clerk like a guillotine... and the front of the office behind him. The cinder-block wall shuddered and collapsed on top of the dead man with a deafening crash.

Holy shit. I *had* to get out of there. But my Bonnie...! There would be time to mourn my bike later. If there was a later.

But Leo's Packmaster was still parked in front of his room, though it had been knocked over and spun a few yards away. The exhaust pipe was mangled and the beautiful red-and-black paint job was a scraped, scarred mess, but the motorcycle was more or less intact. It would run long enough to get me out of here.

If the Packmaster would let me drive it... Suddenly, the idea of a motorcycle not liking me didn't seem so impossible. A tiny church lady turning into a ten-foot-tall glowing angel with wings like an oversized four-leaf clover of death had set a brand new bar.

I ran toward the Packmaster. I didn't want to leave without Leo, but there was only a crater where he had landed when Gabriel pounced on him. I couldn't even see the biker's body.

"Go, Uriel," Gabriel said in that weirdly resonate voice. "Go before Death–"

Metal chains shot up out of the crater like streamers from a demonic party favor. Each of them was as thick as my wrist and wrapped around Gabriel like boa constrictors. Alright, so it's a mixed metaphor. You do any better when an archangel is demolishing a low-rent motel right in front of you.

I thought I was doing pretty damned well just maintaining bladder control.

The chains tightened around Gabriel and whipped the angel up into the air. They smashed through a corner of the motel and blasted huge chunks of concrete, shattered vending machine, and cheap towels across the parking lot. The chains slithered through the night and then dissolved away into black smoke.

What the hell was down in that crater? One hand and then a second grabbed onto the edge, and Leo dragged himself up out of the cracked asphalt. The biker's expression was dazed, but there didn't seem to be any blood or broken bones.

How...? Gabriel must have hit him at fifty miles an hour. It should have been like getting run over by a truck. But Leo was alive... somehow. I spun on my heels and ran toward the crater.

What are you doing, vessel? Uriel asked.

"Helping him," I said.

No! That creature is Death! the angel told me. *Commander of the horsemen!*

"He's my only ticket out of here," I said.

But I staggered when Gabriel shot up out of the wreckage of Arrow Lodge, shedding dust and debris as the angel spread quadruple wings. The figure shone there in the dark sky like a star for a moment and then Gabriel dove straight at Leo again.

"No!" I shouted.

I sprinted the last steps and hurled myself down on top of Leo. He grunted and we fell together back into the bottom of the crater. I threw my arms around Leo and pressed my face into the shoulder of his jacket, squeezing my eyes shut.

Stop! Uriel boomed in my head. *Release the horseman, vessel!*

A hot wind blasted down on us and brilliant light glowed through my closed eyelids. Would Gabriel burn me to cinders to get to Leo? But the light dimmed a little and I cracked one eye just enough to see the archangel pulling up. Gabriel was flying way too fast, though, and plowed right into the other end of the Arrow Motel. The entire building shuddered and then collapsed in on itself like a shitty soufflé.

"Jaz?" Leo asked from beneath me. "What the fuck...?"

"Get up! We have to go!" I said.

Leo pulled us both to our feet and we scrambled together up the side of the crater, then across the parking lot. The asphalt was cracked and burned, strewn with shattered pieces of what used to be Arrow Lodge. Other than the blasted station wagon, I didn't see a whole lot of other cars in the smoke... But how many people had still been inside the motel?

Leo ran through the flaming carnage to his Packmaster. He grabbed the motorcycle and heaved it upright. Leo threw his leg over the bike and it rumbled to life. Exhaust billowed from the battered pipes and kicked up its own cloud of dust.

"Jaz, get on!" Leo shouted.

I jumped up onto the pillion behind him and the Packmaster bucked hard beneath me like a pissed-off horse. Was it that badly damaged, or was the bike actually trying to throw me off? I flung my arms around Leo, who didn't seem to be having any trouble holding on as he pulled the motorcycle in a tight arc. The tires spun and screeched, billowing black smoke.

"Come on..." Leo growled.

The damaged Packmaster stopped screeching as the tires finally caught and we shot forward. I squeezed the bike between my knees and clung to Leo as we raced into the road. But behind us, Gabriel stood up from the rubble of the ruined motel. The angel shook out glowing wings and leapt into the air.

"That thing is chasing us!" I shouted.

"Hold on," Leo said.

"What the hell do you think I'm doing?"

Leo shifted and his engine roared like an angry lion. The road became a blur of black pavement and yellow streetlights.

The glowing red needle of Leo's speedometer arced around and then buried itself somewhere south of the one hundred twenty mark. I shrieked and had to grab onto Leo's belt.

Wind screamed in my ears and whipped through my hair. My helmet was still somewhere back in the motel rubble that had already vanished into the distance behind us. If I fell off at these speeds, I was going to be a bloody smear on the asphalt. But Gabriel's celestial glow faded swiftly into the night and then finally went dark.

"Did we lose them?" I shouted.

Leo didn't answer, but Uriel did.

When we eight chose our forms for the final battle, the angel told me, *the four forces of chaos invested a great deal of power into their mounts. That is why they are the horsemen... And nothing can outpace a horseman on its steed.*

"So we're safe for now?" I asked.

You are never safe while you ride with Death.

CHAPTER 9

By the time Leo throttled the Packmaster down to non-jet-fighter speeds, the town of Arrow was far behind us. So were the remains of my Bonneville, all of my tools, spare clothes and most of my mental health.

We were back on Highway 44, gunning it west toward San Diego. Toward answers, maybe. Though I couldn't imagine any answer that would make sense of what the hell just happened.

Leo and I both tensed when a dozen police cars, fire trucks and ambulances raced past with their lights flashing and sirens blaring. They were heading in the direction of Arrow... I guess the local emergency responders needed backup when an entire motel exploded.

After the highway went dark again, Leo pulled over onto the gravel shoulder and braked to a stop. The Packmaster's engine idled quietly under us – at least, quietly as a big-ass motorcycle ever got. It purred like a tiger that had just finished a large meal. I was grateful that meal hadn't been filet of Jaz.

Leo half-turned in the driver's seat to look at me. His bare chest was every bit as thickly tattooed as his arms and it shone with sweat as he struggled to catch his breath.

"What the fuck just happened?" Leo asked.

You must leave this mortal, Uriel said. *He is the chosen vessel of Death. When the horseman manifests, it will destroy you.*

"Shut up," I muttered.

Leo frowned.

"No, not you," I told him. I pointed with a shaking hand back in the direction of Arrow. "Okay, this might sound kind of unhinged, but let's keep the context in mind. Leo, are you hearing voices? Inside your head?"

Leo's frown deepened, but he looked as though he was actually considering my question.

"No," he answered at last. "Just the dreams and visions. Are you hearing things?"

I nodded. "Yeah, I am. I might be losing my mind. I hope that won't be a problem."

You are not mad, Uriel told me. *You are serving a purpose. The purpose of your entire universe.*

Of *course* the voice in my head would say that I'm not crazy.

"Did you get hit in the head during all that?" Leo asked. He rubbed his eyes. "Hell, did I? I may not be hearing voices, but there are some uh... blank parts tonight. What happened after that winged thing hit me?"

That is the influence of Death, Uriel told me. *The horseman has not fully manifested, but it will protect itself.*

Well, that probably explained the weird chains that threw Gabriel like a rag doll. But Leo didn't remember doing any of it. Had he been knocked out when the angel slammed him into the ground?

"And what do the voices in your head have to do with that... monster tearing up the motel?" Leo asked.

"Just one voice," I said. "It says it's an archangel, like Gabriel back there."

"Gabriel? That was that thing's name?"

If a disembodied voice could sniff, that's exactly what Uriel did inside my mind.

We are older than names, they said. *But there are... approximations in the myths of this planet.*

"It's apparently sort of a nickname," I told Leo.

"What's yours called?" he asked.

"Um... Uriel," I said.

"Isn't that the angel of death?"

I blinked. Both of my parents went to church most Sundays, but I had spent my weekends working since sophomore year of high school. I had to admit that my angelic knowledge was a bit spotty. Leo's seemed a lot better... But *angel of death* sounded an awful lot like what Uriel called Leo.

We are opposing but more or less equivalent forces, Uriel admitted. *Death and I are the leaders of our respective factions. And so the names found in your stories of us are similar.*

I struggled to make sense of that, but Leo was staring at me. I shook my head and grit fell out of my hair.

"Look, it's not just me," I told him. "Uriel says you're some kind of vessel, too."

"For an angel?" Leo asked, raising an eyebrow.

"No. For... for one of the other guys," I said. Shit, I felt like I was losing my mind. My cheeks went hot as I spoke. "Death, the horseman."

Leo's eyes narrowed to dark, glowering slits.

"What? No," he said. "Bullshit."

I spread my hands. "Look, I don't know if any of this stuff is true. It's only what the voice in my head is saying. But you were attacked by an angel – or something that looked an awful lot like one. It was telling me to run away from you. And while you were down in the crater... something happened, Leo. These chains came up and grabbed Gabriel. Uriel said that was Death defending itself."

"I... don't remember that," Leo admitted. "But... I've had a lot of work done on my bike, and we still must have been doing over two hundred getting out of there. That's *way* over spec. And I felt something when I drove, Jaz. I don't know how to describe it. But it was... good."

Death's bond with its steed, Uriel supplied. *And it will only grow stronger as Death manifests.*

I rubbed my head. It ached and I just wanted to sleep.

"Maybe... maybe we did get sick back there where we found your friends," I said. "Maybe we're hallucinating all this shit. I mean, none of this can *actually* be happening, right?"

Leo looked a little more hopeful at that, but then I remembered something and felt the blood drain from my face.

"Wait, Gabriel said something about one of the other horsemen," I told Leo. "That Pestilence had already come looking for you. And that's the name I heard during that hallucination or vision or whatever it was when we found your friends off the highway. What if Pestilence got to them?"

There was a terrible sort of logic to it and would explain how messed up the bikers' bodies had looked. Leo's hands tightened on the Packmaster's handlebars so hard that his knuckles turned into a row of white spots.

"The Knights," Leo said in a growl. "You're saying you know what did that to them?"

"No," I answered. "I don't *know* anything, Leo. None of this shit makes any sense. The only answers I have are from a disembodied voice inside my head!"

I would not be disembodied if you would yield control of this form, vessel, Uriel said.

"Jaz, what if that voice inside you is lying?" Leo asked. "We've seen what Gabriel is capable of. What if that's who... who killed my friends?"

I do not lie, Uriel said stiffly. *Deceit and disregard for order is the way of our enemies.*

"Uriel says that angels don't lie," I repeated, but sighed and rubbed my face. I really wanted another shower. "But *that* might be a lie. I have no clue."

Leo stared down at the ground and his motorcycle moved beneath me as he shifted his weight back and forth. Just like at Golden Touch Auto, when Leo hired me to leave with him. If I had known what would happen, I'd have told the biker to shove his money where the sun and archangels don't shine.

"Carlos says he knows what's going on," Leo said at last. "He can help us make sense of this."

"Really?" I asked, scowling. "Your uncle can explain an angel trying to kidnap me and throw you through a motel?"

"I don't know," Leo admitted.

He pulled his phone out of a jacket pocket, but the screen was a shattered mess of glass and the whole thing was bent into a distinctly not-factory-standard curve.

"I guess I landed on it when that... angel threw me around," Leo said.

His expression became uncomfortable as he considered that. There was no way Leo should have survived that hit. Not unless the voice in my head had a point.

"Do you still have your phone?" Leo asked.

I found mine in my pocket and unlocked it, but a red battery indicator flashed briefly on the screen before it went dark again.

"Shit," I sighed. "I didn't get to charge it at all before everything exploded. And the cables were in my backpack, so they're buried under about a hundred tons of motel now."

"We can buy a new charger somewhere," Leo said.

I glanced down at the leather saddlebags slung over the tail of the motorcycle. Leo hadn't removed them – they were probably heavy and hard to unload – so he still had plenty of money.

Suddenly, sitting on top of heaps of illicit cash didn't seem like my biggest problem.

"What now?" I asked. "Either we're both losing our minds or something really, really weird is going on. I don't know which one of those is worse."

Leo looked back toward Arrow. We were too far away to see the smoke or emergency lights anymore, but Leo took a deep breath and shook his head.

"I don't think we're crazy," he said. "We just need to get to Carlos. He has answers."

"Unless we want to try calling him from a prison pay phone, we had better be more careful. Let's drive a little slower than a speeding bullet, okay?" I suggested.

Leo nodded. "Yeah, sure. Hey, I've got a pair of spare helmets in there."

He pointed to the saddlebag on my left and I unbuckled the straps. There were more neat stacks of cash inside, but I also found some clothes and a pair of black half-helmets nested together. They wouldn't cover much of our skulls and weren't as safe as full helmets with faceplates – there's a reason that half-helmets were nicknamed *brain buckets* – but they took up less room in a motorcycle's limited storage space and fulfilled most states' helmet laws.

Leo and I might have rented motel rooms with stolen money and run away from the weirdest crime scene in history at speeds that made more sense for a race car than a motorcycle, but at least we would be wearing helmets.

A hysterical laugh escaped me as I held out the larger half-helmet to Leo. When he took it, I pulled on the second one myself while he watched, brows creased. Leo was worried about my sanity, I think, and I couldn't blame him one bit.

The helmet was still a little too large, but my curly black hair was pretty wind-tossed by now and provided enough cushioning to make it work. Hopefully wearing helmets would avoid giving any cops a reason to pull us over... But if we hit something, my brains would be all over the road.

That meant I had to trust Leo's driving and his motorcycle. That didn't seem like a very good idea, but what other option did I have?

You could leave, Uriel said. *And you should. This man is Death, vessel, and you sit astride his steed.*

I opened my mouth to answer, but I was tired of talking to empty air. Instead, I clenched my jaw shut and concentrated.

No, I can't leave, I thought out carefully. *I don't have my Bonnie anymore. And Leo's not the one who cut it in half and leveled a motel. Unless I feel like trying to hitchhike out of here in the middle of the night, I* have *to stick with Leo.*

The subject of my internal argument was watching me, right hand tight on the Packmaster's handlebars. He hadn't put on his helmet yet.

"Jaz... thank you," Leo said.

I stared at him. "For what? I was supposed to fix your bike so you could catch up with the Knights. I haven't fixed shit and when we found your friends, they were all dead."

"That's not your fault," Leo answered quietly. I had to lean in close to catch the words over the deep growl of his bike's engine. "Thanks for not running away when things went all to hell. I wouldn't have blamed you. But you stayed."

"Yeah, well... It's not like I have a lot of other options," I said. "I have no idea what's happening to me and your uncle is the only one with answers. So let's get our asses to San Diego."

Leo nodded and then grabbed a black t-shirt from the open saddlebag. He removed his jacket to pull on the new shirt, then covered himself in leather once more. When he went to buckle his helmet into place, though, I carefully touched his shoulder. Leo stopped and glanced back at me.

"Hey… I'm really sorry about your friends," I said.

"So am I," Leo answered in a thick voice. "They were good people, Jaz. They deserved better and I wasn't there to stop what happened."

"It's not your fault."

Leo put on his helmet and gunned the Packmaster's engine. I pretty much had to read his lips to catch the answer.

"Maybe," he said. "But it will be if it happens again."

CHAPTER 10

W e drove through the night. The Packmaster's back end bucked and forced me to hold on tightly to Leo until my arms ached. What the hell was wrong with the bike? Bad suspension or bent swingarm? The motorcycle *had* been thrown across a parking lot, after all.

Or was the machine just... haunted?

Not haunted, Uriel corrected. *This vehicle is Death's steed.*

Oh, right. I wasn't alone in my own head anymore. No more daydreams about hunky bikers, apparently.

Hunky bikers? Uriel asked.

Stop that!

Arrow had been up in the north of Texas, in the narrow part that people called the Panhandle, and by one o'clock in the morning, we were leaving Texas behind and following Highway 44 across New Mexico. The late night was warm and clear, and we drove beneath the brilliant silver points of a million stars. There were a few long-haul truckers on the highway, occasionally washing out the star-glow with their bright headlights. But then they passed us or we passed them, and we were alone with the heavens again.

Waxing poetic usually meant it was way past my bedtime, and tonight was no exception. I was scared out of my mind by what had happened in Arrow and if I thought about it for too long, I started hyperventilating all over again. But it was also exhausting. I yawned and my head sagged forward until it came to rest against Leo's shoulder. He didn't object, so I left it there.

It's pretty much impossible to sleep on the back of a motorcycle, though, even if it's not a possessed Packmaster trying to shake you off. I held onto Leo as the sky began to lighten from black to violet, and then a blue so deep that it looked like something pulled up from the bottom of the ocean.

My stomach growled nearly as loud as the engine. I tapped Leo on the shoulder and pointed a thumb at my mouth in the standard biker shorthand for *if we don't stop for food soon, I'm going to start chewing on the tires.* Leo gestured to the next green aluminum sign – Novak, 23 miles – and I nodded.

By the time we made it to Novak, my stomach was snarling and I almost wished Leo wasn't throttling back on the demonic speed so much. But we took the indicated exit and followed a road that rose through rocky hills and scattered patches of scrubby green pine trees. As the sun finished rising up over the horizon, we rolled past stores and restaurants all in midwest-styled stucco.

It was still early in the morning, but a restaurant with the name *Country Kitchen Café* printed on a folksy wooden sign was open, so Leo parked along the street out front and I jumped off the Packmaster. I was starving and that run had beat my ass to a pulp. The motorcycle growled metallically as Leo switched it off and I discreetly flipped the damned thing off. You would think a demonic hell-bike could manage a smoother ride. But maybe I was being unfair... It had taken a serious beating last night.

We stashed our helmets back in the saddlebags – which Leo then buckled tightly shut – and went inside. A tall woman in a pink skirt and frilly apron looked up from the coffee pot and told us to take a seat wherever we liked.

Leo pointed to a spot by the door, close to the exit in case we had to run, but we weren't the only people up this early and who needed to eat. There were a few men and women sitting along the counter, and a couple of trucker-looking guys, each at their own table. So I headed toward a booth in the very back of the restaurant where we could talk about bonkers shit without any of the other patrons overhearing.

Leo nodded and followed me through the café. I rubbed my aching tailbone for a moment, then dropped down onto the up-holstered bench. Leo sat across from me and folded his arms on the tabletop.

"How're you doing?" he asked.

"I've got a voice talking batshit inside my head," I said. "And an archangel turned my Bonneville into scrap. I... I worked for years on that bike!"

I pinched the bridge of my nose. Yeah, the loss hurt – a lot – but I wasn't the one who had found all my friends dead on the road from some kind of... demonic disease. I swallowed against a hard lump in my throat.

"It sucks, but I'm okay...ish," I told Leo. "How about you?"

The big biker looked down at the table and sighed. "Shitty, but we don't have much time for that, do we?"

"I guess not."

"Jaz, that angel inside of you..." Leo said, dropping his voice. "Have they told you anything useful? Anything we can do?"

"Not really," I answered. "Mostly they're telling me to give up control of my body and run away from you."

This is what your world and entire universe were created to do, Uriel told me. *And you* should *run. Death slumbers in this mortal and when it meets its brothers, it will awaken.*

"Now they're lecturing me," I said.

The tall woman in the frilly white apron shuffled over to the table, stifling a yawn behind her order pad and then offering up a guilty little smile.

"Sorry," she said. "Early morning for all of us. Hope you slept well."

"Not yet," Leo answered with a tired grin.

I wasn't sure if he was talking about riding through the night or the apocalyptic dreams we were both apparently having. I frowned down at my menu, then up at the server and her name tag – Beth.

"Hey Beth, can I ask you a pretty strange question?" I asked.

"It's early, so I can't promise much of an answer," she said. "But go ahead."

"Have you been having any weird dreams? Like end-of-the-world kind of stuff?" I asked. "Four angels fighting against four horsemen?"

Beth blinked, then raised an eyebrow and shook her head. "I've had a few nightmares about my girl running out on me, but nothing like that. Sounds like you've been having some pretty long nights."

"You have no idea," I said.

"Well, maybe I can improve your morning," Beth said. "How about some breakfast?"

"Coffee," Leo answered, then glanced at me. I nodded. "Two coffees, please."

"And waffles, with lots of whipped cream," I added. "Strawberries, too, if you've got them."

After what we had been through, I figured that I deserved it. Our server dutifully wrote down my order, then turned back to Leo with a smile.

"Any food for you, hon?" she asked.

"Some scrambled eggs and sourdough toast," Leo said.

"Sure thing. I'll have that right out for you two."

Beth yawned again, but she didn't bother covering it up this time, and headed off again in the direction of the kitchen. Leo waited until she was out of earshot, then gave me a curious look.

"What was all that?" he asked. "Why were you asking about her dreams?"

"Until about thirty seconds ago, everyone I've talked to about these... visions... seems to know more about them than I do." I picked up my napkin and twisted it into a knot of cloth between my hands. "Your uncle knew all about the dreams, and you're having them, too..."

"So you're wondering if maybe *everyone* was dreaming about the angels and horsemen," Leo said. "Good idea. But it sounds like the answer is *no*."

"Yeah," I agreed. "But I just remembered something else that Carlos said. How weird a coincidence is it that we met?"

"My bike was giving me a lot of shit. I needed a mechanic," Leo said, but he sounded a little uncertain.

"How long had the Packmaster been acting up?" I asked.

"Before I left Chicago. It started during the job."

"But you *suddenly* decided to get it looked at when you and the Knights were driving past Crayhill?"

Leo frowned. "Yes..."

We four warriors of light and order are drawn together, Uriel said. I barely resisted the urge to rub my temple as the angel's voice echoed in my skull. *As are the horsemen. That is how Gabriel found us, and how Pestilence seeks Death. But the light and the dark are pulled toward one another, as well. We are called to battle. It was... unfortunate that Death got so close before I had control of your form, vessel.*

Leo watched me with one eyebrow raised. "Uriel was talking to you just then, weren't they?"

Apparently, it showed on my face, and so did the flush I felt warming my cheeks.

"Uh... yeah," I stammered. "Uriel says the angels are all kind of pulled together like magnets, and so are the horsemen. That's how they find each other and get stronger. But the two different sides are also drawn together."

"And that's what happened to us?"

I nodded. "According to Uriel. Who is pretty cranky that you got to me before Gabriel did."

"How did my uncle know about it?" Leo asked.

"I have no idea."

Rules were set forth for the final battle, Uriel told me. *It is to be fought by four warriors of light against four warriors of darkness. But the horsemen are forces of disorder and when Death is strong enough, it will not hesitate to kill us.*

I stared across the restaurant booth at Leo. Was there really some kind of evil monster lurking inside of him? Leo certainly looked intimidating with his tattoos, the beginnings of a beard shadowing his cheeks, and all his biker leathers. And I remembered the chains rising up out of the crater in the Arrow Lodge parking lot like impossible metal snakes. I shivered.

Our server returned with two cups of hot coffee, along with a tiny pitcher of cream and a ceramic dish of sugar packets. Leo thanked her as I got to work pouring cream into my coffee, then mixed in five sugars.

Hey, don't judge me. I had a rough couple of days.

Leo stirred his coffee – though he hadn't added anything to it – and licked the spoon. I couldn't blame him for wanting every last drop of coffee, but it was kind of distracting. It was amazing how even when my head was bursting with terror and weirdness, I could still notice how hot Leo was. Which was very.

You must leave him, Uriel told me.

Would you stop that*?* I asked.

Stop what?

Stop listening to all of my thoughts!

We are one, Uriel said. *But you may stop having thoughts, if you wish. I will take control of this vessel.*

And then do what? I asked. *Kill Leo? Or Death or whatever?*

That is not what was agreed upon. When both sides have united, four and four, we shall do battle. Our enemies have little regard for order and law, but we do. Yes, I will kill Death – but only when the time is right.

Leo stared out the nearest window with an intent expression as he drank his coffee in long gulps. Was he watching for cops? Angels? Or maybe the other horsemen...?

Was any of this even really happening?

"Any helpful input from your angel?" Leo asked me, finally turning away from the window.

"No, not really. Just a lot of ranting about the final battle," I reported. "Destroying the horsemen, victory over darkness. Stuff like that."

"Damn it." Leo sighed and raked his fingers through his hair.

"I'm not sure that we can believe what Uriel tells us," I said. My voice sounded too shrill. "Or if they're even real at all. What are the symptoms of schizophrenia?"

"I don't think you're crazy, Jaz," Leo assured me.

Both my heart and stomach clenched. It was nice to know at least one of us believed me... But what if Leo was wrong? What if I was losing my mind?

What if we both were?

I took a drink of coffee. Even with all the cream I had added, it was still hot enough to burn my tongue, but after a long night on the back of a bike that really seemed to hate me, it felt good just to drink something warm and sweet.

Beth appeared again a few minutes later with our breakfast plates balanced on one arm and carrying a coffee pot. She set the food down in front of us and refilled our coffee. Leo looked over Beth's shoulder at a boxy old television bolted up into a corner of the country diner. On the screen, a man with an impressive blond mustache was reporting from... I don't know, a war zone?

I blinked. Wait, no...

That was the remains of the Arrow Lodge. It looked different in the daylight and some of the wreckage had been removed, but there was still black smoke rising from the crater where Gabriel had smashed Leo into the asphalt.

"Holy shit," I said.

Beth finished setting out our food and glanced at the news. "Oh, yeah. There was a big gas leak over in Texas last night. Blew a motel to pieces and everything. A couple of people died. It's a government cover-up, if you ask me."

"Huh?" I asked. "What makes you say that?"

"There was some kind of biohazard thing out on Highway 44 yesterday," Beth said, dropping her voice down into a conspiratorial whisper. "Not far from that explosion. I'm guessing some new biological weapon escaped from a government lab and that 'gas leak' was the military cleaning it up afterward."

Leo stared at Beth with a stricken expression on his face, and I looked down into my coffee. Nope, that wasn't going to do the trick today.

"Hey, can I get a bloody mary?" I asked.

Beth nodded and left again. She detoured to check on her other tables, but I really hoped that she would hurry with that bloody mary. I wasn't driving anymore and I needed a drink.

Leo was still watching the local news over my shoulder and he looked ill. The biker hadn't touched his eggs or toast. I craned my neck to watch the television, too. The mustached reporter gestured animatedly around the ruins of Arrow Lodge. There was no sound, but I wondered if he shared Beth's government cover-up theory. Only when the segment ended and went to commercial did Leo finally look at me again.

"We have to get you a phone charger and some power," he said. "We need to call Carlos."

"Do you really think he knows anything about this stuff?" I asked.

It is highly unlikely, Uriel said. *What would a mortal possibly know about our battle?*

Hey, he knew about the dreams, I pointed out. *That's more than anyone else.*

Uriel didn't answer that. Leo watched me, probably waiting for whatever weird face I made when I was talking to myself to pass. I blushed and dug into my waffles.

"Sorry," I said around a mouthful of strawberries.

"Don't worry about it. Do you want to call your parents?"

I shook my head. "No way."

"You don't get along?" Leo asked. He didn't sound alarmed or surprised by that idea. "You were arguing last night."

"What? No, I love my parents," I said. "But they think I'm off making a bunch of money on the best job of my life."

Leo blinked, then smiled at me a little. "Is that what you told them?"

"Pretty much. But what the hell could I say now?" I asked. "That archangels and the four horsemen of the apocalypse are itching to have it out and I'm somehow caught in the middle? Even if Mom and Dad believed me about any of it, I don't want to worry them. It's not like they could help."

Leo nodded, conceding the point, and then finally picked up a slice of his toast. He kept his eyes on the television, but luckily, there didn't seem to be a story about the 'biohazard thing' off Highway 44. I doubted that seeing his dead friends all over the news would do much for Leo's appetite.

"What about you?" I asked after I demolished my first waffle. "Is there anyone that you need to call? Other than your uncle, I mean. You two seem close."

"I spent every summer with Carlos when I was a kid," Leo said. "He came out to Chicago as soon as school was over and I would ride on the back of his bike all the way to San Diego. He's the one who taught me to drive a motorcycle."

Which was certainly an important skill in Leo's life, but it wasn't quite the same thing as knowing how to deal with angelic and demonic possession. Leo's faith in Uncle Carlos' ability to help seemed pretty strong, though.

"Anybody else to call?" I asked. "Parents, maybe? A boyfriend or girlfriend?"

Leo picked up his fork and stabbed it into his yellow heap of scrambled eggs. He shook his head. "Nope. But my dad's still out there. Somewhere."

"Ran off?" I asked.

"You could say that. He was gone when I got out of prison, which was the smartest move he ever made."

"So... you two weren't close or anything," I guessed.

"My dad's an asshole," Leo said. "Liked to hit my mom whenever he had a bad day – which was a lot – and punch me when she wasn't home."

I winced. I mean, domestic abuse isn't as uncommon as we would all like it to be, but I could see the pain of it right there in Leo's brown eyes. And I worried... Kids who grow up getting hurt often end up hurting someone else.

"Uh... mind if I ask what you went to prison for?" I asked. "Since we're in this batshit together and all."

Leo took a bite of eggs and chewed slowly, but after he had wiped his mouth with a white cloth napkin, the biker was grinning again.

"I finally got big enough to hit my dad back," Leo said. "Put him in intensive care for a week. And me in prison for a year. But it was worth it."

Yay! I mean, that sucks, too.

But if Leo said the time was worth it, then I didn't feel too bad for cheering that his asshole dad got a little taste of what he dished out.

I wasn't feeling quite brave enough to tell Leo that, though, which left us sitting in awkward silence while we both ate. Beth returned with the bloody mary I had ordered and I chugged the spiked tomato juice, then crunched the celery to get the very last drops of vodka. If I was going to be riding on Leo's demon-bike and listening to Uriel whisper doom into my ear all day, then I needed all the help I could get.

When we were finished eating, Leo dropped a pair of twenty-dollar bills on the table, pulled on his leather jacket and we both hurried outside. The sun had finished rising and illuminated the town of Novak in bright golden light.

"I should take a look at the Packmaster," I said reluctantly. "If we have any engine problems now, we're stranded. That thing is our only ride."

"I don't want to be stuck here when Gabriel catches up," Leo agreed. "Need a hand?"

"Nope. This is my job, remember?"

Leo nodded. "Okay. There's a convenience store just down the street. I'll go find a phone charger."

I watched him stride away along the road. A few fluffy white clouds raced across the sky in a warm wind that tousled Leo's wavy mahogany hair. I groaned and clapped my hands over my cloud of thick, dark curls.

"And buy me a bandana!" I shouted. "Or we're both going to be eating my hair all day!"

Leo flashed me a thumbs-up over his shoulder and I turned to face my nemesis. Let's see how smug the Packmaster was after being knocked around the parking lot of an exploding motel.

I knelt down next to the bike to inspect how bashed up the exhaust pipes and muffler had gotten, though I wasn't exactly sure what the hell I could do about it without my tools. The loss hit me all over again and I had to squeeze my eyes shut against tears. Some of the tools were older than I was, inherited from my parents back in their factory days. My kit had hundreds of dollars of my own tools in it, and I had worked hard for every one of them.

But now my toolbox was another heap of slag back in Texas and unless I wanted to end up the same way, I had to keep Leo's bike running. Considering what it had been through last night, it was kind of a miracle the Packmaster was still working and hadn't dumped us unceremoniously onto the pavement.

I opened my eyes again and squinted at Leo's motorcycle, but it was... perfect. The exhaust pipes were straight and the chrome shined in the sunlight. The paint job wasn't even scuffed. My stomach churned and threatened to cover the blacktop in strawberries and tomato juice.

What were the possibilities here? Either I had hallucinated a little old church lady turning into a ten-foot-tall angel, or else Leo's bike had fixed itself afterward.

Such material damage is easily healed by our power, Uriel said. *And that of the horsemen.*

I remembered the news and swallowed against the tightness in my throat. Unless my hallucination had somehow ended up on television, I *had* to accept that it was real. All of this was actually happening. I took a deep breath and smelled bacon frying inside Novak Country Kitchen Café.

This motorcycle is Leo's... steed, right? I asked the angel living in my head. *That's why it doesn't like me.*

Death's steed, Uriel corrected. *It is a part of Death. It answers only to the horseman and will grow stronger as Death does.*

So... what it really hates is you, I thought. *I doubt it cares about some silly little human. But it doesn't want an angel riding on its back.*

Yes, Uriel said. *You must leave now, vessel. Before Death returns.*

Leo, I corrected this time. *And where else can I go? The cops? A psychologist?*

To Gabriel. To Michael and Raphael. Find them, and I will lead them into final battle against the horsemen...

I squeezed my eyes closed, tighter and tighter until I could hear only the oceanic rush of my blood. Damn, Uriel really sang a one-note song.

Shut up! I thought as hard as I could. *I'm not running off to join your angelic circus! I'm not leaving Leo. He has the bike and the uncle with answers. I need that or I swear I'm going to lose it.*

Lose what? Uriel asked.

It was like having a child in my head. One of those possessed kids from a horror movie who can fling shit around with their minds and murders people for poorly explained reasons.

Despite having access to everything I thought about – like shirtless Leo – Uriel was terribly literal. In fact, whenever they weren't lecturing me about apocalyptic battles and things that wanted to kill me, the archangel was pretty clueless.

I am new to this world, yes, Uriel said. I could practically hear the ruffled feathers. *But also ancient beyond your limited ability to understand. We existed before this universe of matter and energy. We created it.*

The angel didn't just speak the words – though they echoed like great bells inside my skull – I could *see* the emptiness before the universe, the impossibly bright spark of the Big Bang exploding out through the void, filling it with fire and substance.

And this *is exactly why I'm going to lose control,* I said.

Good. Then I will take control of this body.

I was sorely tempted to run screaming back into the restaurant for about a dozen drinks. A chill like an arctic ice flow ran through me and I felt the vast, powerful presence of the angel tensing itself within me, but then the Packmaster's motor revved.

I jumped back and spun to find Leo jogging across the parking lot toward me. In one hand, he carried a branded plastic bag bulging with snacks and hopefully a phone charger. How long had I been sitting there, staring at the motorcycle and arguing with Uriel?

The Packmaster growled louder as Leo approached us. He cocked his head as I stood up again.

"Did you start it?" he asked.

"Nope," I said. "Just started itself."

Leo paused, then ran his free hand over the smooth curve of the gas tank. His motorcycle downshifted and the engine purred contentedly. Leo's dark-eyed gaze wandered over the Packmaster and a muscle twitched at the angle of his jaw.

"Fuck," he said. "How bad is the damage? It was shaking a lot last night."

"I think that's because your bike didn't like the passenger." I pointed to myself. "But there's no damage at all. Not anymore. It... healed."

"Fuck," Leo said again. He took a deep breath. "Alright. Can we ride it? Is it safe?"

"As safe as it was last night, I suppose," I answered slowly. "It seems ready to go."

Ready to seek out the other horsemen, Uriel said.

"Uh, Uriel thinks it's in a hurry to find the other ones... like you," I told Leo. "Just like Pestilence was trying to find you when it came across your friends."

Leo looked up from his motorcycle with something burning in his eyes. Not literal fire, thank goodness, but seething rage. I was pretty sure I knew exactly what Leo's dad saw right before his son punched him.

"Too bad," Leo said. "We're going to San Diego."

The Packmaster's rumbling engine hitched ominously under his hand. Leo patted the motorcycle once before standing back and running his fingers through his hair. The biker took a deep breath.

"Carlos will know what to do," he said.

The words were quiet, like Leo was talking to himself. Hey, not that I was one to judge. Uriel said a lot weirder shit and at least Leo was using his own voice.

For now, Uriel reminded me. *By the time you hear Death's true voice, it will be too late.*

Can you ease up on the doom and gloom? I asked.

Doom is coming.

I hated to admit that Uriel had a point, but Gabriel and Pestilence were both out there looking for us. We really needed to get moving.

"Did you buy a phone charger?" I asked as gently as I could.

Leo blinked a few times and then looked down at me. He nodded and opened up the grocery bag to show me the charging cable enclosed in its plastic blister pack.

"As soon as we stop somewhere with power outlets, we're good to go," Leo said. "I also got you these."

He reached into the bag and withdrew a package of folded bandanas. I snatched them so fast that Leo laughed.

"Hey, your hair is always perfect," I told him. "Mine rebels when I keep it under a helmet all day."

I selected a red bandana, then folded it diagonally and tied it into place over my hair. I rolled up the other two and stuck them in my pocket. Leo stuffed his purchases into the Packmaster's saddlebags and pulled on a new pair of leather riding gloves. He caught his reflection in the bike's mirror and squinted at his wavy brown hair.

"Yeah, perfect," I said.

Leo gave me a smile that looked a little bit embarrassed and handed me the extra helmet. He straddled the Packmaster and patted the back of the seat.

"Climb on," he told me.

The Packmaster revved again and I hesitated. That motorcycle *really* didn't like me. Leo choked down the throttle and the engine smoothed out.

Death's mortal vessel will not remain in control forever, Uriel said. *Leave now.*

I climbed onto the pillion and the motorcycle bucked hard under me. Even Leo felt it and he glanced over his shoulder.

"Hold on tight," he said.

I wrapped my arms around Leo. He kicked up the stand and we drove back out toward Highway 44.

CHAPTER 11

I rode through the day on the back of the Packmaster as the bike tried like hell to kick me off. It shuddered and fishtailed, forcing me to cling to Leo so hard that I had the shoulder seam of his jacket more or less permanently printed into the skin of my cheek. I missed my own motorcycle so badly that I cried a couple of times. Luckily, the warm, swift wind whipped the tears away before Leo could see any of them.

At highway speeds, I couldn't really talk to Leo, which left Uriel my only company. The constant urgings to leave Leo and seek out the other angels was getting repetitive. *Really* repetitive. At least Uriel could have mixed in a little epic-sounding scripture or something.

Those are not our words, Uriel said.

What? I asked.

Those... church words in your mind are not our words, the angel told me.

Uh, is an angel seriously telling me that the Bible is bullshit?

No, Uriel said. *Our influence is there in your book and in all holy writings. In all things.*

Good for you, I thought to the angel. *But if you don't mind, I'd much rather concentrate on grabbing Leo's abs for a while.*

I felt the swirl of Uriel's confusion at that, and it was nice to return the favor for once. But I kept my eyes on the sky and the highway, watching for Gabriel and Pestilence.

Leo finally pulled over around lunchtime. We didn't need gas and I was pretty sure never would again. Whatever the Packmaster ran on, it wasn't gas anymore.

But its riders' proverbial tanks *did* get empty – I don't really recommend trying to eat a bag of potato chips on the back of a moving motorcycle – or in the case of my bladder, full.

So we stopped off at a filling station anyway so I could shake out my sore and aching arms. We crammed some junk food into our mouths as we checked the rack of newspapers for anything strange. We didn't see much, but printed news was a little slower than television.

I used a restroom that looked like it had been the site of its own apocalyptic battle. When I was done and on my way out of the little station store, I detoured to buy myself a beer and the highest octane energy drink I could find. By the time I emerged from the shop, I had chugged the energy drink and was halfway through the beer.

Outside, Leo stood next to his motorcycle, staring down at it. I groaned out loud as I approached – my ass was two patties of hamburger meat after a day of riding that thing.

"Is it talking to you?" I asked.

Leo looked up from the motorcycle. "What? Oh, no. Nothing like that. Just wondering about this whole fucked-up thing. How can any of this shit be happening?"

"I don't know," I said. "But I guess that's the point of going to see your uncle."

I upended the rest of the beer into my mouth and swallowed. I didn't even like beer that much, but anything to shut Uriel the hell up tasted like ambrosia.

Leo eyed me as I crumpled the can and dropped it into the trash. He frowned.

"Yeah, I know. we make a pit stop and I promptly fill up my bladder again," I said. "I'm a big girl. I can hold it until the next stop. Promise."

Leo just nodded and held the Packmaster steady until I had climbed on. The motorcycle immediately began jerking like a mechanical bull and I threw my arms around Leo. When I was as situated as I was going to get, he drove back out onto the highway and we raced west.

And I do mean *raced*. There was an angel and a horseman out there with our names on them, but we also needed to avoid getting our asses handed to us by the cops. Leo pulled back on the handlebars of his motorcycle like the reins of a horse to keep it under a hundred miles per hour and barely managed it. Sweat ran down the back of his neck.

I could still feel Uriel in my head, but they didn't seem to be grabbing for *my* reins. Maybe the angel was watching for Pestilence, too, or trying to locate Gabriel again. Or maybe it was the beer... I had guzzled it pretty fast and I wasn't a large girl, so I was already a bit buzzed. I wondered what a drunk angel would sound like, which prompted Uriel to renew demands that I ditch the horseman and go find myself a nice archangel.

Or three of them, to be precise.

Shut up, shut up, shut up...! I told Uriel in a sing-song voice inside my head. *I swear, I'll brain myself with a wrench if you don't shut the hell up.*

Uriel didn't shut up.

Leo and I followed Highway 44 through rocky hills that rose steeply into tree-covered peaks labeled with green signs along the roadside as *Cibola National Forest*. We stopped in a pretty mountain town called Zamora Canyon.

Sunlight fell across the road in horizontal amber lines that danced with motes of dust and pollen. It wasn't dark yet – and the Packmaster had a perfectly good headlight – but I think Leo was eager to stop and get my cell phone charged. The beer and energy drink had finished their own journeys and I was ready for another pit stop, too.

Zamora Canyon had a Mexican restaurant on the main thoroughfare that was a welcome change of pace from the roadside diner food we had been eating. We sat next to a window where we could watch the sun finish setting behind the mountains and keep an eye on the road outside.

When our waiter dropped off some fresh chips and several kinds of salsa, I ordered a plate of enchiladas dripping in cheese and a pitcher of margaritas.

"Skip the drinks," Leo said.

I frowned and the waiter looked back and forth between us, but Leo's voice was hard. The waiter didn't make any cute jokes – he just scratched the pitcher off his order pad and left. Quickly.

"Um... what the hell?" I asked. "It's not like I'm driving. I *can't* drive anymore, remember? My Bonnie's probably been smashed into a paperweight at some scrapyard by now."

I choked a little on the last words and Leo crossed his arms on the tabletop. The thick muscles were tensed under his colorfully tattooed skin.

"Drinking isn't going to make this shit go away, Jaz," he said.

"Yeah? Look, you're not the one with a chatty angel in your head," I snapped.

"My friends are all dead!" Leo hissed right back.

"Then why aren't *you* drinking?"

"Because it doesn't make the problem go away."

"Talk to me again when you're mentally wrestling a demon," I said.

"I am," Leo answered.

Now I froze like a rabbit caught in headlights. "What? Is... is Death talking to you?"

"No," Leo told me. "But there's a reason I believe you about what's happening here, Jaz, and it's not just because of what happened in Arrow. I can feel Death, I think. That urge to throw you off my bike and drag you behind me down the road until..."

Leo bit off the sentence with obvious difficulty, but a line of cold sweat was already running down the back of my neck. Shit. Shit! Death was really in there, somewhere inside Leo.

I warned you, Uriel said. *Leave this place. Leave this man, vessel!*

I grabbed the edge of the table, wondering how fast I could sprint for the door. What was I going to do once I got outside? I doubted that the Packmaster would let me steal it... There were no other motorcycles in the parking lot.

Could I steal a car? No, someone would see me and then it would take about five minutes flat before the cops were dragging me out of the driver's seat by the hair. Could I even hotwire one? It looked easy enough in the movies, but I knew engines better than to believe that shit.

Give me control and I will get away, Uriel urged. *I have no need of wheels. I have wings.*

One of Leo's hands came down on top of mine and I nearly screamed. He leaned over the table and fixed me with an intense stare.

"But that's not what I'm talking about," Leo said.

"Wait... what?" I asked. I had lost the thread of the conversation entirely. "That's not what?"

"Death isn't the demon I'm looking at right now," Leo told me. "Look, I get what you're going through."

"Yeah, I really doubt that."

Leo's big hand tightened on top of mine. It felt like there was an electric current running through his skin and into me. I bit my lip.

"My dad was a shitbag," Leo said. "He was a privileged asshole who went down to San Diego on vacation and knocked up my mother. So he brought her home to Chicago to knock her around. Her life hurt, so she took heroin to make it stop. Eventually, it did – she overdosed when I was in high school."

"I... I'm sorry," I stammered.

"Jaz, listen. You know my dad was the same with me. Hit me a lot, threw me through a glass table once, and left a lot of scars. So for my tenth birthday, Mom gave me a needle."

"Oh, shit."

"Don't judge her," Leo said. "My mom loved me. Heroin was the only good thing in her life and she wanted to share it with me. And you know what? My life sucked, so yeah, I shot up. Dad came home and hammered on me, but it didn't matter anymore. I missed weeks of school, and that didn't matter, either."

"Leo..." I whispered, but then trailed off.

What could I say? The biker's broad shoulders hunched, but his hand remained firm on top of mine.

"Remember those summer vacations I told you about?" Leo asked. "When Uncle Carlos came to take me out of Chicago for a few weeks?"

"Yeah," I answered. That trip must have been the best part of young Leo's life each year, a chance to get away from his father.

"And I told you he saved my life," Leo said. "When Carlos came that summer and found me, he knew *exactly* what was going on. He never got my mom – his sister – off the heroin, but I always looked up to Uncle Carlos. I wanted to *be* Carlos when I grew up. Nothing hurt him. Nothing could. I needed to be strong like that."

I wanted to point out that of the two of us, Leo was the one not melting down and speaking to voices in their head. But he was still talking.

"I wanted to be a Knight of Hell like him," Leo said. "But there were rules, Uncle Carlos told me, and one of them was no drugs. If I ever wanted to be a Knight, I had to kick the habit. And then he left me there in Chicago, all summer."

"What happened?" I asked. "I mean, you're here, not dead from an overdose. And you obviously joined the Knights of Hell. So what did you do?"

Leo finally sat back, smiling a little. "At first, I was just pissed off. I broke pretty much everything that I could in my bedroom, including my window. Which earned me a few smacks in the mouth from my dad."

I winced.

"But Carlos was right. If I wanted to join up bad enough, I could do it," Leo said. "So I made it through the heroin withdrawals. Barely. That fall and spring, I made it through school and my dad's fists. Barely. When summer came around again, so did Uncle Carlos. He took one look and told me to get on the bike."

I could imagine that, little ten-year-old Leo – though I guess he would have been eleven by then – jumping onto the back of a big-ass Harley to drive halfway across the country.

"That's the summer Carlos started teaching me," Leo said. "How to ride, and how to fight when I had to. He taught me to be strong like him. I just wish I could have taught my mother. She tried to get off the heroin, too, but it would never stick for more than a few weeks. She kept going back. And she did her last pop when I was sixteen."

"That wasn't your fault," I said.

Leo sighed. There were tears in his eyes again, but he didn't try to wipe them discreetly away before I could see them or claim it was just dust. This was old pain, and Leo wasn't afraid of it anymore.

"After she died, then it was just me and my dad. He hit me, and my mom wasn't there begging us to stop anymore. So I hit him right back," Leo said, then smirked. "Might have been more than once."

"That's what got you sent off to prison, right?" I asked.

"Yeah," Leo answered. "I was seventeen, but I got tried as an adult and spent a year in prison. When I was in there, it was hard not to go back to the heroin."

I blinked. "In… prison?"

"Jaz, you can get anything in prison," Leo said with a raised eyebrow. "It just costs more than on the outside. But I made it through. I still want the needle sometimes, though, especially when shit like… like this happens. You can't outrun everything."

The waiter reappeared, carrying our dinner and some fresh chips. He stared at Leo's tears as he set everything on the table and the big biker dug into his carne asada without looking up.

The waiter cocked his head at me. Maybe he was giving me the chance to order my margaritas again, but I shook my head. I wasn't very thirsty anymore.

CHAPTER 12

"Any signs of angelic trouble?" Leo asked me as we headed across the restaurant parking lot in the direction of his motorcycle.

I studied the horizon, half expecting to find the bright spark of Gabriel blazing toward us, but the sky remained dark. For all I knew, the angel was on a bus, knitting in the front seat and dispensing unasked for ethereal wisdom to people just trying to sleep away the miles.

"I don't see anything," I said. "And Uriel's being quiet."

Leo nodded. "Let's get on the road before that changes."

I followed him quickly and hoped that the horsemen were far away, too... I never wanted to meet anything that earned the name *Pestilence*. The Knights of Hell had done precisely that and I would be having nightmares about what happened to them for years. I could only imagine what Leo's dreams were like.

He dreams of the coming war, Uriel said.

Oh hey, there you are, I thought. *You were suspiciously quiet at dinner.*

I have no commentary to make on mortal sustenance, the angel answered. *And you refuse to heed my commands to abandon Death.*

"Let's find a motel and get some sleep," Leo said. "We didn't rest much last night and I don't want us making stupid mistakes just because we're tired."

Think you could watch our backs while we rest? I asked Uriel.

That is neither my wish nor my purpose, the angel said stiffly.

No, your purpose is to blow up the guy I'm riding with.

You have thoughts of blowing him, too, Uriel countered.

I glanced over at Leo and hoped he couldn't see the blush that I felt burning in my cheeks.

Not the same thing, I thought. *Trust me.*

Z amora Canyon was a small town, but it was located in the middle of Cibola National Forest and seemed to do some brisk tourism business. There were a pair of cute motels with wooden clapboarding on the outside... but they were both full of tourists.

"I've only got one room left," the clerk at the second motel told us. "Two beds, if that's alright?"

Leo had asked for two rooms, so why wouldn't two beds be okay? The clerk gave us a cheery smirk and a wink that I kind of wished were warranted.

"That's fine," Leo answered. "Can I pay in cash?"

"That's fine," the clerk echoed.

We accepted a couple of key cards and I unlocked our motel room door while Leo hauled his saddlebags inside. There were a lot more cars and people than back in Arrow, he had pointed out, and wasn't sure that he should leave packs outside that were full of illegal cash and firearms. Well, Leo didn't actually say the guns were illegal, but it seemed like a good bet.

Our room was generously sized, though two beds took up most of the space. The carpet was thick and brown, almost the same color as the wooden walls. Cut-out silhouettes of birds and pine cones decorated the curtains and lampshades.

Leo tossed me the cell phone charger and I pried it from the packaging. I plugged the cable into an outlet next to my bed and connected it to my phone, which buzzed and then displayed a battery with a lightning bolt through it on the screen.

"Is it ready?" Leo asked.

"No, not yet," I said. "It needs a while to get enough charge for a call. And fair warning, reception out here will be shit."

I gave Leo as reassuring a smile as I could. The biker growled a little, but he nodded. Unable to be still, Leo paced across the room to the other nightstand and inspected an old brown push-button phone under the lamp there.

"No out-of-state calls," Leo read from a small plastic panel on the side. He picked up the receiver and dialed anyway, then shook his head. "Local calls only, I guess."

"I don't think anyone really uses landlines anymore."

Leo tossed the telephone receiver back and forth between his hands a few times before replacing it in the cradle. Damn, the guy was *really* in a hurry to call Carlos... But after his story at dinner, I understood a little better how much his uncle meant to Leo. And if Carlos had a solution for my brain-angel problem, he would mean a lot to me, too.

My cell's battery indicator was still in the red, so I stretched, groaning and pushing my palms up toward the ceiling. My spine popped loudly in several places. Leo had his hands thrust into the pockets of his jeans now, and watched me closely.

"How was the ride today?" I asked.

Leo blinked, then looked up to meet my eye. Had he been checking me out?

"My bike," Leo said. "Yeah. Kind of a wrestling match, to be honest. I don't think the Packmaster is very happy with me. It feels... pissed off."

"Want me to take a look at it?" I offered.

Leo considered, but then shook his head. "We know what the problem is, right? It's me. Because there's something inside of me."

"Inside me, too," I said. "And I'm the one your motorcycle doesn't like."

The biker shifted his weight between his feet and ran a hand through his hair. He hadn't removed his leathers and I caught a glint of the gun under his jacket.

"Jaz, I'm sorry for dragging you into all of this," Leo said. "I just thought my motorcycle was having mechanical problems. If I hadn't stopped at your shop, you would be safe in Crayhill."

I crossed my arms. "No, I'd be at home trying to explain to my parents and then probably a psychiatrist about the angelic voice in my head. And what about you? What if you had been with your friends when Pestilence found them?"

"Then maybe they would still be alive," Leo answered.

That is unlikely, Uriel said. *Death would have gained strength from the presence of its brother. It is likely that Death's vessel would have destroyed his own companions.*

It took me a second to make sense of that, but then I frowned up at Leo.

"I think Uriel's telling me that you might have just killed the Knights yourself," I said.

Leo's face went suddenly pale. "What?"

"If you were there when Pestilence came, Death would have taken over... Like Uriel did when Gabriel touched me," I said. "And I don't think these things inside us care a whole lot about human life."

Leo pressed his fingers against his temple, then raked them up through his hair again. Eventually, he nodded.

"Thank you, Jaz," Leo told me. "Really. I couldn't do this on my own."

He stared at me with need burning in his brown eyes and my heart sped.

You are producing adrenalin and your body is preparing itself for action, Uriel said. *You wish to throw yourself at Death and I am ready. This battle was decreed before time began. We are called to it!*

Uh, it's not a call to battle, I thought desperately to the angel. *Trust me. Maybe action, but...*

Leo made a rough sound like a growl deep in his chest and sat down on the edge of his bed with an obvious effort.

"We actually have some time," he said. "Do you want to take a shower or something?"

I pinched a black curl of hair that had escaped my bandana. "Yeah, that's probably a good idea."

I went into the washroom and shut the door, then peeled myself out of my clothes while I waited for the water to heat up. I unwound the bandage from my hand to inspect the cut Leo's cursed Packmaster had sliced into it. It hurt like hell at the time, but after everything else that happened last night, I barely felt anything.

Or maybe it wasn't just a matter of perspective... I frowned and examined my hand under the bathroom lights. The ragged gash was already healed up. The new skin was pink and sensitive, but there wasn't even a scab.

Did you do that? I asked silently.

I do not yet have full control of your body, Uriel said. *But when I do, I wish it to be intact.*

...So that's a 'yes'?

Yes.

At least there was one tiny upside to all this bullshit. When the shower was warm enough, I climbed in under the spray and set to work rinsing out my hair. And untangling the curls, which was more of a challenge, especially without my own shampoo. My relatively uninjured hand made the job a little easier, but by the time I was done, the hot water was gone and I glared at the shower head.

"I wanted to shave my legs, you know," I said. "Stupid thing."

I sighed at myself. All my toiletries had gone up in smoke with the Arrow Lodge and now I was complaining to inanimate objects. Days of Uriel in my head was clearly taking its toll.

"Jaz?"

I jumped and only barely managed not to scream, but the voice was Leo's and he didn't sound particularly alarmed. Heart pounding, I peeked out around the motel shower curtain to find Leo's hand thrust through the bathroom door and holding up a t-shirt.

"You lost all your clothes," Leo said from outside. "So if you want to wear something clean..."

"Yeah, thanks," I answered, raising my voice.

Leo flicked his wrist and tossed the shirt over the edge of the sink, then closed the door again. I turned off the water and dried myself with a faded green towel. When I wasn't dripping anymore, I pulled my underwear back on – too bad Leo didn't carry any spare pairs of those – and then the new t-shirt. It was black, with the Knights of Hell flame-crested helmet stenciled onto the front.

I glanced down at my jeans. I had been wearing them all day. Did I need to put them on again, or could I wait until tomorrow morning? The shirt was fairly long and Leo didn't seem to mind the view.

It will kill you regardless of dress, Uriel told me.

Leo's not going to kill me, I thought. I hoped.

Death will.

I stared at my reflection in the mirror... Leo had admitted to some rather murderous feelings at dinner. Even without a voice, Death was somewhere inside the biker. I took a deep breath and put on my jeans.

"The hot water's all gone," I said as I emerged from the bathroom. "Sorry about that. There wasn't much to begin with and this hair takes some work."

"Hey, it's worth the effort," Leo assured me.

He gave me another lingering look that started up at my face, then moved slowly down my body. Leo was good at eye contact, I realized, and when he actually let his gaze wander, I *felt* it. Leo brought his eyes quickly back up to mine.

"Don't worry about the hot water," he said. "I could use a cold shower."

My heart began jackhammering all over again. Leo was dead sexy and even in the middle of this weird apocalyptic shit show, I had noticed. Had Leo noticed back? I fished for something to say, something I could lace with smooth innuendo.

A shadow moved outside the window.

"Shit!" I shouted.

The flimsy motel room door slammed open, banged against the wall and ripped off its hinges. I jumped behind the nearest bed and Leo threw himself down on top of me. I really wished that I could enjoy that more, but I screamed in terror as bullets punched craters into the wall where we had just been, hurling cedar splinters and pink fiberglass insulation up through the suddenly smoky air. Gunfire chattered and the mattress above us erupted into a cloud of stuffing. A framed picture that was probably scenic Cibola National Forest vanished into shards of glass and shreds of paper.

What the hell...? I shouted inside my own head. *Is this one of your people?*

I didn't see Gabriel or anything angelic, but it wasn't like I had that much experience with them. Was it the horsemen? Had Pestilence finally found us?

No, these are mortal weapons, Uriel answered. *We fight our own battles, and with far more powerful forces.*

Oh, *that* made me feel better. Bullets could still kill me just fine.

But they will not harm me, Uriel said. The angel's voice rang in my skull. *Give me control of this body, vessel, and these... bullets... you fear will mean nothing.*

Not a chance!

"Jaz!" Leo shouted. "Are you alright?"

My voice came out muffled against his chest. "Yeah, I'm okay. You?"

The sharp, repeating thunder of automatic weapons turned into the ratcheting of reloading. Leo's weight was suddenly gone from on top of me as he jumped to his feet, shedding dust and broken glass. The biker stood over me and drew the snub-nosed revolver from his jacket. He aimed and then pulled the trigger twice. There was a shout outside that sounded human.

Cursing myself for an idiot, I peeked up over the ruined bed to see a man in dark clothes and body armor slumped in the doorway, sliding slowly down as he clutched his stomach. He wore night-vision goggles and held a matte black submachine gun. There was no blood where Leo had shot him – that armor must have been doing its job – but the guy didn't look good.

Who the hell was attacking us like this? I didn't see *POLICE* or *SWAT* stenciled across the man's armor, no badges or insignia. When we found the Knights of Hell, I had dismissed the idea of the government or military, but what if I was wrong? Uriel said this wasn't the angels, and I doubted the other horsemen would have been taking pot-shots at Leo. Was this the cops? Or something bigger? Everyone just wanted to kill Jaz and Leo – murder gone viral.

"There's more of them," Leo said in a tight voice.

The fallen man's gun was pretty big, but even the magazine on that thing wasn't enough to perforate our walls like that. Leo was right – there had to be other guns out there.

As if summoned by the thought, two new figures in identical tactical blacks charged the door. One of them brought up her gun to aim at us while the other grabbed the man Leo had shot and pulled him back out of sight. The woman in the doorway tensed and Leo fell to his knees behind the bed just before she pulled the trigger.

I threw myself down flat against the floor as bullets riddled the beds and walls and nightstand and everything else in the motel room. Leo snarled something in Spanish and kicked the remains of my bed toward the door, briefly interrupting the submachine gun, then leapt up. His first and second shots impacted Kevlar, making the woman grunt. She doubled over and Leo's next bullet whizzed through the open door.

I didn't know guns half as well as I knew motorcycles. How many bullets were there in Leo's gun? Five or six?

Was I feeling lucky, punk?

The woman stepped back as another man in black charged the door, shouting something in a language I didn't recognize. Leo aimed his gun down at the man's knee and fired, but the hammer clacked hollowly. Only five shots in that little revolver, apparently.

But Leo didn't hesitate. He vaulted up and over the shattered bed, tackling both of our assailants before they could get their guns trained on us again.

"Jaz, run!" Leo shouted.

Uh, where exactly did he expect me to run? The motel room door was full of Leo and thrashing armored limbs. The window was only about three feet away from the brawl.

Do something! I cried inside my head.

Do what? Uriel asked.

Something... angelic!

Give me control of this vessel, Uriel said.

No!

Leo drove his elbow into the woman's stomach, right where his shots had doubtlessly bruised a few ribs, and left her gasping for breath. The man swung his submachine gun around like a black metal baseball bat. Leo ducked and the gun smashed into the doorframe hard enough to splinter the wood.

Alright, Leo was a bona fide badass and wasn't freaking out about being shot at. Hell, this probably wasn't even his first gun-filled rodeo. Leo didn't need my help or Uriel's, right?

I ran to the window and ripped open the curtains. Literally ripped... the window glass was shattered and the drapes so full of bullet holes that they were nearly lace. Maybe I could just jump through and make a run for it.

But I stared through the broken shards of glass. A big black panel van was parked sideways outside, hemming in the scene. The driver's side door of the van burst open and I saw another armored silhouette inside. Leo might have been holding his own against the two in the doorway, but they were about to get reinforcements.

Uriel, help us! I thought.

Then give me control, the angel demanded.

My hammering heart clawed its way up into my throat and I jumped back from the broken window.

Okay... just a little, I told Uriel. *No blowing up motels like your buddy Gabriel did. Just get us out of here!*

Destroying this building serves no purpose. All I desire is to rejoin the others... but I cannot do that if my vessel is destroyed. Very well, I will aid you.

I took a deep breath and ran toward the door. There were people with guns and I was counting on a voice in my head to somehow stop them from killing me.

Leo was on top of his two attackers, punching one of them. The big biker's knuckles were bloody and the woman yanked a collapsible baton off her belt, snapping it out to full extension.

She swung the metal baton at Leo's unprotected head, but I dove at her.

I was trying to football tackle her off of Leo, but I had never actually played football and my aim was off. I missed entirely and the baton impacted against my outstretched arm. I shrieked, ready for the sick pain of my bones shattering... but it never came. The steel rod hit my arm with a flash of light and then bounced off.

"Ange!" the woman gasped.

I was pretty sure that was French for *angel*. She knew what I was... or at least, what lived inside me.

Time for those reinforcements. Another man in assault gear leapt out of the van's open door and swung a powerful-looking rifle around to brace against his shoulder. A laser sight lit up the sheetrock dust and falling puffs of mattress stuffing in a crimson line that pointed right at my head.

He pulled the trigger and I closed my eyes. Well, shit. I had no cover or time to get behind it and I was going to die. The rifle fired and something poked me in the temple, like my mother's finger when I was being a brat. I didn't know how being shot should have felt, but I figured that it would hurt a lot more than that. Maybe he had missed, or changed targets to Leo, or... Or Uriel really could protect me from bullets. I cracked first one eye and then the other to find myself surrounded by a nimbus of bright white light.

Leo was still on the ground next to the door, wrestling with the two black-clad goons. The one that he had shot sat slumped against the wall outside, holding his hands over his stomach. His night-vision goggles had either fallen off or been removed, and he stared up at me with wide blue eyes.

The man in the parking lot switched his rifle to full auto and another drumroll of gunfire boomed in my ears. I flinched, but the light flared around me and all I felt was a flurry of hard jabs.

Bullets rained down around my feet, flattened into little lead pancakes by Uriel's protective aura.

"Jaz, what the fuck–?" Leo shouted.

He had turned his head to look at me and took a gloved fist to the jaw for it. I kicked the soldier on top of Leo – the woman who had tried to bash his head in with her collapsible baton – and she flew out through the motel parking lot. She smashed into the nearest panel van hard enough to leave a dent in the metal door, but groaned and didn't stand up again.

This is taking too long, Uriel told me. *Surrender your form, vessel, and I will end this!*

Hey, give me a break, I said. *This is my first angelic brawl, okay?*

I grabbed Leo by his leather jacket and heaved him upright. He spat out a few more Spanish swear words and held his jaw, but the man with the rifle was drawing a bead on us again. I threw Leo back into the room like he weighed nothing, sending the biker bouncing across the one intact bed.

Where the hell *was* everyone? The motel was a lot more booked up than the Arrow Lodge had been. So why wasn't the clerk at the front desk calling the police? Unless someone had instructed him not to...

"Grab the saddlebags," I told Leo. My voice came out mixed with Uriel's and rang like struck crystal. "We have to get away from here!"

"Jaz, watch out!" Leo shouted.

The guy who had punched Leo was rolling to his feet. He didn't bother with the baton like his companion had – he went straight for a combat knife the length of my forearm. He ripped it from a sheath on his belt and charged at me, bringing the blade up in a controlled slash at my stomach.

I gasped and swatted desperately at the knife, really wishing my parents had been Special Forces soldiers instead of motorcycle mechanics. The blade hit my arm hard enough to snap the tempered metal against my luminous angelic armor. I threw a clumsy punch that only clipped his shoulder, but still sent the man sprawling with a sharp sound that I was pretty sure was breaking bones.

The man in the parking lot ejected the magazine out of his gun and grabbed another one from his belt. I picked up the black baton that had fallen to the ground and chucked it. The guy with the rifle shouted and ducked as the baton left a foot-deep dent in the side of his van, but he still slammed the fresh ammunition into his weapon with what I assumed was well-practiced ease.

"Shit," I said in that church-bell voice.

I leapt. I just meant to jump over the man with the broken arm, but I shot out like a glowing arrow instead, and landed in the parking lot hard enough to leave footprints in the asphalt. The last para-military goon brought up his rifle, but I slapped it from his hands and the gun went skidding across the ground. A single shove threw him back into the van and his head hit the dented metal side. He slumped at my feet – still breathing – and I had to hope that I hadn't done too much brain damage.

"Jaz?" Leo asked.

He ran outside with the leather saddlebags draped over his broad shoulders and my shoes in his hand. Leo staggered to a stop, staring around the scene.

"I'm okay," I said. "Let's get the hell out of here!"

I looked down at my arms and the glow faded. Leo tossed my shoes and I caught them almost gracefully, then hopped not at all gracefully across the parking lot as I pulled them on.

The Packmaster started itself as Leo threw his bags over the tail end. I jumped onto the back and grabbed ahold of Leo when the bike lurched violently, trying to throw me off.

"Not now!" Leo shouted, wrenching the throttle. "We have to get out of here!"

The motorcycle revved furiously and we barely got our feet off the ground in time before it leapt forward. Leo grunted and leaned the Packmaster into a sharp turn toward the street.

Headlights raced at us from the road, blindingly bright like demonic eyes, and Leo shouted. He yanked the handlebars of his motorcycle and we swerved around another oversized black van, passing by so close that I could have touched it.

The van roared past us, followed by two more identical ones. The last was decked out with antennae and a big dish on top like a news van. None of them had any kind of branding or insignia. I turned on the Packmaster's pillion to read the license plates, but the vans screeched to a stop. The second one crunched into the rear bumper of the first, but then all three began turning as quickly as vehicles that size were physically capable of.

"They're trying to chase us!" I shouted.

"Not a chance," Leo growled.

He gunned the engine and the streetlights became glowing streaks as Leo's demonic motorcycle shot through the night. I gasped and held onto Leo. Gabriel hadn't been able to overtake the Packmaster. If an archangel couldn't keep up with us, neither could whoever these people were.

I hoped.

CHAPTER 13

W e raced off into the night again. I had spent more time on a motorcycle in the last three days than my whole life combined. My butt hurt like hell, my hand ached – apparently, it wasn't *that* healed up – and my eyes felt like they were full of sand. I needed rest and sleep.

We roared down the dark highway through Cibola National Forest. Leo's whole body was tensed into knots against me and the Packmaster's back end kept threatening to slide out, forcing him to wrestle for every mile. I held onto him for dear life – if Leo's demon-bike threw me off at these speeds, I hoped Uriel could protect me or I would get a lot more than some road rash.

Who the hell were those people? I asked the angel.

I wanted to ask Leo if he had any ideas, but I doubted that he would be able to hear me over the wind, even if I screamed right into his ear.

I do not know, the archangel answered.

Don't shit me, Uriel!

I do not defecate.

You know what I mean, I thought. *Don't lie to me and don't get me killed!*

That is not my intention, Uriel told me. *We have waited for billions of your years for the right vessels to arise. I would not kill you now.*

Then what was all that back there? I asked. *Minions of the horsemen? Some kind of cult or something?*

That seems unlikely, as they attempted to destroy Death's vessel, too, Uriel said. *And angels do not lie.*

Uriel sounded a little sulky, but I actually believed them. Not just because I really hoped the forces of elemental light and order didn't lie, but because automatic weapons and unmarked body armor didn't seem like the angels' style. I had witnessed Gabriel leveling an entire motel pretty much by accident. Why would a creature like that bother using a gun? Or human agents at all, for that matter?

It had to be well past midnight when the Packmaster finally slowed and Leo turned off the highway. There wasn't a road and he wove between a few starlit pine trees before easing to a halt. I let go of Leo and the motorcycle bucked, sending me tumbling off into the underbrush.

"Ow!" I said.

"Stop that," Leo told the bike.

He climbed off and helped me back to my feet. I brushed the pine needles off my butt.

"Why did we stop?" I asked.

"I don't think those guys tonight are naturally drawn to us," Leo said. "Not like the archangels and horsemen are. Did you see that van with all the gear on top? I'll bet they were listening to phone calls or something."

"But why?" I asked. "Who the hell were those people? Why were they shooting at us?"

Leo shook his head. "No idea."

"Wait, my phone!" I grabbed Leo's arm. "Did you get it from the motel room?"

"No point," Leo said with a deep growl. "There were at least three bullet holes through it. I'm sorry, Jaz."

"Shit!" I cried, then clapped my hands over my mouth and desperately hoped that Leo was correct about the tactical goons not being able to magically track us.

"We can buy a burner down the road," Leo said.

"A burner?" I asked.

"A cheap disposable cell phone. You don't register a name and if you buy it with cash, there isn't even much of a purchase record."

"Oh," I said.

Somehow, I didn't think Leo had just learned that watching television shows.

"So what's the plan now?" I asked. "Ride to the next city?"

Leo rubbed his eyes. "Right now, we need sleep. We haven't really rested in the last couple days. We're never getting to San Diego if I fall asleep and drive us over a cliff."

"We've stayed at two motels and both of them pretty much blew up. No one in their right mind would rent us a room."

"We can sleep out here," Leo said.

I looked around at the upthrust shadows of pine trees and a few bushes that were probably green but were transformed into silver-edged black by the moonlight. Most of the forest floor was a thick carpet of pine needles, with a few outcroppings of pale stone. Not a lot of moss or grass that I could see... it was too arid here in the middle of New Mexico.

"It won't be great rest," Leo admitted. "But personally, I'm too tired to give a shit."

"Alright, but let's get further from the road," I said.

Leo nodded and walked his bike deeper into the woods until we could no longer see the highway... and then we walked for another fifteen minutes. I doubted that camping was allowed in this part of Cibola National Forest, but I almost welcomed the idea of some ranger finding us. At least they would just fine us. No submachine guns, no angelic superpowers.

Finally, Leo stopped and then toed out the bike's kickstand. We walked around the motorcycle a few times, complaining about the shiny chrome and wondering if it would reflect any headlights from the highway. We didn't want to push the Packmaster anymore, though, so Leo repositioned it slightly behind a bush.

"Good enough," I said. "I hope."

I slumped against the nearest pine tree and slid down until my butt hit the ground. I was so tired that my whole body ached, blurring the line between fatigue and pain. Leo sat on the non-bush side of his bike.

"Jaz..." he said.

I turned to look at the tall biker. He was sitting up perfectly straight, not relaxing at all. Did he hear something?

"What is it?" I asked.

"Jaz, what happened to you back there? You were glowing," Leo said. "And pretty much catching bullets. How the hell did you do that?"

"I... asked Uriel for help," I admitted. "I thought we were going to die and I didn't see very many other options."

Leo's jaw tightened up and I wondered if he was about to argue, to tell me that he had things dealt with. We didn't need male pride making trouble for us. We were in enough trouble already.

"And Uriel actually helped you?" Leo asked instead.

"Yes," I said. "They barely even demanded extra control over my body. Uriel calls me *vessel*, you know."

Leo smiled briefly at that, but didn't laugh. "Are they any... stronger now? I mean, is Uriel getting any closer to being able to take over?"

"No idea," I said. *Uriel?*

Yes, the angel answered. *When you accept my power, I make progress in seizing this vessel.*

I sighed. "Yeah. Uriel says borrowing their power is bad and I shouldn't do it much if I want to keep control of my body."

That is not what I told you.

I ignored the angel. Leo rubbed his fingers along the rough stubble of his cheek.

"Do you know who those people were?" I asked him. "Like... like a rival biker gang or something?"

"No," Leo said. "I thought maybe it was the cops. We... I did rob a bank, after all. But that wasn't a SWAT team."

"Are you sure?" I asked. "I didn't see a name, but they had the right kind of gear."

"I know the difference," Leo said.

I gulped. Yeah, I bet he did.

"But they didn't seem very rattled when you whipped out the angelic powers, though," Leo went on with a frown.

I remembered the woman who had gasped at me in French, the feeling that she recognized what she was looking at. Those people weren't happy when I used Uriel's power, but they almost seemed to be expecting it. Luckily, that expectation didn't extend to packing halo-piercing bullets.

"You're right," I said. "They clearly know more about what's going on than we do."

Was there any connection there to Leo's Uncle Carlos? Uriel had insisted that we puny mortals didn't understand shit about their glorious battle against the chaotic forces of darkness–

You don't, Uriel said.

–but obviously, somebody did. I couldn't imagine beloved Uncle Carlos sending a team armed to the teeth after Leo, but there was sure as hell something weird happening here.

Okay, something *else* weird.

"You know, that was badass," Leo said.

"Huh?" I asked. "What was?"

"How you kicked those bastards' asses. It takes some serious mettle to run *toward* a gun. And then to throw the guy holding it through a van."

I laughed. The sound was sudden and strange in the dark, empty forest. At least, I hoped it was empty. There wasn't really anything funny about my situation right now, but I couldn't help it – laughing felt *good*. I laughed until I ran out of breath, then wiped a few hysterical tears from my eyes.

"Thanks," I said at last. "That actually means a lot coming from a professional badass like you."

Leo grinned and gave a short laugh of his own, then leveled a much more serious look at me.

"Did Uriel fight you at all?" Leo asked. "When it was all over and they had to let you go?"

I shook my head. "No. Just enough power to escape and then done. That was our deal."

I honor my word, Uriel said. *We are righteous. But I cannot win against the darkness unless you surrender control.*

Can we stop fighting about this for the night? I asked.

Uriel didn't agree, but they didn't say anything else. I called that a victory and settled against the tree, trying to find a comfortable position.

Yeah, right... There were pine needles poking my ass, rough bark against my back, and it was damnably cold. I wrapped my arms around myself and looked over at Leo, wondering if he was managing any better. But the biker hadn't moved. Instead, he was staring across at me.

"Jaz, I felt something back there," Leo said. "When you threw me into that motel room."

My heart suddenly leapt up into my throat. "What... what did you feel?"

"Death."

I went cold all over and Leo stared down at his hands. They were clenched into fists against his thighs.

"I felt that... thing... inside me," Leo said. "Death is waking up. How much time do we have left until I'm hearing voices, too? Until I'm just like the monster that killed my friends?"

Not long, Uriel answered.

"Hey, stop that," I told both of them.

Leo looked up and Uriel fell silent. I sighed and crawled across the forest floor to sit next to Leo, careful not to touch the Packmaster.

"You can fight this," I said. "I'm kind of pulling it off and I'm nowhere near the hardcase you are. Death isn't talking to you yet, is it?"

Leo shook his head and I leaned over to bump my shoulder lightly against his ribs.

"Then you still have time to get to San Diego," I told him. "To reach your uncle."

That finally did the trick. Leo let out an explosive breath and nodded. He scrubbed at his eyes with the heels of his hands and then smiled at me.

"Thanks, Jaz," Leo said.

"Hey, you rescued *me* from Crayhill," I told him. "I owe you one. Ten thousand, actually."

Leo blinked. "What?"

"Ten thousand dollars," I said. "That's how much you paid me up front to fix your bike."

"And twenty grand more when we get to San Diego. Fuck, I completely forgot."

"That's okay. It doesn't seem very important anymore, does it?" I asked.

"Not really," Leo agreed. "I'm not sure there's any amount of money that could fix this shit."

I nodded and wrapped my arms around myself, shivering.

New Mexico seemed warm enough during the day, but now it was dark and cold. I rubbed my arms, trying to create a little heat, and felt goosebumps across my skin. Leo sat forward from the Packmaster and took off his jacket.

"What are you doing?" I asked.

Leo draped his jacket over my shoulders. It was huge on me, like a big leather blanket. One that smelled like Leo... and was branded with the Knights of Hell flaming helm and the rattle-snake. But you know what they say about beggars and choosers. I wound the jacket tight around me.

Leo searched through the Packmaster's overstuffed saddle-bags until he found a long-sleeved shirt and pulled it on over his head, then settled down next to me again.

"Thanks," I said.

I eyed the tree I had been leaning against. It was uncomfort-able as hell, but maybe the addition of the leather jacket would help cushion me against the rough bark. I had never missed my tiny bed back home so much.

"Come here, Jaz," Leo said.

He leaned against his motorcycle and lifted one arm. I hesi-tated, but accepted the invitation and let Leo pull me close. I laid my cheek against his chest and told myself firmly that we were just conserving heat. We didn't have any blankets and Leo had given me his jacket. The least I could do was share some of the warmth.

It was only fair.

You must leave him, Uriel urged. *I grow stronger every day, and so does Death. If the horseman's vessel yields control, you will die. And without a body of my own, I cannot fight.*

Don't you ever *think about anything besides your stupid war?* I asked.

No, Uriel said. *And it is not stupid.*

Leo rested his cheek on top of my head and his warm breath ruffled my hair. I shivered again, but I wasn't cold anymore.

I lifted my face up to look at Leo. His eyes were open and fixed on me. His fingers slid along my hairline and then slowly down my cheek. I closed my eyes and for a heartbeat, there was nothing, but then I felt Leo's lips pressed against mine. They were surprisingly soft and gentle.

But something exploded inside my head. Light and darkness collided endlessly in the void, hurling forces at each other that would have ripped galaxies apart to atoms – if either galaxies or atoms existed yet.

How could something without form be so violent...?

Leo and I yanked away from one another. I fell over onto the carpet of pine needles, and he banged his head against the Packmaster. We both panted for breath and Leo looked like he was about to be sick.

"Shit, did you see that?" Leo asked.

I nodded, gasping. "Yeah."

Did you do that to me... to us? I asked Uriel.

No, the angel said. *At least, not purposefully. But proximity to one of the horsemen brings us ever closer to the final battle. Our power awakens.*

Can't you... I don't know... hit pause on the apocalyptic visions? I asked.

I cannot, Uriel said.

You can't? Or you won't?

I cannot, Uriel repeated. *The coming war is the purpose of your universe and all life.*

Don't we get a say in that? I asked.

No. It may be our design, but it is a part of your very being.

Wow, that's a mood killer, I grumbled.

Death will kill you, the angel told me. Again. *Not just your... mood.*

I sighed. I wouldn't get anything else useful out of Uriel right now. Leo rubbed the back of his head, then gingerly held his arms open to me once more. He didn't try to kiss me again, but I leaned against his chest and closed my eyes. I heard Leo's heart pounding for a long time.

But eventually, it slowed and the strong, steady sound pulled me down into sleep.

CHAPTER 14

The trees of Cibola National Forest shaded us against the first ten minutes of sunlight after dawn. Maybe fifteen... but then slanting golden light stabbed right into my eyes and I sat up with a groan. The ground was cold and hard under my ass, and even the warmth of Leo shifted next to me as my protests woke him, too.

Leo and I got up and moving quickly, like there were archangels, horsemen and an armored caravan of gun-toting paramilitary weirdos all chasing after us.

Oh, wait... that was *exactly* what was going on.

I returned Leo's leather jacket. I was already wearing one of his t-shirts and couldn't steal *all* of his clothes. I didn't see any sign of Gabriel or the other angels – though Uriel wouldn't actually corroborate that – so Leo started the Packmaster. I climbed on behind Leo and held on tight.

We crept back toward the highway, but saw only one car – an SUV with roof racks loaded down by camping gear. It passed us without stopping, so Leo pulled out onto the road.

Spending the night with a hunky biker as a pillow wasn't as comfortable as I had hoped and I was swiftly developing a kink in my neck from looking over my shoulder for glowing wings or unmarked black vans. I began alternating shoulders just to avoid adding chiropractic issues to our list of problems.

We didn't stop anywhere for long. Breakfast was some fast food we bought on the other side of the forest. We got it to go, then drove a few more miles before pulling over to wolf down egg and bacon sandwiches on the side of the road. I perched on an aluminum rail and guzzled my soda pop.

"At least we don't need to stop for gas," I said, then burped and flushed. "Even if your bike hates me."

"Yeah," Leo agreed. "This is some weird-ass shit. How're you holding up?"

"Uh, getting frighteningly used to hearing an angel in my head. Seriously, I thought there was supposed to be a devil on my other shoulder. Some variety would be nice... Uriel never talks about anything but fighting the horsemen."

Leo crumpled up a pair of greasy wrappers and stuffed them back into the paper bag. He spared a tight grin for my joke.

"What happens if we meet another one?" Leo asked.

I tossed my wrapper into the bag, too. "Another angel? Or a devil?"

"Angel."

"I... don't really know," I admitted. "If they get close, Uriel will become stronger. And when Gabriel touched me, Uriel had total control of my body and took over my mouth. These guys have absolutely zero concept of consent."

You and your world belong to us, Uriel supplied helpfully. *We lit the fire that created your entire universe...*

"But you got control back," Leo said.

I touched a finger to my temple. "Not that I can make Uriel shut up now. And just one angel was enough to stuff me into the metaphorical trunk. If all four of them get together, I'll never be able to retake the wheel."

Leo growled and finished his pop, too. That was everything, so we dumped out our ice and crushed the cups until they fit in the paper sack. That went into the Packmaster's saddlebags until we could find a trash can. I wondered briefly if the demon-bike was ever pissed about carrying our shit around.

"Speaking of visions," I said, then took a deep breath. "That jolt we both got last night... Did it give Death any ideas?"

"It sure as hell got the adrenalin pumping, but no. I don't think so," Leo answered. "Kissing an angelic host doesn't seem to be the same as encountering another horseman. They really are stronger together, I guess."

"So what if we run into Pestilence or one of the other horsemen?" I asked.

"Probably about the same as you and Gabriel. Death gets more powerful... Maybe takes over."

Leo's voice was flat and leaden. He tossed my helmet to me and buckled his own in place. He swung one leg over the Packmaster, which rumbled ominously beneath him.

Precisely as I warned you many times, vessel, Uriel said.

I thought an angel would be above 'I told you so.'

I balanced on the pillion behind Leo and wrapped my arms around him. The motorcycle snarled, but I held on. I would have biceps like iron bars by the end of this. Whatever end that was...

"Let's get moving," I said.

We made good time across New Mexico. Not as good as we *could* have, but shooting down Highway 44 like a speeding bullet didn't seem like a smart idea. Those goons we dealt with last night probably weren't police, but I didn't want to get the cops on our asses, too, and I bet all those radar dishes on their van included a police scanner.

But the Packmaster didn't like that decision one bit. The big black motorcycle tried to shake me off with every passing mile, and the engine raced and revved constantly, too. I couldn't help thinking of a very large, very dangerous dog pulling against its leash. If Leo let go for a second, someone would get bitten.

I really hoped it wasn't me.

At least the sky was clear and brilliant blue. I wasn't thrilled about the idea of Leo trying to control his over-excited Packmaster in the rain. The highway remained dry and open as we rode. Well, except for other travelers and drivers, many of them hauling trailers or RVs as they headed across the country. We even passed a few other bikers. Most of them took in the predatory red and black beauty of Leo's motorcycle and flashed us a thumbs-up.

Around dinnertime, though, I checked the cloudless sky for the gazillionth time. We were driving through the outskirts of a small city – Gallup, if I was reading the roadside signs right – and I wondered if we should stop to pick up that burner phone Leo talked about yesterday. The sky overhead was still blue, not a cloud in sight... But I felt something prickling my skin, like a sunburn. Skin as dark as mine didn't burn easily, though, and most of it was covered up.

What the hell was that?

But when I turned back to the highway, I forgot all about the tingle. Something shone black and white in the sun up ahead, half-hidden beneath one of the peeling green-painted interstate signs. I could barely see it around the big rig in front of us, but I reached up and patted the top of my helmet – the hand signal warning for a cop.

Leo couldn't see me sitting behind him, of course. So I swore to myself, thumped Leo on the arm and pointed urgently... But it was too late. We were already shooting past the parked cop car. I looked over Leo's shoulder at the speedometer. We were seven miles over the speed limit, but so was everyone else on the road. We were wearing helmets and *should* be fine…

But two seconds later, the highway lit up in flashing red and blue. Shit! I stabbed my finger at the rearview mirror and Leo nodded shortly. Station wagons and SUVs were all pulling over behind us, clearing the way for the police. I felt the vibration through Leo's body of him saying something, but I couldn't hear a single word.

It must have been a warning… Leo wristed the throttle and the Packmaster finally got exactly what it had wanted all day. The engine roared and the huge motorcycle's front wheel actually lifted a few inches into the air as we shot forward. The back tire screamed on the asphalt and left a burnt black streak down the highway in our wake.

I screamed, too, as the speedometer needle blasted past a hundred and kept going, but I didn't try to make Leo stop. The rattlesnake patch on his jacket, saddlebags full of stolen cash and doubtlessly illegal handguns… Getting caught with that shit was a one-way ticket to prison – if we were lucky. And if we were held even overnight in some New Mexico jail, how long until the other angels and horsemen found us? If that happened, nothing much would matter anymore…

So we ran.

We raced down the highway so fast that my eyes watered and the wind shrieked in my ears. I had to press my face against Leo's jacket and it took every ounce of strength to clutch onto him. I had no idea how Leo could steer or even see at those speeds, but we swerved smoothly back and forth, around trucks and family cars that seemed almost to stand still by comparison. The police cruiser fell swiftly behind and then vanished into the distance.

I clung to Leo until the cop was too far away to catch up and he finally throttled his motorcycle down to a less suicidal speed.

Not without difficulty... the bike growled and surged when Leo tried to brake, nearly ramming us right into the branded back end of a big freight hauler.

"Stop that!" Leo shouted loud enough for even me to hear.

The Packmaster slowed down with a deep metallic grumble and the truck driver honked her horn at us. I waved one shaking hand in apology.

We drove carefully through the slowing evening traffic and I was growing swiftly dizzy trying to watch the road for more cops – on top of everything else I was paranoid about. We didn't stop for dinner, and kept driving long after the sun had set. But then Leo and I were both yawning, and neither of us was very excited about the idea of sleeping rough again.

Reluctantly, we pulled off the highway and drove another twenty miles along the Arizona-New Mexico border before stopping at a motel. It was even later now, and the place was full up, forcing us to share a room again.

"Fine by me," Leo said as we went to our latest rented room. He had left the saddlebags on his motorcycle, but stuffed a few stacks of money and most of the guns into his pockets. "We don't want to be separated if any more of those paramilitary dickwads show up."

It would save Leo a couple bucks, too – he had paid in cash again – but I didn't really think the bill mattered very much at this point. I followed Leo into the room and locked the door, then eyed the beds. I remembered the heat of our kiss the night before and my head swam. Just because we had two beds didn't mean we needed to use both of them...

Why do you sleep? Uriel asked.

Because we're tired, I thought. *Because we've been riding all day and we need to rest.*

Rest?

Wow, Uriel was beyond naïve.

Are you serious? I asked. *How do you not understand this? You're an angel! Don't you... watch people all the time? You know, waiting for your vessel so you could go fight the horsemen?*

This universe was created to provide a physical battleground for our war, Uriel said. *We set all energy and matter into motion, then waited for suitable vessels to develop. The details are unimportant.*

I rolled my eyes and Leo frowned. I pointed to my head and he nodded.

There's a whole universe out there, I thought. *And the only things you paid attention to were your weapons? That's the only bit you cared about?*

Yes, Uriel said.

Well, that certainly explained why the angel didn't understand sleep. I couldn't imagine the need for rest being the trait that sold them and the horsemen on human bodies. And then I wondered why they *had* chosen us.

Uriel didn't answer me about that, though, so I looked over at a clock sitting on the table between the narrow motel beds. It had a fake wooden finish and was so ancient that the term *digital* barely applied. But the flickering amber numbers there weren't very encouraging.

"It's too late to go buy a cell phone, isn't it?" I asked.

Even if there were an electronics store or something hidden somewhere in this cluster of fast-food chains, filling stations and motels, it was well past midnight.

"Probably, " Leo said with a sigh. "I was looking for anything still open this late on the way through. There's a shitty-looking bar down the street, but that's about it."

"Could we borrow someone else's phone?" I asked. "Do you know your uncle's phone number?"

I doubted I could remember more than a couple of phone numbers – the rest were programmed into my cell. But a sudden hope lit up Leo's eyes and he nodded.

"Yeah, I know my uncle's number," he said.

"Umm... wait a sec," I interrupted, shaking my head. "What did you say last night about all the gear on that black van? That they were tracking our phones, right?"

"Well, the joke's on them... They shot up their own damned tracking device," Leo said with a laugh.

"Maybe, but do we really want them coming down on some soccer mom just because she helped us make a call?" I asked.

Leo heaved a sigh and shook his head. "No, we don't. I'm not about to get some little league team caught in the crossfire."

He sat down heavily on one of the beds and I plopped down onto the other to face him. Leo pulled the revolver out of his jacket, checked the cylinder – which he had reloaded with fresh bullets – and set it down on the nightstand.

And then he took a second gun from another pocket. It was a black pistol only a bit larger than Leo's snub-nose. He put it on top of the nightstand and pushed it across the scarred laminate toward me. I didn't pick it up.

"Just in case," Leo said. "Ever used one?"

I was born and raised in Kansas, so I had encountered a few guns... but that was mostly hunting rifles and shotguns, and I had never been a big fan of either. My grandfather lost most of a hand screwing with some buckshot and that didn't inspire a lot of confidence in little Jasmine O'Neil.

"Uh, I'm not really a gun girl," I answered after an awkward hesitation.

Leo gave me a reassuring smile. "Don't worry. It's pretty easy. This one is semi-automatic, so you don't need to cock it between shots. But you can't just hold down the trigger."

I didn't pick up the pistol. I looked at it on the nightstand, but didn't recognize the make or model... I do motorcycles, not guns.

"How many bullets are there?" I asked.

"Seven shots before you have to reload," Leo said. "I've got two more magazines for that one."

I nodded and really hoped I wouldn't have to use any of that information. Gingerly, I positioned the gun next to my bed. It was cool and surprisingly heavy for its size.

"So what's our next move?" I asked.

Find the other angels and prepare for battle against our enemies, Uriel answered.

I wasn't talking to you, I thought.

"Well, that shitty bar might have a pay phone," I suggested out loud. "We can use it to call your uncle."

"I wondered about that, too," Leo said. "But you're right, Jaz. We don't know who is listening in. I hate all this spy shit, but we can't call Uncle Carlos or anybody else until we actually get to San Diego."

"What if he has some... I don't know... advice?" I asked. "A trick or secret to help us get there?"

"We have to figure it out on our own," Leo said.

I gulped. "So... ride like hell tomorrow?"

"Hopefully not *too* much like hell," he said.

Neither of us laughed. Leo looked down at his hands, which had closed into fists again. The biker stood and stripped out of his leather jacket.

"My turn to shower," he said. "I feel like crap and I smell like a parking lot."

Leo pulled his shirt up and off, revealing more tattoos and a whole lot of hard muscle. He kicked away his well-worn boots and then... unfortunately, Leo stopped his undressing there. He draped his shirt and jacket over the back of the room's single chair. Leo hesitated for a moment, then took his gun into the bathroom with him.

That object is a weapon? Uriel asked.

I nodded and apparently, the archangel could see or feel that confirmation from inside me.

You should not let him have a weapon, Uriel said. *He will use it against you.*

God, you're paranoid. You know what that word means, right?

Uriel ignored the question.

I am growing stronger, the angel said. *And Death is, too. Leave that... man... behind.*

Not a chance. Leo's my only shot at making it through this thing alive.

I shuddered and internally braced myself to fight Uriel for control of my body. I still wasn't exactly sure how to do that... But despite the archangel's ominous words, there was no sense of gathering power inside me... Just that faint, sunburn sensation that I had felt all day.

In all the panic of police and phones and guns, I had almost forgotten about the feeling. I pushed myself off the bed and went to the lamp in front of the window to squint at my skin. No burn, and the sky outside was dark and moonless, though it glittered with a thousand silver stars. I sure as hell wasn't getting a sunburn now...

What is that? I asked inwardly. *What am I feeling, Uriel?*

The angel was quiet, though, and I wasn't really in the mood to get into another weird mental debate with them. I actually felt almost alone inside my own head, and it was a nice change of pace.

From the washroom, I heard some muttered Spanish that sounded like swearing followed by the hiss of running water. I paced in front of the window and rubbed my hands against my jeans. Even without Uriel's voice in my head, my thoughts were chasing each other around in circles.

Leo and I were possessed by ancient, powerful magical entities that absolutely *hated* each other. There were unmarked but heavily armed whackjobs after us, and now we were running from cops, too. Well, at least Leo was familiar with that last part.

I spent my whole life wishing I could run away from Crayhill. But somehow, none of my dreams or fantasies had involved my body being taken over by an archangel and hitching a ride on the back of Death's steed. I was pretty sure this fell under the heading of being careful what you wish for.

I leaned against the window, cheek pressed to the glass, and watched the stars sparkle outside. In the next room, the shower shut off and the bathroom door swung open. I smelled warm, wet air and soap as Leo stepped out. His reflection moved across the dark window in front of me and I watched a few droplets of water winding their way down the muscles of his chest and stomach.

Leo was rubbing a towel over his head, drying his hair, and I don't *think* he saw me staring. I managed to get my eyes under control by the time he was done and had tossed the towel back into the bathroom. He stretched, lacing his fingers behind his neck and showing off every inch of tattooed chest.

"Much better," Leo sighed. "Do you want a go?"

At the shower. Leo was asking if I needed a turn washing up. I shook my head, though.

"No, I'm alright," I answered. "I wasn't the one wrestling the Packmaster all day."

Leo dropped his hands back down to his sides and then gave me a long look that I struggled to interpret. He walked across the motel room and made no move to retrieve his old shirt or get a new one.

"Want to go to bed?" Leo asked.

Was I imagining the invitation in his question? I didn't know, but Leo took a step closer to me, not toward either of the beds. He stood close enough that I felt the heat coming off his skin.

There was an electric charge in the room and a hot thrill ran through my whole body.

I turned away from the window to look up at Leo. If his eyes smoldered any more, he was going to spontaneously combust... But then I stopped. I remembered our kiss last night, but I also remembered the visions of Uriel and Death fighting endlessly, impossibly through the void before the universe. Leo froze, too, a troubled look on his face.

"The gun," he said. "Shit, I forgot."

Leo went back to the bathroom and then came out holding his revolver. He replaced it on the bedside table with a sigh. I sat down on my bed.

"So... how about some TV?" I asked.

Leo nodded a bit unconvincingly and we both climbed into our separate beds. I pulled off my shoes, then leaned against the headboard and busied myself puzzling out the remote controls. It took a few minutes to get the television turned on and find something besides late-night infomercials.

Finally, I settled for a bland sitcom and slipped under the bed covers without getting undressed. Sleeping in jeans wasn't very comfortable, but if anything went wrong – and something *always* went wrong – I didn't want to make a run for Leo's motorcycle in a t-shirt and panties. I left my socks on and made sure my shoes were right next to the bed, too.

Leo sat up, watching the television without seeming to really see it. He kept his shoes and shirt nearby, too. The biker looked like he wanted to say something a couple of times, but remained silent. So I pulled the blankets tight around me and fell asleep staring at the door.

CHAPTER 15

My dreams were full of angels charging through Cibola Forest at shadowy demons on motorcycles. Fire burned so hot that the trees were dancing blades of blinding white. All I could see against the incandescent flames was Leo astride his Packmaster and a halo of seething metal chains lashing out at me like a nest of angry oversized snakes. I flew at Leo on six out-stretched wings, bright angelic power blazing all through me. I dove, slashing through cruelly barbed chains with a sword made of light until I reached Leo... and kissed him.

Finally, the rising sun woke us. Without our cell phones and unwilling to trust the sleepy clerk at the motel's front desk to manage a wake-up call, Leo and I had left the curtains open, and now the sunrise stabbed metaphorical golden knives right into my eyeballs. It wasn't as early as a morning at the garage back in Crayhill, but I still groaned and stuck my head under the pillow. We had stopped late last night and dreams of flying into some demonic war didn't make for very peaceful sleep.

But hey, we actually got to sleep through the night in beds! Unless I wanted my nightmare to come true, though, we had to get back on the road to San Diego.

I heaved myself out of bed with a grunt while Leo pulled on his boots and yawned. He offered me a fresh t-shirt, this one branded with the Harley-Davidson name and shield logo. It was huge on me and hung like drapes. That much fabric flying in the wind on the back of a motorcycle would get real annoying real fast, so I twisted the hem up into a knot just above my navel. I was a little self-conscious about displaying so much skin, but I felt Leo's eyes on me and he didn't object.

It didn't take us long to pack. After two nighttime attacks, we didn't have a lot of stuff left. I considered the gun still sitting on my nightstand. Finally, I picked it up – carefully – and held the weapon out to Leo.

"I don't have any way to carry this thing," I told him. "I mean, unless I want to just stick it in my jeans. But that doesn't seem very safe."

"It works in a pinch, but not particularly well," Leo admitted. "I'll hold onto it."

He took the black semi-automatic and tucked it away into a pocket. I wondered how much safer that was... Leo didn't seem to have holsters for those guns. If any of the dead Knights of Hell had carried their weapons more securely, Leo hadn't collected their holsters. And remembering the Knights' contorted bodies and their blackened, bulging veins, I couldn't blame Leo for not touching them.

"But, uh... keep that gun nearby?" I suggested.

Leo nodded and then we headed out into the little truck-stop town to get a quick breakfast. Outside, my impromptu midriff seemed like an even better idea than it had in the motel room. The early morning was warm and growing swiftly hotter. It was already too hot for leathers and Leo stuffed his jacket into one of his saddlebags. He pulled the gun from his pocket, gave me an apologetic little smile, and then thrust it into the waist of his jeans.

I smirked at Leo, but the back of my neck prickled with the sun's heat. Already? We had just stepped out the door... I eyed the sky. A few fluffy white clouds obscured the sun, but were swiftly burning off in the bright morning warmth.

"Let's grab breakfast to go," I said.

"Yeah," Leo agreed. "Something feels..."

"Weird," I finished.

Leo nodded slowly and rubbed his temple with one hand.

"You know what? Forget breakfast," he said.

Leo put on his helmet – riding without his jacket was questionable enough – and swung one long leg over the Packmaster. The engine purred in immediate answer. At least the motorcycle seemed to be in a good mood today and I jumped quickly onto the back, circling my arms around Leo's waist.

The bike was in a good mood... God, my life had gotten strange in the last few days.

Leo took us back out onto Highway 44 and we moved west, toward California. I watched the road for more police cars. Why the hell had that cop tried to pull us over yesterday? Were they looking for Leo? He *had* robbed a bank... Which was the least of our problems right now, but the cops might not see it that way. So I kept my eyes peeled for flashing lights.

The sun rose higher overhead as we drove across the border into Arizona, and shadows shortened under the trees and road signs. The warm morning became the hot one I had predicted and both Leo and I were soon sweating.

Something still felt... off, though. Alternating flashes of hot and cold raced all through my body. The waves of feverish heat weren't just like a sunburn now, but more like I was standing *way* too close to a raging bonfire. But the chills were deep and icy, as cold as a northern wind. You know those cartoons where a dark rain cloud follows some sad sap around? It was as though the sun and that animated cloud were warring to see who could get me to claw my skin off first.

What the hell is this? I asked. *What's going on?*

Uriel remained silent inside my head. The angel had been strangely quiet since last night. Why? It wasn't like Uriel to pass up a chance to pick a fight with me. I actually worried a little bit about them.

The day only got hotter as we drove. Heat shimmer turned Highway 44 into a black river of mirages and cars were pulling over on the gravel shoulder with their hoods up, steam billowing from their radiators. A few cranky overheated drivers shouted at Leo as he wove his way through the slowing vehicles, but even their curses seemed lackluster and tired.

A huge green Cadillac slowed down next to us, then began angling into our lane. Another car honked urgently, but the big land-yacht continued sliding across the highway. Leo swerved around the Cadillac, but I turned to stare. The driver wasn't on his cell phone or anything – he was doubled over in some kind of coughing or sneezing fit. His car kept drifting until it went all the way onto the shoulder... then over and into a ditch on the other side.

Leo braked to a stop and swung the Packmaster around. The motorcycle growled hungrily beneath us as Leo eased it back along the edge of the highway toward the crashed car. Its rear end stuck up out of the roadside ditch, tires still spinning. The main airbag had deployed and was now deflating like a giant scoop of melting ice cream. The middle-aged man inside seemed uninjured – it hadn't been a high-speed collision – but there was definitely something wrong. He was too pale and his head lolled forward. The man coughed again and clutched at his throat.

"What the hell?" I asked. "Is it heatstroke?"

"No," Leo said.

His voice was tight and I could feel his body tense so hard in front of mine that his muscles were trembling.

"It's something else," Leo growled. "Something's coming…"

Another car slewed and skidded to a stop halfway over the double yellow line. A pickup truck heading the other direction plowed right into it, sending both vehicles spinning out across Highway 44. That cold sensation inside me was tightening into a knot of uneasy ice in the pit of my stomach… even as it felt like my skin was on fire.

"Shit," I said. "We need to–"

What? Call the police or an ambulance? Neither Leo or I had cell phones anymore. And even if we did, being here when cops showed up was a really bad idea.

A slick, shiny red motorcycle suddenly appeared out of the heat shimmer, slicing its way through the scattered cars like a bloody knife. It was a Baracca Cavallo V4, a professional-level street racer. Packmasters were more big, brutal cruisers, but that Baracca was all about speed.

The bike's rider didn't match his motorcycle at all. He wore an expensive but wind-rumpled gray suit instead of protective leathers, and no helmet. The man was tall, thin and white, with short pewter hair that had probably been meticulously styled before he climbed onto the back of the Baracca. He looked a lot more like he belonged in a boardroom than astride that road-rocket.

"That's him…!" Leo growled in a voice that sounded like a thunderstorm.

"That's who?" I asked.

"The man I saw in the vision. When we found the Knights."

Pestilence! Uriel snarled from inside me.

"Oh, shit," I said.

The cherry-red Baracca sliced smoothly toward us between stalled and crashed cars. The driver of the crumpled pickup staggered out of his truck, clutching at his throat. He fell to his knees as black lines crawled up the sides of his neck. The man's eyes bulged and then blood ran from them like horrible scarlet tears. My whole body was burning and freezing, and I couldn't stop shivering.

"Leo, we… we have to go!" I said through chattering teeth.

But if Leo heard me, he didn't move. He was a knot of tensed muscles as the other biker stopped in the middle of the highway. Pestilence dismounted and the red Baracca's kickstand snapped itself out as the horseman in the charcoal suit walked toward us. The Cadillac driver began vomiting all over his steering wheel. Pestilence's skin was an ashy white-gray color, but its wide eyes were pure and unreflecting black, more like empty sockets than actual eyes.

"Death," Pestilence said. "I have been searching for you."

Its voice was so loud that I wanted to clap my hands over my ears, and it buzzed like a nest of wasps. I could feel the sound crawling over me and the acidic urge to throw up clawing at the back of my throat.

"Leo? Leo, that's Pestilence!" I gasped. "We have to get out of here!"

I shook Leo. At least, I tried to… but Leo was a big guy, all tensed muscles under those tattoos. I might as well have tried to shake a statue. Leo's hands clenched into fists so tight that the leather of his gloves creaked. Sweat soaked his shirt and it clung to his skin.

"No! That thing killed my friends," Leo snarled.

He jumped off the Packmaster and charged the horseman closing in on us. Leo grabbed his revolver from the waist of his jeans, whipped it up to aim at Pestilence, and pulled the trigger. He thumbed back the steel hammer and fired again, over and over, until the cylinder clicked empty. But Leo's bullets punched right through the insurance adjustor or whatever the man in the gray suit had been before Pestilence took over. But it didn't fall or even slow in its march toward Leo.

Something dark seeped from the wounds... No, not seeped. *Crawled.* Insects buzzed as they poured out of Pestilence's body. I wasn't close enough to see what they were – flies or locusts or some unknown species – but thousands of them crawled from the ragged gunshot holes and flew up into the air. Bugs swirled in a shifting, chittering cloud that blotted out the sun.

"Leo, let's get the hell out of here!" I cried.

"Death, control your vessel," Pestilence said in a monotone buzz.

Leo flung his empty gun aside with a shout, grabbed Pestilence's fog-gray silk tie and punched him right in the face. Leo was well over six feet tall and more than two hundred pounds of muscle, but the blow barely rocked Pestilence.

"It is time, Death," said the pale horseman. "Lead us against the angels and we will claim final victory."

The insects still pouring out of Pestilence darkened the sky like storm clouds. Leo hauled his fist back for another punch, but Pestilence seized his broad shoulders in an embrace like a long-lost brother.

"No!" I shouted.

Leo's fist dropped to his side again, but it didn't unclench. A rictus smile spread across Pestilence's stolen face and Leo turned around to face me. I never realized how much emotion there was in Leo's brown eyes – anger and pain and surprising warmth – until it was gone.

Leo's eyes had vanished, leaving only black, bottomless pits like the sockets of a skull. And those empty shadows stared right at me. The Packmaster growled like a hungry wolf.

Death is manifest, and it will not wait until all eight are gathered to begin the battle, Uriel said. *You must give me control of this body, vessel! Now!*

If I gave up control, I was just as lost as if the horsemen got their hands on me. Shit!

I jumped off the Packmaster and backed away, shaking and probably sobbing. There was no way Leo's motorcycle was going to run for me, not with its master glaring literal death down the highway at me. The livid green-black sky boiled with insects.

"Uriel," Pestilence rasped. "Face us."

Flashes of red and blue lit the cloud of bugs and the sharp wail of a siren finally tore my attention away from Death's empty eyes. Another motorcycle roared up the center of the road from the opposite direction as Pestilence. It was black and white, with a stout cop sitting astride the leather seat. My body burned with ethereal fire as he cruised up the highway without even glancing down at the crashed cars or fallen bodies. Heat shimmer caught the police bike's colorful staccato lights and smeared them out into a glimmering cloak.

No, not a cloak. Wings.

That is the one your mythology calls Michael, Uriel said. *My greatest warrior.*

Uriel seemed to somehow swell within me, suddenly taking up more space inside my head. I threw my hands over my ears as though I could physically hold the archangel at bay, but I felt Uriel's light coursing through my body like a fever.

"No! I... I thought you didn't want to fight yet!" I shouted at the new angel.

The motorcycle cop stopped his bike and had to kick out the stand as he dismounted. Only the horsemen could control their vehicles by will alone, apparently. Michael strode toward me, shiny knee-high boots hitting the asphalt with a sound like gunshots.

The shimmering glow streaming behind him grew brighter – though the storm cloud of buzzing insects above us was still eclipsing the sun – and spread out into four long glowing wings.

They weren't feathered, exactly... unless feathers were made of fire and molten glass.

Pestilence turned to face the newcomer, but Death's empty black eyes remained on me.

"I finally found you, Uriel," Michael said. The angel's deep voice rolled and reverberated like thunder. "My vessel's brethren were most helpful in locating yours. These mortals are surprisingly resourceful."

Was *that* why the police had chased us yesterday? Because Michael put out an APB on me? And the other angel closing in had to be the source of that burning sensation I kept feeling. Uriel must have known... and hadn't told me. That bitch!

"And I have arrived just in time, it seems," Michael said. The angel pointed to Leo and Pestilence. "Go now! The final battle shall be fought when we are *all* gathered, as was agreed. Stand down, horsemen!"

"Your unyielding adherence to the law will only end in your defeat," Pestilence buzzed.

The horsemen have no respect for order, Uriel said. I felt my lips forming the words as Michael's presence strengthened the archangel within me.

"Death, restrain your brother!" Michael boomed. "This is not the time for our battle!"

But Leo's eyeless gaze remained fixed on me, and he didn't answer. Pestilence laughed and its hovering cloud of bugs drew together into something glistening and solid, ending in a terrible needle point. It flew at the winged motorcycle cop like a massive black arrow. But light flared around Michael and the storm of insects caught instantly aflame, falling out of the sky in burning orange embers.

"Uriel, take your vessel and go find the others," Michael said. "We must gather our strength!"

"Death!" Pestilence shouted. "It is time to fight!"

Michael spread four luminous, sharp-looking wings and rose into the air. Pestilence snapped its fingers and the Baracca's wheels spun, churning up thick black smoke and the stink of scorching rubber. Greenish fog and shadows billowed out from the seams of Pestilence's suit, covering the horseman in a cloudy cloak as it leapt into the seat of the already charging motorcycle.

At Pestilence's touch, the Baracca's bright cherry finish darkened, turning the red-black of infected blood. The powerful engine rumbled, as dry and rasping as a death rattle.

Fiery golden light exploded from Michael to collide with the rancid shroud surrounding Pestilence and its diseased-looking motorcycle. The fire struck and deflected, carving a molten line across the blacktop. The earth shuddered and I stumbled as one of the crashed cars collapsed in on itself, cut entirely in half by the celestial blast. The gouge went right through the highway and down into the ground so deep that I couldn't see the bottom of the sudden crevasse.

I screamed and threw myself down on the highway. I didn't need any angels to tell me it was time to get the hell out of there. But smoke and dirt obscured Leo and his hollow eyes. Could I really abandon him to Death while Michael and Pestilence tore the entire road to pieces?

Pestilence isn't touching Leo anymore, I thought desperately to Uriel. *Can I still get him back from Death?*

The horseman's hold is incomplete, Uriel admitted. *Death's vessel fights to maintain control, just as you do.*

I can't leave him here with those... things!

Your mortal form is no match for Michael's power and that of a fully manifest horseman, Uriel said. *And if you are destroyed, then the four warriors of chaos will fight against only three of light and we will fail.*

But if I get Leo away from Pestilence, he might be okay? I asked.

You cannot take that risk, vessel!

Leo came to help me when Gabriel showed up in Arrow and you took over. I can't just abandon him when Pestilence is doing the same thing!

Michael dove at Pestilence, all four fiery wings pointed at the horseman. The dark red Baracca may have sounded like a dog on its last legs, but it sure didn't move like one. The street racer screeched around in an impossibly tight arc and Michael missed, slamming to the ground like a lightning strike and blowing a house-sized crater into Highway 44. Pestilence charged at the grounded archangel with an arm outstretched. The limb lengthened and sharpened into a barbed lance dripping with poisonous-looking green ichor.

Uriel pushed and shoved from inside me, pulling me away from Leo. I was too damned close to Michael... I groaned with the effort of taking a single step toward Leo's indistinct shape in the dust and darkness.

The road shuddered again as a huge oil tanker barreled into the cloud of insects and smoke, horn blaring, but the driver was slumped down in his seat. Michael rose from the sundered earth beneath the truck, lifting it as easily as if it were just a toy, and flung it at Pestilence. The tanker slammed into the horseman hard enough to crumple like a tin can, but then the metal began to blacken and blister.

From underneath the ruined truck, Pestilence let out a laugh that sounded more like a loud, racking cough.

"Leo!" I shouted.

The tall biker's silhouette turned away, marching toward his Packmaster. His steed. The engine roared as he climbed into the black leather seat. Death brought the growling bike around to face me.

Go! Uriel urged. *Run or fly, but move now! Death will ride you down, vessel!*

Leo won't, I thought desperately.

Uriel felt my terror. You can't hide much from the voices in your head. And the angel fought me for every inch as I faced Death and its steed. It was like trying to walk into a tornado.

Out in the darkness, the Packmaster revved again – a growl from the throat of hell – and the back tire spun up a billowing cloud of black smoke. The churning cloud clung to Leo in a dark cloak and he gunned toward me.

I'm not ashamed to admit that I shrieked as Leo's motorcycle raced down the highway at me. Uriel grabbed the reins of my body with both metaphorical hands and pulled, trying to throw us out of the way. I could feel the urge to fly, to fling myself up into the air and away from all of this.

Move, vessel! Uriel demanded.

But I fought the angel and the terror, and stood my ground. Because I'm a stubborn idiot. The Packmaster went from zero to sixty in a single fear-sped heartbeat, shooting toward me like an oversized bullet.

"Leo!" I screamed. "Stop! I'm not your enemy here. Pestilence killed your friends!"

Leo screeched to a halt two inches from my knocking knees. The sudden stop should have thrown Leo right over the handle-bars and into the road, but he still sat astride his motorcycle, as motionless as a statue.

"My friends..." Leo said.

The words echoed hollowly, as though they rose up from the bottom of a deep, empty hole.

"Yes! The Knights," I answered. My voice cracked with fear. "Audrey, Sam and Jack... No, Jett! Pestilence killed all of them trying to find you. Remember?"

Leo lashed out, reaching over the front of the Packmaster to grab me by the throat. He yanked me close. I writhed, but his grip was like steel. Death stared down at me and I would have given anything right then to see Leo's dark brown eyes instead of those bottomless pits.

Fight the horseman! Uriel told me. *I will give you the power!*

I'm not fighting Leo!

Something glowed at the edge of my vision. Michael...? Was the other angel flying to my rescue? But the radiance came from my own hands. They blazed with Uriel's power and I clenched my fists. Light flared between my fingers.

"Leo..." I gasped. "Leo, please...!"

He didn't let go of me, but Leo's head turned slowly toward the gray-green shape of Pestilence.

"*You* killed them," Leo's hollow voice grated. "You killed my Knights."

"Yes," Pestilence hissed. "War knew your vessel was bound by mortal ties. They gave him strength. But alone, he is weak."

Leo's hand remained around my throat and no matter how I kicked and thrashed, I couldn't break free. Uriel's light blazed in my hands. Michael circled overhead, parting the black cloud of insects in a searing arc.

"Uriel, leave this place!" the archangel was shouting. "Find the others!"

I cannot! My vessel is a fool! Uriel snarled.

I had no idea if Michael could hear Uriel without control of my mouth, but there wasn't enough time to find out. Michael folded their luminous wings for a dive and Pestilence snapped its attention skyward again. The horseman coughed and disgorged a swirling pillar of green from its mouth that rose unnaturally fast toward Michael. Pestilence's cloud engulfed the angel, but then lit up with an orange glow like a sunset. Four molten wings sliced through, cutting the horseman's venomous smoke into ribbons.

I was running out of breath. My throat ached where Death gripped me and my lungs burned for air. Michael rained fire down over the highway, but Pestilence's demon-Baracca hissed and raced between the lances of golden flame.

Leo pulled me in until our faces almost touched. His eyes were closed, but tears streamed down his cheeks, reflecting fire and shadow.

"Leo..." I whispered.

"Jaz, I can't do this," he said, voice still hollow. "Pestilence is right... I'm too weak on my own. I can't fight Death without the Knights."

His unbreakable grip was tight around my throat, as cold and hard as steel on my trachea, but I wasn't trying to get away from Leo.

"Your friends died fighting," I gasped. "Fighting that... thing. Fighting for you, Leo. Now fight for them!"

What are you doing? Uriel cried. *You cannot argue with Death, vessel! Use my power and fly!*

The iron grip on my throat jerked, tightening with bruising force, but then wrenched open again. The ground beneath us heaved in another explosion and I fell to the buckling asphalt. I didn't know if that was the work of Michael or Pestilence, but when Leo opened his eyes, they were brown again.

I sobbed in relief, then threw myself down flat on the road as a flaming engine block whistled through the air. Leo ducked over the Packmaster's handlebars, then straightened and shook his head. Fire and blackened metal rained across Highway 44. Leo held out his hand to me.

"Jaz, get on!" he shouted.

I took Leo's hand and he heaved me back to my feet. I leapt onto the Packmaster behind Leo, flinging my arms around him. The swift, strong beat of Leo's heart pounded through his body and I felt the throb of it against me. Pestilence snapped its head toward Leo.

"Death!" the horseman bellowed. "Join us!"

Something boomed and buzzed behind us like thousands of angry hornets. I didn't dare look back, but I heard the roar of Michael's celestial fire and the sky lit up above us in red and gold. Heat blasted out in a burning wave, whipping my shirt and making the sweat on my skin sizzle.

"Uriel!" Michael thundered.

Leo stomped the Packmaster into gear, but the motorcycle snarled at him and refused to move. It didn't want to leave Pestilence and its horrible clotted-blood-colored brother.

"I said *go!*" Leo growled right back.

The big motorcycle's engine guttered, but Leo tightened his grip around the handlebars until his whole body went hard with the tension of... whatever fight for control was going on between Leo and his bike.

The Packmaster ground, groaned – and then finally roared. Leo twisted the throttle and I hung on for dear life as the motorcycle leapt into motion, racing away from Michael and Pestilence. I buried my face against Leo's shoulder as the thunderous sounds of their battle faded into the distance. Within moments, the only ominous rumble left was the demonic Packmaster beneath us. But I kept my eyes squeezed shut and let the hot wind whip my tears away.

CHAPTER 16

Fire trucks, cop cars and ambulances raced past us toward the dark cloud on the horizon where Pestilence and the archangel fought. We shot right through a storm of red and blue flashing lights, but the police and paramedics had more important things to worry about than one speeding motorcycle.

Or maybe Michael was covering my exit... I didn't know and I was too frightened to care.

Why did you do that? Uriel asked. *Death was gaining control... Why do you fight for its vessel?*

Wind and sirens howled in my ears, but it didn't drown out the voice in my head.

Leo's my friend, I answered. *He didn't ask for any of this, either. And I couldn't just leave him there with the thing that killed his gang!*

Why? Uriel asked. *He is not like you.*

The question sounded innocent and curious, not disapproving. I hesitated and struggled to answer.

Because Leo's a good guy, I thought at last.

He is a criminal, Uriel argued. *He violated your mortal law. This man is a vessel well-suited to the leader of the horsemen. They are forces of chaos and darkness.*

I remembered Pestilence's swarm of bugs and shuddered. Uriel wasn't wrong about the horsemen... but that didn't mean they were right about Leo.

You don't give a shit about our laws, either, I thought. *I'm pretty sure there's a rule somewhere about not possessing mechanics who just want to get out of their shitty little hometowns. But that's never stopped you.*

I am not mortal, Uriel said. *I am above your laws.*

And in a way, so is Leo. He cares about more important things than rules, too, I told the archangel. *He's a bit of a bad boy, sure, but he's not a bad guy.*

I do not understand the distinction.

I sighed. Neither did I, exactly...

Leo fights for the people he loves, I thought. *Whether it's against Pestilence or the police. He's been through some serious shit in his life, but it hasn't turned him cold. Leo's tough and kind of rough, but he cares a lot.*

And these qualities are... admirable? Uriel asked. *Worth risking yourself?*

I um... guess so, I answered. *Look, I didn't have much time to weigh my options. I just knew I couldn't abandon Leo.*

And for this man, you risked the loss of light over the darkness? Uriel asked.

Fighting is all *you think about! That's why you didn't tell me Michael had gotten so close, isn't it? I had that weird feeling since yesterday. That was mister fiery cop-angel and you didn't say a word!*

I did not warn you, Uriel admitted. *Michael's proximity made me stronger and I could not risk you evading them... I did not realize that Pestilence had gotten so close, however. You sensed the horseman, as well, but not until it was too late.*

I sighed. *I'm too tired to be pissed. But Uriel, you want me to go racing off across the world to collect the other three angels—*

Yes.

—and you don't even know what else *exists, do you? All the other stuff you're missing out on. You made a universe full of things that you never bothered to learn about!*

The archangel went quiet and I figured they were off to sulk in my medulla oblongata, but then Uriel spoke again.

Like what? What am I... missing?

I let out an unexpected laugh and hoped that Leo couldn't hear me over the rush and hiss of wind. Was he having his own internal conversation with Death?

How about chocolate? I asked Uriel. *Or sex?*

There was a sort of fluttering sensation somewhere behind my eyes as the angel rummaged through my brain for answers. I winced a little at what they might find, but decided to let Uriel have a look around. I was too tired to fight them much more today, anyway.

But if I was giving Uriel an all-access pass to my thoughts and memories, I figured that I had better show off some of the good ones. I remembered how proud my parents were when I graduated from high school – not everyone in Crayhill did – and hoped they were okay without me. There were probably a dozen panicked voicemails waiting for me if I ever got a new phone.

I thought of the day I got my Bonneville and the tantalizing taste of freedom that it represented. The first time I rebuilt a motorcycle engine. And then the second time, when I actually got it right.

When I saw Leo outside Golden Touch Auto, riding into my life to change it forever.

These things are important to you, Uriel said. *You resist me for their sake. Your strength has been... unexpected.*

Uh, I guess I'll take that as a compliment.

It is one, the angel told me. *We did not know what form our vessels would take. Only that they must be strong enough to bear us. To fight. You are not what I thought you would be...*

I felt that soft fluttering, searching sensation behind my eyes again as Uriel went looking for some other bit of information.

...Jasmine.

That was a first. I wasn't sure how any of this had upgraded me from *vessel* to an actual person in Uriel's ephemeral eyes, but decided to cut the archangel a little slack. For an immortal and omnipotent force of light and order, Uriel didn't know very much about the universe. The entire cosmos was just a machine to churn out the equivalent of guns for their divine turf war.

That is... accurate, Jasmine, Uriel agreed.

Jaz, I thought. *You can call me Jaz.*

You are more than you seemed, Jaz, Uriel said.

And so is Leo. Don't try to make me abandon him again.

Uriel quieted once more. I wasn't sure how much respect I had earned from the angel, but I doubted it was enough to talk them out of trying like hell to murder Death. You think human biases are entrenched? The hatred between the archangels and horsemen was older than our universe. I didn't think they had *ever* known anything else.

I watched the highway over my shoulder for the rest of the afternoon. There was no signs of smoke or a billowing green-black cloud of bugs on the horizon now, or even the police cars and ambulances that had answered the call. Were any of them Michael's buddies? Well, friends of his vessel, at least...

I didn't feel that electric sunburn tingle anymore, either. Even if Uriel wouldn't warn me about other angels, I knew what that sensation was. If I felt anything like that again, it was time to run.

We were doing a lot of that these days.

But for now, I hoped it meant that Michael was far behind us. The angel would come hunting after Uriel again, but maybe we could make it to San Diego and Carlos' solution before that happened.

Once we put some distance between us and the Pestilence-Michael battleground, highway traffic picked up again and Leo had to slow down to sub-demonic speeds. It wouldn't do us very much good to escape our fellow horsemen and archangels if Leo plastered the Packmaster across the back of a garbage truck.

Somehow, both Leo and I still had our helmets and despite being streaked in ash and grime, we cruised into Flagstaff without issue. As the afternoon turned into evening, the highway slanted up again and mountains rose in angular violet shadows on the other side of the city. We drove past a big concrete tower with a red and white checkerboard logo on it that looked like something seriously industrial, but most of the signs and billboards along the road advertised hotels and tours of the Grand Canyon.

I had never seen the Grand Canyon before and really wished we weren't on the run for our lives. I was a born and bred Kansas girl. Back home, the land was so flat that you could see the curve of the Earth. I knew what the Grand Canyon looked like – I had seen pictures my whole life, like any American – but was pretty sure that my fantasies would utterly fail to live up to the glorious rocky reality.

A big commercial airliner flew over the highway, roaring like a great mechanical dragon as it descended over Flagstaff, and yanked my attention back to the present.

There had to be a major airport nearby. It was another two day's drive from here to San Diego – depending upon traffic and our route – but what about on an airplane? A couple of hours, max...? We could be knocking on Uncle Carlos' door by the end of the day.

But how would we pay for airplane tickets? With Leo's stolen money? I was pretty sure that airlines got suspicious when ash-streaked weirdos paid cash for same-day flights. They might not actually arrest us for that, but it would certainly get logged into someone's computer system. And then how long until Michael's police came looking for Leo? Or those paramilitary guys who tried to kill us in Zamora Canyon?

What about all of Leo's guns? I doubted that we could just dump them in a trash can. And what about the Packmaster? Did airlines transport vehicles? Did that happen by truck? Would Leo be able to leave the possessed motorcycle for that long? I remembered Leo's utter unwillingness to buy a replacement back in Crayhill with new understanding – Death bound him to that bike and would not let go.

But that wasn't even the worst potential problem with taking an airplane to California. I had no idea if a horseman's steed could fly, but the angels had wings. What if Michael or Gabriel caught up to us while we were in the air? Our encounters with the archangels had already leveled a motel and blasted a mile-long section of Highway 44 into craters. Just the thought of that happening on a plane thousands of feet above the ground sent cold shivers through me.

Nope.

We drove deeper into Flagstaff and without the sickly-sweet smell of Pestilence at work, my stomach growled. I was *starving* and felt an answering rumble roll through Leo where my arms were wrapped around him. The Packmaster grumbled, too, but I doubted the possessed bike suddenly wanted gasoline. It was just bitchy about leaving another horseman behind, and bucked under me.

I tightened my grip around Leo, but I was already tired and my muscles trembled. I leaned in closer until I could put my lips right against Leo's ear.

"We've got to stop," I shouted over the wind. "We need food and we need rest."

Leo nodded and signaled, taking the next off-ramp. There were usually plenty of motels, restaurants and filling stations near a highway or freeway, and Flagstaff was no exception. But Leo passed up the diners and fast food, then drove through the collection of cheap motor lodges that had been our homes for the last four days. When we finally stopped, it was in front of the twelve-story tower of a chain hotel.

Leo parked and sat for a moment, rubbing the bridge of his nose while I scrambled off the back of the Packmaster.

"Are you okay?" I asked.

"Not really," Leo said. "Are you?"

"Not really."

Leo laughed shortly and then climbed from the Packmaster. He turned it off, but the engine kept rumbling. Leo's brows drew down and he pressed one hand against the seat.

"That's enough!" he growled. "Stay here."

His bike grumbled and lurched forward. Leo grabbed the pillion and heaved, but the motorcycle dragged him a few feet across the asphalt before finally braking to a reluctant stop.

Leo grunted and wrestled the bike back into its parking spot. The sun was setting and Michael's golden flames had long since vanished, so Leo put his leather jacket on again. He considered, then unfastened the saddlebags from the tail of his motorcycle. I eyed the red valet counter set up outside the hotel.

"This place is going to cost more money," I told Leo as he shouldered the heavy bags. "A lot more."

"We've got plenty of cash and I'm not worried about holding onto any of it," Leo said. "I just want to get to San Diego and put an end to this shit."

"I hope your Uncle Carlos is as good as you think."

"He is," Leo promised me, then cocked his head toward the hotel. "I'm hoping that anyone looking for us will be searching all those cheap roadside motels. And places like this have room service. We need dinner, but I don't want to spend a minute longer off the road than we have to."

I nodded. "Good idea. And I'm not going to complain about a little luxury."

I followed Leo in through a pair of sliding glass doors frosted with the hotel's name and logo, past a row of luggage carts with brass rails and then into the lobby. It was a long room tiled in a lot of cultured marble and tourist brochures. A chandelier hung from the high ceiling and cast tiny glittering motes of light all across the lobby.

A woman with smooth black hair stood behind the counter, backlit by a glowing starburst logo. Were they even called a clerk at a real hotel? The woman wore a neat burgundy jacket and I glanced down at myself – torn and oil-stained jeans, biker shirt tied off at the midriff, with a big, leather-clad tattooed guy at my side. Probably not her standard clientele, but the maybe-clerk at the counter looked like she was trying her best not to judge.

"Good evening," she greeted us. "My name is Tanvi. How can I help you tonight?"

"One room, please," Leo said. "Two beds."

"Of course, sir. Just let me take a quick look at what we have available."

Tanvi tapped at a keyboard with long, shiny red fingernails. I couldn't help staring a little... Nails like that wouldn't have lasted an hour in a garage. My own fingernails were clipped short, but I kept them religiously clean.

Hey, I had an angel living rent-free in my head. If anyone can use that phrase, it's me.

Leo rubbed at the skin between his eyes again, like he had a monster headache. I tried to give him a reassuring smile, but I don't think Leo noticed.

"I've got two rooms available," Tanvi said. "One on the fourth floor, and one on the ninth."

That was a long run or elevator ride back down to the Pack-master if we needed to escape.

"Anything on the first or second story?" I asked.

Tanvi couldn't seem to help raising a well-shaped eyebrow at that. She covered it with a professional smile and tapped a few more keys.

"I have one king room on the second floor, overlooking the pool," Tanvi said. "Nothing with two beds, though."

"We'll take it," Leo answered.

Somehow, I doubted that he was inspired by the promise of a view and our chances of having the time for a swim were pretty slim. I hadn't packed my bikini, anyway. But that reminded me of something else that real hotels had in movies.

"Hey, do you have concierge service here?" I asked.

"We do. Our guests can order anything they need up to their room," Tanvi said, then hesitated. "Except tobacco, lottery tickets or any illegal substances, of course."

I bristled at whatever assumption Tanvi was making, but Leo nodded... Though it looked strained.

"How about room service?" he asked. "I don't need cigarettes – I need dinner."

Tanvi's perfect smile returned. "The kitchen is open all night and there's a menu in your room. I highly recommend the pilaf."

"Thanks," Leo said.

"If I can just run your card, then we can get you heading toward dinner."

Tanvi glanced back and forth between us, clearly uncertain who was paying for this suspicious little getaway. Leo pulled a few hundred-dollar bills out of his pocket and placed them on the high, glass-topped counter. Tanvi blinked.

"We require a credit card to charge any incidentals," she said slowly. "The minibar, pay-per-view... Room service."

Leo bit down on a growl and put a thick stack of bills on the counter. It was smaller than the one he had given me in Crayhill what felt like a lifetime ago – but not by much.

"This should cover everything," Leo said.

Tanvi's smile faltered and there was naked suspicion on her face... But she pinched the money between those long, shiny red nails. I wasn't sure if she was bending the rules or taking the cash as an outright bribe, but I didn't care.

Wahoo, I was a real criminal now! I was officially a bad girl... with a rule-obsessed angel in my head.

I'm a complicated woman.

"Is there anything else I can do for you this evening?" Tanvi asked.

"We'll need a wakeup call," Leo said. "Five o'clock tomorrow. We have to get back on the road again."

"Of course," Tanvi answered.

She sounded relieved. Whether it was because Leo wasn't asking for something against hotel policy this time or because we would be gone when the sun rose, I wasn't sure. But Tanvi typed for another moment, then tucked a pair of slick black and gold key cards into a tiny folder. She held them out to Leo.

"The wi-fi password is printed inside," Tanvi told him. "Have a restful night."

"Here's hoping," I said.

Leo handed me a key and we crossed the lobby to a row of elevators with polished brass doors that slid open as soon as I pressed the button. It wasn't a long ride up to the second floor, but we were exhausted. We made our way down a carpeted hallway to our room.

I unlocked the door and Leo followed me into a room three times the size of anything we had stayed in so far. He dropped the leather saddlebags on a padded armchair and I went to the window. Outside was the hotel swimming pool, a glowing turquoise rectangle against the skyline of nighttime Flagstaff. The city shone with lights in white and pale amber, flickering like terrestrial starlight as the cooling air stirred up into a brisk wind.

The surface of the water below rippled in the breeze and a line of palm trees danced around the colored spotlights in front of the hotel.

I sighed and closed the heavy blackout drapes. The view was beautiful, but up on the second story, we were still all too visible, and Leo had bags full of money and guns that we didn't want anyone to see. I left just a little sliver open between the curtains, though. Leo and I should be able to sense incoming archangels or horsemen, but there were humans with guns and riot gear we had to worry about, too.

Leo rummaged around the tourist brochures on the desk, then held out a large folder with a leather finish and hotel logo embossed on the front.

"Room service," he said.

"Uh, this stop is already getting expensive." I took the menu and sat down on the edge of the bed. "Are you sure?"

"Yeah," Leo answered. "We got over a million dollars off that armored car, and I'm carrying more than half of it now. Plus, we might not even live long enough to spend it."

He gave me a small smile and raked his hands through his hair.

"Besides, I'm saving on gas," he added.

"Fair point. I guess... But I've still got most of the money you paid me."

I leaned up onto my hip to pull the wallet from my pocket, opened it and held out a hundred-dollar bill.

"Can dinner be my treat this time?" I asked.

Leo hesitated, shifting his weight as he thought, but then nodded. He didn't argue or get all chivalrous – he just accepted the cash and tucked it into his pocket.

We went through the room service menu. Everything was ridiculously overpriced, but as Leo had said, we might not live long enough to spend all of the money. So we called the kitchen and asked for two orders of the pilaf Tanvi had recommended, a hamburger and fries for Leo, a steak for me, and a pair of the chef's specialty brownies. I wasn't sure what those were, but I deserved something sweet. The woman who took our order – I couldn't tell if it was Tanvi or not over the phone – promised us that the food would be up in about twenty minutes.

"Sure," I said. "Thank you."

I put down the phone receiver and rubbed my eyes. My skin felt gritty and greasy. I made a face.

"I bet the water heater in this place is up to the challenge of two hot showers," I said.

Leo ran his fingers along his cheek. "Yeah. And I could use a shave. But you can go first."

"Thanks," I said. "My clothes are filthy, though."

"Is that why you asked about the concierge? New clothes?"

"I think just washing them would be a nice change of pace," I said with a smirk. "Do you want to see if there's a laundry service here?"

"Sure," Leo answered. "Toss your clothes through the door and I'll find out."

I went into the washroom, stripped, then pushed my grimy jeans and socks out the door with one foot while the water heated up. Which didn't take long – the shower was gloriously hot and came down like cleansing rain from an oversized head set into the ceiling.

I took more time in the shower than was strictly necessary – including finally shaving my legs with a disposable razor from the cabinet next to the towels – but it felt *amazing*. When I was done, I patted my hair dry, twisted the black curls back into a damp knot at the nape of my neck, and then wrapped myself in a fluffy white hotel robe. I emerged from the washroom as Leo was closing and locking the front door.

"Food?" I asked hopefully.

"Not yet. Just pickup for your clothes," Leo told me. "They'll drop them off in the morning. I told them we need to leave early."

"I hope we get to stay here that long."

We didn't have a very good track record for that, but Leo just nodded. He grabbed a well-worn toiletries bag and headed for the washroom. Leo passed me on his way, close enough that I could smell the sweat and leather scent of him. But I also saw the tightness in his clenched jaw and across his shoulders like knotted steel cables.

And I felt Death inside Leo. A sudden chill went through me, so cold that it was a wonder ice didn't form on my damp skin. Uriel tensed and drew somehow back from the horseman, even though I hadn't moved at all. Leo looked over his shoulder at me and I could see in his eyes that he sensed it, too. He closed the bathroom door firmly behind him.

I let out an explosive breath and hit the minibar. Not for alcohol – although it was tempting and there were plenty of tiny bottles with foil labels – but nothing felt as good on a dry throat after a day on the road as an ice-cold, bubbly pop. I grabbed a red can swirled in silver, pried open the tab and guzzled half the contents before coming up for air.

Much better. I sighed and then flopped down into one of the armchairs. I stretched out my legs and wiggled my toes, then tensed as someone knocked on the door. I stood up so fast that my head swam, and stared around the hotel room. Leo's revolver was gone, flung across Highway 44 when it failed to kill Pestilence, but the semi-automatic he offered me last night sat on a pristine white table next to the bed.

I picked up the gun and stuffed it into my hotel robe before hurrying to the door. With one hand in my pocket, I looked through the peephole. The man outside wore hotel colors and branding, but I didn't relax at all. Remember that time a little old church lady showed up at my door, then turned into an archangel and leveled the place? Yeah, so do I.

But the guy in the hallway actually had a pushcart full of covered dishes, so I ran back, found my wallet – also on the bedside table – and opened the door.

"Room service," he said. "Can I bring it in for you?"

"No, thanks," I answered.

I didn't really want to let anyone into our room, but when I accepted the food and the bellhop still didn't sprout wings or burp up a creepy bug cloud, I grabbed another hundred-dollar bill and held it out.

"Uh... everything will be on the final invoice tomorrow," the bellhop said.

"I know," I told him. "This is for you."

Can't spend money when you're dead, remember? The man blinked a few times, then took the tip and thanked me before beating a hasty retreat in case I changed my mind. I closed the door and slid the chain into place.

Why did you do that? Uriel asked as I brought the food inside.

What? The tip?

Yes, Uriel said. *You are aware that it is too much reward for the service rendered. There is a rule, and you broke it.*

I rolled my eyes. *Wow, it sounds sexy when you say it like that.*

Why did you do it? Uriel asked again.

I pulled the metal lid off the pilaf and inhaled the steam. It really did smell delicious.

Because it's a nice thing to do, I told Uriel. *Because working at a hotel in the middle of the night has got to suck and maybe that money will make some bill easier to pay this month.*

Why are you being nice?

Because... I hesitated, trying to pull my thoughts into some kind of coherent answer. *Because I wish people had been nicer to me. Not my parents – they were great. But guys like Craig and Leo's asshole dad... Maybe if everyone was kinder, the world would be a better place.*

And you want to improve this world? Uriel asked.

Uh, of course I do...? You are brutally naïve, you know.

I am an immortal force of light and order, the archangel told me stiffly. *I existed long before your universe was born.*

I smirked. *Yeah, and you don't know about sex or chocolate.*

Leo stepped out from the washroom, wearing nothing but a towel wrapped around his waist. Maybe he needed fresh clothes, too, but I didn't question – I just enjoyed the view.

"Jaz, how can you stand it?" he asked.

Leo's voice was so tight that I worried it would break. He dug his finger through his wet hair and into his scalp.

"Stand what?" I asked. "You look great."

"Having that... thing... in your head," Leo said. "How do you not lose your mind?"

I forgot all about the food, arguing with Uriel or even Leo's near nakedness. My mouth went dry.

"Is Death talking to you?" I asked.

"Not exactly. Not with words," Leo answered. "But I feel it inside me. It's like... like this rage. And I can't make it stop."

I flinched. "Pestilence touched you. I mean, I felt weird when you came into the garage, but Uriel didn't actually start talking until Gabriel grabbed me."

"I wanted to kill that woman at the front desk," Leo told me. "Tanvi. Just put her face right through that glass counter."

He looked down at his hands. They were shaking. Hard. Leo clenched them into fists.

"But not as bad as I want to kill you, Jaz," he said in a barely audible whisper. "I want your blood... It's like the heroin all over again. I don't know if I can do this..."

I wanted to give Leo a hug, or just rub his shoulder, but I was afraid to do anything that would make Death stronger.

It may, Uriel said. *Touching him with your lips before was a terrible risk.*

You mean kissing him back in Cibola? I asked.

"Enough!" Leo snarled suddenly, then looked down at me with a guilty expression. "Not you... Sorry, Jaz."

I waved my hand as nonchalantly as I could manage under these messed-up circumstances.

"It's okay," I told Leo. "I get it. Really."

Death will not speak to its vessel as you and I do, Uriel said. *The horsemen are too wild.*

I'm not leaving Leo, I answered at once, before they could start telling me to go find the other angels.

...I know that you will not abandon him, Jaz, Uriel said. *But you must learn caution.*

Leo was rubbing his head again, hard enough that I worried he was going to leave a bruise and throwing his freshly washed hair into utter disarray.

"The food came while you were washing up," I said. "And it smells amazing. Let's eat and get some sleep. The nightmares aren't great, but at least we're both used to those."

We moved the saddlebags off the chairs and sat, then got to work devouring the food we had ordered. My steak was a little overcooked, but the protein felt good in my stomach. The pilaf was just as delicious as Tanvi promised, but the huge, caramel-topped brownie was even better. I licked the plate clean and hoped Uriel was paying attention.

When we were finished, I placed the empty dishes outside while Leo watched the hallway with suspiciously narrowed eyes. He closed the door and secured both locks after I came back inside. I replaced his gun on the nightstand.

"Now I just want some sleep," Leo said, then gestured toward the bed. "There's only the one, but I can take the chairs. They're pretty soft."

I shook my head. "That bed is huge. I think we should be able to share it without getting into much trouble. I don't know the next time we'll get to be anything like comfortable, so let's both take advantage of it while we can."

Leo looked like he wanted to argue, but then he nodded and headed for the bed. I raised my hand like a student in class.

"Um, are you planning on sleeping naked?" I asked, eyeing the towel around his waist.

Leo glanced down, turned and went back to the bathroom.

"Sorry," he called from inside.

"I wasn't actually complaining," I muttered under my breath.

You're thinking of some of those pleasant things, Uriel said. *Is this... chocolate?*

Close enough, Uriel.

CHAPTER 17

C lothes were a good idea if we needed to run, so I went to bed in another one of Leo's oversized t-shirts. At least, oversized on me – they seemed to fit Leo just fine.

It had been another long, screwed-up and exhausting day, and I expected to fall instantly down into apocalyptic dreams... But I laid in the huge king-sized bed, staring at the hotel room ceiling as Leo tossed and turned just a couple feet away. He mumbled in Spanish and I didn't catch most of it. But *no* means *no* in any language, so I understood that much. Leo called out Carlos' name a few times, too.

I clutched the covers up under my chin. I wished that I could scoot over and wrap my arms around Leo. Not because having my hands all over the big, well-muscled biker sounded like fun – although it did – but because I remembered Pestilence's horrible wasp-voice telling Leo that he was weak on his own. Was that true?

I didn't know a whole lot about motorcycle gangs – I was more interested in the machines than the culture – but I knew that road captain wasn't a position they handed out on a whim, especially to a guy as young as Leo. If the Knights of Hell had followed him, it was because they trusted Leo, because they could rely on him. I remembered how much Leo had wanted to get back to his friends, and how it crushed him to see what Pestilence had done to them.

For all of the big scary biker thing that Leo had going on, he didn't seem to do particularly well on his own. Rather like the horsemen and archangels, actually. They were stronger together. But with the Knights dead, Leo was a wolf without a pack, and he was lost alone.

At least Leo still had his uncle. Even without me riding behind him and being an almost literal angel on his shoulder, I guessed that Leo would have driven straight for San Diego. He was desperate to reach Carlos.

In his sleep, Leo snarled something that I didn't understand, and just about kicked the blankets off the bed. I wished that I could help him sleep better, but couldn't think of any way to do that.

So I just waited. Eventually, Leo quieted and settled into a deeper slumber. I let out a long sigh of relief. Finally... We both needed rest and I hoped that after a good night of sleep in a big, comfortable bed, we would have the energy to deal with all of this shit tomorrow. I snuggled down into the covers beside Leo and fell quickly asleep.

And then woke up with Leo's hands locked tight around my throat.

Uriel! I shouted frantically.

I couldn't get the actual word out through Leo's grip. He was on top of me in the bed, looming over me with his long fingers wrapped around my trachea. My vision was going swiftly gray at the edges and swam with little bursts of red light. But I could see Leo's face, and his eyes were squeezed shut. He was still asleep, but I had the terrible feeling that under those closed lids were empty black sockets.

Death waited until Leo slept, Uriel said. *And then overpowered its vessel while his guard was down.*

Okay, useful information, but not really helpful right now. I thrashed in Leo-slash-Death's grip, kicking the extra pillows across our hotel room as I clawed at the big hands crushing my throat. I swung my arm in a wild punch, but it glanced off Leo's temple with a clang like hitting metal.

Uriel, help me!

Light flickered at the corners of my vision. Not red this time, but bright and incandescently white. It rippled down my body just like when I was fighting back in Zamora Canyon, and the pressure on my trachea eased.

I coughed, then grabbed Leo's wrists and pulled. There was no way I could overpower a man of his size and build, but things can get weird when you ask an archangel for help. I pried Leo's hands off of my throat, then planted my foot against his stomach and pushed. Leo flew up and off of me, through the air and then crashed down into the armchairs.

His eyes were still closed, but Leo rolled swiftly back to his feet. His eyelashes were thick and dark, almost long enough to brush his cheeks. It's strange what you notice when you're being murdered...

I tried to jump out of bed, but my legs tangled in the blankets and I fell back into the mattress. Leo advanced on me again and I could *feel* Death inside of him. It was cold and quiet, like falling through ice and deep into the frozen lake beneath.

"Leo!" I wheezed.

My throat was a bruised, aching mess and all I managed to get out was that single rasping word. Leo grabbed for me again, and I rolled across the bed away from him. I came up into a low crouch on top of my pillow and Uriel's glowing aura flickered, concentrating around my fists until it looked like I was holding a pair of lit flares. Strange shadows danced and jumped, but I kept the burning blades of light lowered.

"Leo," I gasped. "Leo, please wake up!"

He took another step and I raised Uriel's weapons. But then Leo opened his eyes and blinked sleepily.

"Jaz...?" he asked.

Leo stared at the nimbus of angelic power surrounding me and whirled, suddenly awake as he searched the hotel room for threats. He grabbed the gun off the bedside table and swept it around in an arc.

"What the hell happened?" Leo asked. "Horseman?"

"Yeah," I wheezed. "You. Death."

I wanted to stand down, but Uriel kept my fists blazing with light that shone like beacons.

Leo's back in control, I told the angel. *Let go of me!*

I shook my hands out, trying to wave the light away.

Death is patient, Uriel said. *And cunning. It will use any ploy, any tool at its command to secure victory in the coming battle. You cannot lower your guard, Jaz.*

Leo stared down at his body, maybe expecting to see some dark aura of his own. He touched his chest and then his face, but didn't seem to find anything amiss. Leo swallowed hard and put his gun down on the nightstand.

"What happened?" he asked quietly. "Did I hurt you?"

"Death took over while you were sleeping," I answered with a cough. "It's not strong enough to run the show when you're awake yet, Uriel says. But when you're asleep, your defenses are down. It can take control."

Leo sank to his knees, with his elbows on the bed and hands covering his face like a little boy at prayer. His broad shoulders shook and I turned on one of the bedside lamps as Uriel's light finally faded from around me. I still felt the archangel tense and watchful inside me, though.

"Is Uriel telling you to run away?" Leo asked me through his fingers.

"Not at this precise moment. Why?"

"Maybe you should listen," Leo said. "You have to get away from me, Jaz. That's twice I've hurt you. I'm dangerous."

"Leo, I'm okay," I told him.

Actually, my neck was sore as hell and my vision still swam with shimmering gray specks from lack of air. But now didn't seem like a very good time to mention that and besides, I was recovering quickly.

I can heal your body, Jaz, Uriel told me. *But not if Death kills you. Go.*

"No, not a chance," I told both the archangel and the biker. "Carlos says he has answers and I need them, too."

Leo looked at me through his fingers. Tattooed flames shone red and orange along the back of his hands.

"I could call you after I make it to San Diego. Tell you everything Carlos has to say," Leo offered. "But you don't have to ride with me."

"Hey, we're staying off the phones for a reason," I pointed out. "You might not be able to call me."

"Jaz, it's too dangerous for you to stay." Leo pushed himself slowly upright. "What if I attack you again? What if I hurt you even worse?"

I crossed my arms over my chest. "No. I'm going with you, Leo. Stop trying to talk me out of it. You're not doing this thing alone."

I thought that Leo would argue, maybe get all blustery and macho about some girl half his size telling him off. But Leo closed his eyes and nodded.

"Alright, Jaz," he said.

This is unwise, Uriel told me. *But... I admit admiration for your loyalty.*

Well, Uriel must have chosen me as a vessel for *some* reason. Leo opened his eyes and watched me with a hard expression on his face.

"What?" I asked.

"Alright. We can't let Death ambush me again," Leo said.

I blinked. "Um, how exactly can we stop a horseman?"

"Death was able to control my body because I was asleep, right?"

"Right..." I answered slowly.

"I'm not giving Death the chance," Leo said. "I can't sleep."

"So you're going to stay awake until we get to San Diego?" I asked.

"Yeah. It's not that far," Leo said. "I'll need to tank up on a lot of caffeine, but it's only two or three more days. I can make it work."

Leo went to the minifridge and grabbed a pop from inside. He showed me the green can, pried up the tab and drained it in a few long gulps. Before I could quite process how fast the guy could drink, Leo had taken out another soda.

"Leo, do you really think this is a good idea?" I asked. "It's not like I can drive the Packmaster if anything goes wrong. I'm pretty sure it would throw me into the nearest ditch. And then run me over for good measure."

True, Uriel agreed.

"I've stayed awake for a night or two before," Leo said. "It's tough, yeah, but not impossible."

He finished the second soda just as quickly as the first, then took a deep breath and pointed to the gun sitting beside the bed.

"But take that," Leo said. "I shouldn't be near it, in case I get sleepy. If Death had shot you..."

"Uh, no need to finish that sentence." I approached the gun like it was a snarling dog and picked it up gingerly. "How do I unload it?"

"You should keep it armed and ready," Leo told me. "In case you need it."

"I'm not going to shoot you," I said.

Leo scowled, but then nodded. "Hold it by the grip, but don't put your finger on the trigger. There's a little round button near your right thumb. Push it."

I found the button that Leo described and pressed it carefully. The magazine slipped out of the gun's handle – or the grip or butt or whatever it was properly called – and thunked to the floor, almost smashing my bare toes. I yelped, then sighed and moved to drop the gun back onto the table.

"Stop," Leo said, holding up his hand. "There's still a bullet in the chamber."

"Shit, what?" I asked.

I had no idea what that meant and held the gun away from me like a live spider. A really big, heavy one.

"Hold the grip again, but not the trigger," Leo said. "Pull the slide. That's the top part. Bring it all the way back, and the bullet will pop out."

I did as Leo instructed and was ready this time when a bullet jumped from the gun. I wasn't ready enough to catch it out of the air – which would have been badass – but at least I didn't shriek again. The bullet bounced across the bed and I breathed a sigh of relief, then glanced up at Leo.

"It's actually unloaded now, right?" I asked.

"Yeah," Leo answered. "And the safety was on, anyway."

"What? Then why did you let me get freaked out?"

"First rule of gun safety – a loaded weapon is *always* dangerous," Leo said.

"Says the guy who carries one in his pocket or jammed down the front of his pants," I grumbled.

"I've been shooting since I was eight years old," Leo told me. "I know how to handle a gun safely."

"Carlos taught you?"

Leo nodded. He picked up the loose bullet from the bed and pushed it back into the magazine, then I tucked the gun and its ammunition under my pillow. That was going to be lumpy as hell, but at least it would be nearby. In case I needed it.

"Go ahead and get some sleep," Leo said. "One of us should be rested."

I felt really guilty about it, but Leo had a point. When something inevitably went wrong, it might help if one of us was alert.

"Are you sure you'll be okay?" I asked.

"No," Leo said. "But I'm sure that you won't be if Death takes over again."

He turned one of the chairs, grabbed a third can of soda and sat facing the door. Reluctantly, I replaced the disheveled bed covers and slid beneath them. I pulled the blanket up under my chin, but left the light on. Darkness would only make it easier for Leo to fall asleep.

I didn't like the idea of him staying awake for days... but I couldn't think of anything better. I threw an arm across my face to block out the light, since it would keep me awake, too.

Hey, why didn't you *ever try taking control while I slept?* I asked silently.

I am not certain that I would succeed. You are strong, Jaz, Uriel told me. *Even in slumber. But Leo is emotionally compromised by the deaths of those close to him.*

And what if I was that vulnerable? I asked. *Would you take over then?*

Uriel was quiet for so long that I wondered if I had fallen asleep.

Nothing is more important than victory, the angel answered at last.

That wasn't very reassuring, but the sharp surge of adrenalin had faded and I was suddenly exhausted all over again. Finally, I fell asleep listening to Leo's deep, even breathing.

CHAPTER 18

The smell of coffee woke me in the morning. I sat up and rubbed my eyes. Leo had opened the curtains a crack and sat in a slice of golden dawn light. He held a cup of coffee and the pot provided by the hotel was about half full on the minibar. Leo's brown eyes were bloodshot.

"Gah, ugh... what time is it?" I asked him in a sleep-roughened voice.

"About seven thirty," Leo answered. "I cancelled the wakeup call, since I was already up. Somebody from laundry dropped off your clothes, too."

"You look tired."

"As long as I still look like me, I can live with that," Leo said. He yawned. "I got some maps from the lobby. I think we need to stay off Highway 44."

"Huh? Why?" I asked.

I blinked and then stretched my arms up over my head until my spine popped. We had been following Highway 44 ever since we left Crayhill.

"Pestilence," Leo answered. "It found the Knights and then us on 44. They're expecting us to follow the highway."

"So you're trying to make it harder for that thing to find us again," I said. "And Michael had cops watching the highway for us, too. Alright, makes sense."

"There's a business center downstairs, so I printed up some alternate routes to get us to California."

Leo pointed to a small stack of papers on the desk, next to the phone. I rubbed my eyes, willing them to focus until I could make out the printed map that Leo was indicating.

"And I set up a new email account to message Uncle Carlos and the San Diego chapter of the Knights of Hell," Leo said.

"What?" I gasped. "Leo, you contacted your uncle?"

I swung my legs over the edge of the bed and jumped to my feet. Leo watched me with bloodshot eyes.

"I didn't use my real name on the new account or say anything about where we are," he told me. "I only wanted Carlos to know when we would get to him."

Most bike clubs these days had their own website and email lists, and I doubted that the Knights of Hell were any different. Though I didn't think they exactly posted about robbing banks. *Hey everybody, don't forget the monthly meeting. We'll have donuts and guns without serial numbers.*

Yeah, it was funny to imagine Leo's badass biker uncle Carlos sitting behind a laptop, maybe wearing some reading glasses as he tapped out emails with two fingers and lots of little skull emoji. But I shook my head.

"You're the one who told me that we can't call anyone, Leo!" I said. "What if those armored van bastards are monitoring the Knights' email server? Or the horsemen?"

Leo frowned and leaned forward in his chair. "What? Do you think they can do that?"

I waved at the window in the direction of the rising sun. "We just talked about how Michael put out an APB on us! We don't know what the angels and horsemen can do. That's the *point!*"

Leo's frown deepened and he tapped the side of his coffee cup in a thoughtful staccato.

"Look, I know you miss the Knights," I said. "But you can't just email your uncle because you're lonely! We have to be more careful than that!"

Leo's grip tightened around the mug and it shattered in his hands. Coffee and white shards of stoneware fell into the carpet at his feet. I gasped and jumped back as Leo suddenly stood up. A dark, painful fire burned in his eyes and my heart leapt into overdrive.

"They're not just gone, Jaz." Leo's voice came out deep, rough and raw. "My Knights are *dead* because Pestilence was looking for me!"

Oh, shit. I felt Uriel tense inside me and light leaked from my fingertips.

"Carlos is *all* I have left," Leo snarled. "The only family that matters, Jaz!"

He shifted his weight and a piece of the coffee mug shattered beneath his bootheel. Blood thundered in my ears, but I didn't back down.

"You'll see your uncle again," I said. "We're running straight to him, Leo. But if we're not careful, Carlos will be identifying your body in a morgue. Or the one who finally shows up on his doorstep will be Death instead of his nephew. What do you think will happen then?"

Leo stopped. His jaw was clenched hard enough to make the tendons stand out under his tattooed skin, but he nodded and took a long step back away from me.

"You're right, Jaz," he said. "And I'm sorry. I... I shouldn't have messaged Carlos."

"Hey, I get it. I want to call my mom and dad, too," I told Leo. I held out my hands toward him. "Are you alright? Did you cut yourself on that coffee cup?"

Leo put his hands palm-up in mine and we both winced as our heads swam with apocalyptic visions. But I inspected Leo's hands and didn't see any sign of cuts or burns from the coffee.

"How're you feeling?" I asked.

"Not great," Leo admitted. "But I've been through worse."

"Are you good to drive?"

"I should be fine," Leo said.

I examined his hands one last time, then let Leo go wash the coffee off them in the bathroom. When he came out, he got to work cleaning up the broken cup on the floor. I watched and considered offering to help, but it seemed like the kind of thing Leo should take care of on his own. His mess, his job.

So I went to the washroom and splashed some water on my face, then scrubbed at my skin with a towel and inspected my hair. Which ended in me just staring at my reflection.

You cannot save that man from Death, Uriel said.

No, I agreed. *But maybe I can help him save himself.*

There is no avoiding what is to come, Jaz.

I ignored the archangel as best I could and when I emerged from the washroom, Leo held out a cup of coffee in one of the remaining hotel-branded mugs. I accepted it gratefully, holding the ceramic between my hands and inhaling the warm brown scent. The smell was sweet, too – Leo had stirred in cream and sugar, just like back in the diner our first morning together. He had been paying attention.

I smiled and took a long drink.

"I can't get the coffee out of the carpet," Leo said. "I'll leave an extra hundred for housekeeping when we go. Which I think we better do soon... in case someone tracked down that email I sent."

I nodded in agreement. "Yeah. I don't know how exactly IP addresses are connected up to physical locations, but let's not risk it."

Leo did most of the packing while I drank my coffee and then got dressed in my freshly laundered clothes. I laced up my shoes and scanned the room, but there wasn't much to collect. Everything that I owned had either been destroyed by an over-zealous angel, or left behind when well-armed strangers kicked in our motel room door and forced us to run.

As promised, Leo left a stack of money on the sideboard for housekeeping, then shouldered his saddlebags and I followed him out. The door was swinging slowly shut when I gasped.

"Shit, the gun," I hissed.

Leo jammed his foot into the door and I ran back to the bed. The matte black semi-automatic and its full magazine were still under the pillow. I guess the gun fairy skipped me last night.

In the hallway, Leo waited a moment to see if I would pocket the gun, but I didn't like the damned things any more than I had yesterday. Leo sighed, then smiled and pulled open the flap on one saddlebag. I looked up and down the hall, then dropped the gun and ammunition inside. Leo buckled the bag shut again.

"Let's ride," Leo said.

"Easy for you to say," I told him. "That motorcycle likes you."

Not that I minded an excuse to hold onto Leo, but I didn't really want to get thrown off the Packmaster at sixty plus miles per hour. Would it be weird if I tied myself to Leo?

Yeah, probably.

We hurried to the elevator, but there was a pair of chattering families gathered in front of the doors and talking about their rafting trip, so we took the stairs. Down in the lobby, Tanvi must have gone home and her replacement gave us his own brand-new surprised look. But there were no problems as we checked out and the morning guy – Marco – told us to have a good day.

There was no way we had spent several thousand dollars on drinks and room service, but I noticed that Leo didn't get back any of the cash he had given Tanvi last night. So it *had* been a bribe, not a deposit.

I wasn't quite sure how I felt about losing that much money, but we had far more important things to worry about. Leo and I hurried across the parking lot to the Packmaster.

"We'll cross the southern tip of Nevada tonight," Leo said as he draped the heavy saddlebags over the end of his bike. "And then we're in California. It should only be a day after that to San Diego."

"Good," I said. "The sooner we get there, the sooner we get solutions, and you can take a nap."

Leo laughed at that, but his dark eyes were rimmed in red. "Let's go pick up some energy drinks from a store. Do you want anything?"

"Pretzels would be nice," I said. "I've been sweating out a lot of salt. Maybe some water, too. Also because of sweat."

"Sure. We'll follow the highway long enough to buy some food, then get off the main drag."

I waited until Leo climbed onto the Packmaster and got the engine started before I carefully perched up behind him. The motorcycle jerked under me and I almost fell.

"Nice to see you again, too," I said. "Asshole."

I wrapped my arms around Leo's waist and we drove through the parking lot, along a steep frontage road that let out onto the highway. We stopped at the first convenience store that we could find, then detoured to a grocery store when the clerk wouldn't take any of Leo's hundred-dollar bills. She was afraid they were counterfeit.

So we filled up a green plastic basket with caffeinated energy drinks, bottled water and as many snacks as we could imagine eating. At checkout, a suspicious clerk scribbled a marker across one of the bills. But Leo's money was stolen – not fake – so it checked out just fine.

When we finished our shopping, Leo and I loaded up the Packmaster's saddlebags, then examined the map that he had collected from the hotel lobby while we ate. After comparing it to the printed directions and taking a few minutes to gripe about our lack of GPS, we settled on a route that looked like it would keep us off Highway 44 without wasting a lot of time on winding scenic roads.

I crammed the last handful of pretzels into my mouth and Leo chugged his second energy drink, then he mounted up on his Packmaster again. But the motor guttered and coughed. Leo frowned.

"We're leaving," he said.

Leo gave the engine some gas – or whatever the demon-bike used instead of gasoline – and the motorcycle wheezed. Then it stopped again.

"I *know* we're going a different way," Leo said. "Because it's the way I want to go. Now start!"

The Packmaster whined and then rumbled reluctantly back to life. Pretty much literally... The engine's pitch dropped into a menacing growl as I gingerly climbed on behind Leo. I gulped.

"Jaz *is* coming with us," Leo told his angry bike. It revved and he yanked back hard on the throttle. "Yes, she is. Because I need her!"

The deep grumble finally eased grudgingly up into a throaty idle more like what a non-possessed motorcycle would make. I finished settling my weight and then steadied myself awkwardly on Leo's broad shoulders.

"Who were you talking to? Death or the bike?" I asked.

"Uh... Both, I think," Leo answered. "They're sort of the same thing. Or at least related."

Well, *that* sounded creepy... As if to underscore the point, I felt Uriel poised and ready to fly if I released control. But Leo put his helmet on and then patted his stomach, so I pulled my own helmet on, too, and wound my arms around his waist. Leo kicked the Packmaster into gear and we rolled out.

Leo drove us past signs and arrows all pointing back toward Highway 44, and then out onto narrow, winding rural roads that reminded me of being home in Crayhill... if the corn fields were replaced with banded red and yellow stone. Within an hour, sweat ran down the back of my neck and Leo's soaking wet shirt clung to his skin. It wasn't even that hot, but the Arizona sun was unrelenting.

The Packmaster snarled and sputtered all throughout the morning. Its shocks bounced me on the pillion, making me hold on tight to Leo. My arms grew swiftly tired and sore again, and I was seriously reconsidering the awkwardness of tethering myself to Leo.

He didn't seem to be doing much better, though. Leo grunted and swore as the Packmaster fought every turn. It growled and pulled, swerving like the very first day Leo and I rode together... Back when I still had my Bonneville.

Damn, I missed my Bonnie. And my tools.

The momentary reminiscing almost cost me when the Packmaster suddenly shuddered and began decelerating. Leo cursed again and shifted, but the motorcycle slipped out of gear with a loud metallic thunk. Leo twisted the throttle again, but his bike only wheezed, still slowing down. A rusty pickup truck swerved around us and honked as the motorcycle coasted to a stop on the gravel shoulder of the road.

"Uh, what happened?" I asked, looking over Leo's shoulder. "That didn't sound like we ran out of gas or anything."

Leo shook his head. "It fried the clutch."

Okay... that happened to bikes sometimes, if the rider feathered the clutch too much and too often. But it didn't typically happen to bikers as experienced as Leo, and motorcycles sure as hell didn't do it themselves on purpose just because they were cranky about their route or passengers.

The kickstand snapped out and the Packmaster whined like a petulant puppy – a puppy made of half a ton of leather, steel and chrome. Leo kicked the stand up again.

"No, I'm not turning back," he told the motorcycle.

You know the noise a switchblade makes when a badass in the movies whips it out to carve someone up into lunchmeat? That's the sound the Packmaster made as it shot out its kickstand again. Leo climbed off the bike with a snarl and I followed. No way I wanted to be alone on that thing. It might not run Leo into a brick wall, but I was pretty sure the motorcycle had no such qualms about me.

"Now what?" Leo asked. "Jaz, can you fix the clutch?"

I blinked. "What? Me?"

Leo nodded.

Holy shit, I had entirely forgotten the reason I was here in the first place. I was Leo's mechanic... That had just become so unimportant next to the war between archangels and demons.

"Um, yeah," I answered after a moment's thought. "I can fix it, in theory. I'll need some stuff to do it, though. I don't have my tools anymore and we'll have to get new throttle plates."

Leo wedged his bootheel under the Packmaster's kickstand and heaved it back into place, then grabbed the handlebars. He cocked his head toward a green aluminum sign.

"There's a town about seven miles away," Leo said. "I guess we're walking."

Seven miles wasn't very far when you were driving, but it was one hell of a walk – especially in the midday desert heat while pushing a pissed-off motorcycle. The Arizona sun beat down so hard that I worried Michael had caught up to us again. I didn't feel any burning angelic tingle, though, and Uriel assured me that none of their buddies were nearby.

Unfortunately, Uriel said.

It was way too hot to talk, so I let Leo focus on rolling the Packmaster along the side of the road. I felt like I should help, but walking a motorcycle is kind of a one-person job and I didn't really want the demon-bike taking a chunk out of me this far from civilization. We couldn't even call an ambulance if something happened... I missed my cell phone almost as much as my Bonnie.

The Packmaster didn't make the trip easy. It kept applying the brakes until Leo growled at the motorcycle, then sulkily allowed him to heave and shove it another mile down the road.

It senses the rift between Death and its vessel, Uriel said. *Leo cannot control the horseman's steed.*

Good thing he has me along to fix it, then, I thought.

The road wound through hills of banded orange and yellow stone, spotted with low shrubs that had silver-green leaves and bright red cone-shaped flowers. They might have smelled nice, but I was sweating so hard that all I could smell or taste was salt. There were a few wispy clouds earlier that morning, but they had all burned away before the clutch did and left the sky a sunbleached blue so pale that it was almost white.

The town seven miles down that heat-baked strip of asphalt was called Jasper, located just outside of the Petrified Forest. Jasper was a mid-sized tourist trap with a lot of brick buildings designed to look older and more rustic than they actually were. By the time we rolled the broken Packmaster into town, Leo and I had drunk everything we bought back in Flagstaff.

We stopped at the first store we saw. It was one of those little shops that sell bits of local stone and shot glasses with the town's name etched onto them. But there was also a refrigerated refreshment case, so Leo and I grabbed two drinks a piece. We paid with some of the change from the grocery store, then each finished a bottle off before we even left the shop.

"We need a break," I said.

The suggestion was more for Leo than myself. I was certainly tired, sweaty and seriously dehydrated, but Leo was the one who had heaved his busted motorcycle all the way here.

"No, I can't sleep," Leo said. He cracked open another drink, an iced tea this time with enough caffeine that it would have kept me amped for hours. "But it might be nice to get off my feet for a few minutes."

I glanced up and down the road outside. There was no shade that wasn't under someone's porch – and even that was watery with heat shimmer.

"Motel room?" I asked. "I could use a shower while I figure out how we're going to fix a broken evil bike."

I felt a little bit guilty for calling Leo's motorcycle *evil*, but he just nodded and finished his iced tea. He tossed the bottle into a nearby trash can, then began wrestling his Packmaster down the street.

Do we have the time to stop? I asked. *How close are the nearest angels?*

The pull grows stronger as we near, but it is weak at the moment, answered the voice in my head.

"Uriel seems to think we have some time before any of the archangels start crawling up our butts," I told Leo. "Any sense of where Pestilence or the others might be?"

"I'm... not sure," he said. "I don't have the dialog with Death that you do with Uriel. But I don't feel like there's an electrical storm brewing inside my skull. So we're in the clear for now, I think."

We both fell silent as a dusty brown park ranger car rolled past along the road. They would surely know where to find the nearest motel, but flagging down a pair of armed government employees wasn't a very good idea. The rangers slowed as they drove past, both eyeing me and Leo, but then seemed to decide we were harmless. Or at least that we were a police problem, not a ranger one.

Their car had vanished into the bright sunlight by the time we reached the next intersection, but as it turned out, we didn't need help finding a motel. Tourist towns liked to post the locations of useful places for visitors to spend their money, and there was a sign bolted onto the corner streetlamp that pointed white arrows toward food and lodging.

We selected the second one and followed another road down to a small, single-story motel. Leo was panting hard when he finally kicked out the stand on the Packmaster and left it in an empty parking spot. I swear the damned bike hissed at Leo as he walked away.

We stopped in the lobby and just savored it. Not because the sight was pretty – unless fake-ass mass-produced country tacky is your thing – but because... well, air conditioning. We stood there under the ceiling vent until an old man in a cowboy hat asked us if we wanted a room.

"Oh, right," I said. "Um, yes. Please."

The motel clerk set down his novel and glanced over a pair of reading glasses.

"Looks like you two are ready to cool off for a bit. Single or double beds?" he asked.

"Single," Leo answered. "I'm not sleeping tonight."

"Oh? Maybe you're looking to heat up, then," the clerk said, then winked at me and tittered.

That's a naughty giggle, right? Yeah, the guy tittered.

He asked us how long we needed to stay and seemed a little disappointed when I said that it was just overnight. But he took Leo's money without any weird looks and handed us a key with a miniature brass horseshoe dangling from it. We headed for the door again and he told us to have a good time.

I wish, mister.

We dragged ourselves into a room that matched Leo's receipt and I flopped down onto the bed. Most of it was done up in that chintzy faux-country stuff, but there was a real quilt on the bed and the air conditioning was going full blast. It was heaven.

"You can shower first," I told Leo. "You pushed that cranky demon-bike the whole way."

Leo nodded limply and then shambled into the washroom. I heard the water start and then the heavy thud of boots hitting the floor, but was too tired to even indulge in a few fantasies. I buried my face in the quilt and closed my eyes.

Wake me up if anyone tries to kill me, I told Uriel.

I will.

I fell asleep for a little while, half out of heat exhaustion and half out of the regular kind. I didn't have much choice but to trust that Uriel would give me a prod if something happened... Or that they wouldn't try to possess me like Death had Leo. Or that the biker wouldn't lose the battle for control of his body and burst through the washroom door with murder in his eyes and no pants on.

The possibilities were endless, shitty, and I was far too tired to sort them all out, so I just napped until something touched my knee gently. I jerked upright on the bed with a shriek as Leo jumped back, hands raised. He was wearing a fresh shirt and some new jeans, but his hair was damp.

I knew for a fact that Leo hadn't taken any clothes with him into the bathroom. So he had dressed afterward, probably out here in the main room.

You couldn't have woken me up while Leo was changing? I asked Uriel.

It did not seem dangerous. Is it?

I sighed and left Uriel to rummage through my brain if they wanted an answer for that. Groaning, I stood up. My legs were sore and my feet hurt from the walk into Jasper.

"Sorry," I told Leo. "I guess I'm getting a little paranoid."

"Can't blame you," he said. "Your turn in the shower."

I stretched and looked Leo up and down. He hadn't dried off very well and his shirt clung tightly to his skin, showing off the muscles beneath. Leo's eyes were still pretty bloodshot, though, and he headed for the sideboard to make some coffee. While the water started heating, Leo grabbed a pop can from the mini-fridge.

My nap couldn't have been very long, but watching Leo flop wearily down into the desk chair, it seemed positively luxurious. I stopped stretching and walked stiffly into the washroom. There was still plenty of hot water and I stood under the shower spray, rinsing off the dust and sweat. The heat felt good on my tensed muscles, too, though it didn't entirely do the job of unknotting them.

My life had gotten too damned dangerous and too damned weird for one shower to soothe away.

I lingered until the water cooled off, then stepped out and wrapped myself in a towel. I couldn't bring myself to get dressed in my sweaty, grimy clothes again. And I just had them washed... I sighed.

As long as we were stopped over in Jasper, I was determined to buy something new to wear. Clean jeans and a few shirts that were actually my size. Not that I particularly minded Leo's big t-shirts, but they had a tendency to whip and snap in the wind when I rode behind him.

I made sure the towel was secure and then carried my dirty clothes out of the washroom, dropping them next to the bed. Leo looked up from the television remote, eyes widening as he took in how little I was wearing.

My heart sped and I burned with heat that had nothing to do with the Arizona summer. What would happen if I kissed Leo? What would Death do? Leo stood, looming over me.

"What now, Jaz?" he asked.

The answer that I really wanted to give heavily involved the motel bed and probably some broken mattress springs, but we had far bigger concerns than how long it had been since I last got laid. I tore my gaze away from Leo to glance at the window, where his motorcycle was parked outside.

"We have to get that Packmaster up and running again," I said. "I don't suppose Death can do anything about it?"

Leo closed his eyes and rubbed his temples. He seemed to be thinking, or maybe trying to speak to the demonic entity living inside him.

"Death could heal... fix... the bike," Leo said after a moment. "But it won't. As far as I can tell, Death is angry because I refuse to give it control. It's like a toddler throwing a tantrum. But instead of demanding a sippy cup, Death won't go anywhere until I murder you."

"Charming," I said.

"Well, it actually wants me to kill Uriel. It doesn't give a shit about you."

"Is it telling you all that?" I asked.

Leo shook his head. "Death still isn't talking, exactly. I just... feel it."

I covered up a wince by searching around the motel room until I found the slender yellow volume of a local phone book crammed into a drawer, next to a battered bible. I spread it open on the desk and paged through, then brought my finger down on one of the entries.

"Chain Gang," I said.

Leo crossed the room to look over my shoulder, standing so close that I could feel the heat of him. I forced myself to breathe evenly.

"It's a garage here in Jasper," I told Leo. "And it looks like they specialize in dirt bikes. I guess people drive them around the desert out here. They should have all the tools I'll need to fix your clutch."

"The Packmaster isn't a dirt bike," Leo said stiffly.

I smirked. "Easy, big bad biker boy. Functionally, there isn't much difference between the biggest Harley and a dirt bike."

"I can't let them touch my motorcycle," Leo said.

"What? Why not?"

"My bike... bit you, Jaz," Leo answered. "It doesn't like being fucked with and I don't want it slicing up some poor bastard just trying to finish his shift."

I nodded in agreement. "And I don't think we can let anyone else see what's going on with the Packmaster. That's a good way to end up with tabloid headlines about hot bikers and demon motorcycles."

A slight flush crept up under the lines of ink tattooed along Leo's neck. He cleared his throat and shook his head.

"But you said you can do the work, right?" Leo asked.

"Yeah, I can fix the clutch," I said. "I just need to convince the mechanics at Chain Gang to let me borrow some of their tools. I... haven't quite figured that part out yet. We could walk in and offer up a bunch of cash, but that's going to be suspicious as hell."

"Or we go in tonight, after hours, and get what we need," Leo suggested.

"After hours?" I repeated with a frown.

"Breaking and entering," Leo elaborated.

I crossed my arms. "What? No! We can't just steal their tools. Trust me, those things are really expensive. If I had sold mine, I could have left Crayhill a long time ago... But that would have been like selling my leg."

Leo glanced down past the hem of the towel I had wrapped around myself, at the smooth brown skin of my legs. His flush moved a little further up, darkening Leo's cheeks.

But he took a stack of hundred-dollar bills from the pocket of his leather jacket.

"We'll only borrow what you need, and we can pay for all of it," Leo said. "We're just not going to ask for permission."

"Leaving a big wad of cash on the counter is still going to be suspicious," I pointed out.

"Yeah," Leo agreed. "But by the time they find it tomorrow, we'll be long gone."

CHAPTER 19

That's how I found myself creeping along the main road of Jasper in the middle of the night with Leo, who pushed the busted Packmaster down the street. At least waiting until nightfall had given us the chance to find a laundromat and run a few loads while we ate dinner. I had bought some new clothes, too, including a couple of t-shirts silk-screened with the name of the town and pictures of the Petrified Forest. I looked just like all the other tourists now.

The evening was cold and clear, but I was still sweating right through my nice clean clothes. Every time a car cruised past, I had to fight not to flee from the headlights. All this badass renegade stuff didn't come very naturally to me, but Leo didn't flinch. He just kept pushing his motorcycle down the road. Either he was that used to this kind of thing, or else he was too tired to give a shit. This was Leo's second night without sleep and he had drunk an entire pot of coffee with dinner.

We checked the address a few times, but Jasper wasn't a large town and before long, we stopped in the Chain Gang parking lot. It was a plain cinder-block building that looked almost identical to the Golden Touch Auto in Crayhill, with a small lobby and a pair of roll-up aluminum doors that were shut and locked. We studied the garage from a distance first, but there was only a single light on in the lobby and no one moving around inside. I didn't hear any tools or music going in the back, either. Everyone had gone home for the night.

I had bought a baseball cap, too, and another one for Leo. We approached Chain Gang with our heads lowered, hopefully obscuring our faces from any watchful security cameras. But we didn't see any and I felt a little silly.

Closer now, Leo inspected the front door – a worn wooden frame inset with glass bearing the garage's name and a picture of a dirt bike. A sign hanging in the window had been flipped over to CLOSED. I tried the doorknob, but it didn't turn. Locked, of course.

"Uh, do you know how to pick a lock?" I asked.

Leo shrugged, glanced back at the road – which was dark and empty – then smashed a leather-clad elbow through the window next to the door. There was a loud crash and shattered glass rained in glittering shards all across the lobby floor. The CLOSED sign swung wildly for a moment, then fell off its hook and out of sight.

I flinched again as a sedan drove by, but either the driver didn't see us and the broken window, or else didn't care. I turned back to Leo.

"Aren't you worried about alarms?" I asked.

"Looks like the door has one, but not the window," Leo said. "Give me a second."

He pulled on a pair of riding gloves – full ones this time that covered his hands in leather – and carefully brushed glass out of the frame until he could grip it, then vaulted over and into the darkness inside. I waited outside, nervously fidgeting, and then jumped when I heard a loud metallic scrape. A chain rattled and Leo heaved up one of the rolling doors.

"Let's get the bike in here fast," he said.

I hurried into the parking lot to the spot where Leo had left his motorcycle. I grabbed the handlebars and started pushing, but the brakes engaged and the handle on my side hit me in the stomach.

"Ouch," I said. "Leo, it's not moving."

He swore and came jogging over to take the motorcycle from me. The brakes didn't release, though, and the tires squealed as he yanked his bike across the asphalt.

"Come on..." Leo grunted.

He pushed, shoved and then finally heaved the Packmaster into the garage. I rolled the door shut as Leo collapsed against a cinder-block wall, breathing hard. He swiped sweat from his forehead.

"That thing *really* doesn't want to be fixed," Leo panted. "So let's do it."

You should not repair Death's steed, Uriel told me.

Give it a rest, would you? I asked. *I need to focus.*

This is my purpose, Uriel said. *And your purpose, too. You were chosen for this. You are unique, Jaz. Special.*

That's flattering. Right now, though, I'm just especially annoyed.

But I felt Uriel's unhappiness inside me. The angel was truly uncomfortable with what we were doing here.

Look, I thought, *Leo's bike... I mean, Death's uh... steed... doesn't want repairs. So by fixing it, I'm doing the opposite of what Death wants. Is that good enough for you?*

Uriel considered for a moment.

Yes, the archangel answered.

Leo and I made a quick search of the garage. But lucky for us, Chain Gang hadn't spent very much money on their security system. There were no motion detectors or lasers to trip, and the building was just as empty as it had appeared from the outside, so we didn't have to deal with an awkward hostage situation.

At least something was going right.

We turned on the lights in the garage and lit up the row of five lift tables – battered metal plates painted yellow and welded to hydraulics that would raise them so mechanics didn't have to work hunched over.

"Alright," I told Leo. "Let's get that monster of yours on a lift."

I pointed and Leo wrestled the resisting Packmaster onto the largest lift table. We strapped it into place and I raised the platform. I reached toward the engine, then hesitated.

"Okay, don't let it... bite me or anything," I said.

Leo grabbed the steel fork that held the bike's front wheel and nodded. "I'll try."

Uriel had healed the gash across my palm and my severely bruised trachea from the night before, but I wasn't in a hurry to repeat any of those injuries. I selected a hex wrench off one of the workbenches and slowly approached the possessed bike. It creaked in the thick nylon straps and Leo tightened his grip.

"Hold still, you cranky beast," Leo growled.

The big motorcycle yanked against the straps again and Leo's muscles tensed to keep it in place as I got to work.

Packmasters have a wet clutch, which means that the enclosure is filled with a lubricating fluid that I had to drain off before I could open it up and replace anything inside. I slid an empty plastic tray under Leo's bike and opened the valve. Primary fluid gurgled and then began streaming into the tray.

I hastily covered my mouth and nose when the smell hit me. There was a sharp burnt scent – which wasn't surprising with a fried clutch – but it was worse than that. The smell was more like gunpowder and sulfur... Or brimstone, as the bible likes to call it.

And blood.

The primary fluid was thick and red, and it stank like something dead. I jumped back and almost needed a tray of my own as my stomach threatened to return dinner in a more liquid form.

"Holy shit," I gasped.

Leo didn't let go of the Packmaster, but he stared. He might not have been a mechanic, but he was a biker and clearly knew that was *not* what primary fluid should look or smell like. I inhaled the graveyard scent and gagged.

"That... that just needs to drain," I said. "Have you got things handled out here?"

"I think so," Leo answered.

I left him to watch over his motorcycle and found my way to the stockroom. Not only to escape the stench – though that was certainly a benefit – but because I needed parts. If Chain Gang didn't have a clutch kit that would fit the Packmaster, then we were back to hoping and praying that Leo could talk Death into healing the bike itself.

The stockroom wasn't large, but the sheetmetal shelves were stacked with boxes and bottles. Chain Gang was a sports shop and I found plenty of kits for Kawasakis and Hondas, but as I wound through the close-packed storage room, I began to despair of finding anything bigger. Just short of giving up, I finally spotted a dusty box crammed into the back of a shelf.

I crossed my fingers and pushed a few import clutch kits out of the way, rescued the one behind them and blew off the dust. It wasn't specifically for a Packmaster, but I opened the box and inspected the clutch plates inside. They looked the right size and should do the job in a pinch. Which was exactly what we were in.

If Leo's motorcycle complained, it had only itself to blame.

I chose a bottle of non-blood primary fluid and carried it all back out into the garage. Leo's tattooed skin shone with sweat under the lights as he held the Packmaster down. The motorcycle revved and ratcheted on top of the lift table.

"Got what you need?" Leo grunted.

"I really hope so," I said.

I grabbed another plastic tray, filled it with some of the new primary fluid and got the replacement plates soaking to prepare them for installation. The tray under Leo's motorcycle was full of blood, so I removed it.

Uh, now what? I wasn't sure if the weird demonic blood was safe to wash down the sink. The last thing we needed was it getting into the water supply and mutating the wildlife. I didn't want to run over some demon-armadillo down the road, so I found a funnel and poured the bike blood into an empty jug. It was one of those big containers for recycling oil and I left it on the workbench to deal with... well, probably never.

With the blood sealed up inside thick plastic, the smell improved a little, but I wasn't really excited about cracking open the clutch enclosure. I pulled down the wrenches I would need and pointed at the Packmaster.

"If you give me any more crap with bolt sizes," I warned the bike, "I'm going to tell on you to Leo."

"Um, I'm right here," Leo reminded me.

"Well, you're still its boss."

The bike heaved to one side in the straps and Leo groaned as he struggled to hold it upright.

"Yeah... I'm not so sure about that," he said.

I fitted a socket wrench over the first bolt. It took me a couple of tries, but the tool fit and after a lot of swearing, pushing and shoving, I managed to remove the bolts. By the time I got the casing off and pulled out the spring retainer, I was sweating as hard as Leo.

I peered into the enclosure and grimaced. The clutch plates inside had been some of those nice expensive carbon-fiber ones, but now they were nothing but blackened, shattered shrapnel.

No amount of feathering your clutch did *that* to the plates. Leo looked over my shoulder and whistled.

"Damn..." he said.

Damnation. Yeah, that was pretty close. I went back to the workbench and found a pair of gloves, then pulled them on before removing the ruined plates. I had no desire to touch them with my bare hands if I could avoid it.

Look, I had no problem with engine grease up to my elbows and smudged all over my face. But gunpowder-smelling demon-bike blood? Hard pass.

The pieces of the broken clutch plates were small enough to dump into the jug of blood-slash-primary fluid. I used some rags and paper towels to clean out the Packmaster's enclosure, then stuffed them into the jug, too. I screwed the cap on as tight as I could, then wrapped it in a couple layers of engine tape for good measure. And wrote *DO NOT OPEN – TOXIC AF* on the side in big block letters with a felt-tip pen.

Well, that was the best I could do there. Now time to get the Packmaster up and running. I carried the new clutch plates over to the motorcycle, picked them out of the primary fluid and silently said a little prayer to the patron saint of mechanics as I began pushing them into place.

They fit and I breathed a sigh of relief. A short one, though. When I maneuvered all of the plates into position and reconnected the cables, I closed the casing up again and then refilled it with fresh primary fluid.

How long would it stay recognizable? The bike was *changing*. As Death grew stronger, it became less and less a motorcycle and more the horseman's steed.

I paid for my momentary distraction as the engine enclosure went suddenly hot under my fingertips. I yanked my hand back as the metal glowed red and a chemical-smelling smoke curled up from the nylon straps.

"Stop!" Leo shouted. "Don't you *dare* hurt her!"

The engine gunned and the exhaust pipes backfired like a rifle shot. Leo snarled at his bike.

"She's already changed your fucking clutch," he said. "That's enough!"

The enclosure flared with ember light for a moment longer before flickering and finally snuffing out.

"Jaz, are you alright?" Leo asked.

"Yeah," I said. "I was wearing gloves."

I reached out toward the bike gingerly, but didn't feel any heat. I finished tightening the bolts and the drainage valve, then stood up. Leo glared at his motorcycle.

"Is that it? Should it run now?" he asked.

"In theory," I answered. "But I can't promise much if your steed here decides to fry the clutch again, or throw a piston."

"It's my job to make sure it doesn't," Leo said.

"Well, let's check that I did mine properly." I gestured over to another machine in the corner of the garage, a large one with steel rollers set into the baseplate. "Can you put that big bastard on the dynamometer? I want to check my work before we try to roll out of here."

I lowered the lift table again and we carefully unfastened the smoking straps that held the motorcycle in place. Leo grabbed it firmly by the handlebars and pushed his bike over to the dynamometer, then up onto the rollers. There were some more straps that I used to lash down the front wheel, but the Packmaster's engine turned over and revved threateningly.

"Would you smack this thing on the fender with a rolled-up newspaper or something?" I asked.

"Easy there," Leo said, like he was gentling a horse. "Easy."

I bet Leo would have looked great riding a horse. Along a beach... Shirtless, just on general principle. But the Packmaster wasn't impressed and growled in a lower gear this time.

"We're only going to make sure you're still working and see how strong you are," Leo said. "Settle down."

The motor throttled back to an idle. I had no idea if that boded well for my work, but it didn't sound like the Packmaster was about to bite off one of my fingers, so Leo and I positioned the rear tire on the dynamometer's roll assembly.

When everything was in place, I turned on the computerized display. An orange progress bar flashed on the screen, and then several rows of yellow buttons. I selected the basic settings and pointed to the Packmaster's throttle. Leo nodded and twisted it slowly, bringing the motorcycle up to speed and cycling through the gears.

I watched the readout and realized my mouth was hanging open.

"Holy shit," I said. "Or maybe more like *unholy* shit..."

"What's wrong?" Leo asked.

I blinked and squinted at the dynamometer. There was no way that these numbers could be right. I had been a slightly unwilling passenger on the Packmaster long enough to know it was far beyond factory specs, but this...

"A... a normal dual-cam engine gets about fifty horsepower at the wheel," I told Leo. "Which comes out to around a hundred at the crankshaft. On a custom bike like yours, I would expect another twenty or thirty."

Leo's dark eyes narrowed. "That's not what you're getting on the dyno, is it?"

"I'm reading four hundred horsepower," I said.

The Packmaster revved and roared in Leo's grip. The best racing bikes in the world had only half that kind of power. Leo's motorcycle was way, *way* beyond street legal. But it was already breaking pretty much every physical and mechanical law... so why not a few mortal ones, too?

"Is everything working?" Leo asked.

"Better than it should," I said.

"Then let's get on the road. We lost a day of driving to this shit."

Leo turned off the engine and hauled his motorcycle off the dynamometer while I shut down the machine. I left Leo to keep an eye on his bike while I wiped down and put away all of the tools. Yeah, I know we broke in and I was a hardened criminal now, but it was habit and I'm not an asshole.

When I was done, Leo took a stack of money from his jacket pocket and I kept nodding until he had fanned out about two thousand dollars. It was more than enough to pay for the broken window, one clutch kit and a bottle of primary fluid, but it still might come up short on therapy bills if someone got curious and cracked open the bloody jug we were leaving behind.

Well, I couldn't solve every problem. I couldn't even solve my own problems at the moment...

I swept up the shattered window glass in the lobby and then left the money on the workbench that I had used in the back. By the time we finished, the first violet light of dawn was creeping over the eastern horizon.

"Do you need something to eat before we go?" Leo asked.

The smells of blood and brimstone were still sharp in the air, and I shook my head.

"No, I'm a little queasy," I answered. "Are you okay to drive? You haven't slept for two days now."

"I'll be fine," Leo said. "I mooched a couple of sodas from the break room fridge and wiped the door down when I was done."

"Why?" I asked. "Did you spill something?"

"Fingerprints," Leo said.

Guess I still had a lot to learn about being a real criminal. I had cleaned off all the tools and worn gloves most of the time I was using them, but I wiped a paper towel over the chain of the rolling door while Leo pushed his motorcycle outside again.

When we closed up the garage as best we could – we might have broken in, but no need to invite more thieves to do so – Leo swung a leg over his bike and started up the engine. The exhaust smelled like gunpowder and the big Packmaster growled. Leo shushed the motorcycle, trying to soothe it. But when that didn't work, he just growled right back.

Is it weird that it was kind of sexy?

I cannot say, Uriel answered.

I wasn't asking you.

Death has chosen a strong vessel, the archangel said. *A horseman's steed acknowledges no other master. But it only grows stronger as Death does. Leo cannot hold it at bay forever.*

What about you? I asked.

You have been a worthy opponent, Jaz. But in the end, I will have control of this vessel. I must.

And here I thought we were becoming friends, I said.

Uriel sifted through the thoughts and memories of my life, childhood and adolescent friends flashing through my mind like the pages of a book flipping by too fast.

Yes, the angel said. *We are becoming friends. To my regret.*

CHAPTER 20

We rode hard across Arizona, trying to put some distance between us and Jasper before someone at Chain Gang called the police to report a break-in. We hadn't exactly been thorough about covering our tracks – Leo may have been a professional criminal, but he was more of a strong-arm bandit than a cat burglar.

So despite the ludicrous amount of horsepower beneath us, Leo drove carefully and legally, and we kept watch every mile for Michael's cops. I mean, we got passed by a minivan and that's just sad.

But some of that might have been Leo... He hadn't slept in forty-eight hours and when we stopped for an early lunch, Leo ordered three coffees. His eyes were bloodshot and rimmed in red, with dark circles under them. I was glad that he *had* eyes – even without Uriel's feature-length apocalyptic dreams, Death's empty sockets were the stuff of nightmares – but I still felt bad for Leo.

And I was damned tired, too. Last night had involved only a few hours of sleep and a lot of fixing a motorcycle that didn't want to be fixed. We took our food down the winding road to a rest stop so that we could remain close to the Packmaster while we ate. I yawned into my hash browns and rubbed my eyes.

"Do you need some sleep?" Leo asked.

"Me? You're the one on insomnia duty," I said.

"More like not-killing-Jaz duty," Leo countered. "And generally maintaining control of my body."

"It's a nice body."

Leo blinked and I clapped a hand over my mouth. I hadn't meant to say that out loud. But you know... tired.

"If you can stay awake," I said quickly, "so can I."

But Leo was shaking his head. "One of us has to be rested and alert, Jaz. Stopping Death from taking over and keeping the Packmaster from throwing a piston requires pretty much everything I have. There are still the other horsemen, archangels and those paramilitary whackjobs that shot up our motel room in... shit, I don't even remember what town that was now."

"Mmmm," I said.

That was supposed to be something along the lines of *Yeah, good point* or *It was Zamora Canyon,* but I was too busy yawning again. We were sitting at a rest-stop concrete picnic table that had been abused by more than weather. Leo patted the bench with a smirk.

"Come on," he offered. "Lay down and get a little sleep."

"Okay, just give me five minutes," I said.

I stretched out on the seat, but I didn't keep my eyes closed for long. The concrete was hard and cracked, impossible to get comfortable on. Sleeping rough sucked.

"Try this," Leo said.

He took off his jacket and I assumed he was going to fold it into some sort of cushion. The leather was old and well-worn, but I sat up and Leo slid down the bench toward me. When my head came down again, it was against Leo's thigh, and he draped his jacket over me like a blanket.

Oh, wow... Leo's muscles didn't make for a very soft pillow, but I wouldn't have traded for the best, most expensive mattress.

Your heart is pounding, Jaz. Are we preparing for battle? Uriel asked.

There's more to life than fighting, I said. *If you can forget about war for just a minute, you might learn about some of it.*

Perhaps. But for now, Leo is correct. You require rest. Sleep and we will keep Death at bay.

I don't know if Uriel was poking around in my brain for some of those non-battle nice things, or if sleeping with my head cradled in Leo's lap set the tone for my dreams... But let's just say that it was a nice reprieve from the nightmares of fighting four mounted demons with a sword made of razor-sharp light.

I slept for a lot longer than five minutes before Leo shook me gently awake. I sat up and wiped my mouth, checking for drool. If Leo noticed, he didn't say anything. I really hoped I hadn't said anything, either... I've never been particularly prone to talking in my sleep, but nothing in my life was normal right now.

You spoke no words while you slept, Uriel assured me.

Thank goodness, I thought. *Wait, did I make any sounds?*

"Ready to go?" Leo asked me.

I stretched and my spine popped as I looked around. Without my phone, I couldn't have told you the time, but the sun had moved and I didn't recognize any of the cars in the parking lot anymore. I wasn't sure how much Leo had let me sleep, but it was long enough that I was glad the cops hadn't picked us up for vagrancy. I felt a lot better and nodded at Leo.

"Let's get back onto the road," I said. "You still know where we're going, right?"

"San Diego..." Leo answered with one eyebrow arched.

"I meant our route," I said. "Since we're not taking the highway anymore."

Leo sighed and stifled a yawn against the back of his hand as he put his jacket on again.

"Oh, yeah. Sorry," he said. "I think so, but maybe you should look over the maps so you can kick my ass onto track if I screw it up."

We pulled out the maps and reviewed our route again. The Arizona maps didn't cover the whole trip to California, but they would get us at least to the Nevada border.

"We can pick up another map there," I said. "Or check on a computer."

Leo nodded wearily and I followed him to the Packmaster. The motorcycle growled at his approach, but Leo snarled at it and put the maps back into the saddlebags.

We mounted up again and kept driving at careful, family-friendly speeds through a town called Whitburn, then Coconino National Forest. I was expecting endless deserts and taco stands – which shows just how badly I needed to get out of Crayhill – and was surprised at how many trees there were in the American southwest. The day was bright and hot, sunlight flickering through the overlapping green of leaves to paint wild golden mosaics across the road winding between them. It was beautiful, and all the more because it was so unexpected.

Unexpected locations lead to unexpected problems, Uriel pointed out.

And unexpected good stuff, too, I thought. *You've never had a surprise party, have you?*

No. The angel riffled around my thoughts for a moment. *And neither have you.*

But if I ever do, I'm going to love *it.*

I wasn't sure if that confused Uriel or they just didn't have an answer, but the archangel fell silent again. Leo drove us through

Coconino National Forest, past trucks and RVs full of families on vacation. By that evening, we left the forest behind and rode toward the setting sun.

It wasn't particularly late, but I felt the exhaustion trembling in Leo's muscles and one yawn after another stretching his chest. He kept the Packmaster moving more or less steadily, though, until I pointed through the fading twilight to a road sign that promised gasoline, food and lodging. If I remembered our maps correctly, this might be our last chance to stop off for a while. Unless we wanted some rocks and pine cones for dinner, and I was pretty sure tree sap didn't have the sort of caffeine content Leo needed right now.

"Let's eat," I shouted into his ear.

Leo gave me a brief thumbs-up and we turned at the next traffic light, then stopped in the parking lot of a hotel flanked by a nice-looking Chinese restaurant and a slightly less busy bar-grill combo. We parked outside the grill and Leo staggered as we went in. I grabbed his arm.

"Hey, are you okay?" I asked.

"Yeah," Leo answered. "Just need some coffee."

At least, I *think* that's what he said. It was loud inside the grill and Leo was mumbling badly.

A host pointed us to a small table and Leo slumped down into his chair without even trying to put his back against a wall. He stared at the menu for five full minutes and when our server came by, I had to repeat Leo's order for him. To be honest, it was mostly coffee with a grilled cheese sandwich chaser.

Luckily, the server seemed to sense the extent of the problem and hastily returned with a cup of coffee. It was still steaming hot, but Leo downed half the mug in a single gulp. He let out a long breath and rubbed his eyes.

Hey, was that you or the horsemen? I asked. *Which one of you invented coffee?*

None of us, Uriel answered. *By agreement, the two sides created a physical universe in which our war could finally be won or lost. But how that universe evolved was shaped internally by its own forces and inhabitants.*

I shook my head. *You should have just taken credit.*

"I'm alive, I swear," Leo said. "This stuff is a miracle."

A little of the light came back to his brown eyes, but the dark circles remained and I wasn't entirely convinced. I drank down some water – it had been a long, hot day and I was thirsty, too – then cocked my head toward the nearest window and the Packmaster parked outside.

"You're exhausted," I told Leo.

"No argument here," he said.

"Do you think there's any chance you could bully your bike into letting me drive?"

Leo looked out the window as he finished his coffee. He had turned off the motorcycle headlight when we parked, but the filament glowed an angry, hellish red and seemed to be staring right at us.

"No," Leo said. "Nobody else can drive my steed."

"Especially some girl with an angel inside her."

Leo nodded. "But even with all the time we lost yesterday, we should be able to roll into San Diego late tomorrow. I can make it one more day."

One more day until answers and hopefully solutions from Uncle Carlos, until Leo could sleep and I could pry the angel out of my skull. I still wasn't sure what that solution might involve and hoped it wouldn't be something like a blessed white-hot ice pick through my ear.

What if it did, though? Would it be worth pain or maiming to get rid of Uriel?

You do not need to worry, Uriel told me.

Thanks, I thought. But then I frowned. *Wait, why not?*

Because I cannot be removed. I am a part of you, Jaz. You are my vessel.

Was that supposed to be reassuring? I was kind of touched, but Uriel's words were disquieting, too. Would the angel fight whatever Carlos wanted to do? And what about the horseman inside Leo? Uriel was a force of light and order, but Death was... well, Death. I couldn't imagine it just letting go of Leo.

Our food arrived, along with a second cup of coffee, and Leo was awake enough to thank the server this time. My pasta was good, but the cheese sauce made me thirsty and my water was gone. I searched around for our server. The grill was only about half full and I spotted him bussing another table. I wasn't *that* thirsty... I could wait until he finished, so I returned my attention to dinner.

But I felt eyes on me and looked up again. It wasn't the server noticing that I needed something... There was an older white lady a few tables away, maybe in her fifties or sixties. I wasn't sure – I was shit at guessing people's age. But her hair was gray and she watched us through a pair of black-rimmed glasses. As soon as she saw me looking, the woman turned away. But she had definitely been watching us.

"Hey, Leo," I said quietly. "There's a lady three tables back. The one with glasses."

Leo finished his swallow of coffee and glanced over at the table I indicated, then nodded slightly toward the left shoulder of his leather jacket, where the embroidered rattlesnake coiled, ready to strike.

"Think it might be the snake patch?" Leo asked. "Sometimes people recognize it and get spooked."

Yeah, I remembered. I had recognized that rattlesnake back in Crayhill and was certainly freaked out. Not that it stopped me from running off with a big, sexy biker. But...

"She doesn't look scared," I said.

The woman was studying her menu way too hard, and she seemed more curious than frightened. She looked up when our server approached her table. Whoever this lady was, she had arrived after us, apparently.

"Is she one of yours?" Leo asked me. "She's not a horseman, as far as I can tell."

Uriel? I asked. I didn't feel anything like I had with Michael or Gabriel – and this close, the feeling would be pretty damned strong – but figured I better ask. *Is that woman over there about to sprout wings?*

She is not an angelic vessel, Uriel answered.

And if another archangel was sitting across a restaurant from us, I was sure Uriel would have control of my body, not me. But I picked up my fork and stuffed some more pasta into my mouth, just to be sure. Yeah, I was still running the show.

For now.

Uriel, will you help me keep an eye on that lady? I asked. *If I look away, can you watch her?*

I can use your senses, but I have others that you do not.

Uh... is that a yes?

Yes, the angel said.

Leo and I ate our dinner quickly. I watched the woman with the glasses from the corner of my eye – and it was clear she was doing the same thing with us – but Uriel didn't alert me to anything fishy.

After about twenty minutes, the lady finished her salad and got up. She put some cash on the table, then left the restaurant. My heart finally slowed and Leo let out a sigh. He ordered some more coffee and I celebrated this small victory by adding a slice of cheesecake to the bill.

We lingered at the grill until we were certain that the woman at the other table was gone, and our server was starting to give us some stink-eye for taking so long.

"Let's get a room," I suggested.

"That sounded bad," Leo said. "Or good. Maybe both."

Even after all of that coffee, Leo was still tired and his smile was sleepy. It was no less charming, but the biker was dragging his feet and nearly dropped the money when he went to pay. Leo left a tip big enough to make our server smile again, though.

"Hotel room?" I asked.

"Yeah. Let's grab one next door."

We left the restaurant and headed across the parking lot toward the dark rectangular silhouette of the hotel. Leo tripped over the edge of the curb and I grabbed the sleeve of his leather jacket to steady him.

"Shit, sorry," Leo said. "I guess coffee just isn't doing the trick anymore. And I don't know when I'll be able to look an energy drink in the eye again."

We made sure that the Packmaster was still where we left it – which it was, and it grumbled at Leo as we passed – and then headed to the hotel. We had the same problem as before with paying in cash, but *enough* cash seemed to take care of the issue and we were quickly heading up to the third story, the first available room that the clerk could find. It was another single king bed, but Leo said that was fine.

We took the elevator to our room, unlocked the door and Leo staggered inside. I followed him, then closed and locked up behind us. It was a simple, boring hotel room, with a lot of mint green and faded sky blue. But the bed looked comfortable and the shower was well-sized.

Leo headed straight for the sideboard that held the coffee maker. No minifridge or pop in here, but I had seen a couple of vending machines out in the hallway. Leo grabbed a foil packet of instant coffee, but it slipped through his fingers and bounced across the floor.

"Shit," he sighed.

I picked up the coffee and replaced it on the counter. Leo ran one hand through his thick brown hair and shifted his weight between his feet a few times.

"How're you doing?" I asked.

"Not great," Leo admitted.

I approached carefully and held out my arms. He nodded and I circled them around him. Leo's whole body was tight and trembling as I hugged him. A shuddering sigh ruffled my hair.

"I keep wondering if heroin would quiet Death down," Leo said. "I'm not sure I could say *no* to a needle right now."

A shudder wracked Leo and I held him tighter, as though I could physically stop the craving. Leo wrapped his arms around me and pulled me close. I heard his heart jackhammering in his chest.

"I don't know how much longer I can do this, Jaz," Leo said. "The coffee and energy drinks are barely keeping me awake anymore. What if I fall asleep? What if Death takes control...?"

Slowly, I reached up to run my fingers down Leo's cheek. It was rough with stubble and the contact made Uriel jolt inside me. Leo jumped, too.

"Death doesn't like that," he growled.

I ran my fingers along Leo's jaw and visions of heavenly fire burned through my brain, but I didn't pull away.

"What about you?" I asked. "Do *you* like it?"

Leo's eyes were so intense that I could feel them on my skin.

"Yes," he said.

"There might be another way to keep you awake."

"Jaz, you shouldn't touch me," Leo said. "It's dangerous..."

He meant every word, I knew, but Leo's hands didn't get the message. They trailed up my arms and then slowly down my back. My head was full of bladed wings and flames, power and violence, but I closed my eyes and leaned into Leo. Maybe there was another way to shut those visions out, too...

I pulled Leo down into a kiss. He stiffened again and I swore that I could hear Death snarling inside him, but Leo put his arms around me, too. He lifted me effortlessly up off the ground and I wrapped my legs around his waist.

Not taking his lips from mine, Leo staggered toward the bed, but he couldn't see and hadn't slept in days. We hit the corner, overbalanced and fell together into the sheets. Fine by me – that's where we were going, anyway. Leo came down on top of me, with every deliciously hard inch of his body pressed against mine.

I clutched the hem of Leo's shirt and wondered how I was going to get it off without breaking the kiss. Would Leo mind if I just ripped it to shreds? He grabbed my hips and let out a deep, hungry growl. Somehow, I didn't think he cared one bit about the shirt.

Someone knocked on the hotel room door. Who the hell was that? We weren't even being noisy... yet. I sat up with a groan.

"What the fuck?" Leo asked.

His heart was still pounding so hard that I could hear it. Leo was wide awake now, but didn't seem to have enough blood in his head to make complete sentences. I wasn't much better and only managed some grumbled swearing as I went to the door to squint through the little glass peephole.

A woman waited in the hallway outside. She stood a few feet back from the door with her hands tucked into the pockets of neat gray slacks. I recognized her, but it took a moment for me to figure out why.

"Holy shit," I whispered. "It's that lady from the restaurant. Did she follow us?"

It would take a lot more than a few nights without sleep and a horny mechanic throwing herself at him to entirely dull Leo's edge. He was on his feet in an instant and racking the slide of a gun that I hadn't even seen him pick up.

"Do you sense something?" Leo asked as he hurried over.

"No, still nothing angelic," I said. "Do you feel anything?"

"Other than pissed off?" Leo shook his head. "Nope. I mean, Death wants to kill her. But it wants to kill everyone, so that's not exactly useful information."

For a second there, I was shamefully tempted to let Death do precisely that. I was tired of being box-locked. The woman in the hallway checked her watch, then knocked at our door again. I jumped and Leo's grip tightened on the gun.

"Now what?" I asked.

"Maybe she'll leave," Leo said.

"Jasmine O'Neil?" the woman called out. "Leopold Valdis?"

I blinked. How the hell did she know our names? I didn't like it, and to judge by how Leo tensed, neither did he. Or maybe he just didn't like being called *Leopold*.

The woman outside adjusted her glasses. "My name is Diane Owens. This conversation will be easier if I don't need to shout through a door."

The lady – Diane, apparently – had a point. I gestured to the chain latch and looked at Leo. He nodded slowly and stood to one side of the door. I hesitated, then moved over to the other side to stay out of the potential line of fire. When we were both in position, I unfastened the chain and turned back the dead-bolt. Leo grabbed the knob and cracked the door open. Outside, Diane smiled.

"Much better, thank you," she said. "Would it be pushing my luck to come in? You've gone to a lot of work to keep what you're doing private, and I'd like to do the same."

Leo glanced at me, and I shrugged. I had no idea what to do, but Diane didn't seem to be either a horseman or an archangel. She wasn't even very big. If something went wrong, Leo could get rid of this woman without breaking a sweat.

As could you, Uriel said. *With my help, at least.*

You would help me? I asked.

Of course.

I wasn't sure if that was Uriel being my friend or just refusing to let some mortal get between them and the final battle. It had been another long day, so I figured that I would take any small victory where I could.

Leo opened up the door the rest of the way and then waved Diane through with his gun. Our visitor stepped inside and eyed the weapon.

"You don't need that, I assure you," Diane said. "And I know that you're both capable of substantially more deadly force than a simple firearm."

Leo pushed the door shut, but didn't lower his gun.

"You were watching us at dinner. Who are you?" I asked.

"Well, I attended seminary, so you could call me *Reverend Owens*," Diane answered. "But I also hold doctorates in astrophysics and history, so you could call me *Doctor Owens*. But if it's all the same to you, I really prefer Diane."

Her voice had a smooth non-accent I always associated with California. If she threw out a *hella* or *dude*, then I would be sure I was right.

"You already told us your name," Leo said. "How the fuck do you know *our* names?"

Diane crossed the hotel room and raised delicate gray eyebrows in a wordless question. When Leo and I didn't object, she sat down in one of the pale green chairs.

"There's some history to that," Diane said. "But the first part of it is because I'm the director of the southwestern division of the Society for the Protection and Observation of the Tellurian."

"The what?" Leo asked.

I blinked a couple of times. There was a lot of information packed into that sentence. And answers, if we were lucky... But none of that was what came out of my mouth.

232 ERICA LINDQUIST & ARON CHRISTENSEN

"So you're... SPOT?" I asked.

Reverend-Doctor Diane Owens spread her hands. "Well, the Latin version provides a somewhat less embarrassing acronym, but... yes. Feel free to make fun. I've heard all the jokes by now."

"I'm more interested in what that name actually means," Leo said. "What are you after, lady?"

Diane sighed. "Well, you've already met some of my people, I'm afraid. Back in Zamora Canyon."

"What?" I asked. I knew my voice was rising and didn't care. "You mean those bastards in the riot gear? The ones who tried to shoot us with big-ass guns?"

"Yes," Diane admitted. "To be fair, however, we had no idea that the hosts – you and Leopold, that is – were still in control of your bodies. We never even suspected that such resistance was possible. I promise you that killing a pair of more or less innocent humans was never our goal."

"Don't call me Leopold," Leo said. "So what *were* you trying to do?"

"To deal with the entities inside you before they could fully manifest and reunite with their factions," Diane answered. "We expected hollow vessels and acted accordingly. I apologize."

"For shooting at us?" I asked.

"I realize that *I'm sorry* isn't much, considering," Diane said. "But it's sincere. Given the fact that the two of you have managed rather shockingly to remain in control of your souls, I thought that we could dispense with the guns this time and simply talk."

Leo hefted his gun. "I'm not putting this down."

"I'd really prefer if you did," Diane said. "I lack the... hmm, resilience granted by the entities within you. But if it makes you feel better..."

"It does," Leo answered.

My heart pounded, but it wasn't just Leo making it thump this time. We had spent days racing to San Diego for answers, but this Diane woman seemed to understand more than even Uriel had ever told me. She knew our names and that there was an angel inside me. How?

I am curious, too, Uriel admitted.

"What do you know about all of this?" I asked.

"I'd really rather discuss that someplace more secure," Diane said. "We can all admit that your... unique spiritual guests... can be rather destructive. There are seventeen people dead so far, a crater that used to be a motel in Arrow, and we retrieved half a gallon of tainted blood from the back room of a bike garage in Jasper."

"You found that shit?" I asked. "Does SPOT uh... know what to do with it?"

"Yes, we do," Diane answered. "And we have disposed of the substance safely."

That was good to hear and I wanted whatever answers Diane had, but that didn't mean I trusted her one bit. Neither did Leo, apparently.

"We're not going anywhere," he said.

"In point of fact, you're both heading to California," Diane countered.

"How do you even know that?" I asked. "How did you find us? We don't have cell phones anymore and we pay for everything in cash..."

Diane nodded. "And those were wise precautions. But Leopold – I'm sorry, Mister Valdis – discarded a gun during an altercation on Highway 44. It was collected by the police, but the Society has chapters in just about every nation, with members at every level of authority. We were able to intercept that particular piece of evidence."

"I was pissed at Pestilence," Leo said. "That fucker killed my friends. But there weren't any serial numbers on that gun. It's not registered to me."

"No, but there were several fingerprints on it," Diane answered. "And your prints are in the system, which we have access to."

Well, Leo *was* a criminal, so I guess that made sense. I really wished that we had thought of it at the time... But to be fair, I had been facing down a Death-possessed Leo.

"Then there was a suspicious break-in at a garage in Jasper," Diane said with a smile. "Where a throttle kit sized for a Packmaster was taken, and cash left behind that could be traced back to an armored car robbery in Chicago."

Leo sighed. "That's exactly why we always take the money to San Diego first. Anything else?"

"Yes," Diane said. "An email sent from a hotel in Flagstaff. It contained no names, but went out to a monitored address for the San Diego Knights of Hell."

Leo turned to me. "I'm sorry, Jaz."

"It's alright," I said. "Sounds like we were screwed no matter what. They had plenty of ways to find us."

"We've been tracking you for our own purposes," Diane told us. "The Society... SPOT... hasn't reported you to governmental authorities. In fact, we've done the best we can to keep the police and state troopers clear of the situation wherever possible."

"Wait, why would you help us?" I asked suspiciously.

"At the risk of further alienating you both, we weren't actually trying to help you," Diane said. "We were helping those first responders. The Society exists to protect this world and its inhabitants from... well, you."

The strange woman stood and adjusted her glasses.

"There's much more for us to discuss," she said. "But there are innocent people here that none of us wish to see harmed. I hope I've proved that we have valuable information."

"Yeah, I guess," I answered slowly. "But can you really help us deal with the... things inside us?"

I do not require 'dealing with,' Uriel said stiffly. *I require only control and victory.*

Diane hesitated, but then she nodded. "Yes... We can help. Does that mean I've convinced you to come with me?"

I glanced at Leo. The biker rocked onto the balls of his feet, weighing the risks of what Diane was asking of us. Leo stopped moving and lifted his chin.

"We've already got answers and help waiting for us in San Diego," he said.

Carlos. I wondered if Leo's uncle had something to do with SPOT. A former west coast member, maybe? If Diane's people were listening to our phones and Carlos realized that, it might explain why he didn't want to talk to us over an unsecured line or whatever. I didn't know much about Carlos... Could a toughened old biker belong to the same group as this preacher-slash-scientist lady?

Diane sighed again and looked over her glasses at us.

"Well, we do have snipers surrounding this hotel," she said. "I would rather talk this out with you. Believe it or not, we're all on the same side. But this is far too important to leave to chance. If you'll forgive the cliché, you're coming with me, one way or the other."

"So much for the good-cop routine," I muttered.

"I'm sorry," Diane answered. "Truly, I am. But the fate of all creation hangs in the balance."

I groaned. She sounded just like Uriel.

This mortal has no part in our battle, Uriel said. *Do not let her divert us from our goal.*

Your *goal,* I corrected. *Not mine. I only wanted to get away from Crayhill and see the world.*

Leo's eyes narrowed and he took a step toward Diane, raising his gun a few degrees.

"If your people start shooting, you won't survive very long," Leo said.

I wasn't certain if he was talking about the SPOT snipers catching Diane in the crossfire, or saying that Leo would shoot her himself.

"I'm not excited about the prospect, but my people have their orders," Diane said. "With any luck, maybe it will help convince you how seriously I take this matter. But other innocents might be injured. Your celestial natures call for terribly large caliber weapons, I'm afraid."

That didn't really leave us very many choices. I was reasonably sure that Uriel could protect me from whatever toys SPOT had brought to this particular party, but whenever I used the archangel's power, their hold got a little tighter.

And that went double for Leo, too. Compared to Death, Uriel was friendly and reasonable. Leo was already fighting Death every moment for control and we didn't dare give the horseman any opening to seize the reins.

"Alright, fine," I sighed. "We'll go to wherever it is you want to talk. Just give us an address and we'll meet you there."

"That's not a good idea," Diane answered. "I'm afraid I can't trust you to make the trip. But we can give you a ride. All of you."

She inclined her head toward Leo, then at the window and presumably the Packmaster outside. I tried to figure out some way to negotiate the point, but the roar of an engine thundered across the parking lot and rattled the windows. Diane flinched a little and Leo snapped his gun up.

"What the hell are you doing?" he snarled.

I ran over to the window and braced myself, hoping that the SPOT snipers weren't too jumpy. No rifle bullets came punching through the glass – yet – but I recognized three of the same big black panel vans that had cornered us in Zamora Canyon down in the parking lot below.

A dozen people in dark paramilitary garb – including bullet-proof vests and reinforced belts all hung with weapons – were trying to wrestle Leo's motorcycle onto a trailer. The Packmaster revved furiously and one of the SPOT guys jumped away with a shout. Blood spurted from his hand and the others fell back, grabbing their guns.

"Shit," Leo growled.

He ran out through the door and down the hall, toward the stairs. Diane and I glanced at each other, then took off after Leo. I was younger and my legs were longer, so I got to the stairwell first – just in time to see Leo leap the final steps and kick open the door at the bottom.

I chased him out into the hotel parking lot as Leo leveled his gun at the Spotters or whatever the hell they were called.

"You! Back the fuck off!" Leo shouted. "Don't touch my bike!"

One of the Spotters rushed their injured friend away from the demonic Packmaster and toward the vans, but the others jumped back behind their trailer and grabbed weapons. There were already red dots wavering all over Leo as SPOT snipers acquired their target from the nearby rooftops. When I glanced down, I found several more of the crimson laser sights centered right over my heart.

You are not dying tonight, Uriel said. *Not before the final battle and not by mortal weapons!*

I felt the angel's light swelling within me and clenched my fists desperately tight as they began to glow. No, not now...!

Diane ran out through the back door of the hotel, holding her hands up in the air.

"Wait!" she shouted. "Stand down!"

The little red dots vanished from my chest and the Spotters on the ground still held guns, but with muzzles pointed down at the asphalt. Uriel grumbled inside me as Diane turned toward Leo.

"Please," she said. "People are watching. You don't want any of them hurt and neither do we. Put the gun away."

Leo glanced around the parking lot. There were a few faces peeking out from between the drapes of their hotel rooms and one man had stopped in the back door of the Chinese restaurant, staring wide-eyed at the scene unfolding outside.

"I only want to talk," Diane said. "And to take you and your steed somewhere safe while we do it."

"Jaz?" Leo asked. "What do you think?"

Why the hell was he asking me? Leo was the bona fide bad-ass, not me. But I shook my head.

"I don't think we can really refuse," I said. "Sounds like they need to talk to us, and we need to talk to them."

Leo replaced the safety on his handgun and slipped it into the back of his jeans.

"Fine," he said. "Let's go talk."

Diane let out a breath that sounded like relief. "I hope that you'll understand when I ask you to ride with me, rather than the steed. It will be right behind us, I promise, but we're on a bit of a timetable here."

Leo and I nodded, but the Packmaster revved again and the rear tire spun up, screaming against the blacktop.

"Can you convince your steed to come along quietly?" Diane shouted over the noise.

"Not really," Leo said.

But he dutifully hurried over to the motorcycle and grabbed the handlebars. The tires stopped spinning, though the engine continued to growl ominously. The Spotters in the parking lot straightened and approached the Packmaster warily. Leo looked at them and every one of the SPOT soldiers froze, watching him.

"You really don't want to load it up without my help," Leo said. "Trust me."

The Spotters all glanced toward the unmarked black van where one of their own was hopefully receiving medical attention. Slowly, they crept closer to the motorcycle and Leo helped them roll the bike into the waiting trailer. It growled, but Leo held onto the handlebars and the Packmaster let itself be strapped down.

"I'll see you again soon," Leo promised. He patted his bike and glared around at the Spotters. "And there had better not be a single scratch when I do."

"I'm not sure we even have the ability to scratch his steed," Diane murmured.

I gave her a sidelong glance. "I doubt you want to try, though. That guy they hauled away could have lost a hand. You realize that Leo is linked to his motorcycle, right? He'll know if you steal that thing."

Diane nodded. "Yes, I understand. We don't tangle lightly with the celestial forces."

"The who?" I asked

"The timeless entities within you and Mister Valdis," Diane answered. "The archangels and the horsemen, as I believe you call them."

The man behind the Chinese restaurant had called out his manager, who was now speaking animatedly into a cell phone. More curtains were being yanked open, and there had to be at least sixty pairs of eyes on us as Leo jogged back over.

"We had better get moving," Diane said. "If you would please follow me..."

I half wondered if Diane was going to offer us candy to get into one of the windowless vans. But the SPOT director pulled out her own phone – it was starting to feel like everyone had a working cell phone except us – and said something into it that I couldn't hear. A moment later, the loud thump of rotors filled the air and a black helicopter flew over the hotel. It descended, making a warm, dusty wind race across the parking lot, and landed on the still-hot asphalt.

All of the watching eyes went wide and tourists stared with mouths hanging open. Diane pointed and then led us to the waiting helicopter. I'm pretty sure she smirked and waved to our audience as she climbed in. Leo jumped into the helicopter, then held out his hand to me.

I took it and let him heave me up. My legs were feeling like overcooked pasta and I appreciated the help. I dropped into one of the seats across from Diane and began trying to figure out the safety harness. A pair of SPOT soldiers slid in on either side of the director and another closed the door from the outside.

As soon as we were sealed up inside, the helicopter took off. My stomach lurched and I grabbed Leo's thigh. He stared down at my hand for a moment, then put his own on top and squeezed gently.

CHAPTER 21

Diane took down an oversized set of headphones from a hook behind her. There was a microphone attached to one side that she lowered toward her mouth. She gestured over our shoulders and I turned awkwardly in my safety harness to find another pair of headsets.

I grabbed one and pulled it down into my hair, but Leo was blindly groping, unwilling to take his eyes off the two big SPOT goons that sat flanking Diane. They were even bigger than Leo – which was saying something – and covered in bulky black body armor, each holding some seriously mean-looking guns pointed right at us.

I helped Leo pull down and put on the other headset. When we were both situated, Diane gave us a thumbs-up.

"First helicopter ride?" she asked.

I could see Diane's lips moving, but her voice came through the headphones. I nodded, and so did Leo. Mine was a little bit shakier than his, though. I had never left Crayhill before all of this began, and that meant no airplanes. If they were anything like the helicopter, I would stick to motorcycles. Even riding on

242 • ERICA LINDQUIST & ARON CHRISTENSEN

the back of a furious demon-bike didn't make my stomach dip and churn like this.

Flying does not need to be unpleasant, Uriel told me. *We have wings.*

You *have wings,* I thought. *I just have motion sickness.*

We can fly.

I'm not jumping out of a helicopter, Uriel.

Leo sat silently next to me, staring down the SPOT soldiers. Diane glanced sidelong at her two guards.

"It's a short flight," she said. "But not one we can risk either of you losing control in the middle of."

I glanced at their big guns again, gulped and looked out the window instead. We seemed to be flying northeast. San Diego was in precisely the opposite direction... I hoped that Diane was being honest with us about the short trip. I didn't know how much time we could afford to waste. Leo was fighting a losing battle against Death for his own body – and I was doing only a little better.

Still, it felt strangely good to be moving north. It was hard to describe the sensation, but it was like smelling the neighbor's barbecue when you're hungry. I desperately wanted to go toward it. Quickly.

That's you, Uriel, isn't it? I asked. *We're getting closer to the other angels. That's what I'm feeling now.*

Yes. I sense my brethren drawing nearer.

Diane's not taking us to them or anything, is she? I asked.

No, I do not think so, Uriel answered. *The others are still some distance away. You have not made it easy for them to find us.*

"Hey, can you SPOT guys track the horsemen and angels?" I shouted at Diane.

My voice screamed back through the headphones, making both Leo and Diane wince. I flushed, cleared my throat and then adjusted the angle of my headset's microphone self-consciously.

Apparently they were designed to let us talk without screaming like groupies at a heavy metal concert.

Good to know.

"Uh... sorry," I said in a more normal voice. "First time. But can you? Do you know how to track the angels and horsemen?"

"Not with instruments or sensors, if that's what you mean," Diane answered. "We watch the tabloids and social media, for the most part. People who report seeing angels or the devil. That sort of thing. We monitor police channels, too. But it's imprecise, to say the least."

"Have you encountered any of the others?" Leo asked.

Diane leaned forward, drumming her fingers on one knee. "Yes. We've had encounters with the chaotic entity you would call Famine, and the angels Raphael and Gabriel."

"Were any of them... like us?" I asked.

"No," Diane answered. "I'm afraid not. Each of the entities were fully manifested. Whoever their vessels used to be, they're only shells now."

What happened to those people? The other... vessels? I asked.

They gave themselves over to us, like Gabriel's host, Uriel said. *Or they were taken, like Pestilence. As Death will eventually take Leo.*

Uriel, those were human beings, I protested. *People that you all just... erased. And you want to do that to me?*

The final battle must *be fought. It was decided at the dawn of your universe.*

"How did those encounters go?" I asked Diane.

I remembered Gabriel at the Arrow motel and could guess the answer. Diane drummed her fingers faster on her knee and shook her head.

"We managed to slow Famine and Gabriel," she said. "But weren't able to stop any of them. Highway 13 will need miles of road work and East Fork, Montana, won't be appearing on any more maps. Which is part of why we're desperate to talk to you."

Mortals are unequal to the task of fighting us, Uriel said.

I squinted at the SPOT director. "You're a priest. Shouldn't you be on the angels' side? Not trying to fight them?"

"It's more complicated than that," Diane said. "There's no true good or evil in this, so let's say that I am on the side of life."

"Did you ever run into that Pestilence asshole?" Leo asked.

"We attempted to isolate Pestilence on Highway 44," Diane said. "While it was chasing you, in fact. But when we closed in, Pestilence charged the line and broke through. Rather easily, I'm sorry to say."

Leo frowned. "What about War?"

"Alarmingly quiet, actually," Diane told him. "We don't know why, but we've barely heard anything from the final horseman."

"But it's out there, isn't it?" I asked.

Diane nodded. "All eight entities have manifested on Earth."

I wanted to lean against Leo's jacket shoulder and bury my face in the leather, but this wasn't exactly the time or place for comfort. This was the time and place to... I had no idea, actually.

When I dreamed of running away from Crayhill, I used to imagine exploring New York or Los Angeles. Maybe leaving the States entirely and heading for Paris or Prague. Being coerced into a black helicopter by some kind of secret society had never occurred to me. My daydreams really should have included the possibility of alien abduction, the Rapture, or maybe a zombie virus outbreak. I resolved to be a little more creative next time. You know, if there *was* a next time.

The SPOT helicopter bumped and I couldn't stifle a shriek. Leo's hand tightened on mine. To reassure me, I figured. There was no way a big, tattooed criminal biker like Leo was scared of flying, right?

"We're just coming in to land," Diane said.

The helicopter descended over an arid, sloping mountainside studded with concrete bunkers. There was a massive tunnel cut into the stone and reinforced with more thick-looking gray concrete.

"Uh, where are we?" I asked.

"Blue Mountain," Diane answered. "It's a decommissioned military base we acquired about twenty years ago. I suppose that if we're SPOT, then this is the doghouse."

Diane arched her eyebrow over her glasses and smiled at us. I didn't laugh, though. Honestly, I had no idea what to make of Diane's friendly demeanor, but I hadn't for a second forgotten about the two armored soldiers sitting next to her. This wasn't some day trip with a sweet old auntie, no matter how nice Diane appeared to be.

I do not trust aunts and uncles, Uriel said. *This one or Uncle Carlos.*

Diane isn't really my aunt, I told the angel. *But yeah, I don't trust this lady. Her people tried to shoot us... But I need to find out how to end this.*

In glorious battle.

Some other *way,* I corrected. *Some way that doesn't get me shot by Spotters or torn apart by horsemen.*

Uriel didn't seem to have an answer for that. The helicopter landed with a bone-jarring thump. Diane removed her headset, so Leo and I did the same and then followed her out as another dark-clad Spotter pulled open the door. Diane waved to us as she jogged away, hunched over with her neat gray jacket whipping in the artificial windstorm. Riding motorcycles always did a number on my hair anyway, so I didn't care about the wind... But I ran doubled over, too, unable to escape the utterly irrational fear of the helicopter rotor chopping my head off.

Diane's two Spotter guards tailed us, weapons lowered but still pointed in our general direction. When we were far enough away, the helicopter lifted off again, probably flying to wherever it was stored when it wasn't ferrying possessed weirdos around.

Diane straightened up and smoothed out her windblown gray hair.

"This way," she told us.

Diane led us toward the concrete tunnel. Leo and I walked close together.

"Where's my motorcycle?" he asked.

"On its way," Diane said.

She glanced back at one of the armored goons following us. He spoke briefly into a radio, then nodded.

"The convoy is still forty minutes out," he said.

"Let me know as soon as it arrives," Diane told him.

"Yes, director."

There were a couple of dozen other people moving through the well-lit base and several of them approached us. They didn't salute, but at Diane's gesture, they all fell into step around us. Each of the Spotters was heavily armed and armored, just like the first guards.

We followed Diane through the concrete tunnel. It angled down into the mountainside and was wide enough for military trucks to drive through. The ceiling was inset with bright lights that cast sharp, dark shadows at our feet.

The tunnel ended abruptly in a pair of huge steel doors with NO ADMITTANCE painted across them in white block letters. Two SPOT soldiers stood at attention to either side.

Um... you could bust through these if we had to, right? I asked Uriel.

Yes, said the angel. *We created this universe. Stone and concrete mean nothing to our power.*

And steel? I asked. *Because that's a whole lot of steel.*

And steel. This mountain will not hold me when the time comes to fight.

That had to be the first time I ever found Uriel's hunger for battle comforting.

400 HORSEPOWER OF THE APOCALYPSE • 247

"Are you okay with this?" I asked Leo.

"No," he answered. "But we don't have much choice."

I took a deep breath and held out my hand. Leo stared for a moment, then took it. Uriel tensed at the contact, but I felt safer with Leo's fingers laced through mine. Diane glanced back at us and smiled a little. She did that a lot and I wondered if it was on purpose.

We were escorted through the huge steel doors. The tunnel continued deep down into the mountain, but now there were smaller concrete corridors and hallways branching off to either side. Diane and her growing soldier entourage led us down one gray hall and then another. They all looked the same and I quickly lost any sense of direction. I began counting the doors and turns in case we needed to make a run for it, but soon lost count and just had to hope that Uriel had a better memory than I did.

Finally, Diane reached a white-painted door and opened it. The room inside was an uninspired concrete cube with a round chipboard table in the center and a few chairs that looked like they had been looted from a hospital waiting area.

"Please, take a seat," Diane told us. "Can we get you something to drink? Coffee, maybe? It tastes terrible, but it does the job. I was going to put some money aside in next year's budget for a decent cappuccino machine, but coffee might not be our biggest concern by then."

"That sounds ominous," I said.

Leo shook his head. "Pass on the coffee. I don't trust you not to drug us."

That actually hadn't occurred to me. I sat down beside Leo and frowned at Diane.

"That would be a really bad idea, trust me," I told her.

"I'm trying to earn *your* trust," Diane said. "But that has the sound of a specific worry. What is it?"

I bit my lip and looked up at Leo. That wasn't really my information to share.

"If I fall asleep or go unconscious, I can't fight Death off," Leo said. "It takes over."

Diane whistled and pushed her glasses up her nose. Seven of the armed and armored Spotters had crammed into the room with us and they all shifted uncomfortably.

"How long has this been going on?" Diane asked.

"A few days," Leo answered.

"And you... haven't slept in that time?"

Leo nodded and rubbed at his eyes. Diane pulled out one of the chairs opposite us.

"Then maybe we can offer you something else," she said.

"Like what?" Leo asked.

"I have access to military-grade stimulants," Diane said. "The kind of thing they give to Special Forces soldiers when they need to be awake for long missions."

Leo sat suddenly forward in his seat. There was a desperate, hungry look on his face that made my stomach knot up. Addiction never entirely goes away, I guess. What Diane was offering wasn't heroin, but it might as well have been. Leo grabbed the edge of the table and the fake wood creaked under the pressure of his grip.

But then he slumped back into the chair and shook his head.

"No," Leo said. "I can't. No drugs."

Diane regarded him for a moment, then held out her hand to the soldiers. One of them took something from a pocket of their tactical vest and gave it to Diane. It was a slender vacuum-sealed cylinder about twice the size and length of my finger. The SPOT director adjusted her glasses and inspected the label, then set the package down on the tabletop. I could see a needle inside now, capped and wrapped safely in plastic.

"Think about it," Diane said.

"No," Leo answered.

"This stuff can keep a Navy Seal in full armor and gear on the move for seventy-two hours without rest."

Diane pushed the syringe toward Leo, who regarded it like a poisonous snake.

"Consider it a gesture of good will," Diane told him.

Reluctantly, Leo picked up the needle. He stuffed the drug quickly into a pocket of his jacket without looking at it.

"How about some answers instead?" I asked Diane.

She smoothed out the lapels of her blazer and sighed. "To be honest, I never thought I would be the one who had to do this. If the four archangels and the four horsemen appeared on Earth, I figured it would be in Rome – that this would all be Director Rossi's headache to deal with. But the apocalypse is happening in the American midwest."

"Answers," Leo reminded her.

"Of course," Diane said. "Let's start with the Society for the Protection and Observation of the Tellurian. Are you familiar with that last term?"

"Tellurian?" I asked. "Nope."

"It's an archaic word for Earth," Diane explained. "Because the Society was founded before its members had an accurate concept of the universe as we know it today. But now we stretch the definition to include all of physical reality, as far as we can comprehend it."

"Alright, got it," I said. "Let's keep it moving toward how you can help us, though."

Diane adjusted her glasses again. "The eight primary entities predate the universe. They have been called by a number of names throughout history and across the world. But I went to seminary, so I hope you don't mind if I call them *archangels* and *horsemen*, too."

"Knock yourself out," I said, then winced and glanced at Leo. "Uh... sorry. That was insensitive."

"Huh?" he asked, then gave me a weary smile. "Oh. It's fine, Jaz."

"This structure of the four archangels and the four horsemen is built into the very fabric of this universe," Diane went on. "There are four cardinal directions, four elements, four seasons, four fundamental forces, four noble truths and four Vedas. The tetragrammaton is the four-letter name of God and the Japanese word that means *four* sounds the same as the one for *death*. Four is the first non-prime number, and our DNA is made up of four nucleotides."

"But none of those are trying to make me strangle Jaz," Leo said. "Death is an asshole."

"Yes, perhaps," Diane agreed. "The angels and the horsemen aren't good or evil, though they've certainly been assigned all sorts of morality throughout the ages. They're not even light and darkness – the light to cast a shadow didn't exist before they set the universe in motion. It's more accurate to call the archangels forces of order, and the horsemen agents of chaos."

That all basically lined up with what Uriel had told me and what little I knew about Death.

"We know this part," I told Diane. "Uriel won't shut up about creating the universe as a battlefield for this end war they really, really want to go fight."

Diane's eyebrows shot up. "The angel... speaks to you?"

I scowled. "Yeah. Ever since Gabriel touched me."

"Fascinating," Diane said. "I wish we had the time to get into the details of that, but suffice it to say that in the universe they created, humans were the first sentient species to evolve the capacity to serve as vessels for the archangels and horsemen."

Did Diane just say the *first* sentient species? Was she talking about smart dolphins or... something else?

Yours is not the only inhabited planet in this universe, Uriel said. *But the species that live on those worlds were not suitable vessels.*

"Holy shit, there are aliens," I said.

Leo turned in his seat to stare at me, but Diane only nodded. Like she already knew there was life on other planets.

"The universe is vast," Diane agreed. "As are the entities that created it. There is a good reason that the God or gods of most faiths are immense, inscrutable beings far beyond the reach of humanity."

"The Greek gods were pretty human," Leo argued. "I knew a guy that might as well have been Zeus."

One of the Knights of Hell, probably. Which would explain why Leo was talking about him in the past tense. I wondered if Leo's friend had a thundering temper or just couldn't keep it in his pants. Diane laughed, but then shook her head.

"And yet the Olympian gods were successors to the Titans, a more elemental race of gods," she said. "Throughout the ages, scholars noticed the similarities between our myths and religions. At first, they came together in small groups to study these common threads. The original Society was based in Alexandria, but as the people of the world learned about each other, so did we. Now the Society has branches and factions located all across the globe."

"So how did a bunch of nerds end up with body armor and sniper rifles?" I asked.

"Because there's something else that most religious mythologies speak of," Diane said. "A final battle or catastrophe – the apocalypse, Ragnarök, the descent of Kalki, the inferno of the Seven Suns..."

I hadn't heard of the last two, but they sounded bad. Diane held up her hand, thumb and forefinger touching lightly.

"You've seen a fraction of what an archangel and a horseman can do," she said. "They will grow exponentially stronger as they come together. And when both sides are gathered for their war, it will destroy everything."

"Wait, what?" Leo asked. "The whole planet?"

Diane shook her head. "No. The entire universe."

The room spun and I almost fell out of my chair.

This lady is shitting us, right? I asked Uriel. *You're not trying to destroy the world, are you?*

There will be... collateral damage when the final battle is fought, the archangel admitted. *But this universe exists only because we required a material battlefield. It is a vessel for our war, as you are for me. Destruction was always the fate of creation.*

Leo looked at me with wide eyes.

"Shit," I said. "Shit!"

"The angel didn't tell you about that part, did they?" Diane asked, brow furrowed.

"No," I answered in a shaking voice.

"Frankly, I'm not surprised," Diane said. "Do we explain to the grass why we need to crush it when we walk? Or tell firewood why we need to burn it?"

"Death doesn't talk to me," Leo said. "I only get impressions. But it's not disagreeing with any of this, either. It doesn't give a shit what happens to anyone or anything else, as long as it gets to thrash the angels."

You should have told me, Uriel! I shouted. You know, inside my brain. *I thought you said we were kind of friends! But you lied... As long as you get your cage match, you're perfectly happy to trash the ring! You'll destroy the entire universe!*

This is my purpose, Uriel said. *And yours, Jaz.*

"I realize this is difficult to accept," Diane told us. "I've spent my entire adult life studying this and still struggle with it every day. But that's why the Society exists. We observe and study the tellurian, but we also hope to protect it."

"Shit," I hissed.

I doubled over with my head in my hands, fingertips digging into my scalp like I could rip Uriel out of my skull. If I could, I would have.

"Alright," I said. "Diane, you rambled something just then about protecting the world. What can we possibly do? You already tried to fight some of the other angels and horsemen with a whole army's worth of weapons."

"Those attacks went even more poorly than the one against you," Diane agreed. "But those forces were all fully manifested. You're not. The two of you are still in control of your minds and bodies. We believe that may well be the key to stopping this final battle before it begins."

"How?" Leo asked.

"Physical forms grant the archangels and horsemen a way to finally end their eternal war," Diane answered slowly. Whatever point she was warming up to, the director didn't like it. "With bodies, they can actually kill each other. And that's what we want to do."

I sat bolt upright in my seat and stared. "What?"

"You have to die," Diane said. "Before the war starts."

Leo jumped up to his feet and his hands closed into white-knuckled fists. The soldiers flanking the door raised their guns to aim at Leo, but he didn't even seem to notice. Diane's face went pale, but she didn't back away.

"We have doctors who can do it quickly and painlessly," the SPOT director said. "Death and Uriel are the leaders of their respective factions. With them gone, neither side can reach their full strength. That alone may be enough to save half the universe from being collateral damage in their final battle. And without the full eight, perhaps they can't fight at all."

I wanted to ask Uriel about that, but what the hell was the point? The archangel had already lied to me about their stupid, universe-shattering war.

I did not lie to you, Uriel said. *I... simply did not tell you what would happen to your world.*

I ignored the voice in my head and gulped, staring at Diane. Leo loomed over us both, fists clenched and shaking with barely suppressed rage.

"You... you really want to kill us?" I asked. "Both of us?"

"Yes," Diane answered. "Please. For the sake of the world and the entire universe."

"If you were just going to murder us, why didn't you just give your snipers the order back at the hotel?" Leo asked.

Diane pushed her glasses up her nose and rubbed her eyes. Her fingers came away wet.

"We're not monsters," Diane said. "At least, I hope we're not. We're trying to save as many lives as possible. But you two aren't monsters, either. You made that clear in Zamora Canyon, and you deserve the chance to make this sacrifice of your own free will."

"Holy shit," I whispered.

"This isn't a choice anyone should ever have to make," Diane said. "And I'm sorry we have to ask it. Would you like some time to consider?"

"Um... yeah," I answered.

Diane raised one hand and Leo tensed like a cat about to pounce, but the director just checked her watch.

"There's a little over four hours until dawn," she said. "After that, we need to act. You have until then to save us all. There isn't much time left."

Diane stood up slowly and left the room, followed by her soldiers. Leo and I stared at each other.

CHAPTER 22

I stood up and checked the little window set into the top of the door. There was a lot more gray concrete outside, but when I squinted off to either side, I could just make out black-clad shoulders and the stocks of large-caliber guns. Diane may have left us alone, but she didn't leave our prison unguarded. I turned to find Leo leaning against one of the cell walls, watching me.

"I hate this shit," he growled. "But we need to consider what Diane's offering."

I blinked. "What? You were about to punch her!"

"I don't want these people to kill *you*," Leo said. "But me... Maybe Death isn't actually evil, maybe it's just amoral or chaotic or whatever. But it's in my head and I do *not* like how it thinks."

And that was coming from a big biker gang road captain and career criminal. My eyes stung, but I forced down a breath to speak. Were we really considering suicide? Leo and I had literally been fighting off death since pretty much day one. But here we were.

"So we... let Diane's doctors kill us?" I asked.

"No," Leo answered.

"You're giving me some mixed messages here," I said with a shaky laugh.

Leo shut his bloodshot eyes for a moment and rubbed them, then looked at me again and offered up a fragile smile.

"That suit had a whole speech about how vital it is that this battle is fought four against four," Leo said. "Eight of them. Two of us don't need to die to fuck up that number. Just one."

I couldn't breathe. I grabbed Leo's arm, feeling his muscles bunched beneath the leather of his well-worn jacket.

"Leo..." I gasped.

"We let SPOT kill me."

I agree to this plan, Uriel said.

Shut up! I thought. *You don't get a vote!*

"No," I said aloud. "Not a chance! Besides, what good would it do? Uriel and the angels follow the rules – even when they shouldn't – but the horsemen don't give a shit. Death and Pestilence have already tried to kill me before the big fight! Without Death, that's still three horsemen against four archangels. How much of the world will survive that?"

"More than if Death fights, too," Leo answered.

"Fine," I said. "But by that token, more than if Uriel leads the angels into battle."

Leo's dark eyes narrowed. "No. I'm not letting you die, Jaz. I can't."

"Why the hell not?" I asked.

I released Leo's arm and threw my hands into the air. My head was weirdly light and my stomach twisted in painful knots. None of this felt real. I began pacing back and forth across our little concrete prison. Leo watched me with a pained look on his face.

"You're a good person, Jaz," he said at last. "You just wanted to see the world. You shouldn't have to die in some anonymous gray room."

"Neither should you!" I cried.

Leo intercepted my pacing. I moved to get around the biker, but he matched me step for step and remained right there in front of me.

"Look, I know what I am," Leo said. "I know the life I chose. You think I ever expected to die of old age? A bullet or lethal injection was pretty much always how this was going to end for me. And at least this way, I'll be dying *for* something."

I tried to push Leo back, but I may as well have been trying to shove a brick wall. I settled for kicking one of the chairs across the room.

"Hey, I'm every inch as dangerous as you are!" I said. "Uriel might be more of an uptight bitch, but they're perfectly willing to destroy the entire universe just to bloody Death's nose!"

That is not entirely– Uriel thought.

"Shut up!" I shouted at the angel in my head, then spun and pointed to Leo. "No. Either we both die here in this stupid base or neither of us do!"

Leo shook his head. "I already let my whole gang die, Jaz."

"You can't blame yourself for what Pestilence did!"

"Maybe," Leo answered quietly. Now it was his turn to put a hand on my shoulder. It was heavy and I felt the warmth of his touch through my shirt. "But I can't lose you too, Jaz."

"Then... then we need some other option," I said. "Anything! What about Carlos? We've been driving like hell to get to San Diego for a reason, right?"

Leo nodded. "My uncle said that he knew what was going on and that he knows what to do about it."

"What if it's the same solution as Diane's?" I asked. "Killing us to kill the things inside us?"

I didn't know how to answer my own question. I was lost, trapped, and totally fucked. Things have gotten pretty damned awful when being back home in Crayhill suddenly didn't sound so bad.

"I have no idea," Leo answered. "But Carlos saved me before. Maybe he can do it again."

At least he was talking about living, even if the hope in Leo's voice was paper-thin.

"Look, I hope so... but Diane and SPOT seem to know a lot about what's happening to us, and she didn't offer up any other solutions," I said, hating myself for the words. "Carlos might not have anything better. He may want to kill us, too."

Leo considered, but then he nodded. "If I'm going to die, I'd rather my uncle do it than SPOT."

"Then I guess we should tell Diane," I said. "But I don't think she'll be very happy about it."

I went to the door. It was locked, but when I knocked, one of our guards appeared at the window.

"We need to talk to Diane," I told him in a loud voice. "We've decided."

The armored man spoke briefly into a radio on his shoulder. I couldn't hear what he said, but only a minute later, Diane came hurrying down the hallway with her row of soldiers following like a line of deadly, heavily-armed ducklings. I stepped back as the lock on the door thunked and Diane came inside. The other Spotters remained out in the hall.

"Mister Valdis, your motorcycle has arrived at Blue Mountain," Diane said. "Intact and unmarked."

"Thanks," Leo answered.

Diane took a deep breath. "Now, Shen says that you've made your decision."

"Yeah, we have," I told her. "Sorry, but the answer is *no*. You made a really good point and we'll die if we have to... But we're not ready yet. There's still one more option for us in San Diego. We need to try."

Diane's brows shot up, but she sighed and glanced back at the armed and armored Spotters.

"I can't tell you how truly sorry I am to hear that," Diane said. "And even more sorry to say your answer is not one we can accept."

"Wait, what?" I gasped, heart sinking.

"We can't afford to release you, Jasmine. The other six are still out there, and the cost of letting you reunite with them is too high. Sacrifices must be made. I'm sorry."

"So you're just going to execute us?" I asked.

Diane's nod looked honestly pained, but I didn't really care. The southwestern SPOT director might not sleep well for the next few years, but at least she would be alive to do it. I should have guessed, though... Diane and her people had already tried to kill us before. Of course she wouldn't just let us walk away.

But Leo stepped between me and Diane, shaking his head.

"Alright. You don't need to kill Jaz," he said. "You only have to mess up the numbers for the final apocalyptic battle, right? So you can have me."

"Damn it, Leo!" I shouted. "No! We talked about this. I'm not letting them kill you!"

"Trust me," Leo said. He held out his hand to Diane. "Do we have a deal? You get me, and Jaz can leave?"

The SPOT director looked at Leo's extended hand, sighed and pushed her glasses up her nose.

"That's noble of you, Mister Valdis," Diane told him. "And I wish I could accept your sacrifice in lieu of Miss O'Neil... But I'm afraid that the combined power of the archangels is just as destructive as that of the horsemen. We require both of you."

"Well, I tried," Leo said. "Sorry."

But he didn't lower his hand. Diane regarded it again, then reluctantly took it. Leo smiled grimly as he closed his fingers around hers. The big biker yanked Diane's hand, spinning her and pulling her arm up behind her back. Diane yelped and shot up onto the tips of her toes.

Before I could blink, Leo had pulled his gun, flicked off the safety, and jammed the muzzle against Diane's temple. The door burst open and all eight of the SPOT soldiers ran into the room with assault weapons leveled at us.

"Release Director Owens!" one of them shouted.

Leo nodded and kept his gun on Diane.

"I will," he said. "Once Jaz and I are safely out of here."

CHAPTER 23

The little concrete room was full of shouting voices and staticky radio chatter as the SPOT soldiers called... everybody, as far as I could tell. The close air smelled of sweat and gunpowder. Inside me, Uriel tensed like a snake ready to strike.

What is happening? the archangel asked.

I had no idea. I threw my hands into the air, but every single eye and gun was trained on Leo. I didn't know what I wanted to happen here, but I was pretty sure a hostage situation and an awful lot of big guns pointed my direction wasn't it.

"You're going to lead us out of this maze," Leo told Diane. "Then Jaz and I will climb onto my motorcycle and leave. After that, we're done."

"You're fighting the wrong people, Mister Valdis," Diane said. Her voice was tight with pain, but otherwise way calmer than I would be. "We're all on the same side here."

"Maybe," Leo agreed. "But you're not God, lady. You don't get to decide who lives and dies."

He shoved Diane toward the door. The Spotters parted reluctantly and kept their assault rifles pointed at him. I jogged after Leo, wondering what the hell to do.

"You know what Death will do if it ever gains control over you," Diane said as Leo propelled her down the concrete hallway. "The strain of holding the horseman at bay is obvious. How much longer can you keep this up?"

Leo narrowed his dark, bloodshot eyes at her. "We still have options."

"Your uncle, Carlos Medina?" Diane asked. "We intercepted your communications with him, if you recall. But what in his extensive criminal history – on both sides of the border – makes you think that he can help you?"

"I don't know," Leo answered. "But we're going to find out. Which way?"

We came to an intersection of gray halls and Diane pointed to the left. The stark concrete corridor didn't look familiar, but that didn't mean anything. I was completely lost – in every sense of the word.

Leo pushed Diane down the hallway she had indicated. Her soldiers fell back a little, but not nearly far enough. They crept after us warily, keeping us in their gun sights. I could still feel their weapons aimed at our backs and their boots drummed out the same panicked, galloping beat as my heart.

"Jasmine, is this what you really want to do?" Diane asked.

She tried to look back at me, but Leo pressed his gun into her temple, forcing the SPOT director to keep staring straight ahead. I swallowed hard.

"No," I said. "I don't know what I want anymore. But I don't want to die."

"And you're not going to," Leo told me.

"How many other people need to die?" Diane asked. "What we're asking seems unfair... and it is. I know that. But you can't run away from the angels and horsemen forever. When they find you, Jasmine, your life is over. Uriel will be all that's left. And they will break the world in half to get at Death."

"Maybe Carlos can help us," I said in a shaking voice.

We came to a wide set of metal-shod double doors, but they weren't the big steel ones that led out of the mountain base. Leo kicked them open and we hurried through into some sort of cafeteria. It was full of tables – enough to seat perhaps two hundred people – but they appeared to have been emptied in a hurry. That must have been what all the radio chatter was about. There was still food and steaming mugs sitting on the tables. I guess the coffee wasn't *that* bad...

A squadron of SPOT soldiers was waiting for us in the cafeteria. They had shoved several tables out of the way and held assault rifles at the ready. I squeaked as the doors banged open behind us and Diane's original guards ran through. They fanned out, surrounding us, and Leo jerked to a stop in the middle of the huge room.

"You led us into a trap," he said.

"Yes, I'm afraid I did," Diane agreed. "Mister Valdis, did you really think that I would ask you to sacrifice your lives and not be willing to do the same?"

Oh shit.

"Open fire," Diane ordered.

Her soldiers didn't hesitate. They fired, but Leo was already moving. He shoved Diane down to the floor and threw himself at me. Gunshots boomed and I fell with Leo's arm around my waist. I was too shocked and scared to even scream. There were bullets everywhere, slamming exploding craters into the concrete and blasting holes through the tables.

My ears rang, and I smelled smoke and cordite; each breath choked me with the stench. Leo lay on the ground, one arm over me and blood pooling beneath him. It spread across the cold gray floor, seeping into the cracks and following their lightning-bolt paths in every direction.

"Leo!" I screamed.

I grabbed Leo and rolled him onto his back, but he didn't move. There was a spray of holes across his chest, all ringed in liquid red. Leo was unconscious and bleeding out. Quickly.

"Please, help him!" I cried.

One of the Spotters was heaving Diane to her feet. Blood ran down her sleeve from a wound in her shoulder. The rest of the SPOT soldiers held their guns ready and moved forward slowly, closing in around me. Laser sights cut glowing scarlet through the swirling gunsmoke, angling for a clear shot at me over Leo's body.

"I'm so sorry it had to come to this, Jasmine," Diane said. She looked up at her soldiers. "Shoot her."

The wall behind Diane exploded inward, hurling concrete and twisted rebar through the dining hall. Leo's motorcycle shot through the rubble toward its master like a missile, bowling over tables and SPOT soldiers without even slowing down.

But that thing wasn't Leo's Packmaster anymore. The motorcycle had... changed. It was beyond custom now. Death's steed was bigger than any bike I had ever seen, as predatory and sleek as a panther. It trailed dark smoke and the headlight shone red like the caldera of a volcano.

Shouting, the soldiers spun to face the new threat. They fired through the smoke and dust, bullets pinging off the motorcycle's perfect obsidian finish. The engine revved, sounding more than ever like a roaring dragon, and the chrome casing shifted. Long chains lashed out from the bike in clanking, clattering whips.

It was Arrow Lodge all over again... but worse. The Spotters' shouts turned into screams.

"Holy shit," I whimpered. I pulled at one of Leo's arms, but he didn't move. "Shit! Come on, please wake up! Leo, we have to go!"

I had no idea how to get away now that Leo's motorcycle had turned into Satan's moped. But I knew that we had to escape.

I tried to heave Leo up again, but the biker was twice my size and the downside of all that well-sculpted muscle was that I could hardly budge him when I needed to.

A soldier ran through the thrashing chaos toward me, still bent on carrying out Diane's original order. He aimed a big automatic rifle at me, but the motorcycle's engine roared and it burst from the swirling smoke. It slammed into the Spotter, spun on one oversized black tire and then raced off across the dining hall once more, billowing black shadows in its wake.

The soldier's body hit the ground next to me, shattered and broken. Not just broken, *ruptured*. What had once been a man was now literal roadkill with the demon-bike's tire tracks cutting through half-burned meat. I screamed and clapped my hands over my mouth.

Leo moved. His fingers curled into claws and raked through the spreading halo of blood to clutch at his chest. His fingertips gleamed strangely in the smoky light, like they had been dipped in something. Blood...? No, Leo's hand had turned to metal. His chrome fingers convulsed, grabbing a handful of leathers with metal claws.

"Jaz," Leo said. "Jaz, I need..."

His voice was a deep, echoing boom and his eyes snapped open, but they were no longer bloodshot. Leo's eyes weren't even there... A pair of empty black sockets stared up at me from his pale face.

No. No more. I couldn't do this.

I hit my limit for terrifying and violent supernatural bullshit. The animal part of my brain took one look at that meat-pile that used to be a human being and Death's hollow eyes, and it threw in the towel.

I ran away. I jumped to my feet and over a tumbled table, then scrambled through the hole in the concrete wall. My sleeve caught on broken rebar and I shrieked as I ripped my way free.

The smashed hole let out into the main tunnel and up ahead were the tortured and twisted remains of the huge steel doors. Death's steed had torn right through them like paper.

But I couldn't help myself – I looked back once through the shattered wall. Leo was on his hands and knees in a pool of his own blood as a cloak of darkness spread from his convulsing shoulders. He grabbed at the front of his black leather jacket like a man trying to tear out his own heart.

Chains and seething shadows lashed, tearing apart anything that moved in the ruined dining hall. I turned away and ran as fast as I could.

CHAPTER 24

The night had turned into a cold, cloudy morning by the time I stumbled down off of Blue Mountain. My legs were sore and my feet hurt, but Leo's demonic Packmaster had destroyed all the black SPOT vans. Even if I knew where the helicopter was, I couldn't fly it. My Bonneville was long gone, and I was all on my own.

So I ran and staggered as best I could through the dim dawn light. The mountainside was treacherously rocky and covered with scrubby, thorny bushes that tore at my ankles. I tripped over a stone I couldn't see and fell, ripping out the knee of my jeans and scraping a shallow, bloody wound into the skin underneath. But I heaved myself up again and kept running toward the rising sun.

Jaz, stop, Uriel said.

I ignored the voice in my head. I was done. Done with archangels and horsemen and secret cabals and even motorcycles. I was going back home to Crayhill.

You don't want to go home, Uriel said.

Or maybe it was me.

I didn't care anymore.

I kicked my way through a rusted and half-tumbled down barbed-wire fence, then stumbled out onto the litter-strewn gravel shoulder of an empty country road. A single cracked lane stretched in either direction and I didn't see any cars, but it was something normal. Human.

The dusty little road ran roughly north and south, so I chose south and began walking. There were blisters in my filthy shoes that already felt the size of softballs, but I had to get away from Blue Mountain. A column of black smoke rose from the slope, back in the direction of the SPOT base. The work of Death and its steed... I squeezed my eyes shut against tears and limped onward, following the road south.

The sound of tires on asphalt made me jump, but it was just a battered pickup truck. My pounding heart leapt into my throat and by the time I thought to stick out my thumb for a lift, the truck had passed and was vanishing swiftly down the narrow road. I sighed and wiped my cheeks. The tears and concrete dust turned into pale gray mud smears on my skin.

I kept walking. My knee throbbed and by midmorning, the clouds had all burned off. The sun was an angry red orb glowing high up over the smoking mountain peak. I found an aluminum sign pocked with birdshot lying face-down next to the road and kicked it over.

Kamin

3 miles

A few more cars and pickup trucks passed me. I held my thumb out, but none of them stopped. I was too tired to switch to my middle finger. And anyway, I couldn't really blame them. I wouldn't have picked me up, either. I was obviously trouble.

I had no idea what time it was when I spotted Kamin floating above the mirage shimmer on the road. It was a tiny little town, about the same size as Crayhill. I limped up to a filling station and was pretty sure I saw one of the cars that had passed me on the way in.

The station's sliding glass doors opened at my approach. At least *they* didn't give a shit about how tired and bedraggled I looked. After a long morning of hiking through the heat, it was shockingly cold inside the convenience store. I wiped sweat and ash off my face with the back of one hand.

I ignored a startled, wide-eyed look from the man behind the cash register and grabbed a map out of a wire rack sitting on the counter. I unfolded it across a freezer half-full of ice cream and searched until I found Kamin tucked down into one corner of the page.

I was still in Arizona, although Diane had brought us north through the state. I wasn't far from the Grand Canyon, actually... but I folded the map up again and picked a bus schedule out of another rack. None of the routes leaving Kamin went all the way back to Crayhill, or even to Kansas. But there was a bus heading east to Holbrook. From there, it looked like I could change buses and make it as far as Oklahoma City.

It was a start.

I checked my torn jeans and was shocked to find my wallet tucked into the pocket. There were still a few of the hundred-dollar bills that Leo had given me inside. Was it just me or was Ben Franklin smirking? I didn't want to hear '*I told you so*' from my money any more than an angel, so I closed my wallet and stuffed it into my pocket again.

I felt the attendant's eyes on me as I stalked to a row of glass-fronted refrigerated cases along the rear of the store, but I just pulled out two bottles of water. I hesitated before grabbing a big can of beer, too.

Leo was dead or worse... I didn't need to stay sober for him anymore.

I selected some trail mix, too, and a little plastic bag of cheap hair ties, then carried everything to the front counter. The clerk dutifully began ringing me up.

"Where's the bus station?" I asked.

The man behind the counter blinked and stared like I had asked him how to get to the moon. I could only imagine how I looked to him.

"Umm... go two blocks down Pickard Street," he answered at last, pointing out the window at what I assumed was Pickard Street. "Then make a left on Tiber."

"That's it?" I asked.

The attendant shrugged. "It's not a very big town."

He returned to scanning my purchases. There was a spinning rack of sunglasses and phone accessories, but no actual cell phones. I briefly considered asking if there was an electronics store in Kamin, but I was pretty sure that the answer would be a blank stare. Besides, Diane told us she was director of the southwest SPOT division and the Society was everywhere, all over the world.

Even if Death leveled Blue Mountain, it was probably best to stay off the phone. I could call my parents from a pay phone once I got to Oklahoma City.

I would have given every dollar left in my wallet just to hear their voices...

I wiped at my eyes as I paid for my drinks and snacks, then asked if there was a washroom that I could use. The clerk sent me around behind the filling station. The bathroom was small and the single-ply toilet paper was practically sandpaper, but the sink worked and I could finally wash off the dust, sweat and tears.

Sniffling and blinking, I regarded myself in the mirror. My hair was a hopeless tangle and picking my fingers through the riot of curls only helped a little. I pulled out the bag of hair ties and snapped two of them before at last managing a fluffy black ponytail.

Good enough. At least it was out of my face. I limped from the washroom and made my way down Pickard Street in the direction that the filling station clerk had pointed. My knee was throbbing and the sun beat against the back of my neck, but I gulped down one of the waters as I walked.

I turned left at a dusty intersection and found the Kamin bus station. There was another man behind the counter of the ticket kiosk, but he didn't look twice as I bought a ticket to Holbrook. Kind of made me wonder what sorts of people came through here, but I didn't have the energy to care very much.

There was still another hour or so until my bus arrived, so I flopped down onto a bench in the hot gray shade and skipped the second bottle of water to go straight for the beer. I drank about half of it before pausing for breath, then alternated long sips and holding the cold can against my swollen knee.

Jaz, this is not helping, Uriel said.

I squeezed my eyes shut and finished the beer. Screw my knee. I needed to numb my brain even more. But all I could see in the darkness were Death's empty sockets staring up at me from Leo's face. I opened my eyes again and wondered if I could go buy another beer before the bus arrived.

A news van with brightly-colored logos – not one of SPOT's blank black vehicles – raced past the bus station, moving north. Toward Blue Mountain? Five minutes later, a second and third van followed behind. They were driving fast.

But even at full speed, those reporters were pretty late to the show... I couldn't see smoke coming from the mountain any-more. Had some other division of SPOT kept the press away until it made sure the base was safe?

Or was Death still up there? Cold sweat ran down the back of my neck.

I suddenly remembered the news story the morning after Arrow Lodge, about the exploding gas main. Our server at the diner said it was a government cover-up... I never realized just how close to the truth she had been. That gas explosion story must have been the one SPOT put forward, something palatable to the citizens of a world that knew nothing about the angels and horsemen coming to destroy them all.

What would the story be this time? Another gas line blowing up? Or maybe something bigger, like a missile going off... The Society's southwest hideout was an old military base, after all. I would have bought it.

I wondered if any of the tabloids would hit the mark. Diane said that they sometimes managed little bits of esoteric truth. So what would the headlines look like tomorrow? *Satan appears in Arizona and destroys a secret military base!*

Return of Bat Boy, page 9.

I didn't laugh, though. Instead, I chugged the rest of my beer and wondered how many more I could drink before the bus came. But my knee hurt, and I had no desire to miss my ride out of this nightmare while I was off staggering across Kamin.

The bus arrived about half an hour later, just as the thin beer buzz was fading. I climbed in, dropped my ticket into the box next to the driver and then limped to the first empty window seat. Uriel might have been able to heal all of my bumps and bruises, but I didn't want the angel's help right now.

Or ever.

The bus was only about a quarter full, but I was the only passenger to board in Kamin, so the doors closed with a hiss and the driver pulled out onto the road. I leaned against the window and watched the little town vanish swiftly into the distance. The sun was beginning to dip toward the western horizon behind us, but it was still too warm for the air conditioner to compete with and everyone on the bus remained sullenly silent and sweaty.

Within twenty minutes, we were on the open road: Highway 44, heading east. The bus drove through the hot, dusty afternoon, quiet and uncomfortable and boring. Which was exactly what I wanted.

No, it is not, Uriel said.

I'm not talking to you, I thought. *Ever again.*

Then listen.

I rolled my eyes at my reflection in the window. Even after all this time, the archangel was still so damned literal.

You have fought for control of your body, Jaz, Uriel told me. *And fought your enemies at every turn. You have stood your ground, even when it was unwise to do so.*

Well, I'm done with that. I just want to go home. I never should have left in the first place.

Why? Uriel asked. *You fought your whole life to leave Crayhill.*

Because I'm tired and I'm scared, I thought. *Because if I never left, I would be safe back home!*

I stared out of the bus window at the red-banded rocks of northern Arizona as they flashed past. There were more signs for the Grand Canyon, advertising hikes and river rafting excursions. A dirty blue minivan weighed down with a roof rack full of luggage passed us going the other way. I caught just a flash of excited faces inside, and one of the kids pointing at the billboard as he bounced in his seat.

What the hell do you care about me seeing the world, anyway? I asked. *If you get your way, you'll destroy the entire universe!*

I am... sorry, Uriel said. *I did not intend to deceive you, Jaz. I simply did not consider it important.*

I sighed against the window. *Yeah, I know. And that's what scares the shit out of me.*

You have been frightened since the moment I chose you as my vessel, Uriel told me. *But that has never stopped you. And it will not stop you now.*

Stop me from what? I asked.

From fighting me, the angel answered. *From fighting Death to save Leo.*

I shut my eyes and pressed my cheek against the glass of the bus window, shutting out the sights of colorful signs and rocks outside.

I can't, I thought. Even closed, my eyes hurt. *I can't save Leo. Leo's dead. Or he* is *Death...*

The horseman's unbridled demonic chrome steed had rampaged through Blue Mountain, killing an entire room full of trained and well-armed soldiers. How much worse would Death itself be?

He said your name, Uriel reminded me. *Leo spoke with Death's voice, but he spoke to you...*

I rubbed at my eyes, pressing my fingertips against the lids until colors exploded across my vision, but I still heard my name echoing in Death's hollow voice.

Stop dredging up my memories! I told Uriel.

These thoughts are not my doing, Jaz.

I didn't want to believe the archangel, but Uriel hadn't actually lied to me during all of this. Failed to tell me some damned important stuff, yes, but... Death had plenty of time to kick my ass while its steed tore apart the SPOT base. Why had it left me alive? Was Leo still somewhere behind that terrible, blank black stare? What did that matter now? Even if Leo had managed to maintain control, how long could that possibly last?

You are strong, Jaz, Uriel said. *Stronger than I ever would have believed. And Leo may be that strong, too.*

But not alone. Leo couldn't do it without the Knights of Hell, and not without Carlos.

Not without me.

I could run all the way home to Crayhill, but never escape that truth. Leo needed me...

What War told Pestilence was true. Leo couldn't be strong alone. Not for himself... But for his gang, his friends and his family, Leo was made of something sterner than steel.

But what the hell did I owe him? Ever since Leo Valdis drove into my life on the back of a demon-bike, I had been on the run. I had been shot at and possessed by an angel, nearly thrown off a motorcycle at over a hundred miles an hour and literally faced Death every day. I had never been so scared in my life.

Or excited. Leo and I had been together for one week, but I had seen more in that handful of days than all the years before. Sure, a lot of what I had experienced was horrible... But there had been wonders, too. Angels and moonlit forests, new cities and hot shirtless bikers. And that was only the beginning of what freedom had to offer.

What if I didn't go home to Crayhill? The bus would take me to Holbrook, but from there, I could go anywhere. Denver, New York... Or leave the country entirely and head for Paris or Hong Kong. But wherever I went, I would be on my own.

You are never alone, Uriel said. *Not as long as I am within you.*

Okay, not alone. But all Uriel knew was strife and battle, and I wanted so much more. And I wanted to share it with Leo.

If Leo was still Leo... Could he actually be alive and fighting Death even now? I couldn't begin to imagine how, but I would never know for certain unless I found him again. I jumped to my feet, bashing my head into the low bus ceiling, and an old white man sitting behind me frowned over his newspaper.

"Are you alright there, miss?" he asked.

"Stop the bus!" I said.

Holy shit, I was actually doing this. My stomach twisted into a knot, but the man with the newspaper blinked as I stepped out into the center aisle of the bus and stalked up to the front.

"Hey, stop the bus!" I shouted.

"This ain't a stop," the driver told me. "Sit down!"

"No, this is the spot where I kick your ass if you don't let me off," I said. "Just pull over!"

"We're in the middle of nowhere, missy."

"Do I look like I care?" I asked. I grabbed my wallet. "I'll give you a hundred dollars to stop and open the door."

The driver looked skeptical, but I took one of the bills out of my wallet and threw it into his lap. His eyes widened, then the other passengers groaned and complained listlessly as the bus slowed to a stop next to the highway. I hovered over the driver's shoulder until he pulled the lever to open the accordion bus doors.

"Thanks," I said.

I raced down the steps and landed in the dusty gravel. The door slammed shut behind me and the big black tires spun, kicking up dirt, and then the bus pulled back onto Highway 44.

I turned the other direction – west, toward California and San Diego. If Death was done gutting the SPOT base and there was anything of Leo inside that monster, then that's where he would be going. I didn't have much money left now and my motorcycle was twisted scrap in a junkyard somewhere, but I had two thumbs and a nice ass. I could hitchhike my way to the coast if it came down to that. It was getting late in the afternoon and most of the tourists would be stopping for dinner and a hotel room soon, but truckers worked all hours and I hoped that one of them would be lonely for some company.

And if nobody stopped, I would walk. At least my knee didn't hurt anymore, but I doubted that was the effect of the beer – either the cold or the alcohol. My jeans were still ripped out, but the skin beneath was smooth and unblemished brown. No more scrapes or swelling, or even a scab.

Thanks, Uriel, I thought.

Something behind me wheezed and then rattled. I glanced over my shoulder and frowned. The bus had crested the next low hill, but now it was rolling to a stuttering stop. The engine guttered and a single puff of black smoke oozed from the tail-pipe, then nothing. Was the bus out of gas?

I squinted through the failing daylight as the driver climbed out and circled the bus, head lowered to inspect it. He seemed to be swearing and aimed a suspicious look back my direction. I shrugged, but doubted the driver could see at this distance. Hey, he got his hundred bucks.

The sound of another motor rumbled across the rocky hills, something a lot more robust than the handful of family cars that had passed me up. That might be my lonely trucker, so I turned and held out my thumb.

No, Jaz! Uriel shouted.

The archangel's voice was so loud inside my skull that I had an instant migraine.

What's the problem? I asked. *I thought you were actually with me on this!*

A shape crested the hill, parting the watery heat shimmer with a single outthrust tire. It wasn't a truck.

It was a motorcycle, a stripped down and skeletal chopper riding low on its suspension. The finish was a flat matte black that didn't reflect any of the fading sunlight. The rider was tall and feminine, but achingly thin – little more than a skeleton wrapped in dark leathers.

Uriel... what's that? I asked.

It's Famine!

CHAPTER 25

So that sick feeling in the pit of my stomach wasn't just fear – it was the sensation of an encroaching horseman. But there was still plenty of fear as Famine's stripped-down black chopper raced down Highway 44 toward me, and I didn't sense the electric fire of angelic backup this time.

I staggered a step back. Running or flying the hell away from here sounded like a great idea, but the bus was still stalled on the top of the hill, out of gas.

That is Famine's doing, Uriel said.

What's going to happen to those people when Famine gets here? I asked.

Nothing good.

The archangels might not have cared what happened to the Earth and its people, but I did.

I'm done running, I said. *How do you feel about kicking some ass?*

Uriel skimmed quickly through my thoughts to make sense of my words.

In single combat against Famine and without my full manifestation of power, you cannot win, Uriel said. *And killing a horseman alone, before we are gathered for the final battle, is against the laws of our creation… But I believe that we can lead Famine away from the humans.*

How? I asked.

I couldn't outrun a motorcycle – not even a normal one, to say nothing of a horseman's demonic steed. Famine raced down the double yellow line of the road at me. The matte black paint job seemed to devour the slowly fading sunlight.

I recommend flight, Uriel said. *Both literally and figuratively.*

I stepped out into the highway and held up my hand, middle finger raised.

"Hey Famine!" I shouted. "Over here! I'm the one you want!"

The gaunt horseman leaned over the stretched-out handlebars of its chopper and pale eyes glared at me from its deep-set, sunken sockets.

You have its attention, Uriel said. *Get ready!*

Light blazed around me and formed into a pair of luminous wings that spread out from my shoulders. My feet floated up off the asphalt and my cramping stomach shot into my throat. I remembered the lurching, buffeting flight of the helicopter and wasn't excited about this plan.

Your mortal machines are no match for an angel's wings, Uriel said. *Now fly, Jaz!*

Behind me, the bus driver shouted something that sounded like more cursing, but the words came out so fast that they all ran together. A cold, sharp wind whipped out along Highway 44 as Famine closed in.

I didn't know how to drive a pair of wings any better than a helicopter, but my angelic passenger had an eternity of practice. Uriel was a powerful, looming presence inside me and for the first time since all of this began, I was grateful.

My glowing wings beat once and I shot up into the air like a fired arrow. I had the sudden but distinct impression that aerodynamics, Newtonian physics and other such trivialities didn't matter much to an angel in flight. I was terrified to look down, but I had to lead Famine away from the bus, or innocent people were going to get hurt.

I forced my eyes open and found the bony black shape of Famine's steed fifty feet below. The horseman turned its skeletal face up toward me and bone-white eyes gleamed malevolently in its sockets.

Go! Uriel cried.

With a thought, I shot out in the opposite direction along the dark ribbon of Highway 44. The lean chopper revved, growling like an empty stomach as Famine pulled it around in a tight turn and raced after me. Greasy black smoke billowed from the tailpipe and smelled like burnt meat.

I banked along a curve of Highway 44, blasting over a convertible with its top down. A middle-aged driver gaped as I flew overhead, but then her engine guttered and died. The sports car swerved off across the shoulder of the highway and Famine shot past. The convertible's driver grabbed her midsection and then doubled over, gasping.

We've got to get that thing away from people, I thought. *Let's go off road!*

I tipped one shoulder and my glowing wings dipped me into a precipitous swoop. The ground below me changed from black asphalt to cracked earth and jumbled red-brown stones. It was the kind of rough terrain that dirt bikes were made for, not low-riding cruisers like Famine's motorcycle.

Let's see a chopper handle this!

Famine raced right after me, off the highway and across the desert. The chopper's out-thrust front wheel plowed through the rocks, blowing them apart into sand and cutting a deep, dark line through the dry ground.

Okay, I didn't *actually* want to see the motorcycle handle the sudden off-roading. It was just an expression...! But the demon-bike was making short work of the miles between us and gaining quickly on me.

Nothing can outrun a horseman on its steed, Uriel reminded me.

Which had been great news when I was the one on the back of Leo's Packmaster and making Spotters and angels alike eat our dust. But what was I supposed to do now?

We cannot battle a fully manifested horseman, Uriel said. Good thing the angel lived inside my skull, or I never would have been able to hear them over the wind screaming in my ears. *Not unless you give up your body to me.*

Not a chance, Uriel, I thought. But I had another idea. *You told me once that the horsemen invest a lot of their power into their steeds, right?*

Yes, Uriel answered.

Then Famine should be weaker if we can get it off that chopper, I said.

Yes!

I shared the archangel's white-hot rush of joy at my idea and something sweet like hope. My luminous white wings spread wider and I pulled up into a steep and sudden rise. The ground fell away dizzyingly below me until even the biggest red-brown boulders became pebbles casting long sunset shadows across the desert floor. Famine was a blade of black metal at the head of a billowing cloud of dust.

Have we lost our minds? I asked Uriel.

Perhaps, the angel answered. *But if we can dismount the horseman and keep it from its steed, it may flee the battlefield. Famine was never as brave as Death or War.*

"Then let's do this," I said.

Famine closed the gap between us all too quickly, tearing through a stand of joshua trees. They twisted and shriveled as the chopper roared past, and then one of the desiccated trees exploded into splinters when Famine slammed right through in a full-throttle charge after me.

Icy wind howled in my ears. I angled myself, then folded my glowing wings and dove at Famine from one side, screaming in absolute terror the whole way. The ground hurtled toward me and I had nightmare visions of being splattered into a smear of red across the rocks, but I spread my angelic wings and pulled up suddenly. Famine reached out for me with ragged fingernails that I would have bet could rip through solid steel. I shouted and kicked frantically, then slammed full-force into the emaciated horseman.

The speed of my sudden dive and the power of Uriel's luminous wings lifted Famine out of its seat, into the air. But I moved with it, grabbing a double handful of decaying biker leathers. I beat my wings and we sailed together over a rust-colored ridge. Famine hissed like a huge, hungry cat in my grip and pounded one bony fist into my face with the force of a freight train. The blow glanced off Uriel's glowing aura, but the pain still made my eyes water.

We hit the ground on the other side of the hill hard enough to make the earth shudder and throw up a miniature mushroom cloud of dust. Famine lashed out at me with one stick-thin leg and kicked me off. I flew up and around in a barely-controlled arc, but the horseman's kick didn't land as hard as the punch had. I whirled and picked out the distant shadowy plume of the riderless chopper cutting its way across the desert.

I leapt back into the air, beating my wings to get some altitude, but even without its steed, Famine was still eerily fast. The skeletal horseman pounced at me, raking its jagged nails down my back and drawing star-bright sparks off my angelic aura. We hit the ground together like a boulder dropped from high orbit and the shock shivered up my spine, but I remained on my feet – in the center of a sandy crater the size of a hot tub.

Damn, angelic powers were badass. Time to play keep away from the demon-bike.

Famine lunged in the direction of its racing steed, so I threw myself into the horseman's path – even as every human part of me screamed to run the other way – and clotheslined Famine with one wing. The blow slammed us both back, carving foot-deep furrows into the hard-packed dirt.

Somewhere out in the desert behind us, the chopper hissed like a huge snake.

Famine ran at me in a blur of pale skin and tattered leather. Sagebrush shriveled into twisted gray knots as the horseman passed and the wind howled, cold and barbed. It ripped at me and Uriel's aura flared again. Without the angel's help, there's no way I could have stayed on my feet.

My hand glowed with power and I swung it at Famine, but an engine roared and a streak of black and tarnished chrome slammed into me. I tumbled across the earth, then crashed into a big red boulder. It should have smashed me like an insect on a windshield, but the stone shattered into pieces.

I lifted my face and spat out a mouthful of dust as Famine's chopper spun to a stomach-churning stop at its master's side. The bike had torn its way right through the middle of a stony hill to reach Famine, leaving a rough valley between the two remaining halves.

I jumped back to my feet, marveling that I could stand at all after being run over at a bazillion miles per hour. Famine threw a bone-thin leg over the motorcycle's leather seat and grabbed the throttle in one spidery hand.

My entire body pumped and buzzed with adrenalin, but my guts were still twisted into knots as Famine shot toward me.

We need to split them up again, I thought desperately. *Alright, Uriel, what have we got? Flaming sword? Lightning bolts from on high? Give me something smitey!*

If we could separate the horseman and steed long enough, we might have been able to overcome Famine, Uriel told me. *But we are out of time.*

The tightness inside me was worse now than when Famine first appeared. It wasn't just fear or excitement – something else was coming. But was that my backup or Famine's? Did it matter? Even if that white-hot surging sensation inside me heralded the approach of an archangel, one touch would give Uriel all the power they needed to take over.

Famine skidded to a stop, hurling sand and stone into the air. But there was no concession or fear there in the thin horseman's posture as it craned a long neck in the direction of the highway. Famine's razor-blade slash of a mouth curved into a grin. Whatever was coming, it wasn't an angel.

"Oh, shit," I said.

The hot-cold sensation of the approaching horseman made my hands clench and Uriel's light wavered around me. Who was out there? Pestilence again? I wasn't in a big hurry to face that disgusting personified disease a second time, but I doubted that meeting War would be any better.

This was not how I wanted to die, and it sure as hell wasn't what Uriel wanted, either. But there were worse ways to go... At least I would still be me.

I settled my weight into the best fighting stance I knew, ready to show the horsemen every single biting, scratching, crotch-punching dirty trick I learned since grade school.

I am prepared, Uriel agreed. *If this is the end, let us fight it to the last.*

Another motorcycle blazed through the darkening desert, cresting a stony ridge. It was the Packmaster, all shiny black and red and chrome.

Death?

No, Uriel said. *That is not Death...!*

I stared into the dying light, but the angel was right. It was Leo! Bullet holes riddled his leather jacket and blood darkened his shirt, but that was his own tattooed skin and Leo's beautiful brown eyes were wide, fixed on me as he raced down the rocky hill.

"Jaz!" he shouted.

Leo barely slowed as he held out his hand and I tangled my fingers through his. I jumped, beat my glowing wings once, and he pulled me up behind him. I swung my leg over the Packmaster and Uriel's wings disintegrated into a cloud of golden sparks. I wrapped my arms around Leo and he brought the bike in a tight arc to face Famine.

"Death," the gaunt horseman wheezed.

Its voice wasn't loud, but I could hear that name perfectly even over the roar of the two motorcycle engines. Famine's voice echoed, so achingly hollow that it made my stomach growl and cramp with hunger. I never wanted a cheeseburger so badly in my life.

"War knows your vessel's heart," Famine said, leveling one needle-like finger at Leo. "War knows your weakness. You will come to us and the four horsemen *will* ride together."

Leo slammed on the Packmaster's brake, throwing me hard against him, and yanked a handgun out from his ruined leather jacket. It was big and black, with a flashlight mounted under the barrel. I was pretty sure I had seen some of the Spotters wearing sidearms just like it.

"Fuck you," Leo said.

He aimed at Famine and pulled the trigger. Leo had to know that bullets weren't going to hurt Famine any more than they had Pestilence, but it didn't stop him from trying.

Leo's shots hammered into Famine's thin body, then clattered to the desert floor in flattened lead discs. We humans are a stupid, stubborn lot, and I loved us for it.

"You *will* come to us, Death," Famine said again. "And then the angels will die."

The skeletal thing that used to be a human woman twisted the throttle, making the chopper kick up sand and greasy black smoke, then tore off in the opposite direction. Uriel was right – Famine was a chicken-shit.

Leo kept his gun trained on Famine until the other horseman had vanished into the twilight, then sagged forward over the handlebars of his Packmaster. The gun fell from his shaking hand. Leo panted hard, eyes squeezed shut. With the sun swiftly vanishing, the desert temperature plummeted, but sweat beaded on Leo's forehead and dripped down the back of his neck. His grip tightened on the throttle of the Packmaster and the engine revved.

Leo still battles Death for control, Uriel said. *His hold is tenuous, Jaz, and may not last.*

I pulled Leo around to face me on the motorcycle. Stubble roughened his cheeks and there were deep, dark circles under his eyes. But they were *his* eyes and they were the most gorgeous thing I had ever seen.

"I'm so sorry I ran away," I told him. "I was so scared... I still am. But I came to find you. I came back."

"I don't know what to do. I... I know I shouldn't have chased after you," Leo whispered. "Death wants your blood... But I *had* to find you. I had to see if you were okay. I don't have anything else left."

"Leo..." I said.

His eyes were haunted and he sagged in the seat of the Packmaster. The motorcycle snarled and Leo gasped.

"Jaz, it hurts so much," he said. "Death is pulling me apart piece by piece. I don't know how much longer I can hold on..."

"You don't have to do it alone," I told him. "Never again, Leo. Whatever happens, I'll be right here with you."

Leo looked at me with such painful need and hope in his dark eyes that it made my heart skip. I grabbed him by the front of his battered, shot-up leather jacket and kissed him. Nothing coy or sexy, and nothing chaste. Just pure, raw Jaz right from the deepest core of me, and I forgot all about Uriel and Death. For that moment, there was only me and Leo. His hands were still shaking hard, but Leo wrapped his arms around me and kissed me back.

We didn't stop for a long time.

CHAPTER 26

E ventually, Leo and I had to pry ourselves apart. Famine had raced off and we didn't feel the sick sensation of the horseman, but neither of us knew the exact range of Death and Uriel's tracking ability. I still had a lot of questions and Leo was obviously exhausted, but he turned the Packmaster back in the direction of Highway 44.

We drove through the desert until rocks and sand gave way to the winding black strip of highway asphalt. The bus was gone, but to judge by the fresh tire tracks and the reek of diesel in the air, it had taken a tow truck.

Leo turned left, pointing us west – toward San Diego. I wasn't sure if Leo had his steed under control or if the motorcycle just liked our route this time, but the ride was smooth and swift. The gibbous moon had risen and we raced through its bright silver light. We passed a few other cars and some of them honked at us, but Leo knew what he was doing – or else Death did – and the bike wove expertly through the scarlet taillights of nighttime traffic.

I caught one brief glimpse of a Highway Patrol cruiser, but I didn't sense Michael nearby. We blew past so fast that the red and blue lights flashed only once before they vanished behind us. Leo was bent double over the handlebars of the Packmaster and trembling with the effort of maintaining control... I wasn't sure if he saw the cop at all.

We crossed the border of California just after midnight, beneath the southern tip of Nevada. I don't think Leo wanted to stop, but we were both falling over with exhaustion. Even if Leo couldn't sleep, he needed *some* kind of rest.

So we finally pulled over in a town called Empire and staggered through the parking lot of a roadside motel. Between the two of us, I was less bullet-riddled and bloody, so I went into the front office and threw a rumpled fifty-dollar bill on the counter. The clerk jolted awake and opened his mouth to ask a question, but I shook my head and put another bill down.

"One room and don't ask or say anything," I told him.

The guy nodded and collected my money. He typed something into his computer and then handed me a key card with a number written on the little paper envelope. He pointed out the window to the matching door. Apparently, he took my shut-up bribe seriously.

Fine by me.

I thanked the sleepy clerk and headed back outside to Leo, who leaned against the cinder-block wall with his arms crossed and head down. He looked up at my approach, then wordlessly followed me down the row of brass-numbered blue doors until I opened one. We went inside and locked the door behind us.

"I can't pay you back for the room," Leo told me. "Hell, I can't even pay the money I owe you for working on my bike anymore. When the Packmaster went rampaging, it kind of... burned off my saddlebags. We lost it all. I'm sorry, Jaz."

I blinked at Leo, and then began laughing.

"Everything we've been through... and you're worried about fifty bucks?" I asked.

Leo stared for a moment, but then smiled and laughed, too. We laughed until we wiped hysterical tears from our cheeks. I pressed my hands against my stomach and fought for breath while Leo rubbed his eyes. He sat heavily on the corner of the bed, then shook his head and stood up again.

"No. If I sit down, I'll fall asleep," Leo said. "I can't let that happen."

"So what *did* happen...?" I asked. "Back at Blue Mountain, I mean."

"I got shot," Leo answered. "A few times. I thought I was dead for sure. And without my... passenger, I would have been."

Leo looked down again and pushed a finger through one of the bullet holes in his jacket.

"I got distracted," he said. "I lost control of the Packmaster and it went wild. I... I couldn't stop it."

Leo leaned against the locked door and failed to suppress a shudder. He was looking out through the motel room window and I followed his gaze. His motorcycle was parked right outside. That wasn't where Leo had left it... The biker's expression was one of weary horror and I hurried across the room to put a hand on his arm.

"It's *not* your fault," I said. "You were bleeding out. Because you took the bullets for me and Diane."

"Which only happened because I grabbed her in the first place," Leo argued. He drew a shuddering breath. "I was stupid and desperate. So I got shot. I was bleeding and losing control of Death..."

I squeezed Leo's arm. The thick muscles there were knotted like steel cables.

"How did you hold Death off?" I asked.

Leo dug into one of his jacket pockets and pulled out a hypodermic needle. I stared. It was the syringe that Diane had given Leo – and it was empty.

"You took the stimulant," I said. "Holy shit, Leo. That's how you stayed in control?"

He nodded wearily. "Barely, but yeah."

"But after everything you went through with the heroin?" I asked. "And your mother..."

"I can't afford to lose control of Death for a second," Leo said. "The Packmaster destroyed half that base before I could call it off. Imagine what Death could do riding that thing through a city full of people."

I leaned my forehead against Leo's shoulder.

"We can't let that happen," I agreed. "Ever. Death and Uriel can never take control. And we can't let them have their war."

"I'm so tired, Jaz," Leo said. "I don't know what to do."

"We go to your uncle," I answered. "We ride to San Diego as hard as we can. If angels or horsemen get in our way, we push through. Fast, before they make Death or Uriel manifest."

"What if Carlos can't help us?" Leo asked. "The only solution SPOT had was suicide."

I pressed my face into the leather of Leo's jacket and took a deep breath, inhaling the scent of him.

"If Carlos can't help, then we go with Diane's plan," I said. "Both of us. You know we can't let the archangels and horsemen fight. I'm scared to die, but they'll destroy *everything*. The entire universe."

Leo raised one shaking hand and slowly stroked the tangled black curls of my hair.

"The universe is too big for me to understand," Leo said. "I can't fight for that, Jaz. I only know people. That's why I fought in Blue Mountain, why I stuck that needle in my arm... to save you."

"Killing me *will* be saving me," I told him. "You know that. I can't live with the cost if Uriel takes me. If Carlos can't fix this shit, then we have to die. There's no other way."

Leo turned and held me tight against his broad chest. "You heard what Diane said. Blue Mountain wasn't the only SPOT base. There are more of those guys, and they will try to kill us before we reach Carlos."

"We'll outrun them," I said.

"And if we can't?" Leo asked.

"Then Diane's people capture us and this ends," I said. "One way or another. But the Earth survives, and everyone lives."

"Everyone but us. I can't lose you, Jaz," Leo told me in a low, deep voice that made my pulse race and my breath catch. "My world is the people that I love. You know that."

"I don't want to lose you, either," I said.

Leo ran trembling fingers down the side of my face. "There's so little time left. I don't know if I can do this anymore, Jaz. That stimulant is supposed to last seventy-two hours, but I've already been running for so long."

"I can help," I told him. My heart pounded. "I can keep you awake."

I grabbed the front of Leo's battered leather jacket and drew him toward the bed. I felt the fire and rage of Uriel reacting to Death, but there was something else inside me. Something even bigger, brighter and more powerful than the archangel.

"Jaz, no," Leo said. His voice was raw. "I can't... What if I hurt you? Death..."

I pulled Leo down into a deep kiss.

"I'm not scared anymore," I whispered against his lips. "Not of you. We'll run together, Leo, as far as we can. Until there's nowhere left to run."

Leo stared down at me with dark wildfire in his eyes.

"Jaz..." he said. "I love you."

"Then show me," I told him.

Leo lifted me into his arms and kissed me until we couldn't feel Uriel or Death anymore. There was only heat and desire, sweet sensation and racing hearts. I tore urgently at Leo's clothes and his already shredded shirt ripped in my hands. Leo growled hungrily as he carried me to the bed. We fell together into the sheets in a desperate tangle, kissing and groping frantically. And then...

Well, none of your business. Get your own bronzed motor-cycle god.

CHAPTER 27

L et's just skip all the way up to the morning. Well, *nearly* morning... The sky outside was still a deep, dark violet, but we had to make an early start.

Leo and I both showered, but managed to get each other all sweaty again by the time we scooped our clothes off the motel room floor. Neither one of us had slept, but Leo's eyes didn't look quite as bloodshot anymore.

I twisted my wild hair into a pair of knots on either side of my head and pulled my jeans back on, but Leo picked up the shredded and bloodied remains of his t-shirt. There wasn't very much fabric left intact. Leo smirked, sighed and dropped the ruined shirt into a plastic trash can.

"All my other shirts burned up with the money back at Blue Mountain," he said.

"Oh no," I managed to answer with a straight face. "Too bad we don't have time to go shopping. You'll just have to manage shirtless."

Leo laughed, then grabbed his jacket and inspected it. There weren't quite as many bullet holes and the black leather had withstood the abuse a little better, so Leo pulled it on. It left his tattooed chest bare, so I bit my lower lip and enjoyed the view. Surely we had time for that much, at least...

Jaz!

Uriel's voice thundered through my skull and I clapped my hands over my ears before I remembered that it wouldn't do any good. The archangel had been silent all night, so why were they screaming in my head now?

You are under attack!

There was a loud *whoosh* and something smashed through the window on a billowing tail of smoke. I threw myself at Leo, trying to tackle him out of the way of a projectile moving a hell of a lot faster than one human woman could run. But I slammed hard into Leo and wrapped my suddenly glowing wings around us both.

We hit the floor as the motel room exploded into rubble and fire. The thunderclap rang in my ears and flaming splinters of what had been the dresser bounced away. I jumped up to my feet and the glow of my outstretched wings was bright enough to eclipse the morning light now pouring through the broken window. Four of them... Two pairs of angelic wings extended from my shoulders.

Uriel was getting more powerful.

"Leo?" I shouted.

The biker sat up, coughing. I grabbed his hand and pulled him upright.

"I'm okay," Leo said. "But that was a rocket launcher!"

Laser sights flashed through the smoke, filling the gaping hole where the door had been with criss-crossing red lines of death. Leo yanked me to one side as the rattle of automatic gunfire tore through the hazy air and high-caliber shots hammered new holes into the already burning wall.

Under attack in a cheap motel... Just like old times. So which of our many enemies had crashed this crappy class reunion?

Bullets pinged off of my wings as though hitting a steel plate. Voices shouted from outside, some bellowing orders and others screaming questions.

"SPOT?" Leo asked.

"Unless you managed to piss off an entire national army," I said. "Yeah."

"Are we ready to let them kill us?"

Silhouettes moved through the smoke, crouched and still firing. I stepped out in front of Leo and spread my wings. Bullets pounded into them, staggering me back into his arms.

"I'm not prepared to die just yet," I said. "You?"

"After last night? Not a chance," Leo growled.

I grinned. "How far is it to San Diego?"

"About a hundred miles."

Behind you! Uriel warned.

An object flew through the gunsmoke haze toward us, and I spun just in time to knock a grenade away with one extended wing. Maybe if we had played baseball with blazing angel wings in high school, I might have been more interested in sports. The indistinct shapes of SPOT soldiers scattered through the smoke, yelling out warnings and hurling themselves to the ground. The grenade boomed.

"Let's go!" I said.

Leo nodded. He kicked a chunk of flaming bed frame out of the way, then held up one hand. He concentrated, closing his fingers into a tight fist. Something even louder than the shouting Spotters and their guns roared across the motel – an engine. The riderless Packmaster burst through the drywall dust and debris, skidding to a stop about an inch away from shattering my shins. Leo's bike still didn't like me.

The feeling is mutual, Uriel snarled. *Jaz, go!*

Leo threw a leg over the Packmaster and I jumped on behind him. I held my quartet of wings up to either side as Leo yanked the throttle. The motorcycle leapt into motion, cutting a path through the rubble that had been our motel room.

The attacking Spotters had reformed their line and bullets pinged off the glowing barrier of my wings. We charged right through them and out into the parking lot, the Packmaster's tires leaving flaming skid marks across the asphalt.

The motel parking lot was full of unmarked black panel vans with more SPOT soldiers pouring out of the back. They shouted and opened fire as we roared past, then threw themselves down behind fenders or armored doors for cover. I thought I recognized a gray-haired woman with her arm in a sling and a bullet-proof vest over her suit, but another Spotter had snatched up a new RPG launcher and swung it around, tracking us.

Uriel, can your wings take a direct hit from that thing? I asked.

Yes, the archangel answered at once. *But the force of the blast will send us considerably off course. Likely through several buildings.*

Shit. I grabbed Leo's shoulder and pulled. He followed my lead and steered his possessed motorcycle toward the nearest van. I slashed out with a wing and it sliced through the front like a welding torch. Sparks flew and coolant sprayed out from the ruined radiator.

Another sharp wing cut through one tire and then a second. I smelled burning rubber and the suddenly off-balance van lurched to the side, rolling between us and the RPG-wielding Spotter. By the time he dashed around my impromptu barrier, Leo and I had blazed – literally – out of the parking lot.

Still shooting, SPOT soldiers chased us out into the road, which was strangely empty. I looked back over Leo's shoulder and swore. Either Diane's Society had some serious police ties, or else they were going to get into a hell of a lot of trouble with the cops for the roadblock set up at the end of the street.

And I don't mean orange cones and yellow tape – SPOT had cordoned off the entire road with a line of armored trucks and barbed chains across the asphalt designed to tear apart any tires driving over them.

Leo braked hard and the motorcycle skidded around in a circle. I pulled my wings around us and heard bullets ping off the barrier of light.

"Shit!" Leo said. "It's the same fucking thing behind us. Now what?"

Go through them, Uriel suggested.

You mean fly, don't you? I asked, heart sinking.

Death will not leave its stead, and you cannot leave Leo, the archangel said. *Drive through. Now!*

I felt as much as heard the urgency in Uriel's voice. A hot prickle ran up the back of my neck. The sun was just beginning to rise, but that wasn't the source. There was another horseman or angel somewhere. Not close, but at the speed of wings or demonic steeds, that distance was going to shrink quickly.

"Go!" I shouted.

Leo didn't hesitate. He gunned his overpowered engine and we raced toward the blockade. I swept my wings forward until they formed a wedge in front of his motorcycle. Incandescence surrounded us, but I could still see through the glow. Bullets ricocheted off the solidified light and someone hurled another grenade – an incendiary one this time, maybe hoping that the phosphorus flames would slow us down. But we drove right through the explosion and Leo's bike shot out the other side of the expanding ball of flame and shrapnel.

I really wished that I could have seen what that looked like, but then we were driving over the spiked steel chain, the kind designed for ripping tires apart to rubber shreds. Steel spines stuck into the Packmaster's front wheel, which carried them up until they impacted the fork. The chain snapped with a shower of sparks and the shards flung free in a hail of red-hot molten metal.

We didn't slow down and the Spotters scattered as the wedge of my forward-swept wings hit the line of armored vehicles. The impact shivered through my body and I expected to fly right off the back of Leo's bike, but I clung on with angelic strength and the SPOT trucks rose up over the angle of my braced wings. They tumbled through the air and then landed on their sides, skidding across the road with matching snarls of tearing metal.

Leo held up one clenched fist, middle finger raised. I finally lifted all four wings up from the truck-smashing wedge and they stretched out behind me in streamers of light. We were through the SPOT blockade, but that sensation of the closing angel or horseman was growing stronger. When it rained, it really shit-stormed.

"Do you feel that?" I shouted.

Leo winced. "Yeah. Feels like more than one of them... Death is getting stronger. Let's get onto the highway and make some distance."

The Packmaster cut through the center of town at NASCAR speeds. We blasted across surface street intersections and left drivers and pedestrians alike gaping at the flaming trail burning in our wake.

A sign for Highway 44 flashed by in a burst of green, warning us about the sharp turn of the on-ramp. Leo didn't slow, but leaned into the turn and we angled so low that my wingtips carved molten lines into the asphalt.

But we were still moving too fast...! Leo growled and chrome slithered out of his black leather sleeve to cover his hand like armor. He stabbed his fingers right down into the street.

Holy shit... Death really was getting stronger.

The Packmaster turned a tight arc around the new pivot point. Leo yanked his hand free and I caught the glint of skeletal metal claws at his fingertips, but we raced up the ramp and onto Highway 44.

The sun rose swiftly into a clear, bright blue sky and the road was already filling with traffic on their way out to the California coast. A minivan swerved out of our path and the kids in the back seat watched the Packmaster race by with their mouths hanging open.

I twisted on the pillion, studying the highway behind us, and saw the burning track left by Leo's demonic motorcycle. But the sensation of encroaching celestial powers was making my entire body tense and tingle.

When I turned back to Leo, his fingers still ended in sharp chrome claws, and the bullet holes were gone from his jacket. It had... healed. Intact leather whipped and snapped against his bare chest. That wasn't all that had changed – Leo now wore a pair of studded black riding chaps and knee-high boots buckled in chrome. I hadn't seen Leo turn it on, but the Packmaster's headlight burned with light the color of blood.

Oh no. *Please* no...

But Leo looked back at me with his own brown eyes. They were hard and pained, but they were his.

"They're getting closer," Leo said. "And at least one of them is a horseman."

And the pissed-off powers from before time weren't the only ones closing in. Someone honked at the next on-ramp and a little red sedan swerved off the side, almost rolling as it sprang over the rail. A pair of huge trucks roared out into the highway in front of us. Each of them had a machine gun bolted onto the reinforced bed, and grim-looking SPOT soldiers tethered down behind them.

"Jaz!" Leo shouted.

The gun barrels swiveled to aim at us. I jumped up to my feet on the back of the motorcycle, steadying myself on Leo's broad shoulders until I realized that I didn't have to. I wasn't going to fall – I was going to fly.

I leapt over Leo and beat my quadruple wings, soaring up into the morning. I was using those wings to fly, so they weren't protecting my body, but Uriel's voice rang through me like a bell.

You have my armor, the angel said.

Uriel's aura of bright light rippled over me. I grinned and folded my wings. I dove at one of the trucks and slammed down to land in the back like a ton of divine bricks. The entire vehicle bottomed out, leaving a line of sparks and scraped metal down the highway. I couldn't hear the driver in the cab, but I saw him fighting for control. The overtaxed suspension groaned and the truck bounced as it veered into the next lane.

The soldier clung to his wildly wheeling mounted machine gun and yanked it around to aim at me. He pulled the trigger and high-caliber bullets hammered into the glowing nimbus of light surrounding me. Uriel's aura kept the shots from tearing me to bloody rags, but it was still enough to make the breath whoosh out of my lungs in a pained gasp and slammed me staggering back. My knees hit the armored tailgate of the truck and I fell.

For a heart-stopping moment, I plunged toward the highway racing beneath me, but then I remembered my wings. I beat them desperately and spiraled back up into the cloudless dawn sky. I thought that I heard Leo shouting my name, but it was hard to make out over the rush of wind and the roar of engines below.

Your people have created powerful weapons, Uriel said.

Yeah, we've got some ridiculously huge guns in this country, I thought. *And those aren't even the scariest shit that our military makes. War would love them... I think. Are they too much for your powers?*

If an immortal, disembodied force of order could snort derisively, that's precisely what Uriel did. When I raised my hands, the light clinging to my skin flared and took on a metallic sheen like silver or steel.

Mortal weapons will not stop us, the angel said.

Below me, Leo was having no trouble keeping up with my angelic pace or the racing SPOT trucks. He pulled alongside one of them as the gunner struggled to track him with the mounted machine gun. Leo lifted a hand and his skeletal chrome claws lengthened into curved blades. He brought them down through the barrel, slicing the thick steel tube and sending it bouncing off across the highway. An oncoming hauler braked suddenly as the sheared metal nearly punched through its windshield.

I swooped and desperately wanted to get close enough to see if Leo's eyes were still his own, but the other SPOT gunner was aiming right at me again. I didn't land in the bed this time, but held an impossible hover above the truck. The Spotter yanked his gun up to as steep an angle as the mount could manage and fired. Only a few of the big lead slugs hit their mark and I didn't even feel them, not through Uriel's armor. The SPOT soldier stared, probably wide-eyed and gape-mouthed behind his black mask and goggles.

"Leave us alone," I suggested.

And by *suggest*, I mean that I reached down and grabbed the barrel of the machine gun. The hot steel dented in my armored fingers, but I wrenched the gun up off the mounting and flung it out across the highway. The weapon went cartwheeling through the grassy meridian and hurled clods of dirt in every direction.

I soared out ahead of the disarmed trucks and experimentally flexed my wings. Well, I flew before with only two of them, so I really hoped I didn't need all four to stay in the air now. I slashed with one of my new wings, and it cut just like a lightsaber through the front tire and most of the bumper. The nose of the truck dipped precariously under the weight of the engine and armor. The truck's ruined fender slammed into the highway, gouging a deep furrow through the blacktop and kicking up a fountain of sparks. It spun out off the road and then plowed into a heaped dirt berm. One truck down.

I whirled toward the other truck, but the driver had rolled down her bulletproof window and aimed an oversized handgun into my face. She pulled the trigger and the shot impacted right between my eyes. I tumbled back through the air.

"Jaz!" Leo roared.

He swerved into the side of the Spotter's truck. By all rights, the much smaller and lighter motorcycle should have bounced right off, but the armored truck skidded into a wild spin. The driver shouted and dropped her gun to grab the steering wheel in both hands, trying to wrestle her vehicle back under control.

Leo grabbed the front bumper in one chrome-plated fist and heaved. Thousands of pounds of truck arced up and over the highway, landing with a thunderous crash on the other side. I mentally crossed my fingers that the Spotters inside were all wearing their seatbelts.

"Jaz, are you okay?" Leo called out.

His voice had a deep, empty boom that sounded nothing at all like human. I flew alongside the Packmaster, touching tentative fingertips to my forehead. There was no blood or even a bruise there that I could feel. Damn, Uriel's upgraded armor was tough.

"I'm alright," I shouted.

The red headlight of his Packmaster blazed like fire and Leo groaned. I felt it, too... SPOT wasn't the only thing chasing us, and archangels and horsemen were both a lot faster than cars. There was the sensation of blazing light against the back of my neck, though the sun had barely risen and the morning breeze was still cool.

That is Gabriel and Michael, Uriel told me. *And Raphael is not far behind them.*

"Shit," I said. "The other angels are getting close."

Leo looked up at me, jaw clenched as he nodded. "Yeah. The horsemen, too."

His eyes were brown and so beautifully alive, but dark steel veins were crawling over his bare chest like some kind of terrible disease.

"How fast can you fly?" Leo asked.

"Let's find out," I answered.

SPOT knew that we were running to Carlos. They could lay as many traps in our path as their doubtlessly impressive budget would support. The other horsemen and archangels could track us every step of the way... Our only hope was to get to Carlos and somehow get a cure for this before they all converged on us.

Or discover that there was no cure. If that happened, well... I didn't want to die, but we wouldn't have much choice at that point. At least I would die with Leo, and far away from Crayhill.

Cars streaked past and we were going far too fast to read the green-painted signs. But the blocky silhouette of a city darkened the western horizon and Leo pointed with one clawed chrome finger.

"That's San Diego!" he shouted.

Already? Leo said the city was a hundred miles away... But we had to be going more than two hundred miles an hour.

More car horns honked and I spotted police lights flashing far, far behind us. The early traffic was still sluggish and half-hearted, but there were plenty of wide eyes and shocked shouts as Leo and I shot past. At least one driver slammed on their brakes at the sight of a winged mechanic soaring down the road. A compact little hybrid smacked right into their trunk and then skidded into the next lane.

But over the rumbling thunder of the Packmaster and the crunch of metal, I heard the monotone thud of helicopter rotors. It wasn't a sound I had been very familiar with until recently and

I really hoped that it was just some local news-copter drawn to the accidents like an oversized vulture. Does Channel 17 have a helicopter with miniguns on the wings?

The black helicopter dropped toward us and the miniguns spun up. Bullets hailed down on Highway 44, punching craters into the asphalt and through the hood of a nearby SUV. Shit, so much for SPOT avoiding collateral damage. But when the entire universe was on the line, I supposed that somebody's Escalade was a small price to pay.

Bullets ricocheted off my armor and the Packmaster's shiny chrome finish. Leo flipped off the helicopter, then leaned over the handlebars and swerved between the twin lines of minigun fire. I covered him as best I could with my wings, but then the hail of lead suddenly stopped.

I craned my neck to stare. Had the gunner finally given up trying to riddle us with holes? The helicopter was still pacing us, but the miniguns were spinning down and I cheered.

Highway 44 rose beneath us and San Diego leapt into focus. Somewhere in that city was Leo's uncle and our final answer about if we would live or die today. Would you think any less of me if I admitted that I actually crossed my shiny, silver-armored fingers?

But miniguns weren't the only weapons mounted on SPOT's suspicious black helicopter. A pair of rockets streaked out from the underside, trailing white smoke across the blue sky. They weren't aimed at us, though... The missiles converged on the highway in front of us, where it sloped up over the dark ribbon of some other freeway.

"Holy shit," I gasped. "No!"

Both missiles slammed right into the highway overpass and the entire road shuddered as broken concrete blasted a hundred feet into the air. The violent shockwave sent a minivan spinning off through the meridian and the cherry-red sports car behind them hit the brakes, but they were driving too fast and plunged over the jagged edge of what used to be their boring morning commute.

I fell out of the sky like a bullet and grabbed the back of the plummeting car before I had time to wonder if Uriel's power made me strong enough for this insanity. My armored fingers punched through the trunk and metal ripped in my grasp, but it held until I lowered the car to the rubble of the freeway below. It landed with a thump, the driver still shrieking safely inside.

I leapt back into the air, but Leo was less than a heartbeat from the blown-out bridge. If I could catch an entire car, I could certainly grab Leo's Packmaster and fly it over the ruined highway... But that save had already cost me too much time. There was no way I could get to Leo before he fell.

But Leo snarled something that I couldn't hear and twisted the throttle. He wasn't braking – he was accelerating. The blood-red headlight flared with hellish fire and the front lifted up in a wheelie that I had never seen from a bike that big. Leo hit the torn-up edge of the overpass and jumped, bike arcing impossibly through the air. It landed hard on the other side, leaving a flaming black tire track in its wake.

"Yes!" I cheered.

I beat my wings and climbed. If that helicopter followed us into San Diego, I couldn't even imagine the damage it would do trying to take us out. And since I was the one with the wings, I figured that made handling the helicopter my job.

The SPOT soldiers inside saw me coming and one of them grabbed for what seemed to be the controls of the miniguns. The barrels spun and hurled bullets, but the twin guns were designed to converge on something much further away than an angel landing on the nose of the helicopter. Inside, the pilot wasn't masked and the color drained from his face as I scrambled up the hull.

This armor makes me pretty much indestructible, right? I asked.

Death and the other horsemen can harm us, Uriel warned me. *But you have nothing to fear from mortal weapons.*

I hoped that applied to mortal vehicles, too, and reached up to grab the whirling main rotor of the helicopter. Somehow, I was still shocked when it didn't shear my hands off.

One of the blades bent and then snapped, but I held onto the other and the rotor whined to a halt. The helicopter spiraled into a deadly fall, spewing smoke, and I adjusted my grip to seize the central mast of the rotor. I heaved, swore a few times and then guided the damaged machine until it was just a few yards from the ground. Finally, I dropped it into the green-tinged gray of a marshy wetland.

The pilot staggered out of the helicopter and splashed into a puddle, pulling a compact nine-millimeter gun from his belt. He fired at me and I swiped the bullet away with one armored hand.

"Stop that," I said. "Let us go, or I will wing thee to thy rest."

I didn't have time to be proud of my Shakespeare quote. My words rang out like striking a huge gong and I winced. The other archangels were *close.* The pilot braced his gun with his other hand.

"But you... you'll destroy the entire universe," he said in a shaking voice.

I shook my head. "We won't let that happen. If Carlos can't deal with Death and Uriel, we *will* die. I promise. But we get to make that decision, not you."

The pilot's aim wavered, and then fell. I didn't know if he actually believed me or simply realized the futility of trying to kill an angel with a handgun. He holstered his weapon and carefully retreated around the crashed helicopter to help his gunner, who was pulling weakly at her safety harness.

I spread all four of my luminous wings and rose up into the open blue sky. With any luck, SPOT was done and dealt with.

Now Leo and I just had to get to Carlos before the other angels could catch up with us.

And the horsemen, Uriel reminded me. *They are as close as my brethren. We are so near... It is time at last, Jaz!*

Not if I could help it. I flew up over Highway 44 and picked out the flaming trail of Leo burning rubber into San Diego. He waved at me and his hand glinted chrome in the morning sun. I beat wings of bright light and soared after him with all of the speed Uriel could give me.

CHAPTER 28

Leo knew his way through San Diego. He had been coming here to see his uncle his entire life... Good thing, because I kept getting distracted by... well, everything. I had never been in a city the size of San Diego and if we somehow survived all of this, I couldn't wait to explore more of it.

I soared between the steel and glass spires of skyscrapers, staring at the people inside. Office workers jumped to their feet, grabbing their cell phones to either take pictures or call the police. Down below, Leo drove far too fast through the streets for the cops to catch, though that didn't stop them from trying. But while SPOT knew where we were going, they didn't seem to have shared that information with the local law enforcement, so we lost all of the black and white squad cars easily in the dense urban sprawl of San Diego.

We wound our way through the close, shining silver jungle of downtown and I almost missed it when Leo turned suddenly left, heading south through the city. I swore, then banked in a half-circle around a tall building with an angled roofline and a slatted latticework dome perched on top. Some kind of library, to judge by all of the people carrying stacks of books in and out.

A group of elementary school kids in matching red backpacks pointed up at me and their teacher dropped her latte when she looked skyward.

I winged quickly away, flushing. At this rate, I would end up with my picture posted all over social media. There wasn't much I could do to hide a woman flying through San Diego, but as the skyscrapers gave way to shorter, more sprawling buildings that stretched out toward the border, I lowered my altitude and flew as low as I dared.

The Pacific Ocean gleamed blue and silver on my right and from the air, I could almost see Mexico. The dark, tiny shapes of seabirds swooped and played above the crashing waves. It was beautiful.

We've got to be getting close, I thought.

Yes, Uriel agreed. *And so are the other angels.*

I tore my eyes away from the view and glided down closer to Leo again. The streets were becoming a little less crowded as we moved south, and he eased up on the throttle. Leo wove his way down smaller and narrower roads, and then finally stopped next to an old warehouse with corrugated metal walls covered in a colorful mosaic of graffiti.

I landed hard beside Leo, cracking the concrete of the sidewalk. Oops. Well, that was pretty small potatoes compared to all of the other damage we had caused during this wild road trip.

In the street, cars slowed down. Drivers craned their necks to look at the big biker in chaps and a jacket made of shadow, and a girl with two pairs of glowing wings stretching out behind her. Then they sped up to hurry the hell away. Someone was going to wind up rear-ended, but we had more pressing concerns.

Leo's jaw was clenched tight and I heard his teeth grinding together. The biker's bare chest was so covered in chrome that I could no longer see any of his tattoos, and it looked like he was wearing armor.

"Did we beat the other archangels?" Leo asked in that deep, bone-chillingly hollow voice.

"Yeah," I answered. "But not by much. My skin feels like it's on fire."

"The horsemen are close, too," Leo said.

"How fast are they moving?"

Leo shook his head. Sweat beaded in his hair. "I can't tell. But I know they're near enough to start crawling up my ass any minute."

"Are you still in control?" I asked.

"For now," Leo said.

I pulled him down into a desperate kiss. Leo wrapped his arms around me and held me close. His body was cold and as hard as stone against me, but his lips were warm and soft. Beside us, the Packmaster revved.

"Back off, bike," I murmured. "He's mine."

My power is growing, Uriel said inside me. *And so is Death's. If you are to attempt this, Jaz, to reclaim your life and prevent the final battle, then it must be now. There is no more time.*

Reluctantly, I broke the kiss and released Leo. I stood back and after a moment of concentration, I dismissed Uriel's wings and armor. They vanished into glittering sparks, leaving me in my jeans and t-shirt again.

"Let's go," I said.

Leo nodded and I followed as he rolled his Packmaster into a sprawling parking lot in front of the warehouse. There was a long line of motorcycles outside, not a single one of them locked up. Whoever left all those gang tags around the neighborhood seemed to know better than to tangle with the owners of these particular bikes. But when I glanced across the lot, I didn't see any other bikers. Where was everyone?

Leo parked his Packmaster at the end of the row, then turned to me with a grin.

"Excited to see your uncle?" I asked.

"Like you wouldn't believe," Leo answered. He touched one skeletally clawed hand against his chest and took a deep breath. "Alright. He should be inside."

"Holy shit," I said. "This is really it."

My voice cracked. In the next few minutes, I would finally meet Leo's Uncle Carlos. I would find out if we would live free of Uriel and Death, or die to save the world from them.

Would Carlos like me?

No pressure, Jaz.

Leo took my hand carefully. Mine was shaking and his was made of metal, but we walked close together toward an over-sized sliding door painted with a huge flaming red and black helm – the crest of the Knights of Hell. Leo led me across the parking lot, but then stopped dead in his tracks, frowning.

"What's the matter?" I asked. "You don't think your uncle will approve of you hooking up with a mechanic from Kansas?"

"Something's wrong," Leo gasped.

He managed another step forward, then fell suddenly to his knees on the asphalt. Leo clutched his head, sharp chrome claws drawing beads of bright red blood from his scalp.

"Leo? Leo, what's happening?" I asked.

"It's Death," Leo groaned. "I can finally hear its voice... and it's laughing."

Holy shit. Uriel, what the hell is going on? I asked.

No...! the angel hissed inside me. *Liars, deceivers!*

The warehouse door ground open with a loud metallic snarl and three figures strode through. I recognized the gaunt, skeletal shape of Famine, and Pestilence in its rumpled suit crawling with shiny green-gray flies.

Between the pair stood a tall man with long black hair and flames tattooed onto skin turned to leather by years on the road.

The fire glowed and danced as though animated by demonic hands, and his eyes burned like live coals.

"Uncle Carlos," Leo snarled. "War."

The sky that morning had been bright and clear, but now the sun vanished behind a sudden bank of thick, roiling smoke-colored clouds. A jagged fork of red lightning arced high above and a thunderclap made the ground shudder. Down the street, a car alarm went off and people began shouting. A hot wind that smelled like gunpowder tugged at my hair and Carlos – War – grinned at us with sharpened steel teeth.

"The horsemen are united at last," it said. "And now it is time to go to war."

CHAPTER 29

I grabbed Leo's shoulder, trying to heave him back up to his feet and away from... whatever the hell was happening here. But Pestilence flicked one scab-encrusted finger and the parking lot heaved like an unsettled stomach. Lightning flashed again, brighter than before, and I staggered as the ground shook beneath me.

"Leo!" I cried.

War stepped forward and Leo stared up at the thing that had been his uncle with tears bright in his eyes.

"You lied to me!" Leo shouted. "You said you could help. You were supposed to save us!"

"I brought you home," War said. His voice was the auditory equivalent of being hit with a sack full of broken glass and bullet casings. "You were never meant to be alone."

"You're not my uncle!" Leo snarled. "Where is Carlos?"

"Gone," War answered. "Just like you."

Leo struggled to stand, but War put a hand on its nephew's shoulder. Leo convulsed, clutching at his head, and screamed.

"Oh shit," I gasped. "No!"

Leo went suddenly still. Terribly, deathly still... and then he turned slowly to look at me.

Leo's eyes were gone. Face-to-face with the other horsemen, Death was just too strong. Shadows and chrome grew out across Leo's tattooed skin, wrapping him entirely in shining darkness. The black of his leather jacket twisted and flowed like stormy waters, closing up over his head in a deep hood. A metal skull gleamed from inside. Death rose to its feet, looming and hooded and terrible – a true Knight of Hell.

"Leo, no..." I whispered.

Death raised one long arm and pointed a skeletal chrome finger at me. I gasped as a chill like claws of ice closed around my heart. I fell to my knees on the shuddering asphalt and tears burned in my eyes.

Uriel, I'm sorry, I thought. *I should have listened to you from the beginning. We walked right into War's trap and now there's nothing I can do. We lost.*

No, Jaz. You were right in refusing to abandon Leo, Uriel said. *And all is not lost yet.*

I had no idea what the hell the archangel was talking about. How could this do anything but get worse...?

War still had his hand on Death's black shoulder, and Leo's uncle grew. Steel and kevlar crawled across its skin, sprouting spines as long as my fingers. Molten, fiery light oozed from its eyes and mouth, and the air all around War shimmered with hellish heat.

"And you brought the archangel right to us," War said. "Your vessel was a fool."

The ice clenched around my heart turned into a wild red-hot rage. Leo trusted Carlos with his life, his very *soul*...! But War had betrayed that trust and stolen Leo away from me. I wasn't giving up on him without a fight – or at least before kicking War in his big lying cannonballs.

Wings blazed out from my shoulders again and light flowed over me into shining silver armor. Pestilence was the smallest of the horsemen at about seven feet, and War had to be half again that height. I was outnumbered four to one and the horsemen stood together, powerful and united. I was alone.

"The time has come at last," Death told me in a hollow voice. "Die, Uriel."

There was another flash of lightning and a crack of thunder like someone had just smashed a plate the size of the moon. A flaming shape streaked across the boiling black sky and landed beside me in an explosion that melted the asphalt into tar.

"Yes," Michael boomed. "It is time!"

The archangel spread quadruple flaming wings, the body of their motorcycle cop vessel swallowed entirely by golden light. Twin blades of bright fire kindled in Michael's hands, each of them as long as I was tall.

Gabriel alighted on my other side, cloaked in silver light and haloed with shining wings. The angel who had woken Uriel inside me back in Arrow glowed like a star fallen down to earth. It was hard to believe there was an old woman in a cardigan somewhere under all of that burning light.

"This battle shall be fought as it was ordained," Gabriel said in their choral voice. "By all eight of us."

The ground shivered and a widening crack raced out from the sidewalk. I followed the growing crevice back to a little girl standing at the edge of the parking lot. Her hair was braided and tied off with a floppy pink ribbon, but the earth rumbled as she wandered toward us. This kid wasn't here to sell us Girl Scout cookies...

As the child neared, radiance burst forth, closing around her lengthening body in crystalline platemail and glittering wings that shattered the light into a thousand rainbows.

"We stand with you, Uriel," Raphael said.

The last angel put a hand on my shoulder. Raphael's touch was heavy and the shock of it was like being plunged into clear, cold water.

"Together," Uriel agreed. "We stand, and we fight."

Oh shit...! I was ten feet tall now, with six wings fanning out behind me. Uriel's fully manifested glory shone like a sun and my light turned the warehouse parking lot into a blinding white stage. The glow played over the assembled horsemen and was swallowed by their shadows.

Wind howled and the ground shuddered as though in fear. The sky above split open, blazing with a furious aurora of colors, and a thousand windows shattered as the buildings all around us shook. Shards of broken glass melted when they hit the inferno of our heat and rained down in glowing orange drops that burned through the whipping storm of newspapers and trash. Death stared at us with hollow eye sockets and Michael raised two fiery swords.

"War!" the archangel called out. "I have waited all eternity for this battle!"

The huge, bladed horseman laughed, a rumble so deep and loud that it sounded like mortar fire. "As have I. A billion times you and I clashed, Michael, but this will be the last battle!"

No! I screamed inside the prison of my own mind. *Uriel, don't let them do this! You'll destroy everything!*

The archangel's power coursed all through my stolen body, exponentially stronger than ever before. Pulling a helicopter right down out of the sky? That was nothing compared to what Uriel could do now. How about pulling a *planet* out of the sky?

And even as Uriel's manifested might crushed me inexorably into nothingness inside myself, I could feel the entire universe cringing, as though all of creation knew what destruction was about to be unleashed here. Maybe it did... this was why these eight had set it all into motion, after all.

Through Uriel's angelic senses, I could see bits of reality itself being torn to pieces – just like the blacktop of the parking lot – and scattered out through the void. Worlds and stars and so many lives. Humans were only a tiny part of it all, but even we were so big and so beautiful...

Please, I begged. *This world isn't just a battlefield, Uriel! You've seen Earth and the people who live here. We have lives and dreams... I just fell in love. Don't you* dare *take that away from me!*

All around us, the other archangels raised weapons made of light. The celestial glow blazed in my hand, stretching out into something that wasn't quite a sword and not quite a spear. But I knew in my bones that the shining edge was sharper than any razor. It could cut through entire galaxies. The roiling daylight sliced into sparkling colors all along its length.

But when Michael leapt at War, Uriel lowered that luminous blade into their path. Michael frantically beat wings of stellar flame and landed next to me again.

Jaz, as we battled for control, I saw this world as I never thought to, Uriel said. *Through you, I have felt love... It is a bond like the one I share with the other angels. But different... and glorious.*

Michael, Raphael and Gabriel stared at me in confusion, but Uriel had warned me – more times than I cared to remember – that the horsemen didn't give a shit about the rules or fair play. All they had ever wanted was to tear the archangels apart. Death hadn't moved or given a single order, but Famine, Pestilence and War strode forward across the melting asphalt. Darkness gathered around them in gunsmoke and swarms of hungry, biting things.

"Uriel, it is time to do battle!" Michael thundered. "Fight beside us!"

I no longer wish for war. I want... chocolate, Uriel said. *I want to experience this world.*

"What?" I asked.

The question came out of my mouth, even as it resonated with Uriel's power. I raised my left hand and flexed the smoothly armored fingers. There was no way I had taken control back from Uriel, not surrounded by the other archangels. Uriel had *given* my body back to me.

Yes, the angel said. *I will follow you, Jaz. But there will be no chocolate or anything else left unless you can stop the others from fighting.*

"Uriel, what is wrong?" Raphael asked.

But the horsemen weren't stopping for questions. The warehouse rang with a crashing boom and three motorcycles raced out through the open doors. I recognized Pestilence's disease-blackened Baracca and Famine's stripped-down chopper as they fell in beside their riders. The last one was a huge three-wheeled trike that looked more like a tank than a motorcycle. War seized the handlebars in gun-barrel fingers and pulled its massive bulk easily into the oversized seat.

"Stop!" I shouted. "No one is fighting today!"

I stepped in between the two armies of eternal cosmic force and raised my hands. Uriel's sword of light vanished and both horsemen and archangels hesitated.

"What are you doing?" Gabriel asked.

"You created this universe to be a battlefield," I said. "But there's so much more to it than that. There are billions of planets and stars out there, and countless lives that are just as important as yours!"

Famine revved its wheezing engine and hissed at me. "You are trying to deceive us."

"We do not lie," Raphael answered in a ringing voice. "Deceit is *your* weapon, horseman."

"Well, I'm not an angel or horseman," I told them. "I'm just a human woman trying to save her universe. Haven't any of you ever wanted something else…? Something besides killing each other?"

"Our battle is the purpose of this universe," Michael said. "And it shall be fought in accordance with the law that we *all* agreed to!"

Pestilence just snorted, releasing a billowing gray cloud of locusts. Raphael burned them out of the air with a crystal wing and the horseman glared.

"This battle is our purpose," Gabriel said.

"Then find a new one!" I shouted at them. "Humans do it all the time. I hated my life in Crayhill, so I left. And I made a new life… with him."

I pointed to where Death still loomed, dark and unmoving.

"The vessel is unimportant," Pestilence rasped.

"Not to me!" I said. "And not to you, either. You all created an entire universe full of things you've never seen before. Amazing, astonishing things! Maybe your vessels never showed you, or maybe you just never looked. But if you fight this out now, you'll destroy everything before you ever have the chance to experience any of it!"

"My vessel… dreamed of becoming an astronaut," Raphael said. The angel spoke slowly in their chiming crystal voice, as though for the first time.

"Then she was a smart kid," I said. "You made a universe and she wanted to go explore it. Who knows what's out there? You can go find out, if you want."

Raphael stared into the sky, like they could see through the storm clouds all the way to the ends of space. Maybe they could.

"There are other people living out there," I said. "On other planets. Maybe they weren't useful as vessels for your fight, but that doesn't mean that they're not worth discovering."

"Yes," Raphael answered. "I would very much like to see the worlds that my vessel dreams of."

Michael and Gabriel glanced at each other. At least, I *thought* that was what they were doing. It was hard to tell... The archangels' faces were featureless planes of pure, blinding light that then turned toward me.

"What did your vessels want?" I asked.

"To hold her grandchildren," Gabriel said. "And to meet her great-grandchildren. She didn't know them yet, but she loved them."

"You can still do that," I told the archangel. "You could hold those little lives *you* helped to make. You might want to turn down the divine light a bit, though, or you're going to seriously freak them out... But you can go find them. You can love them, too."

Gabriel gazed across the disintegrating road and their wings folded down against their back. But Michael shook their head and spread four fiery golden wings, pointing burning swords at the horsemen.

"My vessel desired only justice," the angel announced. "And we *will* have it!"

Michael swung one flaming sword, but I leapt forward and grabbed the blade in a gleaming metallic hand.

Michael has always been our greatest warrior, Uriel warned me. *And our greatest believer. Convince them!*

"There's a whole world full of assholes who deserve justice out there, Michael," I said. "And you know the human cops have limitations. They sure as hell couldn't deal with me or Leo today. But maybe you can."

"There must be justice!" Michael roared.

"You created a universe of beauty and life," I told the angel. "Destroying it isn't justice. But defending it is!"

We stared at each other and slowly, I released Michael's fiery sword. They didn't raise it again.

"Perhaps... there is a greater battle to fight," Michael said.

"Yeah, go kick some evildoer ass," I told them. "And maybe read a few comic books."

"Comic... books?" Michael asked.

I nodded. "Humans have been writing about superheroes for decades. They might help you figure out the whole guardian-of-justice thing."

Michael cocked their head, but didn't argue. I took a tentative step back, then sort of... pulled Uriel's power inside myself again and looked down at my own small, work-scarred brown hands. I gave the other three archangels a very human thumbs-up. They deserved it.

"I don't think so," War rumbled. "We've waited since before time for the chance to finally kill the angels and we are not stopping now!"

War pointed one huge finger at me. Famine and Pestilence fixed their sunken eyes on me, too, and I gulped hard. Inside me, Uriel tensed.

The horsemen respect no law, the angel said. *Only strength.*

Uriel's power was there within me and if I commanded them to, I was certain the archangels would still come to my aid. But that fight would flatten San Diego. And then the solar system.

War and its massive battle-trike charged right at me. I stumbled a step, but what could I do? The other angels stared at me, waiting for guidance. For me to lay down the law and make the rules... But I couldn't risk letting the angels and horsemen fight. If we couldn't stop this, Leo and I had agreed to die.

Now it was time to live up to my end of the bargain.

But what about chocolate? Uriel asked.

Sorry, Uriel, I thought. *But if anyone else is ever going to have chocolate again, we can't fight. We can only die.*

Death stared at me from the depths of its shadowy hood. But something shone in the darkness.

"No," it said.

The single word echoed up through the abyss in Death's ice-cold rasp. The horseman shifted its immense weight, making the ruined parking lot creak and groan ominously. It clenched its clawed chrome hands into fists as War's bike bore down on me.

"No!" Death said, louder this time.

The Packmaster raced out across the broken parking lot like a streak of black lightning and intercepted the trike. War's steed had ten times the mass, but it slammed into the smaller motorcycle like it had hit a wall.

Death moved faster than I could even think. It was suddenly there in front of War, grabbing the bigger horseman around the throat and yanking it down from the trike seat to face him. War's burning bullet-hole eyes went wide.

"Death...?" it asked.

"No," Leo snarled. "Death is riding bitch now."

He yanked his dark hood back to reveal the face of the man I loved. Haggard and drawn, his cheeks rough with stubble – but it was Leo.

My heart skipped and the angels started, but I held out my arms and the other three actually stopped.

"I'm never letting Death hurt Jaz again," Leo told the horsemen. "And I won't let you, either."

"I hunger!" Famine shrieked.

Pestilence hissed at the Packmaster. "No, impossible! A steed would *never* answer to a mortal!"

Leo turned and flung War at the other two. It carved a yard-deep furrow through the melting blacktop before coming to a stop in a huge burning crater.

"That's *my* motorcycle," Leo said. "And nobody takes my bike from me, not even Death."

Pestilence and Famine glared literal murder at him, and Leo glared right back. War climbed up out of the crater with a high-caliber grin. I swear it *liked* that everything came down to this.

The biggest horseman didn't care who it fought, as long as it got to fight.

"You can't beat us, Leo," War thundered. "Carlos knew you were weak on your own. You *will* lose."

"My uncle was right, but I'm not alone. I love Jaz," Leo said. "I conquered Death to come back to her and I'll beat your ass, too."

"Are you threatening me, boy?" War roared.

"It's not a threat," Leo answered. "It's a promise."

Leo thrust a chrome-plated hand out and chains shot from his fingertips, striking like snakes at their prey. The links coiled around Pestilence's bloody red Baracca and Famine's chopper, and yanked them out from under the two horsemen. Before the riders hit the ground, Leo whipped the bikes up, sending them flying over the western horizon. If I listened hard enough, I bet I would have heard them splashing into the Pacific Ocean.

The violent supernatural storm churning the sky quieted a notch as Leo removed half of Famine and Pestilence's power... but the apocalypse was only on hold. War charged at Leo, joints ratcheting with sounds like the slide of a handgun racking even as bullets the size of my fists plowed out of previously empty air, firing right at me.

Jaz! Uriel cried.

The other archangels shouted like the entire brass section of a symphony, brandishing weapons and wings of light, but they didn't move. Not without their leader's orders. I braced myself. I could *not* let the angels start their battle.

But Leo's shining chrome chains lashed out, tearing the over-sized bullets apart into smoking lead shrapnel, and then they swirled around him as he met War's charge. Leo moved so fast that he was a streak of leather and shadow. He slammed into War and the shockwave tore up broken strips of melting black pavement, flinging them through the air.

"You took my uncle!" Leo snarled.

War hammered a barrel-sized fist into Leo's stomach, but the biker just clenched his jaw. Leo gestured and more chains coiled themselves around the other horseman's thick arms and legs. The metal plunged down into the quaking earth, anchoring War in place.

"You tried to take Jaz!" Leo growled. "You tried to destroy the entire fucking universe... And I should kill you for that."

"You can't kill me, vessel," War said.

The three-wheeled tank of a bike roared and rumbled, and shot straight at them, but Leo reached out and sank skeletal chrome claws into the front suspension. I know that we were at the end of the world, but I gasped when Leo heaved the whole vehicle up off the ground and swung it right at War. The chains lashing the massive horseman in place kept it from flying back through the already devastated warehouse, but Leo hammered the monster down to its knees. Face-to-face, Leo grabbed War.

"You still want to tell me what I can do?" Leo asked. "I *can* kill you... but I'm not Death."

War's balefully burning eyes narrowed. Famine and Pestilence crept slowly closer, but I wasn't sure if they were going to jump on Death to save War or just wanted a better view.

"You heard Jaz. We're not ending the world today," Leo said. "So get the hell off my planet. Go explore, go see the rest of the universe. Learn something. There are these things called black holes that you'll love, Famine. But don't touch Jaz, or you'll deal with me."

Leo's gleaming chrome chains tightened around War and it laughed – a real, whole-body laugh. Pestilence hissed at Leo, but Famine grabbed its arm, fear on the demon's gaunt face. Slowly, War nodded to Leo.

"The final battle *will* be fought," War said. "But... not yet, it seems. There is a universe of weapons and warriors out there.

Maybe even more like you. And when the battle is finally waged, I shall destroy all of you. Including Death, if you stand in my way."

Holy shit, these guys *really* didn't play by the rules.

Leo released War, and the hulking horseman stood as the chains vanished, towering up over us again. But I didn't care – I ran to Leo and threw my arms around him. I was never going to let him go again. The shadows and chrome retreated and left Leo standing in his jeans and leather jacket.

"I love you," I told him.

Leo pulled me close and kissed me until neither of us could breathe.

"Nothing I find in creation will ever be as surprising as this," Raphael said.

Michael and Gabriel nodded in agreement. Leo let go of me and stared up at War.

"Uncle Carlos..." he said.

"Gone," War rumbled. The word sounded almost wistful – if an earthquake could sound wistful. "But he put up a good fight, and I sense his strength in you. If there are more like you on this planet, then it is a world worth exploring."

"We humans make some badass weapons," I said. "Although something tells me that you won't exactly be waiting around on background checks."

"Speaking of weapons..." War said.

The horseman grinned and looked up. The churning storm clouds were beginning to thin and I heard the whirr and chop of a helicopter rotor above us. There were sounds of racing engines and screeching tires in the distance, too. SPOT had caught up with us again. Michael spread their flaming wings.

"Are these the evildoers you spoke of?" the archangel asked.

"No, don't hurt them," I answered quickly. "They just want to save the world."

"With large guns," War said, pointing to the helicopter as it descended through the clouds. "I like them already."

"Get the fuck out of here," Leo told the horsemen. "We'll see you again in a million years."

"That might not be long enough to explore all of creation," Raphael said.

I nodded to the glittering angel. "Take your time. Trust me, we're in no hurry."

"Farewell then," Gabriel said.

"Until we meet again, at the end of all," Uriel said. The archangel wasn't in control of my body, but I figured the least I owed them was the chance to say goodbye. "Fly and find the wonders of this world."

The other three angels bowed to me, multiple wings spread, and then leapt into the air. They flew up past the SPOT helicopter, then through the lightening sky. The angels glittered like stars for a moment before they parted and vanished toward the unknown corners of the universe.

Leo looked back at the other horsemen, his dark eyes hard.

"Go," he commanded. "Now."

Famine and Pestilence glared, but War snapped its massive fingers at them. Engines roared in the distance and then the other demonic steeds came racing up the street. They screeched to a stop beside War's trike, black smoke billowing from their tires. Leo's Packmaster growled at the other motorcycles – there was only room for one alpha in the pack, and it was Leo. The three horsemen mounted their waiting bikes.

"When I see you two again," War said, "it will be for the last time."

"Goodbye, Uncle Carlos," Leo answered.

War's burning ember eyes softened almost imperceptibly, but then the hulking horseman laughed like automatic gunfire and stomped on the gas. War's tank-trike tore out of the cracked warehouse parking lot with Famine and Pestilence scrambling to follow.

A dozen black SPOT panel vans raced toward us, then scattered as the horsemen charged right down the middle of the street. The vans screeched to a stop and squadrons of armored Spotters jumped out, aiming an impressive arsenal of weapons at the retreating demons' backs. I ran into the road, waving my arms.

"No, wait!" I cried. "Don't shoot!"

SPOT soldiers shouted and scrambled out of the way as the horsemen drove through. An armored truck bringing up the rear of the caravan couldn't move fast enough and War's steed knocked it aside like a cardboard cutout. The big truck tumbled, then came to rest halfway through the brick wall of a bodega.

Diane Owens leapt out of the passenger seat of the lead van. Her arm was bound up in a sling, but she heaved a huge grenade launcher onto her shoulder and turned, tracking the horsemen.

War raised its steel middle finger and I placed one hand on Diane's arm. I pushed the launcher down as all three horsemen vanished quickly into the distance. I had no idea how those motorcycles might carry their riders to other worlds, but I didn't put it past them. Diane spun to stare at me with eyes wide behind her glasses.

"Jasmine? Leopold?" she asked. "You're still in control? How? Why are the horsemen leaving? What happened to the angels?"

"It's all over," I answered.

Leo came to stand beside me and settled an arm around my waist. He nodded at Diane.

"For the next million years or so," Leo said. "The angels and horsemen are still out there, and you might run across Michael and War a few times. Guess you're not out of a job just yet."

"You two have a lot of explaining to do," Diane told us. "Ah... if you don't mind."

EPILOGUE

There were no hills in Crayhill, but we found the closest thing that we could. We parked at the top of a small rise outside my tiny hometown. Leo and I leaned against the side of the Packmaster together and the motorcycle purred beneath us like a happy tiger. The bike still didn't like me very much, but it seemed content with Leo's mastery.

Call me biased, but I was pretty sure Leo was a better boss than Death. At least, the Packmaster hadn't burned through the new clutch plates yet.

I pointed to a green-brown rectangle in the distance.

"Over there is my parents' place," I said. "The lawn, at least. You can't see the house very well from this angle. Or the back porch... Dad grows roses out there for my mom."

Uriel sifted through my mind for the memory of roses and I smelled their sweet scent. I smiled and resolved to stop at the next roadside stand to let them experience the real thing.

"That's my middle name, you know," I said. "Rose."

"Jasmine Rose...?" Leo asked. "That's a beautiful name. Your parents really like flowers."

330 • ERICA LINDQUIST & ARON CHRISTENSEN

"Flowers and motorcycles. That was pretty much their whole courtship."

"Sounds nice," Leo said. "Maybe we should try it."

"I think we did just fine."

Leo wrapped his arms around me and looked over my shoulder. He kissed the side of my neck and I reached up to run my fingers through his hair. There were a few strands of white in the mahogany waves that hadn't been there when Leo first drove into Crayhill.

"Diane sent me the confirmation numbers last night," I said, patting my pocket and the new cell phone tucked away inside. "My mom and dad have all the money they'll ever need. They could even leave Crayhill, if they wanted to."

"Think they will?" Leo asked.

"I doubt it," I answered. "But that's okay. Crayhill isn't such a bad little town."

It was strange to say. It was stranger to feel. I had spent my entire life trying to escape Crayhill... But Crayhill was never the problem. I was.

A wind that smelled like sun-warmed grass blew through my hair. You can never go home again, though. That's the saying and I know it's meant to be metaphorical, but this was as close to Crayhill as I ever planned to be. Leo and I were finally free to see the whole world and I was eager to get started.

"Diane texted me last night, too," Leo said.

"Really? Why didn't you tell me?" I asked.

"You were taking a shower. And when you came out, then we were... busy."

I laughed. He had a point. Even now, Leo remained reluctant to sleep at night. He still had dreams, nightmares where Death seized control and called the other horsemen to the battle that would destroy everything. But Leo didn't need military-grade stimulants or drugs anymore. He had something more powerful

– something to hold on to. Leo was the one in charge and nothing in the universe could make him hurt me.

I still heard Uriel's voice, too, but not often. The angel gave me a few words of encouragement when the road became rough or uncertain. But mostly, Uriel just watched and learned about the world they had helped to create.

"Did Diane close your police records like she promised to?" I asked.

Leo nodded. "As far as the federal government is concerned, Leopold Valdis is dead. As long as we steer clear of Chicago for a while, no one should be looking for me."

"I want to visit Chicago, but I guess we can wait a few years," I said. "Maybe we'll hit Johannesburg or Mumbai first. Do you think this guy can get us across the ocean?"

I reached back to pat the gleaming red and black curve of the Packmaster's gas tank. The engine revved eagerly. Flying was fine, but riding double was even better. And nothing could move faster than a horseman on his steed.

"I'm not sure, but we'll find out," Leo said.

"What about your friends?" I asked. "The rest of the Chicago Knights of Hell?"

"Texas Highway Patrol picked up their bodies, but Diane had SPOT claim them and give my friends each a proper burial. I gave her the contact information for their families, too. They'll all be taken care of."

"That's it, then," I said.

"That's it," Leo agreed. "It's time to go."

Our lives were our own now, and all of the world's roads. Leo kissed me under the warm Kansas sun, then swung a leg over the waiting Packmaster. I climbed on behind Leo and wrapped my arms around him. He kicked the motorcycle into gear and we drove away.

Next stop – anywhere.

For more books by
Erica Lindquist & Aron Christensen,
visit us at **LLStories.com**